FATE of the ARGOSI

FATE of the ARGOSI

SEBASTIEN DE CASTELL

HOT
KEY
BOOKS

First published in Great Britain in 2023 by
HOT KEY BOOKS
4th Floor, Victoria House
Bloomsbury Square
London WC1B 4DA
Owned by Bonnier Books
Sveavägen 56, Stockholm, Sweden
bonnierbooks.co.uk/HotKeyBooks

A CIP catalogue record for this book is available from the British Library.

HARDBACK ISBN: 978-1-4714-1371-1
TRADE PAPERBACK ISBN: 978-1-4714-1370-4
Also available as an ebook and in audio

1

Typeset by DataConnection Ltd
Printed and bound by Clays Ltd, Elcograf S.p.A.

Hot Key Books is an imprint of Bonnier Books UK
bonnierbooks.co.uk

For Kim Tough, who dauntlessly walks her own Argosi path.

Zhuban

Northern
Tribelands

Convent of
Scarlet Words

Darome

Great Temple
Road

Jan'Tep
Territories

Oatas Jan'Xan

Cinto Rhea

Monastery of the
Silent Garden

The Seven
Sands

Gitabria

Berabesq

Southern Nomad
Ranges

Eldrasia

Dancing on a Spire

I've been pondering this awhile now, balanced precariously on my tiptoes atop this six-hundred-foot spire where every stray gust of wind seems eager to send me hurtling to the hungry cobblestones below, and I've come to a decision: I've decided that 'glorious' is the most beautiful word there is.

Now, maybe you disagree. Maybe you reckon there's a word that tickles the tongue sweeter than 'glorious'. Maybe you're partial to 'quintessence' or 'diaphanous' or 'loquacious'.

Hmm . . . Loquacious. *Lo-qua-cious*.

Okay, I'll admit it, that's a good one. Matter of fact, I've been accused – righteously, some would say – of being a mite *loquacious* myself. No shame in an eighteen-year-old girl wanting the world to hear what she has to say, is there? You ask me, it's a bigger shame when a body *don't* bare its soul now and then, even if there's no one to talk to up here but a grumbling spire goat who keeps butting me in the leg, trying to topple me off his favourite perch.

Peculiar critters, spire goats. Barely two feet tall with three little horns and twenty miles' worth of bad attitude. Real territorial too. Legend has it they got their name on account of their proclivity for climbing up spires, towers and cathedrals to be closer to the gods. More likely they come for the coppery-blue moss that only grows above the treeline. Chewing the moss is what gives them the malodorous abilities they rely on to fend off predators ten times their size.

Yep, that's right: I was one headbutt away from meeting an undignified end courtesy of a goat no bigger than a house cat and mostly known for belching and farting its enemies to death. Oh, and when they get real angry? Spire goats make this bleating noise that can shatter your eardrums if you get too close.

I reached down a hand to tickle his silvery-white beard. 'But I'll bet you fancy me too much for that, don't you, fella?'

The spire goat growled at me, real quiet like, but that low rumble rattled my bones. Hadn't known they could do that. No wonder these little guys are so bossy. The thing is, here in Gitabria there aren't many mountains high enough for the blue moss to grow, and the ones there are attract a particularly venomous snake whose favourite snack is dead spire goat. But luckily for them, snakes don't take to cities, and Gitabrian contraptioneers are legendary for erecting towers so tall that anyone crazy enough to climb to the top could kiss the moon right on the cheek.

I might be exaggerating a little. I'm prone to a touch of the dramatic now and again. Perched up here though, atop the tallest spire in this whole magnificent city, overlooking copper-capped alabaster towers and crowded streets blazing with a thousand flickering oil lanterns, each one a star beckoning you towards some new adventure or intrigue? Well, it's no exaggeration to say that the view was breathtaking.

Glorious, you might say.

The spire goat gave an enquiring snort.

'I ain't crying,' I informed him, shooing him away when he tried to nibble on the heel of my boot. 'Takes more than one tear before you can call it crying.'

One tear. No big deal. A single, solitary tear for all the places I yearned to explore, the wonders I longed to see, the fights – hard-won, I promise you – it had taken to get me to this moment, when I finally had the skills to travel anywhere on this continent without fear of persecution or peril.

One tear.

As that lonely drop of grief slid down my cheek, and the little spire goat butted my leg for the hundredth time, trying to oust me from his private feeding ground, I reached into one of the dozen pockets of my favourite black leather waistcoat and pulled out my least favourite deck of cards.

Argosi carry all kinds of decks. The *concordances*, for example, are made up of different suits for each of the cultures living on this continent. We paint them so we can comprehend how folks live and the patterns that govern their societies. The *discordances*, on the other hand, represent individuals and events that break those patterns. Anomalies that could alter the course of history. The *teysan* deck teaches the Four Ways of Water, Wind, Thunder and Stone that guide an Argosi's path, along with the seven talents we rely on to survive the journey. I even have a deck of razor-sharp steel cards that my pappy taught me to throw so fast and accurate I could pin a swallow's tail to a tree branch – not that any Argosi worth the name would do such a thing.

Most decks, you hope to build up over time as you learn more about the world. The one I was holding in my hand though? Those cards you hope to shed quick as you can so they don't weigh you down on your travels. They're called *disharmonies*, but that's just a fancy word for what they really are: debts.

The Way of Water says an Argosi should flow past other people's lives like a gentle stream, never taking what others don't want to give, never leaving behind more than a smile and a good story.

No matter how hard you try though, once in a while you can't help but violate the Way of Water. You end up taking something you didn't mean to, or leaving calamity and misery in your wake. We Argosi don't believe in regrets though. Regrets aren't restitution, and an Argosi always pays her debts.

That compulsion had brought me to the top of this spire. I needed to gaze out over this gorgeous city and the gleaming shores beyond to all the places I'd dreamed of visiting but couldn't. Not yet. Eighteen years old and already I was weighed down by more debts than my conscience could bear. The deck in my hand contained painted cards of people who'd done me a kindness only to suffer as a result: families who'd lost a loved one I'd failed to protect and never learned the truth of what had happened; folks who were hurting because of me and would go on hurting until I found a way to make things right.

My hands trembled as I shuffled my disharmonies deck. Chance probably isn't the noblest way to decide which debt to pay first, but we Argosi are gamblers by nature. So I closed my eyes, fanned out the cards and let the breeze guide my fingertips. There are four suits in a deck of disharmonies: thorns, chains, tears and dust. Each represents a different imbalance that needs rectifying.

Nobody likes paying off debts – always feels like you're gonna walk away poorer than when you started. That's why, when I opened my eyes and saw the card I'd drawn, and the tribulations to which I was surely headed, I was utterly unprepared to find myself laughing so hard and smiling so bright I reckoned I'd outshone the stars above and below.

The spire goat gave an angry bleat – not the kind that knocks you off your feet thankfully. This was more of a 'Hey, idiot, what's so hilarious it warrants you giggling like a lunatic while stomping all over my favourite patch of moss?'

4

Now, impoliteness ain't the way of the Argosi. So before I began my precarious descent from the spire, I knelt down to ruffle the goat's fur and kiss him on his grumpy little head. I held out the card I'd painted a few years back of a reckless, sly-faced thief with straw-blonde hair and a smirk that was a magnet for trouble. 'Ain't it funny,' I asked the spire goat, 'how even when holding an awful hand, sometimes you draw a lucky card?'

Part 1

The Thief of Chains

A disharmony represents more than an unpaid obligation. When we abandon those we've wronged, they are not the only ones imprisoned by our mistakes; part of us remains shackled to them. Ignore this simple truth, teysan, and you not only steal from those to whom restitution is owed, but rob from yourself the joy of becoming whole. This is why the Argosi pay their debts not grudgingly but with gratitude.

1

The Moral Dilemmas of Prison Breaks

Six months and seven hundred miles I followed the trail on which that card had set me. From the heights of a majestic spire overlooking the most glamorous city on the continent to the subterranean depths of a prison so notoriously fatal to body and spirit it more than earned the name 'Soul's Grave'.

How awful was this place to which that smug, I-know-better-than-you smirk painted on my disharmony card had brought me? Put it this way: the conditions inside the cramped cells carved into the rock a hundred feet beneath the dried-out heart of a desert are so loathsome that the Berabesq – a profoundly religious people – consider it sacrilege to imprison their own convicts here. Only foreign criminals are consigned to Soul's Grave, and only foreign mercenaries – those convicted of lesser crimes and offered the choice of serving out their sentence as jailers rather than prisoners – patrol its depths.

'Bet you're wishing you'd stayed up on your cosy tower, eh, Conch?'

The spire goat shook his soot-dusted fur and served up a whistling snort I'd come to recognise as meaning, 'Get on with the job, idiot.'

I'd gotten halfway down the spire when I'd heard the clackety-clomp of the goat's hoofs dancing along the tiniest of crevices in the building's mortar. I'd worried he might be inclined to yet another attempt at shoving me headlong to my death, but mostly he just followed behind, bleating in obvious amusement at how slow and clumsy I was compared to him. That only got worse when he trailed me back to my camp outside the city, where Quadlopo was tethered. You wouldn't think a horse and a spire goat would have much to talk about, but those two got on like long-lost siblings. Couldn't tell what they were yakking on about at first, but after a few days it became clear they were regaling each other with tales of my ineptitude.

I didn't mind the extra chatter though. Quadlopo gets real sullen on the long roads. He prefers a sympathetic ear for his complaints. Conch – that's what I'd taken to calling the spire goat, on account of the blaring noise he makes when he wants something (which is all the time) – was happy to fill that role in exchange for a thimbleful of blue moss every few days. It nearly got me eaten by a hill snake one time, but I managed to harvest enough to keep the goat content long after we'd crossed the Gitabrian border in search of a girl I hadn't seen in four years and had no clue where to find.

I'd started in Darome, of course; that's where I'd last seen Arissa, back when she was running with the Black Galleon gang. They were mostly teenage street thieves, with a few rooftop robbers and a couple of long-con swindlers. Turned out Arissa had left them the day after she'd run me out of town at the point of a knife blade. Wasn't her fault; I'd been under a silk mage's curse that twisted the love and affection of anyone who came to care about me into a hatred so deep they couldn't stop themselves from trying to kill me. If I look too close I can still make out the faded sigils of the tattooed collar that mage had etched into my skin. Don't mind them nowadays. Durral Brown, the Argosi who'd instructed me in the four ways and seven talents, also taught me to find beauty even in the ugliest of places.

Places just like this, I thought as I crept round another of Soul's Grave's infamous oubliettes. Hadn't seen a living soul in any of them so far, which wasn't to say they were empty. *Not sure what beauty you expect me to find here, Pappy.*

Conch sidled up on my left. The spire goat could move real quiet when he set his mind to it. Problem was, his temperament generally favoured chaos.

'Don't even think it,' I whispered to him.

As I edged up to the corner of the next passageway, I was greeted by the usual assortment of grunts, dice rolling and ale swilling coming from the alcove at the far end. This was my third visit to the prison in search of a peaceful opportunity to break out my quarry. It ain't the Argosi way to give in to brutality when kindness or cunning can get the job done. So far, both had failed me.

'A *prince's decree?*' the warden vizier for Soul's Grave had exclaimed when I'd unfurled the ornate scroll with its delicate gold and silver engraving. I'd done so on my knees, which isn't a posture to which I'm predisposed at the best of times. I'm even less inclined to genuflection after risking life and limb – not to mention my horse – to recover a priceless sapphire-studded casket containing the ancient saint's bones the prince demanded in exchange for pardoning the thief I'd come to rescue.

My mistake had been pursuing the Way of Water before I'd followed the Way of Wind. That's how I'd wound up making a deal with the prince without first learning about the decades-long theological dispute between him and the warden vizier of Soul's Grave.

'I will not tear it up,' the vizier informed me. He spat on the decree before handing it to one of his shaven-headed clerics. 'Have this framed. Gilded tamarisk oak to bring out the gold inks of His Highness's exquisite calligraphy. Afterwards, place the document behind ironglass and have it bolted into the rock wall opposite the prisoner's cell. That way she may gaze at it through the bars each night as she withers away from starvation, humbly grateful to the prince who pardoned her for the attempted theft of my silver-coated stallion.' Assuming I was an uneducated barbarian, he explained, 'One of only three in all of Berabesq.'

Like I said, when brokering deals involving sleazy princes and even sleazier religious fanatics, it's best to do your research first.

The warden vizier ended our interview by instructing his guards to escort me to the border along with his blessing and profound thanks for saving him the cost of feeding the horse thief who, as was made clear in the prince's decree, was now a free woman.

The Way of Water having failed me, I belatedly travelled the Way of Wind. Two weeks of infiltrating underground taverns and speakeasies, bribing just about the entire criminal population of southern Berabesq, had enabled me to piece together a map of six potential escape routes out of this famously impenetrable prison.

Over the centuries, every time the viziers had expanded the prison, they'd relied on convicts to do the tunnelling. Since criminals are notoriously capricious when it comes to digging what's almost certain to become their own grave, I'd bet correctly that a few enterprising souls might've conspired to leave themselves a way out.

The information hadn't come cheap. In fact, it had cost me one of the only three silver-coated stallions in all of Berabesq. Yeah, I know, but I'd paid for the pardon once already. Besides, if His Illustrious and Most Pious Eminence the Warden Vizier of Southern

Berabesq was so in love with that horse, he shouldn't keep pissing off the wrong people.

Unfortunately, while excellent for sneaking *into* Soul's Grave, my overpriced map wasn't any help in getting to the cells without having to go through the guards. Six men and women, trained fighters who'd committed more murders between them than all the convicts they kept locked up in this hellhole, stood between me and the gal I'd come to rescue.

This was the third night I'd come here, the third time I'd hidden in the shadows, forced to listen to the filthy, degrading jokes they made while placing bets on which convict would die before dawn. Wasn't hard to imagine that when the stakes got high enough an unlucky prisoner might wind up with poison slipped into their greasy soup so that a guard who'd wagered more than he could afford didn't have to pay up to his equally brutal colleagues.

Six is too many, I thought helplessly. Only three guards were ever supposed to be on watch, with the others walking their rounds. The cleric overseers of Soul's Grave never descended from their comfortable offices above to check on the guards though. One more reason I didn't feel so bad about stealing their boss's horse.

'Can't risk it tonight,' I whispered to Conch, kneeling in front of him so the little goat would see my face. I couldn't tell for sure if he could understand my words any better than I could his bleating, but he seemed to get my meaning from my expressions. 'Gonna have to come back tomorrow.'

'Slit their throats! Let their blood bathe the weakness from your spirit, that you may reconsecrate yourself as our most devoted servant!'

My fingers were squeezing something cold and smooth. Without my realising, I'd slipped my hand into the pocket of my waistcoat and drawn a half-dozen steel throwing cards. I put them back, breathed in what calm I could from the stale air of the tunnel and

15

set my thoughts to dancing around the malignant imperative that was trying to grab hold of my mind.

Conch hadn't made that sinister suggestion; even spire goats aren't *that* ornery. What I had rattling around my head was called the Red Scream: a plague of words and sounds so devious that hearing the verses just once drove the victim to spread the disease to everyone they could, and kill everyone they couldn't. I knew this because I was the last person ever to be infected with the Red Scream, and the only one to fight those Scarlet Verses off. But they weren't done with me.

'*Allow us to serve your cause, Argosi!*' they hissed insistently. '*Merely whisper a single one of our verses to the guards, and they will—*'

'*Become mindless lunatics tearing across the continent and spreading you to anyone they don't kill first?*' I asked, my thoughts pirouetting around their attempts to ensnare me. '*Sorry, darlings. My plan may have its flaws, but yours comes with too high a body count.*'

The verses pushed a little harder, murmuring words in a dozen different languages meant to bind me to their will. I twisted those ugly meanings one by one. *Torment* went from being the infliction of pain to the act of annoyance – something more in keeping with my personality. To *scourge* is to whip or flagellate, but its synonym, *flog*, is a contronym that contains its own opposite meaning of 'to promote or talk at excessive length', which as anyone can tell you, is far better suited to me.

'*You cannot contain us forever, that-which-once-called-itself-Ferius.*'

'*The name ain't "that-which-once-called-itself" anything. It's Ferius Parfax. I'm the Path of the Wild Daisy, fellas, and if you intend to keep trailing after me, you'd best be ready for some unexpected twists and turns along the way.*'

I let them tire themselves out, then allowed myself a self-satisfied smirk. The Argosi don't mind a little pride now and then. Even

16

Conch looked up at me with what might've been the spire goat equivalent of a grin. I bent down to scratch his chin. That's when he burped in my face. A faint blueish mist got into my nostrils. I covered my face, but too late. Every muscle in my body turned to jelly as I collapsed in a heap on the cold, uneven stone floor. Conch clambered onto my chest, licked my face, then sauntered off down the tunnel.

Might've been the hallucinogenic effects of his foul-smelling saliva, but I would've sworn the little bastard was whistling a tune as he abandoned me to the guards.

2

Never Trust a Spire Goat

Guess it was the odd whistling echoing down the tunnel that drew the guards to me. It had a haunting, almost melancholy sound to it. Who knew spire goats were such inspired musicians?

Wasn't long before I was staring up at six of the ugliest faces I'd ever seen. Let's be clear about something: ugly don't mean to an Argosi what it might to regular folk. Slack jaws, bulbous noses, big ears, balding hair, bad teeth – these things don't make a person ugly; they just make 'em different.

Behold the world through your *arta precis* – that's the Argosi talent for perception – and those same faces become entrancing, beguiling, even beautiful. When an Argosi speaks of ugliness, they mean the way a person's spirit – their *intentions* – contort those same features towards bitterness, greed and, worst of all, cruelty.

'Blessed and beloved are those who yield,' whispered one of the guards as he brushed aside my red curls with a finger to trace a line down the side of my face and then along my lips. It was like he was checking to see if I were made of wax instead of flesh and blood. His accent was Daroman, former military from the look he shot the others that sent them inching back even as they kept leering at me like a pack of . . . well, no pack of wild dogs ever struck me as quite so ill-mannered.

Blessed and beloved are those who yield, is the proverb Berabesq clerics recite to slaves and prisoners to remind them that submission is better for the soul than a beating. No doubt the saying grates on those who don't share their faith – until they get to use it on someone else.

My *arta forteize* – just a fancy word for resilience – was telling me that roughly two minutes had passed since Conch had paralysed me. Wasn't sure how long it'd take before the effects of his noxious belch wore off, but it was a safe bet I wouldn't enjoy how the guards intended to pass the time.

Come on, you stupid spire goat! Can't believe you hate me this much!

This is what I get for allowing a beast who spends his days atop copper-capped spires, chewing on tasty blue moss while gazing down at his heavenly dominion, to follow me into a dank hellhole. Guess I'd been lonelier than I wanted to admit.

'That's right,' the big Daroman kneeling over me said. His ragged chin-length hair would've been blond were it not for the dust and grime darkening it a muddy brown. He was stroking my cheek like it was an apple he was about to take a bite out of. 'You cry, little girl. Everyone cries down here.' He leaned in close and kissed me on the forehead. 'The clerics that run this place preach that tears are the ink in which the six-faced god writes our futures.'

More chortles from the other guards. Abuse people long enough and the only joy left to them is the suffering of others.

'Few tears to be shed down here tonight,' said a tall, rangy-looking woman – a Zhuban warrior-poet from the high cheekbones and deep, melodious voice. Couldn't have been too good at the warrior part; she had more scars on her face than hairs left on her head. 'Some stinking Berabesq prince is sending his troops to close Soul's Grave for good. The warden vizier's got us sacrificing convicts in protest. Six each morning, one for each of his god's six faces. We ran out yesterday, which means come dawn—'

'Shut up,' said the former Daroman soldier. He was straddling my midsection, making it hard for me to breathe. Calloused fingers slid under the collar of my dust-covered travelling shirt. Whatever I'd expected his intentions towards me, they turned out worse as his hands wrapped around my neck. He sighed, eyes closing as if he were drifting off to sleep, but then a slow smile crept over his lips and he began to squeeze. 'They're going to kill us guards before they shut this place down, we all know that. If this is my last night, I want to imagine I'm back home one last time.'

A tingle in my fingertips told me I could move them again, but not enough to do more than scratch at the unforgiving rock beneath me.

'Home,' the Daroman repeated. I couldn't tell if he was talking to me or the other guards. 'Have you ever visited the southern hills of Darome? This time of year, the orchards burst with apples more golden than any sunset. The fruit practically falls off the branch into your hands. And the city girls . . . oh, they do love a man in uniform. I was a proper soldier, of course, never took advantage. But I did enjoy strolling through those orchards, listening to someone else talk about their aspirations and ambitions. Those silly, giddy dreams of theirs made me feel as if, when I marched off to fight in the border wars, I'd be defending something good and pure rather than just killing people I'd never met.'

All the while his hands were slowly tightening around my neck. I wasn't hardly breathing at all any more.

'Then I got captured,' the soldier went on. 'Consigned down here where nothing grows except an . . . ache to taste what little life leaks out of another's eyes as they die.' His right hand came away from my throat, but his left was more than strong enough to

20

keep strangling me on its own. A fingertip traced a half-circle beneath my eye and then went to his mouth, smearing his bottom lip with my tears. 'Whimper for me,' he urged, eyes still closed, a dreamy smile on his face. 'Whimper as you die so I'll know I'm still alive.'

There *was* a cry then, but it didn't come from me. Instead, the sort of soft, anxious bleating you'd expect from a sheep separated from its herd, soon followed by the clackety-clack of hoofs stumbling across the uneven stone floor.

'Well now,' said one of the guards, a big-bellied man with tattoos all over his face who chuckled as he ambled past where my last breath was being squeezed out of me. 'Can you believe the clerics sent us a juicy dinner to go with our entertainment?'

The Daroman soldier opened his eyes. He didn't laugh like the others, nor did he turn to look at the little goat skittering nervously towards the other guard's outstretched hand. Instead his gaze remained on me, searching my eyes for signs of relief – of a trap about to be sprung.

Too bad you decided to strangle a professional gambler, I thought, giving up nothing but wide-eyed panic and a desperate plea for mercy.

I heard the sound of a knife being drawn from its sheath, then the slow, cautious shuffling of the guards as they began encircling Conch. I'd gone almost two minutes without air and my vision was starting to blur. Didn't matter though; I couldn't affect what happened next. All I could do was play out a thousand times in my mind the precise sequence of movements I'd need to make. That's what an Argosi does when the only path ahead is the Way of Thunder.

Strangely, I *heard* thunder down in that prison a hundred feet below ground. It was the thunder of a spire goat letting out a scream so ear-splitting I half expected the tunnels to cave in on us. The guards closest to Conch cried out in pain. The Daroman straddling me groaned, teeth gritted as he slammed his palms over his ears. Blood oozed between his fingers like his eardrums had burst. My head had been on the ground, so I guess that's why I hadn't gotten the full force of the little monster's fury, which he followed up with a belch of that foul breath of his. The five guards nearest collapsed, unconscious or paralysed, leaving only the one on top of me.

My own paralysis hadn't completely worn off yet, but I didn't care. Instinct and practice can overcome a whole lot when the necesssity demands. My arms being pinned under the Daroman's weight, I bent my left knee, pressed my foot down on the floor and pushed up with my hips, throwing him off me. I didn't try to get up; no point getting into a grappling fight with a trained soldier twice my size. Besides, I knew what he'd do next.

Quick as a hunting hound, the Daroman rolled back on top of me, driving his right knee into my stomach so he could use his weight to prevent any further resistance. I had him exactly where I wanted him.

Back when my pappy was teaching me *arta eres*, the Argosi talent for defence, he'd shown me an old Daroman military injunction that had been around for nearly two hundred years: 'No foot soldier of the Imperial Daroman Army is permitted to keep a dagger sheath hidden in their boot.'

Durral had made me stare at that one line for a whole day until I could explain why it was still on the law books. Eventually I figured it was because the extra dagger would create an imbalance in the soldier's step that would reduce their efficiency when marching long distances. The Daroman military is real big on efficiency.

'*Smart answer, kid,*' Durral had told me. '*Eminently logical.*'

'*You're saying I'm wrong?*' I'd asked, irritated.

22

'I'm sayin' anyone who's ever tried to walk twenty miles with a fifty-pound pack and a knife stuck in their boot knows it's uncomfortable. Only reason to make a law forbidding it is because . . .'

'Because Daroman soldiers keep hiding daggers in their boots anyway,' I'd finished for him.

Turns out Daroman foot soldiers get into a lot of fights. Getting arrested using a military-issue sword against your fellow infantry is treason, but accidentally stabbing them with a knife you just happened to find on the ground when the fight broke out is . . . excusable.

Crazy-ass empire, if you ask me, but I was grateful this one time, because old habits die hard. The former Daroman soldier with his knee on my chest was no exception to the rule. When I slid the fingers of my left hand inside the top of his boot, they found the leather-wrapped grip of a short-bladed dagger.

I hate hurting people nowadays. Even people who fill me with such anger that it shouts down the voices of my teachers urging me to stay on my path. My foster mother, Enna, though, she taught me that while an Argosi might walk a thousand miles around a problem to avoid a fight, when there's no other way but the Way of Thunder, you strike like lightning: no hesitation, no remorse.

Sensing my manoeuvre, the Daroman reached for my wrist while his other hand seized hold of my hair in preparation for cracking the back of my skull against the stone floor. The tip of the dagger I now held hadn't yet cleared the top of his boot, which meant the difference between survival and death existed only in that tiny sliver of time between choosing mercy or murder.

The sharp edge of the blade sliced through and along the vein in his wrist, sending a spray of blood between us. Before the first grunt of pain had even reached his lips, I'd spun the dagger to a reverse grip and jammed three inches of steel into his throat.

23

Two seconds. That's all it had taken from the moment I'd reached for the dagger hidden in his boot until the blood from his throat began to pour down on me. How can nature allow such awful deeds to be performed so quickly?

There's no silence so deep as that which follows the last echo of thunder. I watched through the windows of the Daroman's eyes as a lifetime of military training took over and cold hard calculations told him he was out of moves. His right hand was no good now, not with all that blood spilling from the gash in his wrist. I hadn't cut across; that doesn't work fast enough. That's why I'd sliced vertically along the artery.

The hand yanking my hair might've done some damage if he hadn't needed it to staunch the puncture in his throat that was competing with the laceration in his wrist to decide which would kill him first.

We stared at each other, him and me, as if neither of us had expected to travel this road and we each blamed the other for its destination. The clarity of his eyes, which I only now noticed were an almost sapphire blue, gave way to the watery blur of tears as he teetered to one side and then slumped to the ground.

I rose to my feet, coughing from what would soon be ugly and painful bruises around my neck. The other guards were splayed across the floor, eyes open, still conscious despite the paralysis. The Daroman who'd tried to strangle me whimpered as he waited for death. Fiery wrath rose like bile in my throat, demanding payment for what I'd endured. There are a dozen different civilisations on this continent, each with their own laws, their own courts. Not one of them would've denied me retribution.

The Scarlet Verses acted up something awful. They always do at times like these. They whispered ideas to me. Terrible ideas. But terrible things can be beautiful sometimes. Cruelty is a language

24

that transcends cultural barriers, which makes it useful when you want to send a message to those who speak no other.

Yes-yes! Yes-yes!' the verses repeated over and over like a drum beat that kept perfect pace with my heart. I felt a tightness on my face that turned out to be a grin matching the one I'd seen on the Daroman soldier when he'd tasted my tears.

I have other voices in my head too. My pappy, Durral Brown, who took an angry little Mahdek girl, lost in her own darkness, and shone a light to show her a different path. His wife, Enna, who saw that I couldn't walk her and Durral's path no matter how much I wanted to, and so helped me find my own. Others too, like Sir Gervaise and Sir Rosarite, two knights from a land far across the sea, who used words like *honour* and *courage* a lot, but what they really meant was love and compassion.

I crawled over to my pack near the edge of the tunnel and brought it back to the dying man, who was trying his best to keep from bleeding out. I took out a small clay jar and unstoppered the lid. The smell was nearly as bad as one of Conch's farts, which was probably what brought the little spire goat to sniff at the rim.

'Not for you,' I said. My voice was a raspy growl.

The goat curled his upper lip, took in a breath and I swear was about to belch me into paralysis again before he caught the look in my eyes and thought better of it.

There's not much you can do to stop a bleed as bad as the one on the Daroman, but before I'd come to Soul's Grave I'd spent a small fortune on a jar of *aquae sulfex*. Daroman medics use it to save the lives of their most valued officers. The guard must've recognised the smell, because he didn't fight me when I took his hand away from his wrist. Aquae sulfex has an oily, sticky texture that beats just about anything when it comes to staunching wounds and staving off infection. Wasn't long before the vein on his wrist was sealed up and the blood stopped spilling.

The wound on his throat wasn't as bad as I would've expected. I doubted he'd be singing in any choirs, but he wasn't going to die. Not yet, anyway. His fingers were weak as wet strands of grass when he tried to grab my arm.

'Don't bother trying to talk,' I told him.

He tried anyway. Didn't sound too good. Didn't matter though. I knew what he wanted to ask me. I wanted to smack him across the face and tell him he didn't deserve to know, and the fact that he so desperately needed an answer only made me less inclined to give him one. But there was Durral's voice in my ears, just like always. The savviest fighter I'd ever met, reminding me that surviving is all fine and dandy, but victory? That requires something . . . more.

'You think you can do this, kid?'

I shook my head, which was silly, seeing as how he wasn't there. *'Could you?'*

'Doubt it.'

'Then why the hells should I try?'

It's quiet, even in my imaginings, but somehow I can always hear that smile of his. *'You ever see a wild daisy blooming on top of a dune in the desert? Prettiest thing you ever saw.'*

'Quit it, Pappy. Everybody knows daisies don't grow in sand.'

'How can you know for sure unless you plant a seed now and then?'

Sometimes, I swear, I prefer the slithering hisses of the Scarlet Verses to the memories of that man's gentle laughter.

I slumped down next to the vicious brute who'd tried to kill me and had already admitted to killing plenty of others before me. I'm not as good as Durral at this. He always said my *arta loquit* – my eloquence – was the best he'd ever known. But this? This was beyond my talents. I wasn't even sure where to start.

26

'You believe in miracles?' I asked.

The Daroman's eyes were cloudy from loss of blood, but he was conscious enough to turn and stare at me like I was an idiot who'd apparently failed to notice the hell in which we'd found ourselves.

'Fair enough,' I conceded. 'The Berabesq claim that only their god can do miracles anyway.'

He gave a soft snort. A bubble of spit appeared between his lips.

'Yeah, I feel that way about the viziers sometimes too.' I leaned back against the rough stone wall, searching for words, searching for strength. 'But what if – and I'm just asking here – what if a man who'd descended into this pit of hate and despair, who'd come to delight in the misery and suffering of others because that's what this place had made of him, were to spit in the face of not just the clerics who put him here and their six-faced god, but fate itself?'

Confusion and suspicion spread across features now ashen and clammy. 'N-nature,' he managed to cough out, along with more spittle.

'Sure,' I said, knowing I was losing the fight. 'Nature. Nobody can do such evil as you've done here unless the seeds were already planted long ago. Born a killer, die a killer. But let's pretend a moment. Let's imagine the guy who climbs out of this prison defies both his nature and his destiny. What if he chooses a path better than fate intended? What would we call a person like that? Wouldn't we have to call him a . . .'

I let the silence hang between us. First lesson Durral ever taught me in arta loquit was that you never utter the word a person most needs to hear. Give them the space to find it themselves.

'Mmm . . .' he mumbled. His eyes were blinking shut now. Too much blood lost too quickly. He fought the shadows coming for him and tried again. 'Mmm . . .'

I knew what he was trying to say, and I sure as hell didn't want to hear it come out of his mouth. But I'm trying real hard to be

27

an Argosi, and my path, the Path of the Wild Daisy? It's all about flowers growing where nobody believes they should.

'Go on,' I urged him. 'Say the word.'

He did better than that: got five of 'em out, all in a whisper and too late to do the world any good. I'd wasted my aquae sulfex after all.

'Eighteen's kinda young to be so bitter, don't you think, kid?' Durral would've asked.

'Tried your way, Pappy. Traded righteous anger for a handful of seeds wasted on dead sand. Didn't do anyone a lick of good.'

'That so?'

Sometimes I can almost feel the battered second knuckle of Durral's forefinger under my chin, lifting it up a little higher. This time, though, it turned my attention towards the five other guards down on the floor. Bewildered gazes drifted from me to the dead Daroman, their glassy eyes were filled not just with tears, but something else too.

Hope.

'I could've been a miracle.' That's what the Daroman had said as he died. That's what his fellow guards had heard.

Sometimes you plant a seed in the desert because nobody, not the Berabesq clerics, not their god or anyone else's, not fate or even your own heart, knows for sure what might grow there.

3

Fifty Yards

I sat there a few minutes longer, finding my breath, awakening my
arta forteize. Can't say that the Argosi talent for resilience has ever
been my strongest suit. At times like these I always feel like I'm
made from brittle glass, so I draw my strength from elsewhere.

Enna Brown, now there's a woman with arta forteize. Punch
her, starve her, leave her out in the freezing cold . . . One time
some crazy girl she'd taken into her home and loved like her own
daughter stabbed her through the lung with a smallsword. You
cannot keep that woman down.

That's a sort of privilege, I think. A kind of wealth – no, an
inheritance. Knowing someone like Enna, seeing how all those
limits people impose on their own bodies and spirits don't have
nearly the power we believe? That's gold in your pocket right
there.

I spent a few of those coins getting to my feet, sliding on my
pack. The guards on the floor didn't look like they were going
anywhere soon. Conch must've dosed 'em with a bigger blast of
his belly gasses than he'd given me earlier.

'Come on,' I told the spire goat as I turned towards the tunnel.
It wouldn't be far to go now; we were already in the lowest depths
of the prison. Based on the information that silvery-white stallion

had bought me, the cell I was looking for was maybe fifty yards away. Not far at all.

Conch butted me in the back of the leg with those stubby horns of his on account of how I hadn't moved yet.

'I know, I know,' I said. 'Just give me a second.'

First lesson you learn in arta forteize is that the body hardly ever tells you to stop. Battered, bloody, starved and parched, it'll keep on going if you ask it to. The mind, though, the mind is full of warnings about how bad you'll hurt yourself if you keep following the path you're on, and the awful things waiting for you just around the next bend.

I closed my eyes a moment, stilled my breath. Arta forteize isn't about forcing your body or your mind to deny itself. It's about being patient, breathing in slow and steady as you fill yourself not with calm but with something more potent: trust.

I can do this, I reminded myself, though the voice in my head sounded like Enna's now. *I'm Ferius Parfax, the Path of the Wild Daisy. There's no darkness in this world so cruel I can't meet it with a smile on my face and a card up my sleeve.*

The words are easy. The trick is infusing them with a truth more potent than your own weakness and fear.

My fingers reached into one of the inside pockets of my waistcoat, slid out the card I was keeping there and held it up to my face. Only then did I open my eyes. One of the guards had been carrying a brass oil lantern that was sideways on the ground now, rolling a little this way, a little that way. From that feeble, flickering light, I gazed one last time at the disharmony card to prepare myself for what came next.

Soul's Grave was being shut down within days, the guard had said, likely by the same prince whose feud with the warden vizier I'd stoked in my attempt to secure a pardon. What was that next part again?

30

'The warden vizier's got us sacrificing convicts in protest, Six each morning, one for each of his god's six faces. We ran out yesterday, which means come dawn—'

'I'm ready,' I told the smirking, too-clever-by-half face painted on the card. She didn't say anything back.

I took my first step into the deeper shadows waiting for me. Conch nipped at my heels to hurry up. I took my time though. Fifty yards isn't far, but six months and seven hundred miles is a long way to go just to bury a dead girl.

4

The Remains

Conch kept squirming between my legs as we walked past the cells that weren't much more than roughly hewn alcoves in the rock. Iron bars thick as my wrists dug at least a foot into the stone above and below. Most of these doors probably hadn't been opened since the prisoners had first been shoved inside – not until the guards had started sacrificing them, which explained the rusty debris on the floor directly below the hinges.

There are a lot of different ways to kill a person. Walking those long, winding fifty yards, I reckoned the guards had tried out just about every method they could conceive.

'Seeds in the sand. You really believe that nonsense, Pappy?'

All those different kinds of killing, but the bodies always left the same: flat on their back in the middle of the cell, palms tied together in prayer with the fingers touching just below their chins. A tiny pile of sand covered each eye in accordance with an old Berabesq funerary injunction for the newly dead: *When seeking your place among the heavens, never lose sight of the sand whence you came.*

Strange to think the guards had honoured that tradition. They were prisoners as much as the convicts they'd killed on the vizier's behalf. Guess they'd been right in their ominous prediction about what happened when there were no convicts left to kill.

'. . . six each morning, one for each of his god's six faces. We ran out yesterday, which means come dawn—'

Conch let out a low, keening sound. Wasn't like him to be so skittish. He kept pawing at the backs of my legs with his hoofs. When spire goats get scared, their instinct is to climb high as they can.

'All right, little fella,' I said, keeping my eyes on the tunnel ahead while I reached down to pick him up. The spire goat hadn't been looking for my help, it turned out, only my permission. Somehow he managed to scramble up the back of me, those little hoofs of his finding every fold in my trousers till he was perched sideways along the edge of my belt. I felt him leap up to my shoulder and teeter a moment before nestling against my cheek.

'You're heavier than you look,' I told him, trying to accustom myself to the awkward weight. Conch's nostrils flared like he was taking in a deep breath. 'Okay, okay. No need to paralyse me again.'

With the goat ensconced on my shoulder, I went on down the passage, one foot in front of the other, bearing witness to the dead. Was this my fault? Would I be painting two dozen more disharmony cards to carry around with me forever?

Forget it, I thought. *I'm drawing the line at taking on the debts of butchers and child murderers.* Much as I disliked this place and all it represented, every single felon incarcerated here had committed atrocities such as could not be forgiven. All but the one who'd been stupid enough to get arrested for stealing the warden vizier's prized stallion.

And then I saw her, and all my arta forteize fled.

Behind the bars, a slender figure lay flat on the cold stone floor of her cell. Straw-blonde hair spread out like the rays of the sun around her head. She'd always been about the most sacrilegious person you could ever meet, but now her palms were pressed

33

together beneath her chin, bound with twine. A tiny heap of sand covered each eye.

'Oh, Arissa.' I wept.

I'd hoped the guard had lied, that not all the prisoners were dead. But hope is a bright and shiny coin; staring at it won't buy you spit. And the Way of Water? The one every Argosi follows before any of the others? Sometimes it leads you nowhere but deeper into the desert.

The warden vizier had fulfilled one promise though: on the stone wall opposite Arissa's cell, framed in gilded tamarisk oak behind ironglass so clear you could read every line of the prince's elegant calligraphy, was the meaningless pardon I'd bought for Arissa.

Had she been looking up at it when the guards had been killing off the other prisoners, six each day? Had she hoped that when they finally got to her cell, those pretty words in gold and black inks would save her?

I stormed up to the frame bolted to the stone wall. Ironglass is almost unbreakable, but I'd brought a second clay jar with me, meant for getting through the bars of Arissa's cell. I poured a few drops of the reddish-black syrup on each of the four iron rivets bolting the frame to the wall and stood back to let it do its work. A minute later the frame came crashing down, everything breaking except the ironglass. Careful not to dislodge Conch from my shoulder, I knelt down and retrieved the decree. I turned back to face the dead girl lying cold on the floor behind iron bars that would never again be opened.

My Berabesq isn't too good, but when I'd brought that sapphire casket full of saint's bones to the prince in payment for his pardon, I'd also hired a translator to accompany me to make sure the prince didn't play any tricks on me.

"'Thus, with this edict,' I read aloud, "'by his royal hand and in God's name, the foreign thief known as Arissa is hereby pardoned of her crimes and freed of Soul's Grave upon the public reading of this decree.'"

Like a child giving in to a temper tantrum, I tore the lavishly illuminated vellum into strips and hurled them through the bars. Conch was bleating, struggling to stay balanced on my shoulder, but I didn't care. 'You hear that, Arissa?' I cried out. 'You're a free woman now. I freed you. So go on now. Get off your butt and go make trouble someplace else. You can't be here no more, you understand? You can't be dead because I followed the Way of Water and bought you a pardon, cos that's what an Argosi does and I'm supposed to be an Argosi now!'

I sobbed a while longer before I finally tossed the debt card into the cell to lie among the scraps of that worthless pardon. 'Paid in full,' I said. 'You got a problem with that?' I turned to leave that cursed place behind.

Hadn't even gone two steps before the dead answered me back.

'Now why would anyone rip up a beautiful decree like that when you could've just hired a forger to change the name? You could've sold it for a fortune to free some other prisoner in some other prison.'

You ever see a spire goat spooked so bad his body won't even try to flee because he knows his legs are too short to outrun whatever's after him? Funniest thing you ever saw, right up until terror and instinct make him belch right in your face.

'Damn it,' I swore as my limbs froze and I toppled backwards into the cold, dark and now all-too-familiar embrace of Soul's Grave.

5

Rat Girl

If you don't live your life righteous and proper, one day you're going to wake up with a rock digging into the back of your skull and a spire goat's tongue licking your face.

'Love you, too, buddy,' I mumbled.

I wasn't expecting a reply, but got one anyway. 'Aw, but aren't you the sweetest thing? Maybe we should go steady.'

My eyes shot open, to be greeted by the sight of filthy, matted hair dangling around my face, casting jagged shadows across a smile that was all cracked lips and mischief. She was laughing at me.

Careful not to move too quick, I wiped away the slick wetness and gritty grains of sand from my face. The fact that I could move my hand explained why Conch's belch hadn't filled my nostrils with its usual sulphuric stench, but a sweeter, less punishing fragrance, like rotting roses. Apparently spire goats can spew gasses that just knock a predator out rather than paralysing them. Turning my head a fraction, I caught sight of Conch huddled in a corner, looking mighty sheepish for a goat.

Can't blame you for gettin' spooked, I thought. *Not with the dead rising up from their graves.*

Returning my gaze to the woman on top of me, not at all convinced that this ragged corpse was, in fact, alive, I asked tentatively, 'Arissa?'

36

The grin widened, showing me teeth in worse need of cleaning than the spire goat's. 'Yeah, Rat Girl?'

She was the only person alive who'd ever dared call me that. In fairness, back then I had no other name, and teasing me had been her favourite pastime. Still was, apparently. 'I have two questions,' I said.

'Go on.'

'Are you alive?'

She winked, dislodging more of the sand stuck to her eyelids that had been covering them while she'd played dead in her cell. A few grains fell onto my nose and cheeks, tickling me. 'Simple con, really. The clerics who'd ordered the guards to start executing prisoners a week ago had sweetened the deal by sending down casks of wine and smoking pipes filled with rapture weed. Nice gesture, don't you think? Eases the spiritual discomfort of murdering convicts, one supposes.'

'So, you figured if you pretended to already be dead . . .'

The left corner of her mouth rose higher. 'Those idiot guards were so drunk and stoned by the third morning that they stopped bothering to keep track of who was left to kill. Every night they sat in their alcove, playing drinking games. Loser had to kill the next prisoner. By the time that big Zhuban woman with the scars got to me, I had sand over my eyes and twine around my hands. A little ash diluted in spit and rubbed on the lips looks like the mortification after being choked to death. The Zhuban figured one of her fellow guards must've raped me, then suffocated me to keep me quiet. She walked right by my cell without so much as a prayer for me or a curse for him.'

The casual way she brought up such heinous crimes stirred a terrible fear in me. 'Please, Arissa, tell me no one—'

The smile disappeared. 'Don't ask me that, Rat Girl. Don't ever ask me about what was done to me in this place, or the things I've done of my own free will.'

Durral would've insisted that pain has to be given voice before the body can set it aside. Enna, though, she warned that some memories are like scabs: *'Pick at them too soon, my darling, and the wound gets infected.'* Enna's usually right.

'How did you get the sand and twine?' I asked instead. The answer wasn't hard to guess, but part of arta loquit is making space for others to guide the conversation towards a place they feel safest. Arissa had always loved showing off.

With a filthy, calloused fingertip, she brushed the sand off my cheek. 'One of the few privileges accorded every prisoner is the right to have a duly-appointed cleric descend to your cell once a month to regale you with the horrors awaiting in the particular hell to which God will consign you after your death. Most convicts decline that delightful ritual.'

Now it was my turn to smile. Far from despairing at such a litany of horrific details, Arissa would've revelled in them.

'I did love the sound of those floppy sandals coming down the passageway,' she said wistfully. 'The leather soles always left a few grains of sand on the floor just outside the bars. Never knew why I kept scooping them up and hiding them in the corner of my cell. Lock up a thief all you want, but she'll always find something to steal, I suppose.'

Beneath the rasping cackle I detected a touch of pride in those words, so I kept her talking. 'What about that twine they bind the hands of the dead with? I don't suppose the clerics left any of that behind on their visits.'

Arissa reached into the filthy, mottled rags that barely covered her emaciated bones and produced a ratty tangle of silvery twine. 'Now this – this took some skill. Too distinctive to fake with strips of the sackcloth we wear down here. So I made a length of string from strands of my hair and tied one end around a sliver of rusted iron I scraped off one of the bars to use as a tiny grappling hook. I spent an entire day and night collecting scraps left behind when they'd wrapped the hands of the prisoners killed that morning in the cells opposite mine.'

The explanation made sense. Daring, ingenious and a little petulant. All qualities I associated with Arissa. On the other hand, head wounds are funny things, especially when accompanied by noxious, narcotic gasses expelled from a spire goat's belly. There was a more than even chance I was hallucinating all of this, except for one small, confounding detail.

'Arissa, is there some reason why I woke up imagining a goat was licking my face, but now he's way over in the corner of the passageway?'

Laughter. A thunderclap followed by a downpour of mischievous chortling. 'Couldn't help myself, Rat Girl.' She rolled off me to sit cross-legged on the floor. 'There you were, laid out like the slumbering hero in a fairy tale dreaming of the kiss of his beautiful princess, only to discover it's his horse licking his face. After the goat knocked you out, I used my trusty grappling hook to snare what was left of your little clay jar of solvent. Once that foul-smelling syrup had dissolved the lock on my cell door, I thought to myself, *Arissa, you know how Rat Girl's always had a crush on you?*'

'I neve—'

She ignored me. '*Well, seeing as how she's come all the way down for a visit, why not do the hospitable thing, and let her imagine there's a goat licking her face when in fact it'll turn out to have been a beautiful princess all along?*'

I leaned up on my elbows to get my first proper look at her. Probably shouldn't have done that.

She bristled under the scrutiny. 'What's the problem?' she demanded, a brittle challenge in her tone. She tried to brush her hand through her hair the way elegant ladies do, only her fingers got caught in the knots and muck. 'You implying that I'm not beautiful any more, Rat Girl?'

She wasn't. How could she be? A whole year they'd kept her down here. More beatings than meals, more spit than water in the leaky wooden bowl she'd had to drink from.

And all those other things she doesn't want me asking about, I thought.

Still woozy from Conch's unintentional act of gassy self-defence, I managed to get onto my hands and knees. I crawled closer to Arissa and stared at her long and hard, making sure she saw me doing so. It's not the Argosi way to coddle people with lies and half-truths. Arissa's bottom lip was trembling now, the laughter giving way to something else.

'The girl you once were is gone,' I told her. 'You'll never again see her in the mirror.'

She said nothing, just nodded with a stuttering downward motion of her chin that reminded me more of a servant awaiting the lash than the brash thief without whose teachings and protection I never would've survived long enough to meet Durral and Enna and learn the seven talents that had kept me alive ever since.

My hands went to the knot in her hair where her own fingers had gotten snared while pretending to preen a moment before. It took patience, and more time than we had to waste, but I got the knot untangled, because it's also the Argosi way to see people not only for what they are, but for what they can become.

I rested my forehead on hers. She felt cold as a corpse. I wanted to wrap my arms around her, share my warmth. I didn't though; my arta precis warned me that Arissa's prank kiss, bizarre and inappropriate as it had been, was meant to protect herself from more genuine intimacy than she could handle.

'There's this woman I came down here to meet though,' I went on, feeling the oily filth of her brow dirtying my own skin. 'The one who walks out of this prison tonight, gets a hundred good meals in her, cries herself to sleep a hundred nights. The gal who wakes up one morning and discovers she's still got that same untamed spirit as when I first met her. Only difference is that now it's tempered, not by suffering but by survival, forged into a steel so strong she'll stride across this continent like a titan.' I sat back on my haunches, took another long look at her and let her see reflected in my face what my arta precis saw beneath all the bruises and the grime and the misery. 'That woman? She's gonna be a sight to see, Arissa. A. Sight. To. See.'

They weren't my words, not really. Enna had said them to me a long while back. But some spells work more than once.

Arissa breathed in heavy and held that dank air in her lungs for a long time before she reached up to a nearby iron bar and hauled herself to her feet. She waited for me to do the same before she asked, 'You came all this way because you've still got that crush on me? I mean, I always knew you were inclined in that direction, but I prefer a big strapping man with hair gold as mine who keeps his mouth shut except while he's kissing me, not some annoying, can't-stop-talking-for-five-whole-minutes, scrawny little—'

'Rat Girl?' I finished for her.

Arissa held up the disharmony card I'd tossed into her cell when I'd thought she was dead. 'What is this ugly thing anyway?' She stared with pinched eyes at the painted image of a young woman with hair like sunlight and a devil's smile, dressed in outlandish crimson clothes topped by a dusky red frontier hat coming down at an angle across her brow. 'Is this supposed to be some kind of . . . memento? A token to remind you of a debt you never owed and I never asked you to repay.'

'Pretty much.'

'Doesn't look a thing like me.'

I picked up my discarded leather pack, took out the biggest item inside and handed it to Arissa. It had been almost as difficult to secure as the prince's pardon. You ever tried finding a dark red frontier hat in the middle of Berabesq? Those folks don't take to hats. Damn near had to steal another sacred horse to afford the idiot thing.

Worth every penny.

Arissa stared at the hat like it was a magical artefact dropped into her hands from the stars above. A potent talisman that would turn her beautiful as she used to be the moment she put it on. It didn't, of course. Not until she got the angle just right. Then, just for a moment . . . well, best not make a habit of exaggerating, I suppose.

'I take it back,' Arissa said, standing up real tall all of a sudden and looking down at me with an appraising eye. 'Maybe I will lick your face again since you enjoyed it so much the first time.'

She turned and winked at Conch like the two of them were sharing a private joke. The little spire goat gave a bleating snicker like he sometimes does. It echoed so loud in the tunnel it almost drowned out the sound of another, more bitter laugh.

'Arissa?' I asked. 'Is it possible you're not the only prisoner still alive down here?'

She didn't look surprised, but her expression turned hard as stone and dry as grave dust. 'They were saving him for last.' She pointed at the pack in my hand. 'Did you bring a knife? Something real sharp?'

'Why?'

Arissa took that as assent, turning to walk with a slow, stiff gait towards the last cell at the end of the tunnel. 'Find me a blade. There's somebody down here who needs killing.'

6

Friends in Low Places

Some people, no matter their circumstances, manage to look like they own the place. Dress them in rags and dump them in a palace, they'll dust themselves off and saunter over to the throne like they're expecting to be crowned. Find them locked up in the worst prison on the continent? They'll lean against rusted iron bars, staring at you so smug it's like every step you ever took had no purpose but to bring you to them. To him.

Long and lean, naked to the waist, he wore the dark copper tattoos across his chest and arms like a king's vestments – no, not a king: a priest or maybe a holy man. Only there was nothing holy about him that I could see. Long, curly hair the colour of red wine through smoky glass hung down to his shoulders. His eyes . . . well, if trouble was a colour, those eyes gleamed with pure calamity.

From the moment I saw him, my arta precis picked out three discernible facts. First, this guy couldn't have spent more than a week in Soul's Grave. He was beat up real bad, but the bruises and cuts were all fresh. Second, there wasn't a glimmer of a doubt in him that I would keep Arissa from killing him. In fact, he was absolutely certain I was going to set him free. The third thing I sensed about this rangy, feral-eyed swaggerer couldn't be put into words. It was like staring into the face of a stranger who, looking back at you, sees their own reflection.

'Give me your knife,' Arissa commanded. 'Give me whatever you got that's sharp and long and you won't be needing any time soon, because there won't be any edge left once I'm done carving up his carcass for the sand beetles.'

'Who is he?' I asked.

The prisoner didn't strike me as bothered by Arissa's macabre intentions. He wasn't looking at her at all in fact; his eyes were peering so deep into mine it was as if the two of us were alone down here.

'Don't let him hold your gaze,' Arissa warned, though she didn't turn away herself. 'This snake can do things with his eyes. The guards wore blindfolds any time they brought him food. Some sort of spell, I think.'

'That's no spell,' I told her as I locked eyes with the prisoner. 'And there's no need to fuss over me. Let him stare as long as he wants.'

Some people think the Argosi can work magic on account of the way we can travel just about anywhere we want without fear of the dangers that confine most people to the same seven square miles of the town where they were born. After all, somebody who can face down a mage or a military commander with nothing but a smile on their face and a few cards in their hand has to be magic, right?

It's not though. 'Magic ain't the Argosi way,' Durral's fond of saying. We're gamblers. Wanderers. Mapmakers. The only spells we cast are part of an inheritance shared by all human beings: music, dance, games of chance, languages, swagger, patience, charm . . . Heck, one time I saw Durral turn back a dozen armed bravos with nothing but a dirty joke.

44

It was a hell of a joke.

We're not the only ones with a bag of tricks though. Take the legendary Daroman marshals service, famous for being the world's most relentless fugitive trackers. What's less well known are their skills at interrogation. Some say the first marshals came to study with hermit snake charmers right here in Berabesq. Others claim they travelled up north to learn folk magic from Zhuban warrior-poets who can lure a stag so close they can pierce its heart with an arrow before the beast knows it's in danger. Wherever it comes from, you find yourself staring down a marshal who's mastered the art and before long you'll be spilling every secret you know while polishing their boots for them.

The guy locked behind those rusted iron bars was no marshal, but whatever he was doing with his eyes had to be pretty close. Never in my eighteen years had I felt so small, so powerless and so desperately in love.

Which feels especially weird when you're not partial to boys in the first place. 'Go on,' I told him, drowning in the endless black oil of his gaze. 'You can do better than that, can't you?

He held on a few seconds more, then closed his eyes and winced.

'I hear that when you push that trick too hard it can leave you with a nasty headache,' I observed casually.

The grimace on the prisoner's face gave me all the confirmation I needed. He slammed his palms against the iron bars, betraying his lack of emotional control over himself. Happens with people accustomed to controlling others. 'Arta forteize, I presume?' He managed to make it sound like a pestilence.

'Arta forteize is resilience. That was *arta valar*.'

His lips twisted into a disbelieving smirk. 'Dauntlessness?'

'I prefer to think of it as swagger.'

He chewed on that a moment. Didn't seem to like the taste. 'So I had you the entire time! You weren't resisting my mesmerism at all, you simply hid your submission from me, returning my gaze like some half-witted farm animal!'

I brought the back of my hand to my forehead and pretended to swoon. 'Darling, you keep talkin' so sweet, you're gonna have me fainting.' I let my arm fall to my side and walked past Arissa to the bars so I could get a closer look at him. 'What's lover boy in for, anyway?' I asked her.

'His name is Chedran. He murders people. *That's* his crime.' Murder isn't a word I'd ever heard Arissa shy away from. The way she said it now though was like it woke a whole nest of spiders in her belly.

'Children?' I guessed.

'Twelve of them,' Chedran confirmed, grinning with a madman's theatrical delight. 'Runaways. Stolen from a kindly Berabesq noblewoman who'd given them sanctuary. Throats slit. Bodies bathed in lantern oil and set ablaze in her courtyard until there was nothing left of them but charred bones.' He made a show of licking one of the bars between us. 'Then I arranged their skeletons in their beds, under the covers, for the stupid cow to find the next morning.'

Arissa grabbed me by the front of my shirt. 'Hand me a blade. Now. Otherwise I'll rip him apart with my teeth.'

'The Argosi won't let you slaughter me,' the stranger said. 'Their silly "Way of Water" forbi—'

Arissa shoved me aside, spinning on her heel and holding up a card. It wasn't the disharmony I'd painted of her, but one of my razor-sharp throwing cards. Damn, that girl had not lost her touch! I hadn't even noticed her picking my pocket. 'I wasn't asking her permission,' she hissed.

Chedran didn't flinch, just leaned even closer to the bars. Those copper-coloured tattoos danced across the lean musculature of his chest and shoulders as he moved. He lifted his chin and smoothed the dark reddish curls away from his neck, daring Arissa to cut him.

Back when we were running with the Black Galleon gang, I'd seen her bury a throwing knife in an oak door from thirty yards away. One flick of her wrist and she could've sliced the braggart's throat wide open. Nothing in his manner revealed so much as an ounce of fear. It was like this was all some penny-a-ticket stage play and he was the only one holding the script.

Funny how people get stuck in their ways. Is it nature that makes us repeat the same patterns over and over? Or is the price of mastering a skill forgetting how to do anything else? I'd known Chedran all of ten minutes and already I recognised him as a con artist through and through, tone deaf to any music but that which he could play on people's emotions. Even now, with Arissa poised to slit his throat, he preferred the pretence of being in control over confessing the simple truth that would save his life.

'He's not guilty,' I told her, because calling him innocent would've left a bad taste in my mouth. 'Chedran didn't kill those children.'

Arissa took three steps back from his cell so he wouldn't be able to reach through the bars and snatch the steel card from her hand. Only then did she turn her fury on me. 'He *confessed*! Every night since they brought him here, he brags about how he murdered each of those kids. Repeats their names over and over, rambles on about what foods they liked, their favourite stories. All of it.'

'That was just his fear talking, hiding beneath all that spite.' I turned my arta precis on Chedran, my gaze tracing the jagged lines

47

of malice etched into his features. Lurking in the grooves between his smug superiority and his disdain for me was an all-consuming anxiety over the awful things that might be taking place far beyond these walls. The longer I watched him, the more rigid his mask became, but he couldn't hide the faint salty scent of sweat forming on his brow.

You would've made one hell of a poker player, friend, I thought. *But not even the best card sharps can bluff an Argosi.*

'Chedran couldn't risk anyone figuring out those kids are still alive,' I told Arissa. 'He must've dug up bones from a children's cemetery far enough away that no one would connect the grave robbing to the scorched remains he left under the bedsheets for that noblewoman to find. Charred black so no one would look too closely and maybe notice the ages weren't quite right. He laid a scene so grotesque that when the authorities captured him they were too riled up by the atrocities they'd imagined – not to mention his whole monstrous-villain act – to ask themselves why anyone would go to all that trouble just to murder a bunch of innocent kids.'

'You're saying . . .' Arissa was practically shivering with rage. I couldn't tell whether it was because she thought my explanation was nuts or because his deception made her want to throttle him even more. 'You expect me to believe that this piece of crap *rescued* those twelve runaways? Snuck them away under cover of darkness from some tender-hearted highborn lady who, by all accounts, had provided them sanctuary in her own home? You're telling me *she's* the monster?'

That part *had* confounded me for a minute. Why would a woman of such prominence and thus under constant scrutiny bring a group of strays into her home if she meant them harm? Despite the stories kids tell each other in orphanages, rich folks rarely go to the trouble of housing, feeding and clothing hapless urchins just to make soup out of them.

Arta tuco is the Argosi talent for strategy, but Enna calls it pathfinding, because it's like looking at a map and seeing all the hundreds of ways each place could connect together. On this particular map I saw Chedran, who feared for the children, and the noblewoman, who meant them no harm. Yet he saw her fondness for them as a threat. Fondness leads to attachment. Attachment grows from affinity, a sense of being alike, which is only possible through familiarity. Familiarity emerges from understanding, from learning more about some—

'Who are those kids?' I asked suddenly. 'Why were you so afraid that noblewoman would discover the identities of a bunch of runaways?'

The look in Chedran's eyes changed. Cold and callous they remained, but something else broke through. Bitterness. Loneliness. Resentment against me in particular even though we'd only just met. '*Who* we are means nothing to the rest of the world,' he said. 'It's *what* we are that gets us killed.'

Strange way to talk about oneself – like you weren't a person at all, barely a human being . . .

Oh.

My reaction betrayed me, and Chedran saw it. 'Fate brought you to me, Ferius Parfax.' He spoke now with the fervour of a roadside preacher drunk on his own superstitions. 'I heard you speak of your debt to this smug, self-righteous thief who is entirely guilty of the crime for which she was convicted. What about those innocents you abandoned seven years ago to whom you owe *everything*?'

Arissa was watching me, suddenly suspicious. 'What's he talking about, Rat Girl? How does know your name when this is the first time I've heard it?'

49

I hadn't found my name back when the two of us were running together. Chedran spitting it at her like that had stolen my chance to share it with her.

'Oh, Ferius Parfax is practically a legend among my people,' Chedran went on, smiling with so much venom and arrogance I might've mistaken him for a Jan'Tep lord magus – if I hadn't already figured out what he really was. 'That's why she isn't going to let you lay a finger on me. Instead she's going to break me out of this prison and help me find those children before it's too late.' He pressed his face between the bars. 'There are so few of us now after all.'

I cursed myself for having been so blind. There hadn't been anything to see though. Not really. We don't look so different from the children of other nations who came to this continent after us. Still, those wine-coloured curls of which Chedran was so proud should've been my first clue. We do tend to produce more redheads than most. Used to anyway. These days, there can't be more than a couple of hundred of us left.

'Those kids he snuck out of that noblewoman's house are Mahdek,' I told Arissa. I hadn't said that word aloud in months; that's how little I think about the people I left behind seven years ago. 'Mahdek,' I repeated, a penance or maybe a curse. 'Refugees from a long-dead culture. Like Chedran. Like me.'

7

Unpaid Debts

We made a strange quartet as we climbed up winding stairs from
the cold, crushing embrace of Soul's Grave to a dawn sky so warm
and gentle I felt her sun kiss my cheek. She burnished the desert a
brassy gold while her brother the south wind sent a breeze that made
the sand dance around our feet. An Argosi learns to take comfort
from these moments, to hold them close and smooth them against
our skin like newly woven silk. Such memories become a fine coat
against the chills to come, armour to deflect the slings and arrows
of callous voices that can't let beauty be, not even for an instant.

'How lovely,' Chedran said, twisting the words to mean their
opposite.

The blow hadn't been meant for me. Arissa had been his target,
punishing her for those first tears she'd allowed herself. The kind
that can't make us forget the pains of our past, but remind us that
a kinder future might still await. Her right hand darted up to wipe
away those salty, healing droplets before they could do their work,
smearing the filth and grime of Soul's Grave back onto her cheeks.
Conch rubbed his muzzle against her leg. She shooed him away.

The Way of Water, I told myself, observing Chedran's unconscious
pride in the damage he'd done. *Every desert has an oasis if you look
hard enough.*

It was the manner of our escape that had set him off. Those secret tunnels I'd paid so dearly to discover had turned out to be a myth propagated by shysters to sucker wealthy foreigners desperate to rescue their incarcerated family members. Wasn't anything the victims could do about it either, since complaining to the law about a prison break failing on account of a fraudulent map would only see them permanently reunited with their loved ones behind bars. Chedran had insisted we could fight our way past the guards. Arissa, well, she'd known better than to drink from that particular mirage. Me, I'd held to the Path of the Wild Daisy.

'They're . . . they're all dead,' Arissa had said, emerging from the last row of cells, past the empty guard alcove and into a wider passage where four corpses awaited us on the ground. The last remaining jailers of Soul's Grave stared up at us with dead eyes and placid smiles. All except for one.

The broad-shouldered Zhuban woman was waiting for us by the iron-banded door that led out of the lower levels and up a quarter-mile long set of rough-hewn stone stairs to the surface. She dangled the ring of thick brass keys needed to open the three locks at the top, middle and bottom of the impregnable door. Each trio of guards on duty was only ever given one of those keys, which made the prospect of bribing your way out of Soul's Grave both too expensive and too risky.

'You kill 'em?' I asked, gesturing to her dead comrades.

The Zhuban shook her head, sending sparse strands of stringy black hair whipping around her face. In her other hand she held out a blue flower petal with gleaming yellow edges. 'A gift from the clerics,' she said gruffly. 'To be ingested after we executed the last prisoner. The promise of a gentler passing into their god's embrace than any the prince's troops would offer once they hunted us down for our loyal service.' She tossed her petal into the air, watching it drift away to land on the cheek of one of her dead colleagues. 'The last thing he said before he stopped breathing was that it tasted of oranges.'

She turned back to the door and placed each of the three keys into their respective locks. 'The mechanism is devious and intricate. The keys must be turned at the exact same time or else a fourth lock will engage that can only be opened from the outside.'

'Go on,' I told Arissa and Chedran. 'Should be the two of you who open the way out of here.'

Arissa said nothing. Chedran sneered at the guard. 'You should have taken the poison,' he told her. 'The prince's soldiers won't bother pursuing a pair of escaped convicts. They'll assume you followed the clerics' orders and exterminated every last one of us. The incarceration records will be incinerated to avoid any diplomatic incidents with those nations whose citizens were unlawfully detained at Soul's Grave. No doubt the warden vizier and his clerics have already slithered off to some monastic sanctuary where they'll be left alone. Too much trouble to violate religious laws. Ah, but the jailers . . . you know how it goes. The Berabesq people will demand that someone suffer for the atrocities committed in their name. The so-called Faithful, with their razor-tipped gloves and so, so many ways to torment the body without letting the spirit flee . . .' He leaned closer to whisper in her ear. 'Your suffering will be the stuff of legend long before the Faithful are finished with you.'

'Shut your fool mouth until she gives you the signal to turn the key,' I told him.

Arissa though, she sided with Chedran. 'You didn't see what the guards did, Rat Girl. What *she* did.'

'I saw enough.'

I nodded to the Zhuban, who counted down from three and then slowly turned her key. Arissa and Chedran had no choice but to do likewise. When the keys wouldn't turn any more, the mechanism inside the door kept going for three more long seconds. A click, a thunk, and then the scrape of a heavy bolt sliding back before the door swung open like it was inviting us through. I waited for Chedran and Arissa to go first, giving Conch a gentle kick in the butt to get him to follow after them.

'You planning on running?' I asked the Zhuban as she stood back for me to go next. 'Five can travel as discreetly as four. We might be able to help each other along the way.'

'No, the Mahdek was right. The prince's soldiers and the Faithful won't concern themselves with counting dead prisoners. They will, however, hunt down every last guard.'

'I can show you ways to evad—'

'Perhaps that's as it should be,' she said, cutting me off. 'Lies will be spread about Soul's Grave by the warden vizier and his clerics. Even by the mob, who will pretend they never knew what was happening here. Perhaps someone should stay behind to remind the Berabesq people of the truth.'

Durral once told me that honour was like a dashing portrait of yourself that you hide behind. Looks nice, fools some folks, but no good at stopping a blade. 'They won't believe you,' I warned her. 'The Faithful will have you on the rack in the city square while the prosecutors shout down everything that comes out of your mouth other than a confession. Believin' you can sway 'em with words alone . . .'

I let the warning die on my lips. The Zhuban was grinning at me like I'd just said something hilarious. Which I guess I had. 'Gettin' all them folks ta hear the truth?' she asked, mocking the way I talked. 'Reckon that would take . . .'

She held it there, leaving the last part for me.

'A miracle,' I said.

As I set foot upon the first of those steps out of hell, I imagined daisies growing from the barren rock. Wild daisies.

Alas, not everyone was so sanguine about our departure. With Arissa, it was only the raw, unassailable beauty of her first dawn after a night lasting almost a year that shook her bitterness. Chedran, though . . . Chedran was seething. Knowing his bile couldn't burn me, he'd spewed it at Arissa instead.

'How lovely.'

I crossed the sand between us, turning my back on the sun. He was spoiling for a fight, and I was sorely tempted to give him one. Without the iron bars of his cell to hang on to, he wasn't nearly as steady as he pretended. Seven days in prison may not sound like much compared with Arissa's three hundred, but that first week is when the guards make it their business to break you. Chedran's snake-charmer gaze had made the guards skittish enough to wear blindfolds during his beatings, but it hadn't hindered their determination. He'd been left with bruises on his back so black I'd almost mistaken them for more tattoos. The way he walked, the stiffness not just in his legs but in his pelvis, told me they'd done other things to him too.

That explained why he couldn't tolerate the Zhuban guard seeking redemption, or Arissa hoping a thousand sunny tomorrows might make up for all those awful yesterdays.

'Those injuries of yours need rest and healing,' I reminded him. I kept my voice flat, devoid of anything but dispassionate logic so as not to arouse his cynicism. 'We're likely to encounter trouble on the way, and it's going to be you and me who do the fighting. I used up most of my aquae sulfex on those . . .' Here, I allowed a touch of shame to shade my words; he'd like that. 'Will you allow me to make restitution by offering my shoulder as we walk?'

'You think I desire your help?' He jabbed a finger at Arissa. 'She's far weaker than I am.'

Funny how an assertion can be entirely true and yet utterly false at the same time. 'She doesn't have twelve Mahdek runaways waiting for her to rescue them before some heathen-hunting posse of Berabesq Faithful or a coven of Jan'Tep hextrackers finds them first. Arissa can afford to be stubborn. But can you?'

Chedran's eyes narrowed. Instincts bone-deep had him attempt his mesmerism on me again so he could feel like I was under his spell instead of pitying him. I waited until he'd done giving himself a headache, then once again offered my shoulder. At last he put his arm around my neck and leaned against me as we began our slow, awkward journey towards the hills where poor Quadlopo was waiting for me.

'We'll make for your camp,' Chedran declared, as if doing so put him back in charge. 'Tomorrow we leave the thief behind. She's too weak, too damaged to be of any use. She would only slow us down. Once rid of her, we'll acquire fresh mounts and ride for the meeting place where the children will be waiting for me.'

Arissa shot him a look that could've set a forest ablaze in the middle of a rainstorm.

'You carrying any money?' I asked Chedran.

'What?'

'Money. Gold, gemstones, maybe some lender's scripts we could exchange for horses and supplies?'

Leaning against me for support, Chedran weighed more than I'd expected. All that lean, ropy muscle, I suppose. His attitude was the heavier burden though. 'You found me in a prison cell. How stupid must you be to assume the magistrates, the bailiffs, the clerics and finally the prison guards would've permitted me to hide a single coin on my person?'

56

'Well, that's the problem, see? I spent every coin I had getting into that same prison. Which means the only way we're going to acquire those horses you're so keen on is to steal them. Don't know if you've noticed, but the Berabesq are real protective of their livestock. So unless you plan on ridin' on the spire goat's back . . .' Conch gave a snort that made it clear what he thought of that idea. I shot Arissa a grin. 'Guess we'll need to find ourselves a professional thief to acquire less ornery mounts.'

Chedran was quiet for a while, limping alongside me. Every few steps he tried to walk on his own, then stumbled and had to let me take his arm across my shoulders again. 'So this is the Way of Water,' he said.

'Not so bad, is it?' I asked.

He turned his head and spat in the sand behind us. '*That* for your Way of Water.'

8

Heroes and Horse Thieves

Those next days and weeks came and went in flashes for me, no longer measured in sunrises and sunsets but by the reflexive scowls and reluctant smiles of my companions. There's a price you pay for learning the seven Argosi talents. Arta loquit teaches you to hear what people are trying to say beneath their jumbled words, and how to give them the space to find the right ones. Arta precis reveals both what others are trying to hide from you and what they've hidden from themselves. But what happens when your ears can't take the sounds of their suffering any more? When your eyes can't bear the sight of all those other, deeper pains waiting to be unleashed?

'*You forgot the Way of Water, kid?*' Durral would've asked. '*What business you got hangin' on to someone else's pain? Listen to 'em, that's all. Let 'em cry or scream or spew a thousand hateful words your way. That's what a friend does. Then you take yourself off into the desert and tell yourself dirty jokes until you're laughing so hard all the pain shakes off you like rainwater. Let it sink into the sand at your feet, where it can't do any more harm. That's the Argosi way.*'

I tried, Pappy, I really did. But watching Arissa struggle to keep pace with us, day in, day out, pretending the sandstorms could scrape the miseries of Soul's Grave off her skin, only to relive each and every one of them the moment she collapsed into restless sleep once we made camp? Conch tried to comfort her at night, but she'd wake kicking and screaming when she felt him near her. A couple of times the spire goat got so scared he belched gas from his belly that knocked her unconscious again. Seemed almost a mercy, but I knew it wasn't, not really. After the first few nights Conch slept up against Quadlopo, who never let Arissa near him.

At least we managed to acquire a pair of horses for her and Chedran. Fine Berabesq bronzes that looked like they were posing for a painting every time you put a saddle on them. I couldn't tell the two apart. Arissa adored hers though, and Chedran treated his with respect, even talking to it politely now and then – which is more than I could say for the way he talked to me.

'You think I didn't see what you did?' he demanded the day after our heist.

Thanks to Arissa's ingenious scheming, we'd snuck into the largest and best fortified horse trader's stable I'd ever seen. Forty-seven guards I'd counted while scouting the perimeter; crossbowmen on the rooftops; short, thickly muscled women with wickedly curved cavalry swords waiting next to saddled horses, ready to ride down anyone who tried to get away with their boss's property. Took us three days just to prepare the traps along our escape route so we could delay any pursuers without hurting them or their mounts. That was just one of seventeen components of Arissa's intricate plan. Her favourite was the one she'd devised for Conch.

Can't say I enjoyed the rehearsals.

'That the loudest he can scream?' she'd asked me for maybe the fifth time that afternoon. We were in a dried-out gully roughly twelve miles from the horse trader's fortress.

I took the candle wax out of my ears, which were ringing something awful despite my precautions. Small they may be, but spire goats can let out a scream so loud, so blood-curdling, that most predators would rather claw out their own eardrums than hear it a second time. Conch was pleased with himself, wagging his tail at me – which looks weird on a two-foot-tall goat. 'How much louder do you expect him to be, Arissa?' I glanced up warily at the clifftops above us. 'I thought we needed a distraction, not an avalanche.'

Chedran was in an even fouler mood than me. 'This is madness, trying to steal horses without killing those guarding them!' He was pointing a finger at poor Conch, who was probably wondering why everybody kept yelling around him after his exquisite performance. 'He'll send most of the horses stampeding before we can even steal any!'

'That's the point,' Arissa explained, the smirk I'd painted on her disharmony card appearing for a brief, achingly beautiful instant. She bent down to scratch Conch under his billy-goat beard. 'Most of the horses will stampede, which will keep the third set of guards inside the stable busy. The finest stallions though, the ones bred and trained exclusively for the highest-ranking Berabesq military officers to ride into battle—'

'Those will be the ones that don't bolt!' Chedran exclaimed, so delighted at the prospect of a triumph over the Berabesq that he allowed a little admiration for Arissa's scheme to show in those mesmerising eyes of his.

Nothing admiring about the way he looked at me the next day though.

'You're a traitor and a coward,' he informed me bluntly.

Lucky for both of us, he'd waited until Arissa was out of earshot. She was off singing to herself and her new bronze stallion about the daring thief who came to this lousy country to steal a sacred horse and damned if she didn't wind up stealing a pair twice as fine.

'We got what we came for,' I reminded Chedran, and kept on brushing Quadlopo's coat in long, languorous strokes the way he likes. I didn't want the horse to feel out of sorts, what with us having those two smug bronze stallions with us now. The slow, repetitive motions helped me keep my own temper in check. 'None of us got hurt and none of them got killed. Arissa's plan worked perfe—'

'You let your friend *believe* her plan succeeded,' he countered. He'd been cutting me off more than was healthy lately. 'It was all a sham. A piece of theatre to make a damaged young woman feel better about herself.' His snarl turned so angry it almost made me wonder if he was falling for her. 'I hope you'll spare me from any such acts of "friendship".'

'It was just a note, Chedran. No harm in leaving an apology for the trade lord. We did steal his prize stallions after all.'

'Ah, the "Way of Water" again, is that it?'

'Matter of fact, yes.'

He snorted. Quadlopo's head jerked up like Chedran had just called his sister a bad word. Maybe he had. He was certainly about to. 'You lying, treacherous bi—'

I let the brush fall to the ground, turned on my heel, brought one hand high and the other low. 'You want to dance with me, Chedran? Because you finish that word and I'm taking you for a spin.'

Oh, that look in your eyes, I thought, watching him. *You want a scrap so bad you can't taste nothing else. But it's not because of what I did last night, is it, Chedran? It's something you've been carrying since before we met but won't say out loud. So what's eating you, brother?*

His fists were clenched, but he kept them by his sides. 'As I understand it, the Way of Water demands an equitable exchange to restore balance and avoid conflict. Take nothing more valuable than that which you leave behind, yes?'

61

'It's more of a suggestion, but yeah.'

He jabbed a finger towards my chest that would've soon been broken had it reached its destination. 'And the two red gemstones I saw you leave with the note? Rubies?'

I knelt down to pick up Quadlopo's brush. 'Garnets. More valuable in these parts. Sacred too, when sewn into the palms of silk wedding gloves. The trade lord has two sons getting hitched next month.'

Chedran took this as some kind of confession. In gratitude, he spouted his next accusations quietly so as to make sure Arissa, hair still soaking from the luxury of washing it in a stream so narrow it barely deserved the name, grinning like she'd just remembered something funny, didn't hear as she walked back towards us with her bronze stallion's muzzle looming protectively over her shoulder. 'You knew the trader's sons were getting married because you'd already made an arrangement for the purchase of the stallions from their father. Everything else, this ruse you seem to believe constitutes some sort of gift for your friend, was a lie.'

'I made a deal for two of the horse lord's best horses,' I admitted. 'Two garnets worth more than emeralds in exchange for a pair of Berabesq bronzes. Figured Arissa would need one, and a spare would be wise in case Quadlopo needed a rest now and then.' My perennially offended horse replied with an angry snort that *definitely* involved calling me a bad name. 'Say, Chedran, you happen to know what the Berabesq noblemen call a contract signed with a foreigner of low birth? Because I'm pretty sure it's the same as their word for toilet paper.'

'Then why would yo—' He caught himself, having finally figured it out. 'You suspected the horse trader wouldn't keep his word, and thus planned to steal that which he'd already agreed to sell you.'

'Suspicion ain't the Argosi way. A little judicious spying on the other hand, well, sometimes that's just the cost of doing business.

Ten minutes after we'd signed our contract, I overheard the trade lord order his clerks to have me arrested as a horse thief when I returned – *after* having his guards confiscate the garnets from me and hide them away before the authorities arrived.' I stuffed the brush back in Quadlopo's saddlebag. 'Can't seem to cut a square deal in this danged country no matter how hard I try.'

'So the mission was genuine? We *did* need to steal those horses?'

That gave me a chuckle. 'Chedran, you saw all those guards chasing us.' I bundled up my unruly curls underneath my hat. 'That one cavalry gal must've chopped an inch off my hair with that whip sword of hers. You think I'd risk all our lives just to make Arissa feel important?'

I did not like the smile that came to Chedran's face. 'Then you won't mind if I inform your *friend* of the whole truth regarding last night? Shouldn't honesty be a requisite of the Way of Water?'

I knew it wouldn't matter what answer I gave him. Whether because he believed Arissa deserved the whole truth or from simple spite, he was going to tell her about the deal I'd made and the gems I'd left behind. I couldn't let that happen, not the way he'd go about it.

Arissa rejoined us, breathless and jubilant, like someone who'd finally raced up that last set of stairs out of Soul's Grave. That night, by the fire after our celebratory feast, I knocked her right back down.

She did me the kindness of pretending to understand.

Chedran, though, he knew what he'd made me do. His scowl made it plain that his callousness brought him no pleasure. He sat there on the other side of the fire, self-loathing etched on to his cheeks redder than those coppery tattoos across his chest and shoulders. There was something defiant hidden beneath his despondency though. Something my arta precis couldn't pierce.

63

I painted a card of him that night, stared at it long after he'd wandered off to sleep by himself. The Argosi create such cards to make sense of the world, and I needed to make sense of Chedran. But despite all those subtle shadings and angry brushstrokes, the precise rendering of his tattoos and the more violent abstract lines I used to depict his eyes and mouth, his true self remained obscured.

There was one secret I uncovered in the face staring back at me from the card in my hand: Chedran would rather be proven a villain than let me believe myself a hero.

When I stuffed the card into my discordance deck, it was with the certainty that this was one of those mysteries you can ponder for years without solving. But twenty-three days later, when we arrived at the safe house on the border where twelve runaway Mahdek teenagers awaited their saviour, I found out why Chedran hated me so bad.

Part 2

The Tower of Thorns

There is joy to be found in the repayment of a debt, is there not, teysan? A lightening of the spirit that strengthens the resolve to uphold one's word. How tempting, then, to dance along this path, paying off one disharmony card after another, your heart swelling with pride at the knowledge that each small sacrifice made along the way enhances your sense of righteousness.

Beware, however, the trap being laid out for you by your own cards: when you walk the path of restitution blindly, you grant others the power to play upon your guilt, luring you step by step down a road of their choosing . . .

9

The Tribe

We finally caught up with the twelve Mahdek runaways right where Chedran had sent them after he'd figured out the law was on his tail. No sane person submits themselves to a Berabesq court on a charge of child murder just to keep the authorities from discovering that the alleged victims are alive and well. Boundless courage and unbridled determination aren't the sole province of storybook heroes, it seems.

'Stupid fools,' he muttered as we stalked towards a long-abandoned miners' camp a mile north of the border into Darome. 'I'll be surprised if any of them are still alive.'

'Can't help but feel sorry for those kids when he gets his hands on them,' Arissa said quietly as we followed a few yards behind.

Four weeks of solid meals and a couple of hundred miles' distance from Soul's Grave had done wonders for her health. Shedding those tattered, filthy clothes I'd found her in proved equally curative to her spirit. I kept catching her rubbing the various fabrics of her crisp new linen shirt, leather riding trousers and silk scarf between her thumb and forefinger. It was like she needed to remind herself every few seconds that she wasn't encased in prisoner's rags any more. Back when she ran with the Black Galleon gang, Arissa had been legendary for wearing only crimson. Now though, for reasons

I could only imagine, she insisted all the clothes I bought for her be white, and washed them in every stream or fountain we passed.

In the evenings we'd catch each other's eye across the campfire sometimes. My arta loquit would pick up all kinds of conflicting clues when she looked back at me. Some nights, if I was especially exhausted, every subtle squint, wide-eyed stare or sleepy, limpid gaze turned into a confounding monologue in my mind – like she was talking to me but nothing she said made sense.

'I'm happy you're here, Rat Girl.'

'I owe you a debt now. I hate owing people.'

'Every time I look at you, it reminds me I couldn't escape that hell myself.'

'Quit looking at me like I'm some injured dove, Rat Girl. Do I need to come over there and kiss—'

No. That part was just my own yearnings playing tricks on me. Arissa had always made it plain she favoured men, not women. Why then did she taunt and tease me so often? Was it just to give herself a fleeting sense of power to banish the helplessness that still haunted her? When she talked about sex – never love, of course – she always made it sound as if, to her, romance was this . . . afterthought. Like if she really thought about it for more than ten seconds, she might decide maybe she liked girls as much as boys.

Idle thoughts, the kind many a forlorn lass has surely pondered. Problem was, in me those thoughts awoke more than just wistful longing.

'We will give her to you,' the Scarlet Verses promised me, soft as the gentle tickle of a snake's tongue flicking in your ear. 'Go to her tent tonight, speak our words, and the thief will be yours. Her mind, her soul and, most especially, her body.'

Resisting temptation ain't hard, even for something you find yourself craving more and more. Submitting to such impulses is no different than submitting to an iron collar around your neck. No Argosi ever fools themselves into believing you can take from another something they don't want to give and still call yourself free. That's why, over the weeks that followed, the verses would add this little tidbit: *'Alone, the thief is miserable, whatever mask she wears to hide it. Soon she'll crave the touch of flesh so badly that she'll give herself to the man. He will not make her happy. You would.'*

This is how they get you. Charlatans. Con artists. Deadly mystical mind plagues. They begin with that which you most desire, then turn that desire into a virtue and eventually an inevitability. That's when you give in. That's when you break. But I am Ferius-gods-damned-Parfax, and I *do not break*.

I started messing with my own arta loquit, twisting the meanings of Arissa's glances across the fire or when our hands touched on occasion, sometimes by accident, sometimes on impulse. All those different looks and gestures, the shifting shape of her eyes, varying degrees of softness in her gaze, the length and warmth of any touch between us . . . I collapsed all their manifold possible meanings down to one. A single sentence, repeated with every moment of contact between us.

'We're friends, Rat Girl, and that's how I like it.'

An Argosi's not supposed to mess with their own talents, especially not arta loquit and arta precis, since those ones are crucial for following the Way of Water. But it made the nights go by easier. Soon, I'd reunite Chedran with his runaways and get Arissa into some big Daroman city where she could go back to thieving and laughing at the world. My debts would be paid and I could finally set out on the Path of the Wild Daisy, alone, sure, but that's not the same thing as being lonely.

Chedran had recovered from his time in Soul's Grave too, more or less. His bruises were gone, along with whatever other hurts had

71

made it hard for him to walk unaided. We'd tied up the horses back a ways so as not to leave a trail, but we hadn't slowed our pace one bit. Chedran moved like a feral cat on the hunt, his quick footsteps almost completely silent – which he more than made up for with his endless stream of invective.

'Idiot children,' he repeated.

The source of his ire was a trail of footprints, crushed leaves, broken twigs and about a dozen other signs of his errant teenagers having done an impressively poor job of hiding their tracks in and out of the camp. The Daroman ridge where the abandoned mine lay also bordered northern Berabesq and the southern tip of the Jan'Tep territories. Not a good place for a pack of Mahdek runaways to be seen, which made me wonder why Chedran had risked sending them here.

Our people aren't exactly known for their talents for subterfuge. Lacking a homeland, what's left of the Mahdek tribes survive by never staying too long in one place, selling what services they can to those generous enough to hire strangers for jobs their own kind can do just as well. Begging is no sin to the Mahdek; it's a simple fact of life. Three centuries of charity takes its toll on a culture. Children learn quickly that it's safer to appear weak than dangerous, gullible and ignorant rather than cunning.

It's easy to mock those who live that way, and, I'll admit, I'm as prejudiced against my people as anyone else. But the Argosi are gamblers, so we know that anyone, whether an individual or an entire society, can be dealt a bad hand. What can you do but play each lousy card, one after another, until the game is over?

'Listen,' I said to Chedran, risking a hand on his arm to make him slow down a moment, 'when we step inside that camp, if those kids are there and alive—'

72

'Of course they're alive,' he snapped, peeling my fingers off his arm more forcefully than necessary. 'Can't you hear them? It's the middle of the day and those simpletons are chattering louder than your goat.'

Conch, who'd taken to riding on my shoulder when we had to move quickly since his legs were too short to keep up, produced a warning rumble in his belly.

'Try not to paralyse me when you're belching on him,' I said.

Chedran was right though: now that I was listening more carefully, I could make out the faint sounds of shouts and laughter in the distance. The kids must've been playing some kind of game.

'I'll kill them myself,' he said, upper lip curled like he meant it.

Arissa and I exchanged the same glance we had a dozen times before: the one that wondered whether the quiet rage eating Chedran from the inside out was too far gone, and maybe today was the day we were going to have to put him down. I gave a small shake of my head.

I'm not walking the Way of Thunder with him, I vowed silently. *Not yet. Not until it stops being so damned tempting.*

'From what you have told us, you saved those children from their own ignorance many times,' I said, my arta loquit framing the sentence more in his manner of speaking than my own. 'Now you must protect them from your own ire.'

Chedran spun on me, his body loose, ready to fight. Only his eyes betrayed how badly he wanted to beat me bloody once and for all. Arissa reached into the small leather pouch strapped to her right hip where she kept a few of the steel throwing cards she'd never returned to me.

So much for keeping off the Way of Thunder, I thought bitterly. *Fate makes fools of those who hold their vows in high esteem.*

An old Mahdek saying. Funny that it came to me then, especially since fate had found a far better way to make a fool of me.

'Chedran!' screamed a young girl's voice.

She didn't sound scared at all. She sounded ecstatic.

More voices followed, shouting his name in delight, and then it was all bare feet slapping against soft dirt and arms and legs all over the place. One after another those kids hurled themselves at Chedran, hugging him and grinning stupid kid grins up at him and yapping so many disjointed pieces of what had happened since last they'd seen him that poor Conch leaped off my shoulder and went running into the bushes.

I felt Arissa's arm around my shoulder. She leaned against me and asked, 'Ferius, did that goat of yours unleash some kind of hallucinogenic fart without us noticing? Because I cannot be seeing what I think I'm seeing.'

I'm rarely lost for words, but this time I couldn't do anything but stare at the way those kids kept grabbing onto Chedran, and the way that mean, sour-faced cuss couldn't stop smiling, or the wetness in his eyes he tried and failed to blink away. 'You are, quite simply, the most idiotic pack of half-witted clods it has ever been my misfortune to be saddled with,' he growled.

That unleashed a torrent of laughter and giggles, which made the kids seem all the younger, even though most were teenagers and a couple were almost our age.

'They love him,' Arissa murmured, her head resting on my shoulder as if the incomprehensibility of the world had exhausted her too much to stand on her own. 'Those kids absolutely adore him.'

I nodded, and found the words that had eluded me moments ago. 'He's their hero.'

I guess Chedran's ears really were sharper than mine, because he began slowly extricating himself from his admirers and said,

'No, I'm not.' He turned to me, all the bitterness I'd seen these past weeks returned to his eyes, his jaw, even the tightness in his shoulders. With an almost accusatory gesture he pointed to me and said, 'Everyone, this is Ferius Parfax.'

Silence fell harder than a ten-ton rock on a patch of wet sand. All the frantic enthusiasm, incoherent babbling and mad jumping around came to a stop as all twelve of the Mahdek runaways stared at me with eyes so wide it was like a giant golden statue had sprung up right behind me.

Arissa found this hilarious. 'Hate to say it, Rat Girl,' she whispered in my ear, 'but you seem to be a lot more famous among your people than you thought.'

She was right. I didn't need my arta precis to recognise what was unfolding before me. Two versions of the same tale: one written on those twelve awestruck faces, the other in Chedran's disgusted scowl.

Few Mahdek ever get famous. Most of us either die young or live too long by staying small and quiet. Me though, I'd done things. Big things. Some of my actions had been good and noble, others . . . others less so, but each had left behind a story. When a people don't get to build cities or erect statues of their heroes or monuments to their past, stories take on a fierce power. And a good story? The kind where a young Mahdek girl fights off Jan'Tep war mages and puts an end to mystical plagues, defies generals and princes, and most of all . . . most of all gets to live free of despair?

'Go on,' Chedran said to the runaways, who had abandoned their kin on account of all the stories they'd heard of a Mahdek girl who'd decided she was too special to live poor and humble. A girl who'd decided she didn't need to be Mahdek at all, but could call herself an Argosi and take for herself whatever name, whatever destiny, she chose.

What those stories likely hadn't mentioned was all the friends who'd saved me from my own stupidity along the way: Sir Rosarite and Sir Gervaise, two foreign warriors-of-honour who'd sacrificed their lives to give a terrified little girl a chance at happiness; Arissa, who'd protected me from thieves and bully boys and made me her partner in crime; Durral Brown, who'd showed me the Argosi ways and freed me from a Jan'Tep curse; Enna, his wife, who'd freed me from my own rage and bitterness.

Chedran never had that, I finally understood. But that's not why he resents me. It's those numbskull teenagers he's no doubt rescued a dozen times since they ran off from their families, and yet I'm the one they're looking up at like I stepped out of a storybook. Chedran's their saviour, but I'm their—

'Go on,' Chedran urged the kids again, not unkindly. 'Say hello to your hero.'

10

Never Meet Your Heroes

'We . . . we had to leave,' said a girl about my age with hair near as blonde as Arissa's, mingled with enough tawny red strands to make you think of strawberries when she was smiling and a match flame when she wasn't. Kievan was her name, which meant 'summer berry' in the Mahdek tongue. When she spoke, the other runaways paid attention.

'Why?' I asked, glancing around at the shadows filling the rickety old mining barracks. The rotted crossbeams holding up the sagging roof looked ready to give up the fight any second now. 'You must've known the dangers out here on the frontier. Why flee the safety of your clans?'

'There are no clans,' Kievan corrected me. 'Not any more. The massacres perpetrated against the Mahdek –' She glanced nervously at Chedran, who was sitting cross-legged on the dusty wood floor with two of the littlest ones wrestling for his lap. 'Our people,' she amended, 'huddle together like fugitives hiding from the world. Our elders have given up on our future.'

'Perhaps it is difficult to envision the future when your children have abandoned their own culture,' Chedran observed drily, one hand mussing the hair of the chubby-cheeked ten-year-old girl on his lap who'd successfully shoved away a boy so like her they had to be twins.

Murmurs rose from the other kids, most of whom I would have put at a year or two younger than Kievan. You can learn a lot watching the reactions of those who listen rather than talk. Durral likes to say that to an Argosi a conversation is a kind of music in which the silences are as important as the melodies, and the audience a choir whose whispers, mumblings and even intakes of breath are all part of the performance.

What I heard in the back-and-forth between Kievan and Chedran had the rhythm of an old argument to me. A familiar song repeated for the benefit of a newcomer, in hopes I might compose the ending that had eluded them for so long. Chedran though . . . the gentleness with which he treated those runaways gave my arta precis a headache. Bitterness and casual cruelty still burned beneath the surface, but around those kids he tamped it down like he was the flame of a hearth desperately trying to bring warmth without setting the house on fire.

'I still hate him,' Arissa muttered from the doorway, just loud enough for me to hear. Night's chill was coming on fast, but she still hadn't stepped inside the barracks. No surprise there: with its decomposing wooden bunks bolted along the floor and decaying grey walls bathed in shadow, this place didn't look so different from a prison.

The silence left behind by Chedran's discordant accusation was broken by an unexpected outburst of innocent, delighted laughter from the far end of the room. Conch was playfully butting the head of a boy seated on the floor whose unruly mop of brown hair was lustrous as polished oak. Say what you want about the Mahdek: no money, no magic, no military, but we sure do have pretty hair. Strange thing was, every time Conch tousled the boy's hair, the kid's hand jerked up to smooth it back across his forehead. He didn't strike me as the type to fret over looking presentable.

78

'Remeny, shush,' one of the older kids hissed.

'Why not let him play?' Chedran asked acidly. 'It's not as if he's a runaway child in the middle of hostile territory being led to certain doom by petulant teenagers who think themselves too grand to toil alongside their people.'

'You're being unfair!' Kievan shot back. 'You haven't lived among us for years. You ran off an—' She stopped herself, wincing at her own choice of words before trying again. 'Forgive me, Chedran, I misspoke. I meant only that a great deal has changed since the Jan'Tep massacres decimated our numbers. Despair bedevils our elders, leaving the rest of us . . . unmoored.'

Shame stabbed me right in the gut. I'd barely thought about my people since I was eleven years old. It never occurred to me that the slaughter of my clan had been only one of many.

'Grief, guilt and shame are just three words for wasted love,' Enna would've reminded me. *'Make restitution if you can, walk on if you can't.'*

'We brought their protector back to them, Rat Girl,' Arissa said quietly, almost like she could see my guilt in the slump of my shoulders. 'Time for you and me to hit the road.'

She was right. There was nothing here for me, for us. Happiness awaited on a long road far from this place. All I needed was to turn around and walk out the door. Quadlopo and Arissa's poncy bronze stallion were waiting for us a quarter mile up the path. Once we'd saddled them up, we'd ride fast and far, put a hundred miles between us and the past before it even knew we were gone. Not even the certainty of our paths diverging soon after could keep the itch to get moving from my soles of my feet. Instead, I found myself staring at Kievan, and the flame inside her that burned just as bright as Chedran's. 'You said the elders had changed. How?'

She was only too eager to answer, and Chedran's groan told me he'd heard it all before. 'They huddle among themselves, endlessly bemoaning the long-lost glories of the Mahdek,' Kievan replied. 'The council makes no plans for our future, no efforts to educate the young – all while forbidding us the chance to forge our own destinies.' She pointed to the giggling girl nestled in Chedran's lap. 'They offer the youngest among us nothing but the conviction that fate has cursed her people to end in dust and misery. Would you condemn a child to a life without purpose, without hope?'

Chedran lifted up the girl by her armpits, rubbed his nose against hers before setting her down next to her brother. 'I would see her grow to a ripe old age.' He rose and approached Kievan, his steps slow, relaxed and reminiscent of a mountain cat preparing to pounce. 'You denounce the elders for excessive caution, yet I came upon you half-starved and already rounded up by a coven of war mages after having stumbled into Jan'Tep territory.'

Kievan held her ground. 'Why must you always defend the elders who cast you out? Forgive me, Chedran, but it's true, and though it breaks my heart, I must be grateful for the council's callousness, because when we were captured, it wasn't our elders who came searching for us. It was the boy they'd exiled years ago, grown strong and cunning – through hardship, yes, but also because he'd been free to become so.' Her tone softened, the plea in her voice full of admiration and, maybe, something more. 'Our people were once strong, like you. We were the first mages on this continent. We had *magic*, Chedran! Mahdek shamans and spellshapers erected wondrous cities and—'

'Magic?' Chedran cut her off, suddenly leaning in so close that I could've sworn he was about to rip out her throat with his teeth. He stopped though, his lips next to her ear, making me wonder if maybe they were lovers. When he spoke though, barely over a whisper, it became obvious he was just making sure the little ones

80

playing at the back of the barracks wouldn't hear. 'The Jan'Tep teach their initiates that all Mahdek are demon spawn. Imagine you were a young war mage, eager to test out your spells of ember, iron, blood and all the rest. Imagine you believed with all your heart that the great and noble Jan'Tep were endangered once again by the filthy, devilish magic of the Mahdek.'

'I wasn't saying th—'

Again he cut her off. 'Have you ever witnessed what those brave young mages do when they capture us, Kievan? They cheer each other on, competing over whose magic can inflict the most spectacular and painful executions. Sometimes they perform experiments on us . . .' Chedran's head turned just enough for his eyes to lock on mine. 'I wonder which is worse?'

'Rat Girl?' Arissa gripped my shoulder. I hadn't noticed her walk up behind me, any more than I'd realised how bad I was shaking.

Kievan and the kids were all staring at me. My hand had gone to the collar of my shirt and tugged it down, my fingernails scratching at the faded symbols engraved around my neck. They still itched sometimes. Suddenly, I was twelve years old again, strapped to a table inside a cave, begging for mercy over and over. The stench of molten metallic inks was choking me, silver and copper instruments burning as they pierced my skin. I could hear the old lord magus again, praising his young, handsome apprentice for such elegant work as he etched his first mystical collar into the throat of a filthy Mahdek.

'Hey,' Arissa said, squeezing my shoulder. She sounded worried. The kids looked terrified. Chedran, though . . . Even through the haze of those horrible memories, I saw the sneer come to his lips. All those awful things he'd said to Kievan? They'd been meant for me. The girl had tried to use me to strengthen her case against his insistence that the runaways needed the guidance of the elders to survive. All my so-called adventures, spun into myths with each

81

retelling, were a tool for her to convince a bunch of teenagers that they too could wander the world, wild and free, never having to settle for unrelenting gloom and despair. Never having to be Mahdek.

Chedran, though, he'd had his own adventures. He knew there were gaps left out of those stories. The bad parts. The ugly parts. Scars left behind that never stop itching. And mixed in with the memories of my own screams, the Scarlet Verses whispering promises of vengeance over all my enemies if only I'd give them voice.

'*Remember what I told you about not dragging around somebody else's pain?*' I could hear Durral asking. The memory of that smooth frontier drawl of his was the only thing that ever drowned out the verses.

'*Some crap about it being a bad idea, Pappy.*'

'*Well, that crap goes double for your own pain, kid, especially when someone's playing your suffering like an ace snatched from your own hand.*'

The problem with Durral's endlessly obscure proverbs is that they get under my skin twice as deep when he's not there. '*You think I don't know what Chedran's doing? He's trying to make the others see that I'm messed up, that it's a dangerous world out there and those kids should go back home where it's safe. And you know what? He's right!*'

'*Maybe, maybe not. But he ain't the only one playing those cards right now.*'

'*Who else is . . . ?*'

I'd gotten so wrapped up in the anguish of my own memories that I'd almost missed what Kievan, with her strawberry hair and earnestly clenched jaw had been doing to Chedran. Twice she'd played him, just like he'd tried to play her, each time when he was getting too close to a topic she didn't want discussed. The first had been when she'd implied he'd 'run off' before things got tough for the Mahdek. That was to keep him from making the other kids feel guilty over abandoning their families. An obvious gambit.

The second time she'd played that 'exile' card had come when his accusations had been probing something specific, something she'd been keeping purposely vague . . .

'You found them in the Jan'Tep territories?' I asked Chedran.

'What of it? I told you, they're stupid, petulant little chil—'

I raised a finger to shut him up. 'No Mahdek child, petulant or not, would ever be stupid enough to "stumble" onto the lands of those who've been slaughtering our kind for three hundred years.' I strode up to Kievan, grabbed her by the shoulders and worked hard to keep my fingers from clenching so tight I'd leave her with five bruises on each one. 'You didn't accidentally wind up in Jan'Tep territory. You went there on purpose. Why?'

Give the girl this much: she knew how to bluff. 'We aren't so easily frightened as our elders would have us be. We believed we could stay hidden from any—'

I didn't slap her, but I did shake the stupid out of her. 'Every Mahdek alive knows that Jan'Tep sentry mages set breath spells along their borders to warn against outsiders entering their lands. Why do you think all those clan princes and lords magi don't get assassinated by foreign agents of Darome, Berabesq and all the other countries that would love to find a way to take control of the oases and find out if maybe some of their people could learn to wield magi—'

Oh, three hells and a hangnail, I swore silently, letting go of her.

'What is it?' Chedran demanded. The full weight of that mesmerising glare of his settled on Kievan. 'What have you been hiding from me?'

He never even gave her the chance to answer. That fire inside him was raging fit to set ablaze the whole barracks.

'You've all been hiding this from me, haven't you? After all I've done for you, the sacrifices I've made, you keep secrets from me? Laugh behind my back?' He jabbed a finger in my direction like this was all my fault, which for once it wasn't. 'You wanted to emulate her, is that it? Prove you could strut about the Jan'Tep territories, play at being Argosi wanderers, tell yourselves that neither borders nor armies nor spells could keep you out? Perhaps even ambush some unwitting Jan'Tep initiate, leave them bruised and bloodied so you could return home with tales of your daring.' Again he pointed at me. 'Did you think such brazen arrogance would make you just like your hero, the glorious "Ferius Parfax"?'

Anger blinds us as much as pain. Love is even worse. Put anger, pain and love all together, though? You can't see what's right in front of you.

'They weren't lookin' to beat up any Jan'Tep initiates,' I said. 'They weren't trying to follow in my footsteps at all. I was just the inspiration for them to pursue an even dumber path to get themselves killed.'

'Why then?' Chedran asked, still turned away from me. I guess he figured if he saw my face at that precise moment he wouldn't be able to stop himself from throwing the first punch. 'Why did they venture into Jan'Tep territory?'

'Because the Mahdek were once strong.' I gestured to Kievan. 'How did you put it, sister? We were "the first mages on this continent"?'

'Don't be ridiculous,' Chedran barked. 'No Mahdek has felt the pull of magic in generations. Even if a shaman or spellshaper *was* born, only an oasis could awaken th—'

He froze, looking for the first time like prey cornered by a predator. His gaze swept over the twelve kids he'd risked so much to protect, searching for which of them had been the secret the others had kept from him.

84

It's in the silence that secrets reveal themselves, in the nervous giggles and awkward gestures that a proper Argosi should've picked up on right away if she weren't so busy resurrecting bad memories. Durral might have a point about leaving your pain out in the desert where it can't do anyone any harm.

The laughter from the back of the barracks was almost frantic now. Remeny, the kid with the tousled brown hair, was pushing Conch away forcefully because the spire goat kept trying to knock his fringe away from his forehead. 'Quit it, you silly goat!'

Kievan tried to stop me, but I shoved her aside. The rest of the kids – even the little girl and her twin brother – rose to form a wall between me and Remeny. They looked like they were ready for a scrap.

So much for being their hero, I thought.

'Please, Ferius, let me explain. It's not wh—'

'Shush now, sister,' I said, a weariness coming over me as my arta tuco – that's the Argosi talent for figuring out the workings of things – began putting together the disparate pieces of what the runaways had kept from Chedran, and what one of them had been hiding from the others.

I don't want this, I thought, my hand instinctively reaching into one of the pockets of my waistcoat, where my disharmony cards waited. *I just want to leave here with Arissa and Conch and Quadlopo, then pay off a few more debts until I can walk the Path of the Wild Daisy without this deck weighing me down.*

'*Who's stopping you, girl?*' I could hear Enna ask.

'*You, Mamma. You and Pappy and all the lessons you taught me about following the Way of Water.*'

'Come on now, Remeny,' I said, talking over the kids blocking my way. He kept trying to smooth that lustrous brown hair down to cover his forehead. 'Nobody should have to grow up so fast, and never all at once, but today's your day. Today is when you learn the hard lesson.'

'Wh-what lesson?' he asked, stuttering as he tried to hold back the tears.

The others were still walling me off from him. I gave them a look. The Argosi don't meddle with snake charming or mesmerism. We do have our own talent for persuasion though. *Arta siva* is less about hypnotising someone and more about letting them see the truth of your intentions. The runaways parted, a little reluctantly maybe, but they made a passage all the same.

Remeny was cuddling Conch to his chest now. The spire goat hated that. There must be a deeper kindness in his species than he usually showed me, because he didn't belch the poor kid into oblivion. I knelt down so that me and Remeny were eye to eye. 'Here's the lesson, kid. The difference between the boy you were a few minutes ago and the man you're about to become is in the hard truths you're willing to admit and the responsibilities you're willing to accept.'

The dam broke. Sharp, soul-wrenching sobs of guilt and grief burst out from the boy. 'I'm sorry,' he cried, shaking so hard I thought he might come apart. 'I'm so sorry! I didn't mean to . . . I never should have run away from camp. The others came to find me, but I wouldn't go back. I needed to find the magic. It kept tugging and tugging me until—'

'Remeny's always been drawn to the oases,' Kievan said, coming to kneel beside me. 'Even in our encampment in Darome, the silver flow called to him. It was driving him mad, but the elders wouldn't listen. They insisted he was just acting out. The rest of us, we thought if we could get him across the border, maybe within a few miles of an oasis . . . But we were captured, and Chedran rescued us.' There was a quiet note of defiance in the way she ended that sentence that told me she wasn't done yet. She looked back up at Chedran. 'It worked too. Remeny hasn't been feeling the pull any more. He's cured.'

'Not the word I'd use,' I said, watching misery and guilt, too long contained, shaking his whole body with each heart-wrenching sob. 'It's time now, Remeny. Time to show them what's been scaring you so bad you couldn't let anyone else see it.'

A trembling finger inched up slowly to the mess of brown hair that Remeny had no doubt been using to cover up his forehead from the moment Chedran had rescued him and his fellow runaways from those Jan'Tep mages. The shaking got even worse as he brushed the hair away so I could make out the traces of intricate silver lines his captors had etched there.

'D-do you know what it's called?' Remeny asked, tears streaming down his cheeks. 'I don't know what I'm supposed to call it.'

I did, of course, though I badly wished there was some kinder name I could put to the maze of silver lines gleaming across the landscape of his skin. 'It's called a spell warrant,' I told him. 'Those mages burned a spell warrant onto you.'

11

Fight or Flight

I'd never seen a spell warrant up close. You could blame my disinterest in the mechanics of Jan'Tep magic on the tribulations I'd suffered at the hands of its practitioners, but that would be a half-truth at best. All those incantations, conjurations, bindings and bewitchments, awesome and deadly though they might be, never filled me with any sense of wonder.

The Argosi talents, on the other hand? Those are nothing more nor less than a birthright that belongs to all of us: music, dance, language, daring, insight, even plain old stubbornness. Taken further, though, studied and elevated to their full potential, those simple, human gifts become far more wondrous than petty hocus-pocus spells.

The Argosi aren't stupid though. As soon as I recognised what the silver scrawls on Remeny's forehead must be, I pulled out my deck of ruse cards and rifled through them in search of a countermeasure. Regardless of our attitude towards magic, the Argosi keep track of all the different tools of violence and subjugation wielded across this continent. We paint cards as a record of the tricks others have used to escape those traps. My own deck was based on Durral's, and contained gambits to counteract iron-binding hexes and silk mind chains, blood crown summonings and ember cataclysms. What I lacked was a card to suggest how I might break a Jan'Tep spell warrant.

'It's . . . it's almost beautiful,' Kievan murmured, unconsciously reaching out a slender finger towards the entanglement of silver lines shimmering across the boy's forehead. 'Like a magnificent labyrinth that can only be walked in a dream.'

I batted her hand away. 'This ain't no corn maze, sister. It's a cattle brand, plain and simple. Permanent as scorched iron burned into a steer's hide. With this, any Jan'Tep mage worth the name can track Remeny across this whole continent.'

A scream of pure, blinding frustration exploded behind us. Chedran was in a rage, his vehemence so personal you'd think this was a prank that had been pulled on him alone. 'This cannot be!' he shouted. 'I killed those mages myself! Four of them, all dead at my hand!'

I tried to ignore him, having more urgent problems to contend with than his pride. Maybe that's why he grabbed me by the shoulder and swung me around so hard it was all I could do not to let my arta eres get the best of me and punch him in the throat.

'I killed the mages!' he repeated helplessly. 'I saved us all!'

I should've listened deeper to the disconsolate notes beneath his outrage, but I was too focused on our tactical situation. I have a bad habit of giving my arta tuco free rein at the wrong times. 'Did you bury the bodies? Haul the corpses at least a hundred miles from any Jan'Tep oasis?' I asked, pelting him with questions to which I already knew the answer. 'Did you drag the dead down a tunnel or into an underground cave deeper than Soul's Grave?'

'What? Of course not! I had twelve terrified runaways to sneak across the border. Why would I waste time on—'

'Sand magic, you idiot.'

I shouldn't have belittled him. Chedran was as confused as everyone else in that rotting mining barracks, too bewildered by the intricacies of Jan'Tep magic to understand the danger. Everyone except me.

I settled myself some. 'When those Jan'Tep sentry mages failed to report to their commander, hex trackers would've been dispatched within hours. Plenty of adepts have sparked their tattooed bands for iron and blood magic, but all that would do is lead them to the bodies. Figuring out how they died would require a mage who'd sparked the sigils for sand magic. Probably took a lord magus to sift through the passage of time until they could latch on to the killer's echo.'

'Is this lesson in Jan'Tep mysticism intended to frighten me?' Chedran demanded. 'Let them send all the hextrackers and bounty mages they want. After I'm done with them, I'll toss their ashes to the western wind and send them back to their families as a gift.'

Bluster, I thought. *Not daring, not arta valar. Nothing but hubris drowning out reason and common sense.*

'You're not thinking this through,' I told him. 'Jan'Tep spells require an anchor to bind them to a target. In the case of sand magic, the anchor has to exist both in the present *and* during the events the mage is witnessing. A corpse is only a shell that once contained life, not the life itself.'

'Doesn't that mean we're safe?' Kievan suggested. 'If the mage who branded Remeny with this spell warrant is among the dead, then there's no way for anyone else to track us through it.'

I tugged down the collar of my shirt once again to show her the fading sigils around my throat. 'The metallic inks they used on me and Remeny are no different from the ones tattooed around the forearms of initiates to help them draw on the magic of their

90

oasis. These inks don't just mark the skin; they seep all the way into your bones.'

One of the other runaways, a boy of maybe fifteen with grey-green eyes like mine but hair an even darker red than Chedran's, stepped forward and smoothed the front of a ratty grey side-buttoned marshal's shirt two sizes too big for him. 'Forgive me, Lady Ferius, but would not the inks in the dead mage's bones serve only to link back to the oasis, therefore preventing any sand spell from reaching us?'

Something about the way that he called me 'Lady' really got my goat. Not literally, of course, since Conch was curled up on one of the bunks, snoring loud enough to wake the dead. Regardless, being addressed as if I was some highborn noblewoman with smooth skin and painted nails, who'd never set foot outside a palace, made my teeth ache. I was an Argosi, damn it. I wore the scars of my travels. 'Ain't no lady, kid,' I snapped at the indecently mannered boy. 'If I look one to you, then best you wipe the stupid from your eyes.'

A couple of the other children giggled nervously at that. The kid glanced at Kievan for support. 'Elozek was merely being courteous,' she said, giving him a quick smile to show that she had his back before serving up a glare at me so I'd know I'd overstepped. 'We found a box of old Daroman shield romances beneath an upturned ore cart. We've been using them to help teach the younger ones to read. Elozek became fascinated by the protocols of courtly etiquette.'

Mahdek teenagers learning manners from a bunch of Daroman knight's tales. Now I'd heard everything. I bent down to pick up a tattered bit of rope from the dusty floor. I held it up for them to see. 'Look, Jan'Tep bands aren't just a tether between the mage and the oasis from which they draw their magic.' With my thumbnail, I pushed apart the frayed strands from each other. 'It's like a web

91

of filaments that stretches between their tattooed bands and any spell they cast that hasn't faded yet. Some of those spells persist awhile, even after death.'

I saw a lot of confused looks from Kievan and the others. Remeny, though? That poor kid was staring at the frayed end of my rope like it was a coiled snake about to strike.

'One of those mages took you aside, didn't he, Remeny?' I asked. 'At night, maybe? When the others were still unconscious from a sleep binding, someone came to rouse you?'

The boy nodded, cheeks red with tears as his hand came up reflexively to cover the spell warrant with his hair again. 'He was younger than the other three, but he said he was already a proper silk mage. He had brown hair like me and his nose was flat like mine. He said I was special, and he smiled like . . . like he wanted us to be friends. But then pushed me down and sat on my chest. His knees pushed into my arms and it hurt really bad. I started crying, but he didn't care, just took this long silver needle from his robes and . . .' Remeny's hand had strayed up to his hair again. He brought it back down to his side. 'It only took a few seconds. There wasn't even any pain until he was done. He laughed like it was all a big joke, then grabbed me by the hair and dragged me back to the others. He put me to sleep again, and when I woke, I thought it had all been a bad dream until I saw what he'd done to me.'

Kievan was staring curiously at the spell warrant. She frowned. 'But these markings are so elaborate, so detailed. They must have taken hours.'

'What does it matter?' Chedran roared as he stalked towards the boy. 'Remeny knew he'd been marked and he hid it, putting all of us at risk. He betrayed his own people.'

'I don't think so,' I said, and got between them. Chedran was terrifying the boy and making my card-throwing fingers twitch. 'It

92

didn't look like anything at first, did it, Remeny?' I turned to him, lifting his chin so he'd look at me. 'I'll bet those marks were so tiny you figured they couldn't be important, right?'

'At first,' he admitted. 'The symbol was so small and . . . pretty. I felt kind of special when I looked at it. But then the silver lines got bigger and longer. Every time I saw my reflection on a piece of metal or in a bowl of water, the markings had grown. They kept getting more and more complicated. Like a word that turns into a poem, then a song, then a whole story.' He touched the markings once more and let out a heaving sob so full of terrors I wondered how he'd held them back this long. 'I don't think it's got a happy ending.'

Chedran's voice was cold, not so much angry as defeated. 'You've given every Jan'Tep bounty mage on the continent the means to find us wherever we go.' I heard a sound, like a hand brushing leather. Neither Kievan nor any of the other kids reacted. I guess none of them had noticed Chedran draw the short curved dagger from behind his back. 'They'll be able to follow Remeny as long as he lives.'

Nobody missed the sound of a second blade being drawn. 'One hair,' Arissa said from close behind Chedran. I didn't need to look back to know the tip of her knife was at his throat; she'd always been sneaky. 'Touch so much as one hair on that boy's head, and these dull grey walls get a cheerful coat of red paint.'

'Ferius, please,' Kievan cried, clutching at my arm. 'Make them stop before they turn misfortune into tragedy!'

Little late for that, I thought, but couldn't tear my eyes away from the spell warrant gleaming across Remeny's forehead. 'A *magnificent labyrinth that can only be walked in a dream,*' Kievan had called those markings. But it was the weeping, terrified boy, already resigned to the fate Chedran intended for him, who'd had the right of it. A story was being composed on his flesh that would surely end badly unless a way out of this could be found for all of us.

'Don't be afraid,' I wanted to tell him. 'There's a way to wipe those markings off, I'm sure of it.' Lies wouldn't do either of us any good though. I'd told this boy he was going to have to be a man now, and that much was true. I knelt down in front of him again and brushed aside his brown hair, which was now slick with sweat. I closed my eyes, and with the tip of my little finger began tracing the lines of the spell warrant, guided only by the cold metallic sensation of the silver ink.

'What are you doing?' Kievan asked.

I kept my eyes shut. 'Trying to get a feel for whoever's on the other end of this thing.'

'I told you, woman, the silk mage is dead.' Chedran's voice was tight, like he couldn't take a deep breath for fear Arissa would get too enthusiastic about redecorating the barracks with his blood. 'I killed them all.'

Arrogance. That's what had blinded me this long. Not my own – which can be bad enough – but Chedran's pompous boasting. I'd let him get under my skin, which had prevented my arta precis from asking the obvious question.

'No doubt you did kill that silk mage, brother,' I said, moving my fingertip almost imperceptibly, searching out the sensation of another's touch. 'So how come the spell warrant kept growing instead of fading?'

'Forgive me, Ferius,' Kievan intervened, no doubt hoping to restore calm to the proceedings before things got further out of hand. 'What good does tracing the lines with your finger do?'

Patterns, I thought, but didn't say aloud. *An Argosi seeks understanding in the patterns people leave behind. Follow the pattern, and you come to know its maker.*

Patterns are everywhere if you know how to look: rituals, paintings, games of chance, the seemingly random order in which a culture strings its words together, the way they arrange the houses in their towns and villages. Sometimes, though, it's the absences that hold the clues to a civilisation. Take the Jan'Tep for example. On the surface, just about the least romantic folks you'll ever meet. No love songs, no flowery vows tearfully spoken at their weddings, and you'll never, ever catch them dancing.

Watch the way they cast their spells, though, and you'll be struck by something . . . carnal. A mage can't work magic unless their mind is perfectly calm, and yet, beneath that unyielding sense of control, all kinds of emotions ripple across their face. The way they perform their somatic gestures and utter their incantations – even the hatred with which they look upon their foes while casting a spell – betrays a troubled intimacy.

Enna, an inveterate hugger, always did claim that those who avoided intimacy weakened their mind and body both. Bet she never predicted her foster daughter would one day use that altogether sappy piece of motherly wisdom to whoop a Jan'Tep mage's arse. Then again, knowing Enna, maybe she did.

'Can you feel this?' I asked silently, my fingertip tracing the silver lines of the warrant – an act of profoundly intimate desecration to a Jan'Tep mage. 'The metals of this ink are tied to the silk spell you took control of, which means it's now tethered to the sigils of your own silk band. Bet this feels real uncomfortable.'

As I followed the flowing silver contours, an ache began to travel up the tiny bones in my finger to my hand, along my arm and through my shoulder all the way to my neck until the pain settled behind my eyes.

'Rat Girl?' Arissa asked quietly. She was right next me, so I guess she'd decided not to kill Chedran yet. 'I'm thinking you'd better stop what you're doing. You've got streaks down your face.'

'No big deal,' I said – grunted, more like. My hand was trembling. 'My new friend's just a tad ornery, is all. Besides, didn't I ever tell you that tears are just sorrow leaving the body?'

'Those aren't tears, Rat Girl. You're bleeding from the eyes.'

'Is that how it's going to be?' I asked whoever was tethered to the other end of the spell warrant. *'You think I don't know that whatever agony you put me through, you're feeling it too? Let's dance then, stranger. Let's you and me see who stumbles first.'*

'Ferius, I don't feel right,' Remeny complained. 'I don't . . .'

He went quiet, then I heard the shuffling of feet as someone – probably Kievan – rushed to hold him up. 'Ferius, he's fainted. Please, you must stop what you're doing!'

My whole body was shaking from the effort of trying to trace the last line. I could feel wetness dripping down from my nostrils to my upper lip. 'I'm almost there. I can feel them givin—'

My body shot backwards like I was a rag doll tossed by a child in the midst of a temper tantrum. My eyes opened, but all I saw was the rotted rafters going by, the grey tinted pink by the blood of my tears. That all came to a stop when my head and back slammed onto the floor, knocking the wind out of me.

'Rat Girl!' Arissa called out.

I could tell she was running towards me, yet her footsteps were virtually silent. That's how stealthy she moves: a natural-born thief, through and through. Then again, my ears were ringing pretty badly, so maybe Arissa was thumping up a storm and I was too deaf to hear it.

'I'm okay,' I said, rolling onto my stomach before pushing myself up to my hands and knees. I wiped the blood from my eyes before accepting Arissa's arm. 'So, who won?' I asked after she'd gotten me to my feet.

My vision was still blurry, but Arissa's arched eyebrow was hard to miss. 'Well, you bled out your own eyeballs, made the kid faint, got hurled about fifteen feet, probably gave yourself a concussion and almost certainly alerted whoever's in control of that spell warrant that we're on to them. Was that the glorious victory you'd envisioned?'

'Damn it,' I swore. 'I'd hoped if I could reach through the spell somehow, I could force the mage to parlay or at least send us a—'

'Look, look!' shouted the little golden-haired girl who'd sat on Chedran's lap earlier. 'The lines are talking!'

I ran – stumbled mostly, but Arissa kept me from falling on my face – back to where Kievan was holding Remeny up with her hands under his arms. The boy wasn't unconscious, but he was definitely woozy. He cried out as the lines on his forehead twisted and turned, pulling themselves apart before reshaping themselves into something new. No longer the intricate, labyrinthine design, but now an elegant calligraphy: letters scripted in a language most of us in the barracks could speak but few had ever seen. Nobody bothers to write anything in Mahdek any more.

'What does it say?' Arissa asked, but by then the words had disappeared, the lines returning to their earlier convoluted design.

'Tickles,' Remeny said, eyes still unfocused. He giggled. 'It really tickles.'

The other kids had probably never learned to read Mahdek. Mostly the young are taught Daroman, the most widely used language on the continent. After that, a little Gitabrian, Zhuban, Berabesq and whatever else a refugee needs to know to beg for charity. Chedran had seen the markings though, and he'd gotten the message, same as me. He didn't look angry any more, or even sad. He looked grim.

'They're changing again!' Kievan shouted, craning her neck from behind Remeny to see what the others were pointing at.

We all watched as the silver unwound itself, stretching as if pulled by invisible fingers. The lines gave up their intricate curves, some straightening like roads and trails, others flowing like rivers or inclining up one side then down the other like hills. On the far right of Remeny's forehead, two vertical lines were crowned with a jagged parapet: a tower of some kind. On the far left, a tiny silver rectangle appeared, its proportions identical to the barracks in which we stood.

Kievan beckoned for two of the older kids to hold Remeny up so she could step out from behind him and try to make sense of this strange change to his markings. 'Is it some kind of map?'

'Not quite,' I replied. I wiped the last stray drops of blood from the corners of my eyes before looking around for my pack. Outside it was already dark, but a wide gap left by broken boards in the wall above the door frame revealed a full moon that would light our way. I decided that Kievan deserved a fuller answer. Precision is important in these matters, after all. 'A map is a tool for navigating wherever you want to go. What that mage just inscribed on Remeny's forehead? Those are directions.'

I'd only gotten a glance at the words that had so briefly appeared in those silver letters, written in the tongue of my people to let us know that whoever was in control of the dead mage's spell warrant knew who these kids were and could find them whenever they wanted. Now I understood precisely what they meant.

'They're threatening to slaughter the children,' Chedran said, stomping up beside me to make it clear that if I were stupid enough to follow the trail laid out for us, I wouldn't be going alone. Arissa was right behind him of course; someone needed to keep him from killing me. 'They want to goad us into facing them in battle on their terms and their terrain.'

98

'Could be,' I conceded. 'But me, I prefer to think of it as a hastily worded invitation.'

Chedran's scorn could have curdled milk. 'And if you're wrong? If this asinine Argosi optimism in which you place so much faith leads us into a trap?'

I traded him his sneer for one of Durral Brown's most irritating smiles. 'One thing folks always seem to forget about us Argosi? We're awful good at ensnaring ill-mannered hosts in their own traps.'

Better that you come to us, the message had read.

Damn straight I'm coming to you, pal.

I stepped outside into the darkness, looking up at that bright silver moon overhead. Daroman gamblers claim she's the goddess of good fortune. I offered her my cheek so she could kiss me for luck. Had a feeling I was going to need some.

12

The Ruined Tower

Four days of riding at a slow but steady pace brought us to within sight of the tower. We could've gotten there sooner, but that would've meant Arissa, Chedran and me were exhausted, not to mention irritating the two bronzes, and especially Quadlopo, who had, with some reluctance, accepted his status as lead horse. Truth be told, I was in no rush to walk into a nest of Jan'Tep mages. Moon-kissed I might be, but Lady Luck has never been so magnanimous as to grant me just one enemy to fight at a time.

'What are the odds they'll fall for it?' Arissa asked, lowering the brass spyglass I always carried with me for occasions like this but which she seemed determined to keep for herself. 'There's still no sign of anyone leaving the tower.'

'Why should they?' Chedran asked, that dismissive sneer of his on full display as it had been this whole journey. 'We're handing ourselves over to them like lambs to the slaughter.'

I know what you're thinking: *Tell him to shove his incessant smugness up his own arse or at least have the decency to come up with a less gruesome metaphor.* Well, I could remind you that part of arta loquit is knowing when someone's offering you the first verse of the song just so they can hit you hard with the chorus. The honest answer, though, is that Arissa already had that covered.

'Hey, Ferius? You remember last week when I cut some guy's tongue out of his head, then made him swallow it, then waited until he had to go to the privy so I could make him fish it out of his droppings and eat it again? Whatever happened to that guy?'

In case you're wondering, that particular incident hadn't taken place.

Yet.

'Oh, right,' Arissa said, smacking her palm on her forehead. 'That wasn't last week. All my time in prison, I get my yesterdays and tomorrows mixed up. No, that was five minutes from now unless the arsehole in question shuts the hells up.'

Fallen in love yet? I swear, I was getting close.

'The others won't have gotten more than fifteen or twenty miles from the barracks yet,' I pointed out, then gestured to the ruined tower some sixty yards through the trees ahead of us. 'The coven might not bother getting on the move until they know for sure the kids are making a break for it.'

I'd instructed Kievan to wait about six hours after we left the barracks and then take her crew north towards the Mahdek enclave in Darome, making it look like they were running home. The whole point of a spell warrant being to make it easy to track a fugitive, the mages hunting them would want to catch them before they got too deep into Daroman territory where Jan'Tep hunting covens aren't exactly welcome – especially when they're in the business of murdering teenagers. By the time the kids had set out, Arissa, Chedran and me would've reached the only decent road between them and the tower. With a little judicious scouting, we'd know when the Jan'Tep were coming, allowing us to take cover and set up an ambush.

Good plan, right? Only problem was, the mages hadn't shown up on the road, and the smoke coming out the top of the tower and the signs of movement inside that Arissa had spotted earlier through my spyglass made it plain they'd never left.

'Complacent,' Chedran said, the hunger for violence in him so strong he was practically smacking his lips. 'They know they've more than enough time to ride down the children. They'll cling to the comforts of their tower until the last moment.' He glanced up at the position of the moon in the sky, then back at the flickering light barely visible through one of the slatted windows of the tower. 'There's been no movement for an hour, which means they're asleep. Jan'Tep mages are too lazy and arrogant to set a sentry, and their concentration is weak when newly roused. If we attack now, we can slit their throats befo—'

'I didn't come here to slit nobody's throat. Ain't plannin' on letting you do so either.'

We had argued this point so many times on the way here, I was pretty sure he only kept bringing it up to annoy me. Guess I was doing likewise. Enna used to say that the simplest lessons are the hardest to teach. Killing leads to more killing; every ounce of blood you spill stains the ground at your feet, flowing into a path that goes in only one direction. Seems obvious as a toothache to me now, but it had taken a while – and nearly cost Enna her life – for me to finally grasp that unbending law.

Chedran turned to me, the belligerence in his gaze giving way to a challenging stare that said: *If you were Mahdek, you'd do what it takes to defend those children.*

This was just another kind of mesmerism to him. Another tactic to tear down my convictions. Wouldn't be hard to get lost in those dark eyes of his, especially when part of you couldn't help but believe he was right. Too bad he hated the Argosi so much; he might've made a good one, what with all his cunning, courage and even that blunt eloquence that made you think he was the one speaking the truth, while everyone else was just playing with words. I'll bet he would've been happier if he'd followed the Argosi ways, maybe called himself the Path of Boundless Steps or the Path of Copper Smiles.

The ugly truth was that love would forever keep Chedran from those brighter roads. Even as an exile, his intense, unrequited love of our people remained the yoke across his shoulders, the shackles around his ankles that yanked him back every time. I had to admit, there was something noble about his unwavering devotion. Chedran was Mahdek in a way that I could never be. He revered our culture and embodied our heritage; bled from every cut we'd suffered, seethed over every slur we'd ever been called. All of it – *all* of it – made him proud.

I guess I really *had* abandoned my people seven years ago after Sir Rosarite and Sir Gervaise had rescued me from the Jan'Tep coven that had massacred my clan. They'd given me a nice home, put me in a fine school – I still remembered all my comportment lessons from Master Phinus – and offered a life to which I'd taken as if I'd never known another. After their kindness had seen them murdered by the Jan'Tep mage who'd tattooed that collar on me, I'd wandered aimlessly through the Seven Sands until at last I'd met Durral Brown, and he'd shown me you don't need a destination to have a path. Never once had I tried to find another Mahdek family to take me in. Never once had I considered the debt I owed the clan into which I'd been born.

Was that what had me out here, staring through the darkness at some old ruined tower, risking my neck to protect a bunch of Mahdek runaways, yet refusing to kill on their behalf? Holding tight to the Argosi ways and my own path, yet desperate to prove to Chedran that I hadn't abandoned the people who'd given me life?

'*Ruminations are a fine way to pass a lazy afternoon,*' Durral used to tell me. '*Problem is, they tug you into the past so you can worry about the future, and by the time you've figured out you've been ruminating too long, someone else has decided the future for you.*'

'Damn it,' I swore, shaking off my stupor. This is why the Argosi say that guilt, shame and grief are three words for wasted love: because they don't do nobody any good and all too often trap you inside your own regrets.

'What's wrong?' Arissa asked, pulling her horse close to mine. Her eyes were glazed, unfocused.

Guess he'd gotten to her too. I leaped off Quadlopo's back and landed quietly on the soft ground – though not nearly so quiet as Chedran had been after he'd mesmerised me and Arissa.

She snapped out of it, glanced around and then swore in at least three languages that I was pretty sure she didn't speak. She was so pissed off I could hear her footfalls as she followed me through the forest towards the tower. Too late now for philosophical debate or crisis of conscience. Chedran had decided for us that when it came to protecting the lives of twelve innocent kids whose only crime was the blood that ran in their veins, spilling someone else's was just the cost of doing business.

Ruminations. They'll get you every time.

13

The Climb

Silver-barked birch trees tall as oaks encroached on the grey tower's domain – a ponderous siege fought across decades. Thick roots had displaced the foundations, tilting the three-storey building to one side as branches poked through cracks in crumbling mortar already weakened by vines wrapped like garrottes around the stone structure.

The three of us climbed in silence towards an upper window whose wooden slats had long ago rotted to jagged teeth. I couldn't help but wonder who had built this long-abandoned stronghold, and for what purpose. Had sentries once stood upon its parapet to keep watch against Berabesq incursions from the south? Had pilgrims travelled here for quiet contemplation? What if these weary fortifications had once housed a grand library where books from every nation inspired scholars and diplomats from across the continent?

Chedran, who ascended the outer wall faster than either Arissa or I could keep up with, would no doubt have insisted the question was pointless. Whichever architects and masons had erected this tower were long dead, the aspirations they'd nurtured rendered irrelevant by the crumbling remains of their labours. Maybe I should've shared that view; wistful nostalgia isn't a virtue espoused by the Argosi. And yet I couldn't help but wonder what right any of us had to trample blood and mayhem across the ruins of someone else's dream.

Night was fading fast, but dawn was still an hour away by the time we'd reached the top and squeezed ourselves between the busted wooden slats of the partially collapsed window Chedran had picked as our entry point. Moonlight seeped through the gaps left by crumbling mortar all around us, lending an eerie gleam to Chedran's self-satisfied grin. He had good cause to be pleased with himself.

The roof above us looked sturdy enough, but the wooden beams supporting the top and middle levels must've rotted away years ago, giving us a clear view of the ground floor below where six mages slept on silk bedrolls around a cosy fire. No sentries, no telltale scents of the sorts of spells Jan'Tep mages sometimes use to ward against intruders. A grey haze hung heavy in the air thanks to the excess moisture and dust inside the tower, a welcome boost to the shadows that would help us sneak down the inner walls before the mages had any idea their sanctuary had been infiltrated.

'Two each,' Chedran said in a whisper so quiet that, even perched right next to him on the remnants of a rafter, I'd barely heard a thing. He brought a finger across his neck, his way of conveying that the obvious move was to slit their throats. Mages don't do so well uttering their incantations when they're choking on their own blood.

When I signalled my refusal, he tried to lock eyes with me. I made sure the moonlight glinted off one of my steel throwing cards so he'd be in no doubt as to what would happen if he tried to mesmerise me.

Arissa though, she put a hand on my shoulder and whispered in my ear, 'He's right, Rat Girl. Too many of them, too few of us. Only chance is to do this ugly work quick and clean.'

Nothing clean about it.

Twelve Mahdek runaways. Six Jan'Tep mages. Three bloodthirsty killers. One lousy result. The same old arithmetic of violence I'd sworn never to let rule my life again.

'*Your equation is incorrect, that-which-once-called-itself-Ferius,*' the Scarlet Verses informed me.

'*Shut the hells up. Last thing I need right now is advice from a homicidal language plague.*'

'*Heed us,*' they hissed insistently. '*You fail to underst—*'

I shoved them away, sending my thoughts in a whirl that gave me a headache but spared me having to listen to their vile tactical suggestions. As they often reminded me, the Scarlet Verses were capable of strategic insights far beyond my own feeble understanding of warfare. Funny to think that I was probably carrying around more military genius in my thick skull than a hundred Daroman generals. Too bad all that shrewdness was good for was spreading madness and mayhem.

Not that this situation required a whole lot of cunning.

'We'll never get a better chance,' Arissa whispered.

I shot her an angry glare to remind her that none of this was what I'd intended when I'd busted her and Chedran out of Soul's Grave. She shot one right back to remind me it hadn't been her idea to free him in the first place.

'It's perfect,' he said, looking down at those sleeping, stupid, *stupid* mages.

The hazy mist was catching the dim beams of moonlight, filling the tower with an eerie yellow glow. I could see just fine, but everything seemed blurry to me somehow. Even without the advice of the Scarlet Verses, my own arta tuco was showing me the dozens and dozens of ways to get down there before the mages noticed us, along with which one we should kill first, which one second. I saw all the spots to hide if one woke up, where to take cover if any of them happened to be sharp enough to fire off an ember spell so soon after waking. A hundred paths were open to us. It was almost like these Jan'Tep were already dead and all that was left was for us to go through the motions of murdering them.

'Ready?' Chedran asked quietly.

I wiped my brow, expecting to find sweat from the climb. My fingers came back bone dry. My muscles were limber, my mind sharp. I was breathing slow and easy. Chedran stripped off his shirt to eliminate even the faintest rustling sound when he moved. He looked ready for a fight. So did Arissa, who I'd worried about far more. A few weeks of freedom and good meals can't make up for a year of deprivation. She'd always been strong though. Balanced precariously on one of the rafters as she prepared to vault down to one of the wooden beams below, Arissa looked like the fearless, reckless thief I'd met years ago: tough, graceful and utterly lacking in self-doubt.

Maybe that should've been the warning. I'll never know, I guess, because by then Chedran had already started leaping down from one cracked rafter to the next, landing quiet as a cat. Arissa followed, and the only decision left to me was whether to kill those mages or watch as they killed my friends.

I chose wrong.

14

The Red Path

Blood spattered against the wall, the streak so straight and true that I couldn't stop staring at it. The edge of the steel throwing card in my hand dripped more drops onto the white silk robes of the mage pinned beneath my knee. He – was it even a he? I hadn't looked – gurgled up at me, the sound as familiar and reassuring as the babbling of a brook as you dangle your feet in the water. Hands clutched at the front of my shirt, grasping nothing, the fingers having lost all their strength. If there was such a thing as a perfect murder, I had just committed it. And still I couldn't seem to tear my eyes away from that spray of blood along the tower's curved wall.

'Quit dawdling!' Arissa shouted.

It was the first sound any of us had made. We'd climbed down the sides of the tower, quiet as shadows, and crept towards the six slumbering mages so lightly our footsteps were drowned out by the whispers of their breathing. The three of us moved with such practised ease it was almost as if we'd done this a hundred times before. Not once did any of us block the other's sight lines even as we pointed out unseen obstacles and loose boards that might give us away. The only hitch had been when Chedran had slit the throat of the first mage before Arissa and I had gotten into position.

Even then, the fellow died without a fuss, his passing marked only with a sigh as his spirit fled to wherever Jan'Tep mages meet their ancestors.

I'd expected more trouble with my target. Maybe it's more accurate to say I'd *hoped* it would be harder. If only my hand had been less steady, the edge of my steel card not so hideously sharp as it drew a red smile across the mage's neck. Had he opened his eyes at the last instant, seen the cold stare of his killer before everything went dark for him? It had all happened only a couple of seconds ago, so why couldn't I remember?

It was that damned spray of blood on the wall. The light from the fire made it gleam like a necklace of rubies. So familiar, somehow, like I'd seen that exact same trail of red before.

'Damn it, Rat Girl!'

A harsh murmur of guttural syllables set off a sizzle in the air right behind me. Whatever spell had been about to end me died with a scream and a warm splash of blood against the back of my neck.

'You made me kill three of them,' Arissa said, shoving me forward. She sounded like a Daroman prosecutor reading out an indictment in court. *'The defendant's inaction forced me to kill three of the victims myself, your worship. Murdering two would've been fine, but three? I demand restitution!'*

'It's over,' Chedran declared, sounding far too pleased with himself and far too close to me. He must've been looming over me, yet still I couldn't tear myself away from the blood of my victim sprayed along the wall, mesmerised by its flawlessness. 'You hesitated,' Chedran accused me.

'Indeed, your worship, I, too, demand restitution, for as we callously slaughtered those sleeping men and women, the defendant hesitated in a fashion most discourteous.'

110

'Don't listen to him,' Arissa said, shoving him away. I felt a cloth wiping the blood off the back of my neck, soft and smooth as silk bedsheets. I supposed she was withdrawing her indictment.

With far more effort than I would've thought possible, I finally tore myself away from the wall to survey our righteous victory. Neither Chedran, Arissa nor I had suffered so much as a scratch. Our enemies though – had to call them 'enemies', otherwise I wouldn't have been able to breathe – had all died on their backs. Most still lay underneath their blankets, like weary codgers who'd been awaiting death all this time, waiting for us to come and grant it to them. Only, five of the faces peeking out of those blankets weren't old at all. They were . . .

'Teenagers,' I tried to say, but no breath came with the word. I made myself try again, then a third time until at last my confession found its voice. 'Most of them were just teenagers, no older than us.'

'Jan'Tep,' Chedran corrected as though their people were somehow incapable of anything so innocent as youth. He dug his toe into one of the bodies and rolled it over so we couldn't see her face. 'No more deserving of pity than they were of mercy.'

No! I screamed inside my own head, though I had no more business shedding tears for a girl my own age than I did for the old lord magus who'd died next to her. I looked down at the other faces, determined to burn every detail of their features into my memory, yet unable to make myself see them as anything but the evidence we would leave behind to rot unburied amidst the ruins of this place. *Please, Pappy. Please, please come find me so you can tell me I didn't do this awful thing!*

'We can free you from your pain,' the Scarlet Verses whispered in a soothing, slithering lullaby. '*Let us out. A few dozen words from your lips and we will carry away all your suff—*'

'No!' I shouted back at them. '*I don't want you! I want Durral. I want his teachings, his love, his forgiv—*'

'*My teachings?*' I heard him say. There was more than a touch of annoyance in that smooth drawl of his. '*Grand word for somethin' that never seems to stick with you, teysan. But since you asked so sweet and all, how about this old chestnut: shame ain't the Argosi way. So how about you quit starin' at them faces and get to work?*'

'*What work? What's left to—*'

Teysan. He'd called me *teysan*. Even in my imagination, Durral only ever calls me teysan when I'm failing to heed my Argosi talents.

'*Where should I be looking, Pappy?*'

I turned to Arissa, whose arched eyebrow and tight-lipped grimace told me she was about ten seconds away from slapping me silly until I stopped acting crazy. I wasted two of those seconds on Chedran, searching that smug fox-in-a-henhouse smile of his for any sign he'd somehow gotten control of me with that snake charmer's gaze of his. My fingers squeezed the thin, cool surface of the throwing card still in my hand.

If you did this to me, Chedran, if you mesmerised me into committing murder, I'm going to see your blood mingle with that of all these Jan'Tep you so despi—

I imagined a pressure under my chin, the familiar touch of Durral's busted second knuckle lifting my jawbone up and then a few degrees to the left, guiding me right back to the spot I'd been staring at moments ago: a cracked tower wall painted with a single, perfect line of sprayed blood.

'*What am I supposed to see, Pappy? It's exactly as it was just—*'

Stupid.

Stupid, stupid, *stupid*.

'*Don't say it,*' I warned Durral. Well, myself really. Didn't work though. In my recollections, he's even more stubborn than I am.

'You wanted the lesson, teysan, so you tell me. When's the last time you saw blood splash on a wall and not—'

Arissa grabbed my shoulder with her left hand, which told me she was winding up to slap me with her right. I lifted my arm straight to catch the blow, then down hard to trap her wrist against my ribs. Both of us knew she still had a dozen ways of taking me down from that position.

'Don't,' I warned her. 'We didn't do this.'

'Yes, we did,' she said, not bothering to free herself, instead pulling me closer. 'We did this thing, Rat Girl, and now we have to live with it.'

'Enough!' Chedran shouted, a clarion horn blaring in my ear. 'This was a victory. A *righteous* victory! Look—' He kicked the corpse of the old man. 'Those robes mark him as a lord magus. A *lord magus!* How many of our kind has he murdered in his time? Now he's dead, and every Mahdek should rejoice. I'll not have this triumph sullied by your pathetic mewling self-pity!'

'You're wrong on two counts,' I told them both. I let Arissa see that I was calm now so that when I released her hand she wouldn't make a move on me. 'First off, there ain't nothing righteous about slaughter. Not even when it never happened in the first place.'

Suddenly Arissa was wary. Even without moving a muscle, you could tell she was readying herself, which told me she too had sensed something was wrong; she'd just confused it with the guilt we'd both felt but she'd been better at suppressing. 'Rat Girl, what's going on?'

I pointed to the wall and waited for them to follow my finger. 'You ever see blood splatter on a wall that didn't drip?'

'Sand magic?' Chedran asked, crouching low, his curved knife back in his hand as he spun around searching for enemies in every shadow. 'How? They were asleep when we killed them!'

113

Took me longer than I would've liked to get the words out. There was a reason the pattern of that blood spatter had been so familiar: it was exactly the same one that had sprayed from the Daroman guard's neck back in Soul's Grave all those weeks ago. A perfect replica. That having been the only time in my life I'd ever slit somebody's throat, it was the only image that could be used to convince me I'd just committed a murder.

'We never got the drop on them,' I said. 'We never even made it inside the tower.'

I looked back down at the six dead mages. They looked exactly the way you'd expect dead bodies should look, only the dead never quite look right, do they? And had the corner of the youngest's one's mouth just moved a fraction?

'What's wrong with you?' Chedran demanded. 'Why are you standing there when we—'

Without so much as a whisper, the six dead mages vanished from the floor of the tower. In their place lay three different figures whose faces were all too familiar. Arissa, Chedran and I stared down at our own corpses gazing back at us. They looked happy.

'It's called a mind cage,' I said. 'We're in a mind cage.'

15

The Mind Cage

Silk magic.

The most devious of the seven forms of Jan'Tep sorcery, silk is
the magic of the mind: an intricate web of hidden forces that can
tether one consciousness to another. Only those initiates who've
sparked the middle band of sigils tattooed in platinum inks on their
left forearm can wield its subtle spells. The lords magi boast of silk
magic being incontrovertible proof of the superiority of the Jan'Tep
intellect over the weaker minds of other cultures. Never understood
how anyone could brag about the wilful desecration of their fellow
human beings like that.

Now, the Argosi may not be keen on magic, but we keep track
of its presence across this continent, same as we do wars, plagues
and famines. Most would agree that the vilest silk spell ever
conceived is the mind chain: a spell that prevents the victim from
ever speaking or otherwise revealing a secret the spellcaster wishes
kept. Doesn't sound like such a big deal, right? Now imagine your
mind straining against those invisible shackles, day after day, year
after year, until at last your spirit breaks and insanity becomes a
blessed release.

A close second, though, Is the mind *cage*. This nasty piece of
business traps the victim's consciousness inside a prison constructed

from their own memories. The mage picks through your most intimate and private recollections then weaves in their own, refashioning them into a cell from which you can never escape because you can't even see the bars.

'How can this feel so real?' Arissa asked, rubbing the tips of her thumbs and forefingers together. 'I can feel everything, taste the spit in my mouth, see, hear, smell—'

'You remember a time when someone pinched the skin on the back of your hand real hard?' I asked.

'Sure.'

I reached out and took her wrist, turned it over and pinched her. Arissa swore and tried to pull away. 'What the hells—'

I held on. 'How's that feel?'

'Like one of us is due for a black eye.'

I pinched her again. She yelped and yanked her hand out of my grip. Knowing it was coming, I ducked beneath the straight jab that would've forcefully reminded me of a bloody nose I'd once gotten years ago.

'What purpose does this childish game serve?' Chedran demanded, interposing himself between us.

'Aw,' Arissa said, chuckling. 'Seems the big bad wolf's gone sweet on you, Rat Girl. Don't suppose you'd mind me taking him to bed, what with your romantic inclinations leaning in other directions?' She winked at me and cocked one hip. 'Then again, this being in our heads and all, maybe I'll finally let you have your way with me.'

I did my best to smile the lurid taunt away. Arissa had a bad habit of teasing me about my attraction to her. One minute she'd be flirting outrageously with me, the next she'd find some way to remind me that she preferred men. Many a sleepless hour over these past weeks I'd contemplated sitting Arissa down and explaining the profound discourtesy of stoking affections she couldn't return just because she enjoyed the thrill of being desired. What held me back all those nights troubled me even more now.

Arissa had been imprisoned in Soul's Grave for three hundred days. Three hundred days of beatings, near starvation, torture and being relentlessly, mercilessly demeaned. Strange word that, 'demean' – like you could literally erase the *meaning* from a person. Yet that's what the warden vizier and his clerics had done to Arissa. That was why part of her needed me to fall for her, even if she could never fall for me the same way.

That's why I was so scared for her now, because bad as Soul's Grave must've been, inside the insidious silk magic of a mind cage there was nowhere to hide. Whoever had us locked up inside our heads could demean Arissa in ways only she could imagine.

'Pinch the back of your hand again,' I told her.

'Why?'

'Because you trust me.'

'That's dirty poker, Rat Girl.' She turned her palm down and pinched the skin. 'Damn it!'

'How'd that feel?'

She scowled at me. 'What were you expecting? Pretty much the same as all the other times.'

'Wrong. Not "pretty much" the same, *exactly* the same, right?'

Her eyes narrowed as she pinched herself again, gentler this time, and yet she winced same as before. 'What the hells? How could it hurt this much when I barely squeezed at all?'

'Mind cages are incredibly hard to maintain. The mage can only create them from sense memories, ours or theirs. The strongest ones, like the time someone pinched you so hard it made you wince, are easy to pick out. Subtler memories take more effort.'

117

Arissa turned, slowly taking in the entirety of the tower. 'So none of this is real? Every stone, every sound, even the stench of decay are nothing more than bits and pieces of past experiences cobbled together like a badly made quilt?'

'No,' Chedran murmured, so quiet I knew something was wrong. 'No, no, no.'

He was staring down at the trio of corpses on the floor that looked and even smelled like us: a faint whiff of cinnamon I always associated with Arissa back when we both ran with the Black Galleon gang mixed with Chedran's earthier, salty musk. He kept shaking his head like a drunk trying to shake off too much whisky. All the while, he kept repeating that same *no* over and over.

'Hey, handsome,' Arissa said, laying a hand on his arm, 'probably isn't healthy to obsess over your own body, especially after it's dead.' She made a show of leaning closer to hers. 'Even if mine does look rather gorgeous in repose, I must say.'

Humour can be a fine tactic, and one the Argosi employ more than most to stave off despair. Arissa never trained in arta precis though, which was how she'd misjudged Chedran so badly.

Like an avalanche, he crashed down on the corpses at our feet. His long, curved knife, designed for slicing rather than thrusting, stabbed over and over into the flesh of the one that bore his face. 'I'm not dead!' he bellowed. 'I'm not dead!'

I let him rant awhile. Doesn't do much good to reason with someone oblivious to how gleefully they're stabbing their own cadaver. Besides, I was waiting for what was sure to follow.

'I'm not dead,' he said, this time bringing the curved edge of his blade to his own throat. 'I can prove it.'

I keep an extensible steel rod in a hidden pocket in the back of my waistcoat. With one smooth motion – or at least, the memory of a particularly skilful draw – I flicked it open and slammed the shaft down on his wrist. The dagger went flying and Chedran yelped from the pain. Guess he had a strong recollection of once being struck on the wrist bone.

I walked across the debris-strewn floor to retrieve his blade. 'I happen to know from experience that you can't kill yourself in a mind cage,' I informed him. 'But attempted suicide probably ain't good for the spirit.'

Chedran expressed his gratitude for my intervention in the fashion to which I'd grown accustomed. 'Damn you, Argosi. This is your fault.'

Nothing like being trapped inside a prison made of memories with a guy who manages to forget it was his idea to rush in here and start slitting throats without a backup plan.

'Why isn't the blood dripping?' Arissa asked. She was walking over to the splatter on the wall that had been the first clue that something wasn't right about this tower. She stopped about a foot away, then leaned in closer. 'Funny – it *is* dripping now, but it's still off somehow.'

'Simple,' I replied. 'Whoever's doing this to us doesn't know precisely what dripping blood should look like. Jan'Tep mages rarely get their hands dirty. They rely on iron bindings and ember blasts instead of slicing their enemies open. What their own memories can't provide for the mind cage, they draw from ours.' I went to join her by the wall. 'This one was from the Daroman guard I killed when I came to get you out of Soul's Grave.'

'But you've seen plenty of blood,' Arissa countered. 'You know what it looks like when it splatters.'

'Memories aren't perfect portraits of the past. They're like . . . pieces of stories we recount to ourselves later.' I reached out and touched the blood. It was still warm. I dabbed my fingertip on my tongue. It tasted of copper and shame. 'When my blade went through that soldier's throat, all I could see was that spray of blood, almost like it was frozen in the air, reminding me that what I'd done was permanent – a stain on my soul that would never wash away. The memory is fresh and strong in my mind, making it the easiest one for the silk mage to use.'

'You seem to know a lot about these mind cages,' Chedran said accusingly. Apparently he was finally done stabbing himself and was looking for a new target.

'I was caught in one a couple of years back.' I glanced around at the tower. 'Different place, different memories, but the feeling of it . . . the *flavour* of the magic, is kind of similar, now that I think about it.'

'Can the mages hear us?' Arissa asked, whispering under her breath.

I chuckled. 'Oh, they can hear us all right.'

I looked up at the collapsed ceilings above and the night sky beyond. Not sure why I bothered, since it's not like the mage was up there. Still, you have to look somewhere when you're trying to look someone in the eye.

'I offer you the Way of Water,' I told the mage. 'Release us from your cage and we can talk this through like civilised folk. Try to keep us here, and you and me are going to walk the Way of Thunder.'

There was no answer at first. Mind cages are tough to maintain because they require continuous concentration on the part of the mage. Splitting their focus to get into a debate with their victims requires additional effort, which explains why our captor sounded mighty irritable when at last they spoke.

'*Do not speak to us of civility!*' a voice echoed throughout the tower. '*Your own memories betray the litany of barbarity each of you has committed, crimes so vile as to defy even our people's worst fears about you!*'

Rude way to start a conversation, I thought. Whoever had spoken tossed in a headache to emphasise their displeasure with us. Then the real show began.

'Witness what passes for heroes among the Mahdek!'

Suddenly our corpses were gone, along with the rubble and debris, the campfire and everything else that had lent the illusion of realism to the tower. All that was left were the curving walls surrounding us, and upon them exploded images of our respective violence and criminality. Neither Arissa, Chedran nor I appeared in them, but only because the scenes were shown from our own vantage points, through our eyes. Stolen memories – private, intimate recollections – hurled against the walls to lay bare our most shameful secrets.

Arissa was the first target. Turns out it's not just the Argosi who don't waste time on shame or guilt.

'Oh, I remember that one!' she said, feigning almost childish excitement as a robbery unfolded before us. An elegantly dressed Daroman woman in her seventies was bound to a chair in the middle of a private study walled in mahogany and filled with enough trinkets to keep a thief's eyes darting this way and that. I was getting dizzy just watching.

'How proud you must be to steal that which is most precious from an elderly woman who couldn't fight back!'

The heist continued, with Arissa's crimson-gloved hands coming in and out of view as she snatched jewels and curios with no discernible method to her madness, even dumping out a gold box to steal the letters inside.

Arissa shrugged, seemingly unconcerned. 'Go a bit further back in my memories and you'll discover the nice little old lady wasn't so nice after all.'

But the mage casting the mind cage banished that memory, superimposing upon the wall a far more violent one. A young

121

Jan'Tep, maybe seventeen years old, was struggling to cast a spell through bloodied lips and broken teeth. Every time he tried to utter his incantation though, a fist shot out and smashed into his face. A girl's fist.

'Go on,' the attacker's voice – my voice – shouted. 'Hit me with an ember spell! Prove the superiority of the Jan'Tep race over a filthy little Mahdek bitch! Do it!' But my fist kept striking over and over, even after the young mage had passed out and that stupid, prideful girl's knuckles were split and bleeding.

'*Would you still seek to instruct us on civility, Mahdek?*' asked our captor.

That one hit hard, but I followed Durral's advice and left my guilt and shame back in the desert where they belonged. Regret isn't restitution, and you can't pay your debts when you're dead. I stilled those dark thoughts, promising them a visit when time and wisdom revealed a path for me to make peace with them. In the meantime, I awoke my arta precis and dug through the hard shell of our jailer's outrage for what might be hidden beneath.

Anger. Bitterness. Resentment. But why? You don't resent an enemy for proving themselves as barbaric as you've always believed. You resent them for failing to live up to your expectations.

Before I could pursue that deduction, the scene on the tower wall unfolded beyond my recollection of the fight with that young Jan'Tep mage. The violence became even more savage. At first I worried that I must've blocked out the cruelty I'd inflicted on him, but then I saw through the blood and bruising that the victim wasn't a teenager any more but a grown man. He wasn't being struck by mere fists either, but with a sharpened rock held in the hand of a skinny boy who looked no older than twelve.

I'd never witnessed anything so brutal before in my life.

16

Unforgivable Crimes

'Thirteen,' Chedran said. 'I was barely thirteen. Small and weak for my age.'

'Old enough to butcher men and women who were parents to children far younger,' our captor countered, the words discordant and painful as a church bell ringing in our ears even as the silk spell stripped away any discernible characteristics of tone and pitch that might've offered some clue as to the identity of our jailor. I'd assumed it would be the lord magus, but in both tone and emotional intensity, this sounded like someone far younger.

On the curved inner walls of the tower, Chedran's crime of long ago played out in startling detail. Over and over, the narrowed point of the chiselled rock in his scrawny fist came crashing down, an endless storm of merciless lightning strikes that tore through the mage's robes, darkening silver and white silks a glistening oily red. Ragged pleas for mercy gave way to a wheezing struggle for breath, lost in the sobs of the boy who kept hitting him again and again as his own tears mixed with the blood of his victim.

When at last exhaustion caused the rock to slip from the boy's hand, he got up off the dead mage and rose to his feet, stepping back to survey his handiwork. The image torn from Chedran's own memories stilled, frozen in time as if it had been painted on the tower wall years ago, waiting only for someone to come and witness the bloody vista he'd left behind. It hadn't only been the one mage he'd killed. Three more Jan'Tep lay dead on the ground around his feet. Two of them were women. One showed a swelling at her midsection that strained against her blood-soaked robes.

I turned to Chedran, the broad-shouldered man who'd once been that skinny, terrified boy. He wouldn't meet my eyes, just kept staring straight at the wall. 'I won't be judged by you any more than I will by them,' he said quietly. The look on his face was grim, but not the least bit sorry. There was pride in the flat line of his lips. 'Those four mages killed sixty-eight Mahdek men, women and children. The pregnant one? When the little boys and girls of my clan threw themselves at her feet, begging her to spare them, she placed a hand against her belly and, with the placid smile of an expectant mother, rained ember spells upon the children.'

In his darker moments, when Durral worried I mistook his teachings for cunning tricks and facile frontier philosophy, he'd remind me that the Argosi talents are an awakening from which there's no return to the peaceful slumber of ignorance. There's a price for learning about people. All people.

'She was thinking of her unborn baby,' I said – mumbled really.

'What?' Arissa asked. She'd heard me though.

On the tower wall, the image of the dead pregnant woman haunted me. 'That mage Chedran killed. When she was massacring all those Mahdek children, she was thinking of her child, and how she'd do anything to give it a safer future.'

Chedran barked a laugh, a hyena circling its prey. 'What do you suppose she was thinking when I killed her?' He didn't wait for an answer, instead tilting his head all the way back to shout at the whirling grey mist seeping through the gaps in the tower roof. 'Would you like to know how I tricked her coven? How a boy –' a

124

sob slipped past the iron bars of his pride – 'a *child* convinced your fellow lords magi to take him into their camp and make him their plaything?' He jabbed a finger towards the wall. 'Why not show us *that* memory? It shouldn't be hard. It's as fresh in my mind as the night it happened!'

The silence lasted a long time. Arissa and I stared at each other, uncertain what comfort either of us could or *should* offer him. When I looked back at the image staining the wall, all I could see was a trail of cruelty and murder passing from one generation to the next with no end in sight.

'*It's over then,*' the reply came at last. No denial, no outrage, only . . . resignation. '*Fate will have us all. Blood will beget more blood, and a three-hundred-year war continues until the last Mahdek's bones bleach beneath an unforgiving desert sun.*'

'It doesn't have to be that way,' I called out. 'You sent for us! You could've used that spell warrant to hunt down those kids any time you wanted, but when you sensed me reaching out to you, the lines became a map leading us to this place!'

'*And you came with murderous intent, proving what our elders have warned us our entire lives – that the Mahdek heart is filled with hate from the moment of conception.*' I felt a blast of nausea so thick I couldn't stop choking long enough to deny the accusation. '*So be it. Sleep, little Mahdek. Dream of sweet sailings upon an ocean of my people's blood until thirst and hunger return you to your ancestors.*'

Chedran's and Arissa's eyes started to blink closed, my own vision began to blur. Another favourite of silk mages? Sleep spells.

'You're making a mistake!' I shouted, drawing on every ounce of my arta forteize to stave off unconsciousness. 'Drop the cage and let's talk like civ—'

'*Like "civilised folk"?*' the voice mocked. '*Again you speak of civility with a frontier drawl reminiscent of a man who was, indeed, civilised.*

A man determined to prove to his mortal enemy that nothing she could do would make him hate her, who instead taught her that the only real cage that binds any of us is the past, and we all have a duty to help each other escape those bars.'

'Wait, that sounds like my papp—'

'Enough! We offered the Mahdek a peaceful invitation. In return, they sent a thief, a killer and a monster whose thoughts are so infected by rage and madness that I cannot even see your face through the miasma of hate and violence that shrouds your mind!'

They can't see me through the Scarlet Verses. Whoever's behind this doesn't know who I am because my mind's so messed up . . .

Probably wasn't the best time to be ruminating on the perceptual limitations of mind cages, because they hit me with a second sleep commandment, pouring more of that damnable silk magic into the spell.

'Sleep, now, Mahdek. Until the end comes, may slumber grant you peace from the insanity that infects you.'

Arissa and Chedran had already fallen unconscious to the floor, and I was fading fast. No way could I resist a third time, which left me with precisely one option for busting out of this prison.

The mage must've sensed something shifting within my mind, because their next words sounded awful nervous. 'Why have your thoughts begun to still? Before, they swirled and spun, as if the words in your mind were an ever-shifting maze seeking to confine the madness within you, but now—'

Part of me wanted to try to negotiate with our captors one last time, but Enna, she taught me that the Way of Water can only carry you so far when someone's pouring sand down your throat.

'It's like this, friend: since I can't get you to listen to reason before one of your sleep spells takes me down, and you seem so powerful concerned about the monstrous insanities rattlin' around

126

inside my skull, how about I give you a taste of what's gonna happen if I let 'em out?'

A second later, the tower echoed with the mage's scream.

I felt terrible about that.

I mean, not *too* terrible. Like Enna always says, if you're gonna walk the Way of Thunder, you gotta expect you're gonna make an impression on people.

17

Parole

The first lesson Durral ever taught me about breaking out of mind cages was, like most of his teachings, a paradox.

'Problem with trapping another person's mind inside your own, kid, is that you're also locking yourself in with all their thoughts.'

My pappy had gotten us out of that particular mind cage by having us share the stories of our lives. Stories full of love and pain, laughter and sorrow. The mage in question, being a stuck-up little Jan'Tep princess who'd never faced an honest emotion in her entire privileged life, broke under the weight of our experiences. I swear, when Durral throws a punch, he finds a way to do even that with dignity and compassion. Me? I didn't have that kind of time. What I did have were allies . . . of a sort.

'You boys having fun yet?' I asked the Scarlet Verses.

'Yes! Yes, yes!' they cooed in rapturous delight. If mystical language viruses had legs, these would've been dancing up a storm. *'Freedom, Argosi! That's a word you love, isn't it? Free yourself now by unleashing our sublime eloquence on those wh—'*

'Okay, okay, don't get all pompous on me.'

Despite how hard they tried to push me, I still didn't speak the verses aloud. All it took was to permit those sick, twisted syllables to take shape in my mind, unleashing words I'd bound into notions of beauty and mischief back into disfigured meanings full of horror and despair. That alone was enough to drag a coven of silk mages kicking and screaming to the brink of madness.

'No!' the first one screamed so loud it was like her fists were pounding the inside of my skull, trying to get out. Confusion and terror had weakened the mind cage enough that I could make out the feminine tones of her voice – along with a defiant nature I would've found admirable under different circumstances. '*You will not break me, monster. Though my mind be torn apart by your foul disease, still you will not—*'

'*Don't be an idiot!*' a somewhat less hardy soul cried out. '*We must abandon the spell before it's too late!*'

'*Jir'dan is right!*' said another mage, this gal sounding even younger. Where was the lord magus in all of this? '*Sever the bond and I will rupture the Mahdek's—*'

A fourth voice chimed in. '*Something's wrong. She can't release the spell. Look, her lips are quivering. I think she's trying to tell us . . . Ancestors! What are those sounds coming from Ala'tris? They're like snakes slithering inside us!*'

Wait . . . Ala'tris? Why did that name sound familiar? Damned mind cages – mess with your memories so bad you can hardly recall any but those the mage chooses to draw out of you. Ala'tris . . . Ala'tris . . . Repeating that name made my palm itch, like I was remembering the touch of a young woman's hand, squeezing mine tight, almost like we were sis—

Oh, crap.

'Stop!' I commanded the verses, but they weren't listening to me.

I'd been so proud of myself for keeping them from escaping through my lips that it hadn't occurred to me the bond between the silk mage casting the spell and me might allow the verses to pass through her!

129

'Oh, no, you don't,' I told them, clawing back the Scarlet Verses before they could burrow all the way into her brain. Those nasty syllables tried to squirm from my grip, determined to unleash their foul meanings on the world. I bound them with contronyms, nullifying each word with its counter-meaning. *Sanguine* went from bloodthirsty to cheerful. The *slither* of a snake about to strike softened to the sensuous, deliciously sinful feeling of silk sliding down a naked thigh. One by one, I beckoned those verses back inside me, dancing, always dancing, until their curse was mine alone.

I might've cried out from despair, but truth be told, I lacked the words.

'If you're still of a mind to kill me, now's as good a time as any,' I informed our captors, plunged into a desolation so deep I wasn't sure I would ever drag myself back out. 'You won't get a fuss from me.'

It's a strange thing to hear panting in your mind. I mean, a person who's out of breath doesn't actually *think* their huffing and puffing, do they? Slow rasping breaths filled the tower, causing the walls to expand and contract with each one. After a time, they slowed and finally settled.

'*You had me,*' the young woman holding the cage together admitted. '*You could have destroyed us with those . . . what do you call this horror that hides you from my mind? It's as if you're a figure dancing inside a crimson mist, the tendrils of that insidious fog grasping for you from all sides.*'

Well, that was just about as depressing an analogy for what I carried around inside me as I could imagine. Too bad she was spot on.

It took me a moment to respond. I was panting too, as it turned out, even though my body probably wasn't even inside this tower.

A chill was coming over me, which suggested I was actually somewhere outside in the cold. 'You showed me your hand and I've shown you mine,' I said. 'How about we set our cards down and call this one a draw?'

'Show yourself to me first. My comrades have left the tower. They're heading for where your bodies lie on the ground. They will kill you rather than risk a second attack.'

I tried to tell her my name. It is, after all, the one possession I prize above all others. Maybe it's vanity, but I love that name. Took me a long time to find it, and it means everything to me – which was precisely the problem.

The trick I used to prevent the Scarlet Verses from taking me over was to shift the meanings of their words, preventing those noxious ideas from solidifying inside my mind. It was a neat trick. Unfortunately, they'd started learning it for themselves. When I felt low, if I let sorrow or loneliness get the best of me, the verses would start . . . playing with my name. They'd strangle every joyful word until I was too scared to say my own name out loud for fear it would no longer mean anything at all.

'A *bargain*,' they whispered, convinced, as always, that this time they had me. *'Speak us aloud. Let your lips take on the beautiful forms of our syllables but once, and you will forever be free of—'*

'Nah, you ain't getting away that easy.'

Maybe the reason I hate mind cages so much is the way a silk mage will turn your own memories against you. That's both a crime and a mistake, because my memories aren't just treasures, they're like . . . magic spells. The bad ones you survived can strengthen your resolve, wrap you in armour strong as steel. The good memories, though? Those rare moments of laughter, surprise and fascination that most people let slip away? You'd be amazed the wonders you can work with them.

131

An orphaned Mahdek girl of fifteen stands before hundreds of Jan'Tep and their clan prince. She's angry, confused. She's just revealed to them the perfidy of the crimes committed against her by a cabal of mages. Even then, even after the evidence has come out, thanks to the brave daughter of one of those self-same conspirators, the prince has decided to wipe the Mahdek girl's memories to prevent a war. He's going to steal from her even the truth of her suffering in the name of peace. But then she feels something – something unexpected. Something their two cultures may never have seen before . . .

I send my thoughts hurtling back to that Jan'Tep city with all those people looking so relieved that the horrors performed in their name were about to be wiped away, and then that hand slipping into mine . . . fingers smooth, not calloused like my own, intertwining, squeezing. An unspoken promise to stand beside me no matter what happened next. The unexpected gift of sisterhood, more precious and powerful than I could ever have imagined, even if we were never meant to see each other again.

'There are such things as miracles,' I whispered. 'No matter what people say, there are miracles in this world. It's just that they don't come from gods or magic. They come from us.'

I heard a sob then, somehow both in my mind and in my ears, and the sound of footsteps running towards me. I was just noticing the sticky wetness of the mud seeping through the back of my shirt when a young woman's arms grabbed hold of me, barely courteous enough to yank me to a sitting position before crushing me in a frantic embrace. Then a voice unclouded by magic, chiming like a bell, still sounding like she couldn't believe it was me.

'Ferius Parfax?'

Yeah. That's how you say the name.

18

The Captors

The world is full of injustices. Some great, some small. But surely the most annoying is when you wake up shivering, your best travelling shirt soaked through on account of you being flat on your back in the mud, hair matted and filthy, thoughts murky and a headache pounding out a funeral lament in your skull. All that though, that's just circumstance. Bad luck.

The injustice begins when you open your eyes and the first thing you see is a girl your own age, slender like you, with hair nearly as red. Like looking into a mirror, right? Except her skin is smooth as silk and there's not a scar to be found anywhere. Oh, and give her a face so beautiful the sight puts an ache in your belly. Brown eyes, not green like mine, but they shone with brilliance in every sense of the word and brimmed with tears like she'd just found her long-lost sister. You can bet I was bawling like a baby before I'd even gotten my feet under me.

'I thought I'd never see you again,' Ala'tris said, holding my hands in hers – now that she'd finally stopped trying to hug the life out of me. The fabric of her fitted robe, silver and black, shimmered in the moonlight, bound with purple cords the colour of silk magic that crossed from each shoulder down to the other side of her waist. The sleeves, like those of most mage's garments, were thin as gossamer to reveal the shimmering glyphs of her tattooed bands. The cuffs ended in a narrow strip of loosely woven velvet that made it easier to slide them up her forearms and keep them there when casting spells that required total concentration.

Ala'tris gave herself a little shake and her robes shed the dust and mud that clung insistently to my own ratty shirt, waistcoat and trousers. I probably looked like a mangy mutt by comparison, but you wouldn't've known it from the way she was smiling at me.

I could feel Chedran's gaze burning a hole in the back of my neck even before the inevitable disdain burst out of him. 'What a charming reunion. The Mahdek beggar girl kissing the feet of her Jan'Tep oppressor. No wonder you never returned to your tribe, Ferius. Why fight for the impoverished and persecuted when you can befriend the children of tyrants?'

There wasn't a shred of anger in me for Chedran at that moment, not one drop of resentment. On the walls of that imagined tower in which we'd been confined, I'd watched my fists pounding our enemies the same as I'd witnessed his rock crashing down on them. We'd both had our reasons, both been given plenty of cause to despise the Jan'Tep. But my darkest impulses had been tempered by gifts Chedran had never been given: a handful of precious memories filled with kindness and grace. One of those memories was Ala'tris of the House of Tris.

The first time we'd met, the *only* time really, had been after Durral and me had broken out of a mind cage only to discover that our captor was a young Jan'Tep girl my own age who'd been commanded by her mother to imprison us so she could steal the secrets of the Argosi from Durral's memories. Waste of a costly and painful spell, if you ask me. The only reason the Jan'Tep can't learn the seven Argosi talents is because they're hard work, and magic makes you lazy. Also arrogant, craven and blind to your own people's culpability.

Not Ala'tris though.

Boy, had I railed against Durral after we'd busted out of that mind cage and he'd refused to let me kill her. Worse, he'd spoken to her with gentleness and reassurance, as if she had every right to be as confused and scared of us as we were of her. He'd praised – *praised* – her skill as a mage then challenged her to become something more. Durral Brown had showed her the first step on the Way of Water, and Ala'tris had walked the rest all by herself.

After her mother's cabal and their crimes against innocent Mahdek refugees had been revealed, their clan prince ruled that the only way to prevent the entire continent from turning against the Jan'Tep was to shatter my memories so that I could never reveal what had been done to me. Ala'tris, in direct violation of her prince's command, helped me thwart that spell.

Mostly.

I'm still pretty nuts, and my memories are a jumble of images and impressions, never entirely reliable and hardly ever in the right order. But they're still mine, and that's what matters. All thanks to a girl raised to despise me.

Ala'tris might've looked a little like me, but Chedran was my true mirror: the person I would've become had it not been for people like her and Durral and Enna and all the others who'd helped me find my path. That's why I couldn't be mad at Chedran, even if he was doing his level best to sour this unexpected reunion.

On the other hand, him having used that bitter laugh to muffle the faint hiss of the curved blade sliding out of the sheath at the back of his belt? Downright rude.

'Arissa?' I asked quietly, not wanting to let go of the warmth of Ala'tris's hands.

135

A sharp *shhhick* broke the quiet as the steel rod made from three interlocking cylinders that Arissa had apparently pilfered from my pack extended to its full length. 'So, you're expecting me to bash our travelling companion's brains out if he makes a move on your girlfriend?'

'Yeah.'

'Give me leave to bind the savage in iron and blood, Ala'tris!' a higher-pitched voice called out. A girl, maybe fifteen or so, short and compact, with hair dark as night and amber eyes bright as starlight stepped out of the forest. The tattooed iron band around her forearm gleamed with an unnatural grey incandescence. Her blood band sparked crimson.

'Ba'dari, no!' Ala'tris called out.

Three other Jan'Tep mages, all of them teenagers, joined her with hands raised, fingers contorted into an assortment of somatic gestures, lips ready to unleash some dastardly incantation or other. The forest was aglow with the reflected magic swirling around their tattooed bands.

'Spells down!' Ala'tris commanded them. 'Especially you, Jir'dan.'

The guy she'd directed that last part to was tall, skinny and mightily self-righteous. 'You witnessed for yourself the darkness inside them!' he insisted. With his golden hair, magnificently hooked nose and drawn-back shoulders, he looked like an especially pompous eagle posing for a portrait. His fingers had formed the somatic shape for an ember spell I recognised and wouldn't fancy being on the receiving end of. 'A thief, a murderer . . .' Finally his eyes darted to me, narrowing in suspicion, making him look even more hawkish. 'You said it yourself, Ala'tris, this one carries a mind plague the likes of which none of us have ever encountered. How long can she possibly contain it befo—'

136

'Forever,' Ala'tris said with such finality that even I was taken aback. 'Trust these words, Jir'dan, all of you. Forever and a day will pass before Ferius Parfax allows such anguish to be unleashed on anyone but herself.'

'How can you know for certain?' the raven-haired girl asked. 'You claimed to have known her less than a day.'

'Indeed, but I have been inside her mind twice now.' Ala'tris bowed her head. 'An offence for which I fear I may never be able to make restitution, save in this one thing.' Her eyes rose again and met mine. 'Fate intended for us to be enemies, but we defied that destiny and chose to be something very different to one another. So let me be clear: anyone who bets against my sister bets against me.'

Damn it. She was going to set me to bawling again.

'That makes no sense,' argued a boy about the same age as Ba'dari. He shared the raven-haired girl's squat physique, but the short, curly locks sticking straight out of his head were a sandy brown. 'No one can "defy" destiny. By definition destiny is inevitable.'

Ala'tris grinned at the boy's stubborn certitude. 'You will find, Ga'brel, that Ferius Parfax makes a habit of flouting the inevitable.' Her smile changed, becoming so confident it was almost sly, like she was holding on to a secret none of her fellow mages knew and was about to raise it on high like an amulet. 'How else can you explain a smart-mouthed teenager with no magic of her own saving the entire Jan'Tep people from the scourge of . . .' She held them in rapt attention for so long even Durral would've called it theatrical, until finally, she finished her performance with, '. . . the Scarlet Verses?'

'What?' asked Jir'dan, his nose looking even more beakish as his eyebrows rose up in disbelief. 'This . . . this scrawny, pinch-faced, gap-toothed—'

137

'Hey!' Arissa interrupted, coming to my defence. 'Rat Girl doesn't have a gap in her teeth!' She leaned in close and peered at me. 'Well, maybe a little one?'

Jir'dan didn't seem concerned with debating though. All his doubt was directed at Ala'tris. 'You expect us to believe that this dishevelled scarecrow is . . . the Argosi?'

'The Argosi . . .' Gab'rel marvelled, followed soon after by Ba'dari, who walked right up to me like I was an exhibit at the zoo and asked, 'You're the Argosi?'

It never occurred to me that accounts of the Scarlet Verses would reach the Jan'Tep. My fellow Argosi do travel those lands sometimes, and we're awful prone to bragging. Still, I would've expected the Jan'Tep repeating the tale to alter the details to make like one of them had put an end to the Red Scream.

Ala'tris started laughing at me, pointing at my face. 'Ferius Parfax, I don't believe I've ever seen anyone look quite so uncomfortable at being admired.'

'Not like it's a problem I encounter too often. Now, is there any chance we could make our way into that tower and one of you all-powerful mages can spell me up some hot water for a bath? I'm starting to smell like my horse.' I glanced around the sparsely wooded forest and then the tower beyond. 'Speaking of horses, where are yo—'

'What about her companions?' the final member of the group asked. The woman who stepped out of the shadows was tall and graceful. The silk of her sleeveless sand-coloured robe clung to curves that, judging by Chedran's audible intake of breath, was making him reconsider his prejudice against the Jan'Tep. Her head was shaved, her skin bronze. She was the only one of the group wearing make-up: vibrant shades of pale cerulean and darker azure that accented her lips and the magnificent blue of her eyes. She

138

caught Chedran's stare and didn't seem offended by it; nor was she persuaded to trust him though. 'Will you vouch for this murderer as well?'

'A fair question, Sar'ephir.' Ala'tris crossed the muddy ground to stand before Chedran. Like a card sharp who can't stop pulling the same buried ace out of his sleeve, he tried his snake-charming on her. I caught a glimpse of her fingers twitching, a faint flash of purple from the sigils on her forearm. Chedran winced like she'd flicked his earlobe with a rusted nail. 'No,' she said then. 'There is no path to friendship for us, is there, warrior of the Mahdek?'

His only reply was a slow shake of his head.

Ala'tris surprised all of us by taking his hand and kissing the back of it. 'Fortunate for both of us, then, that peace is not negotiated with friends but between enemies.' She let go of Chedran's hand and turned to Arissa. 'Might I hope, however, that Arelisa Talédra, Contessa of—'

'Arissa's fine,' she said.

Arelisa Talédra. That was the first time I'd heard Arissa's real name. And she was a contessa, of all things? I guess Ala'tris hadn't had as much trouble rifling through her thoughts as mine.

Arissa shot me a familiar look from back in our Black Galleon days – the one that said, *'You want to stay friends? You don't dig into my business.'* To Ala'tris she added, 'Besides, I'm not here to negotiate some treaty or whatever it is you people think we're about to do. I just tagged along with Rat Girl on the off-chance there'd be something worth stealing in that tower of yours.'

'Rat Girl?' Ala'tris asked, unable to keep a smirk from her lips.

I shrugged. 'It's a compliment really. You should see the folks she usually hangs with.'

Laughter eased the tension a little. We were, all of us, dangerous people who'd come perilously close to bloodshed. Would've been

139

nice to leave it there, maybe share some proper food and a little wine, a few dirty jokes, maybe even a stolen kiss here or there. Too bad I couldn't allow that, not yet. Friendship was the card that both Ala'tris and I had played. Now it was time we showed the rest of our hands.

'Ala'tris,' I said, tugging at the hem of my leather waistcoat with my right hand to mask drawing a half-dozen steel throwing cards from one of the pockets with my left, then coughing to conceal the cards sliding into the cuff of my shirt. 'I sure hope you have a good explanation for cursing an innocent twelve-year-old boy with a spell warrant.'

Ala'tris, the unexpected friend from my past who I dearly hoped wasn't about to prove herself an enemy, replied with a single word. She spoke it clearly enough, but still I stared at her until she repeated it. 'Again,' I insisted, because it was the kind of word over which wars get started.

'Restitution.'

19

Restitution

In retrospect, Chedran had displayed admirable restraint up until Ala'tris had used that particular word. After that? He pretty much erupted like a volcano.

'Restitution?' he demanded, jaw clenched so tight I thought his teeth would grind out sparks and set the forest ablaze. '*Restitution?* You would seek *restitution* from a subjugated people for some perceived crime against their oppressors? We could slaughter a thousand Jan'Tep and still barely begin to—'

'Chedran . . .' I began gently, which didn't help matters at all.

'Don't you dare pacify me, *Argosi*. I'm sick of you siding with everyone but your own peop—'

'I'm pretty sure Ala'tris didn't mean that Remeny owes the Jan'Tep restitution.'

I pointed to the coven of four mages beside her. Warring with the inevitable tension and mistrust on their faces was a look of unbridled idealism. Before I'd met Durral Brown, I'd mistook that look for gullibility. In his eyes, though, wistful romanticism was like a force of nature. An unquenchable need to prove the world was a better place than anyone wanted him to believe. Ever since, I'd sorely tried to keep a little of that faraway stare in my own eyes. 'I think . . . I think they're the ones intending to make restitution.'

Chedran wasn't persuaded. 'Restitution begins with confessing one's crimes,' he reminded me.

Arissa picked that moment to chime in unhelpfully. No soul on this continent as cynical as hers. 'The snake charmer's not wrong – for once. Those pretty words and adoring gazes between you and your little girlfriend might melt my thieving heart, but they don't explain why she took control of that spell warrant on Remeny.'

One might've expected Chedran to be grateful for the support, but that would require not having met him. 'Spirits of Fire and Fury!' he bellowed into the darkness. 'Are you both blind? Am I the only one who sees the obvious?' He jabbed an accusing finger at Ala'tris. '*She* took hold of the dead silk mage's spell after I rescued the runaways.' A feral smile twisted his mouth into an ugly shape as he stalked towards Ala'tris, arms outstretched as if to show he was unarmed. I knew that smile though. I'd worn it on my own face plenty of times when facing off against a mage, knowing I had a trick up my sleeve. 'Would you like to know how your fellow Jan'Tep died?' he asked her.

'Don't even think it,' I warned him.

Chedran stopped but didn't turn to face me. He wanted me to know that this was a pause and not an ending to what he planned. 'She's been using the spell warrant to track the runaways. She knew that, sooner or later, the endless dangers facing them in the outside world would send them scurrying back to the last Mahdek enclave, unwittingly leading the enemy to our doors.'

'I do not deny that I reshaped the other silk mage's spell warrant,' Ala'tris admitted, her tone calm yet respectful, her gaze steady but not challenging. 'That is, however, only half the story. I urge you

142

to hear the rest without allowing bigotry to blind you to the possibility that not every Jan'Tep wishes to be your enemy.'

The gal was a born diplomat all right, but there's a reason diplomats don't negotiate peace treaties with wild dogs. Chedran heard, but didn't listen. Every word out of her mouth was a barely veiled admission of guilt. He stabbed his finger in the air at each of them in turn, hurling one accusation after another as if casting his own personal brand of magic. He started with Ala'tris. 'A silk mage to sedate the Mahdek sentries.' His arm swung towards Ba'dari, the raven-haired girl whose red and grey bands sparked instinctively when Chedran's venomous glare startled her. 'Blood and iron magic – the weapons of a filthy chaincaster who binds her enemies into submission.' He saved his finest sneer for Jir'dan, who loomed behind Ala'tris, doing a poor job of hiding the fiery orange shimmer of the spell he was preparing. 'Ember magic to incinerate his victims with gouts of fire and bolts of lightning.' The next indictment was against Gab'rel, the short, heavy-set lad with the glimmering blue band. 'Oh, and a touch of breath magic to spread the flames and ensure no one escapes?'

'Would you shut up and listen for five seconds?' I asked, hoping to at least turn his ire on me before he spooked one of these kids into firing off a spell they wouldn't be able to take back.

'No,' said Sar'ephir, the statuesque woman with the shaved head who, it seemed to me, wore far more make-up than anyone so beautiful required. She stepped forward, coming to stand so close to Chedran he could've leaned forward and torn out her throat with his teeth. Not a shred of concern showed in her placid features. 'Let the poor, frightened beast continue gnashing his teeth at us with this litany of insipid accusations. Heavy-handed Mahdek moral superiority always makes me nostalgic for my childhood.'

'Sar'ephir . . .' Ala'tris warned, but the other woman waved her concerns away.

143

'Go on,' she told Chedran.

Undeterred, he leaned in close and whispered in Sar'ephir's ear.

'They gonna kiss?' Arissa asked, propping an elbow atop my shoulder. 'Wouldn't mind seeing if he's any good at it, though I suppose it's more likely he'll chew her lip off.'

Whatever Chedran said caused the tall Jan'Tep woman to laugh. She stepped back a foot or so, then raised her fists tauntingly. 'Shall we settle our dispute with fisticuffs, Mahdek?' Without waiting for an answer, she dropped her hands and curled her upper lip. 'Or would you prefer we continue baring our teeth and snarling at each other like rabid ferrets to better suit your people's natural temperament?'

What in the name of the Way of Wind had Ala'tris been thinking, bringing this woman with her? Sar'ephir clearly had issues with the Mahdek and no concern at all about goading one into a duel. I was pretty sure the only thing stopping Chedran from slitting her throat then and there was that he knew she wanted him to make a move and he preferred going berserk on his own terms.

'Your peace parlay is going swimmingly so far, Rat Girl,' Arissa observed.

I didn't respond. Idle mockery was just her way of letting me know she was waiting for my signal, since things were clearly about to get ugly.

I glanced at Ala'tris, wondering what her plan had been, summoning us through that spell warrant. She must've known that whoever answered would be expecting a fight. There was too much suspicion between the Mahdek and the Jan'Tep. Too much history, leading to a complete inability to perceive events from the other side's perspective. I used to wonder how any two civilisations could go to war, when the cost of victory would always be too high no matter who won. Now though, watching the way Chedran and

144

these Jan'Tep couldn't seem to cool down around each other, it seemed like armed bloodshed was baked right into our bones.

Ala'tris surely knew this as well as I did, which was probably why she wasn't meeting my eyes. Disappointment sharper than it had any right to be stabbed deep into my belly. Seeing her again, sharing that unexpected and unearned bond of sisterhood with this girl who was so unlike me and yet seemed convinced we were two of a kind . . . I wasn't prepared for whatever betrayal was coming my way.

'*You know your problem, kid?*' I could hear Durral asking. It was a memory from long ago, just a couple of months after we'd first met.

'*What now, Durral?*' I'd asked. I didn't call him Pappy back then.

'*You ain't near gullible enough.*'

When a notorious gambler informs you that your primary defect of character is a lack of gullibility, you can't help but get suspicious.

'*See what I mean?*' he asked, laughing at my dour expression.

I could practically see him in front of me now, standing in the patch of moonlight slipping through the canopy of trees outside the tower. That frontier hat of his was casting a shadow across a smile that could charm the claws off a squirrel cat. '*If you can't trust Durral Brown, the Path of the Rambling Thistle, then how's your arta precis going to pick up what that pretty young Jan'Tep girl's trying not to tell you?*'

'*Since she's hiding it, isn't my suspicion entirely justified?*'

Durral grinned, wagging a spectral finger in my direction – which was quite a feat for someone who wasn't there. '*Oh, is that a riddle you got goin' on, girl? I do enjoy a good riddle. Go on then, riddle me this: why would an Argosi admire someone for keeping a secret from her?*'

'Ferius?' Arissa asked quietly.

145

'Yeah?'

'You know you're just standing there staring off into the distance while Chedran and a couple of these Jan'Tep are pretty much just waiting to see who blinks first before they go at each other, right?'

'Give me a second.'

Why would an Argosi admire someone for keeping secrets from her?

I glowered at my imagined Durral. True to form, he wasn't there any more. Even my memories of him insist on getting drunk on my moral dilemmas and then sticking me with the bill.

I sighed, letting my arta precis slide down over my gaze like a pair of spectacles that blurred everything but what others were trying to hide from me. My eyes settled on Ala'tris – well, not *her* precisely, mostly on her mouth. She was frowning at Chedran, and her lips were pursed like she was trying real hard not to let out something she badly wanted to say.

All right, sister, you're keeping secrets from us, but that's okay, because I am presently filled with nothing but admiration for you. See? I'm admiring how you're standing there like an oh-so-pretty gossamer-gowned statue while my crew and yours are one dirty look away from a good old-fashioned knock-down, drag-out punch-up. I'm positively in awe of the way you keep glancing at Chedran like you could shut him up with a few words, some simple spell that you won't let pass your lips on account of you're so nice and decent and you'd never want to hurt a fella's feelings by righteously knocking him off his high hors—

'Damn it, Pappy,' I muttered. 'You got me again.'

'Who now?' Arissa asked.

I strode over to where Chedran was staring down Ala'tris's coven with his unwavering determination to prove there was nothing he wouldn't do to protect those twelve Mahdek runaways from a half-dozen scheming Jan'Tep mages.

Well, not quite a half-dozen actually. Five.

146

'Go on,' I told her. 'Tell him about the sixth mage.'

'What?' Arissa asked, eyes darting across the darkened forest.

'We saw six dead mages in the mind cage,' I explained, then gestured to the ones surrounding us. 'Five teenagers and one old man. A lord magus.' I caught Ala'tris's gaze again. 'Tell him about the lord magus.'

Never seen someone look so uncomfortable admitting something most people would've already flung in our faces. 'Ferius, no. It's not important.'

I chuckled. 'Actually, I think it *is* important. Once you get to know Chedran better, you'll find he doesn't suffer from a lack of pride. A little humility could only improve his disposition.'

'Stop talking about me as if I'm not here,' he snarled at me, then turned on Ala'tris. 'Go ahead, Jan'Tep, make your confession. You'll find there's no trap you could set for which I'm not prepared, and I'm eager to settle accounts once and for all.'

Even after *that* ungracious invitation, still she began with kindness. 'You were correct, warrior. We *did* follow your runaways after they'd fled Jan'Tep territory.'

'They're *our* territories,' he countered. 'You're an occupier. A genocidal mob slaughtering all who—'

Turns out there's a limit even to the considerable diplomatic restraint that Ala'tris worked so hard to maintain. *'Occupier?'* she repeated, shoving Gab'rel and Ba'dari aside to stand defiantly before Chedran. 'You believe the Jan'Tep were the first and only conquerors who coveted the oases? Perhaps you should learn your own history.'

'What new lie is th—'

She stuck a finger right up to his lips. 'No, you've had your say, now you can listen for once, no matter how hard the truth might be to hear. I've travelled far and wide in my studies, and seen historical treatises recorded by the first Daroman settlers who crossed the ocean to this continent. Those accounts describe tribes scattered from their lands by foreign mages who predate my people.'

'The so-called "Darvanil"?' Chedran sneered. 'Legends. Folk tales. There's no evidence they ever existed.'

'How could there be?' Sar'ephir asked. 'You Mahdek drove every nomadic tribe from the oases, slaughtering whole families to ensure only your own shamans and spellshapers would have dominion over the magic contained within.' The dismissive shrug she gave with her bare bronze shoulders struck me as almost cruel. Personal, somehow. 'One could argue that we Jan'Tep merely returned the favour.'

Chedran looked fit to be tied – which might well prove necessary if this kept up.

'Get on with it,' I told Ala'tris. She shot me a glare that could've stopped a rampaging bear in its tracks. I didn't much care. 'That wasn't the truth I meant, and you know it. Tell him what happened after he and the runaways crossed the border. If it makes you feel any better, *that's* gonna get under his skin way worse than all this ancient history.'

'Fine,' she declared, for once striking me as a proper pissed-off Jan'Tep noblewoman rather than the placid peacemaker she was always trying to be. She wrapped her fingers around the purple cords crossing the front of her silver robes.

'She gonna strip?' Arissa asked. 'Because if that's how these folks make peace, I might develop a fondness for Jan'Tep cultural exchanges.'

'Thought you weren't into girls.'

I felt her hand snake around my back to settle on my waist. 'Maybe you're starting to rub off on me.'

Don't keep playing me like this, I thought, stepping away. *It's not fair and it's not right.*

148

Arissa shot me a confused look, but by then we had other matters to occupy us. The gossamer of Ala'tris's right sleeve billowed outward, then began to ripple as if tiny figures were racing across her arms beneath the fabric. The cloth shaped itself in greater and greater detail, until soon we could make out what appeared to be Chedran leading the twelve Mahdek runaways away from a Jan'Tep oasis.

'More silk magic demonstrations?' Chedran asked. He almost sounded disappointed. 'Will you show us how I killed those other mages, or perhaps this time you'll reveal what *they* were intent on doing to the children?'

'Neither,' Ala'tris replied. She held out her left arm now, parallel to the ground. The sleeve undulated for a moment before shaping itself around new figures. The smooth silver fabric began to change colour, adding more detail to what appeared to be nine robed mages pursuing the runaways from a distance. The one in the lead was an older man who shared the colouring of Ba'dari, the short raven-haired girl. It was the lord magus whose corpse we'd seen in the mind cage. 'Her uncle,' Ala'tris said as if she already knew what we were thinking. 'A legendary hextracker whose coven was charged with hunting down the assassins who left four dead sentries to rot in the sand outside the oasis.' She brought her right arm back in line with her left, only now the ripples in her sleeve took the form of Ala'tris and her followers. She gave her arm a shake, and the gossamer fabric billowed as if a cloud were encircling them. 'I had to summon disguises for us, so that after Ba'dari was forced to bind her uncle in an iron spell that broke his ribs, he would never know it was his own niece who'd attacked him!'

'I can't get him out of my mind,' Ba'dari said softly, gazing down at the soft earth as if expecting to find a corpse there. 'I keep imagining that he died.' She turned to Ala'tris. 'I'm sorry, it's my fault he appeared in the mind cage. I just can't stop picturing how lifeless he looked, lying there on the ground as we fled. What if the broken bones of his ribs made their way to his heart and I—'

'You didn't kill him,' the hawk-faced Jir'dan said firmly, coming to place his hands on the younger girl's shoulders. 'But he would've killed all of us if you'd given him the chance. You saw the look in his face, in all of our fellow mages' faces when they realised they were fighting their own kind.'

'No!' Chedran yelled, his features as pale as if he were the one staring at a ghost who'd come to haunt his dreams. 'No one could've tracked us from the territories. I kept watch every night!'

Ba'dari snorted. 'My uncle's coven got within fifty yards of your camp. He used a breath spell to hide the sounds and smells of their approach. You sat there, oblivious, while we fought our own kind for you. While I fought *my family*.'

'That's not all!' Gab'rel, the short kid, gestured extravagantly to the tall, eagle-beaked blond fellow. 'Jir'dan nearly had his arms ripped right off by a lightshaper who would've torn those Mahdek kids limb from limb.'

Sar'ephir, still sounding more amused than self-righteous, added, 'Let's not forget the Berabesq Faithful who on three separate occasions nearly found the runaways while their oh-so-clever protector was rotting in the depths of Soul's Grave.' She turned to me and winked. 'Our gratitude for saving us the trouble of breaking him out of prison ourselves. I doubt his pride could've survived the experience. Then again, if he knew how we'd also had to—'

'Okay, enough,' I said, shooing them all away from him. I was more in awe than ever over the fact that Ala'tris had managed to keep her comrades from rubbing all this in our faces before now. I turned to Chedran. 'Well, what now? You reckon they're all lying or can we skip the stand-off and get down to business?'

150

Watching mistrust and loathing fade should be a joyful thing, but with Chedran it was like the blood was draining out of him, leaving him so weary he might fall asleep and never wake up. 'I . . . I've been a fool.'

I got up on my tiptoes and, gesturing back at the mages, whispered, 'In case you hadn't noticed, there's a lot of that going around.'

To his credit, he made a sincere effort at a wry smile. Alas, it barely reached his lips and got nowhere near his eyes.

Ala'tris shook the magical stage show from her sleeves, then came and gently put a hand on Chedran's bare chest. 'We all share the same disease,' she said sadly. 'We're born to it. A sickness buried so deep we hardly know it's there, yet we can't seem to live without it.'

Sorrow, deep and desolate . . . and yet, one thing you learn in poker is how to tell when one of the players has been dying to turn over their hole card. That's how it was with Ala'tris; the acknowledgement of hopelessness hadn't been the end game, merely the bluff before she revealed her hand.

It began with an ear-to-ear grin that lit her up like the sun rising before the moon had even set. 'The five of us, we're part of a faction within the Jan'Tep searching for a way to redeem our people for the crimes that have continued long after the war with the Mahdek should have ended. Our elders mock our efforts. They call us "restitutionists" as a slur, claiming any attempt at resettlement would only incite more conflict. They're convinced that bloodshed is inevitable so long as a single Mahdek still walks this continent.'

Arissa arched an eyebrow. 'But you and your little club of "restitutionists" think you have a better solution?'

Ala'tris glanced at the members of her coven, waiting for each one to nod their assent before turning towards the derelict tower. 'There's one final secret we've been keeping from you. A gift.'

'A crumbling Daroman ruin on the edge of the Berabesq theocracy?' I asked. 'You think *that's* gonna make up for centuries of abuse? Because I gotta tell you, sister, my horse is gonna be awful irritated if I rode him all this way just to—'

Damn it. First principle of arta precis: don't waste time staring at the thing in front of your face when you should be asking what's *not* there. In this case, how had five Jan'Tep mages travelled this far from any town without horses?

Ala'tris and Sar'ephir stood side by side. The silk mage raised her hand first, lustrous purple sparks bursting from the tattooed sigils around her forearm. Sar'ephir mirrored her, the subtler gold of what I now recognised as sand magic pulsing in waves from her own sigils. The tower appeared to crumble, as if a thousand years had passed in mere seconds. That was all illusion though; the real magic was in the heap that had been hidden there all along. Half-buried in the sloping ground, branches of trees seemingly melted through the oak planking of its massive hull, was a galleon bigger than any I'd ever seen.

'Spirits of Sea and Sky,' Chedran murmured. 'How could such a thing exist this far from any ocean?'

Five masts rose up from the three-decked ship, its elongated prow towering over us. The sails were unfurled, yet they rippled to their own rhythm, ignoring the direction of the breeze. The incongruity of a monstrous ship in the middle of a forest a hundred miles from a body of water capable of floating it left me and Chedran dumbstruck.

Arissa never liked seeming surprised by anything though, and so managed a passably snarky tone to cover up her own amazement. 'I'm not usually one for pranks, but I've got to admit, gifting the Mahdek with a ship that can't sail anywhere does have a certain flair.'

'This ship doesn't sail on *water*,' Ala'tris corrected, sweat on her brow from the effort of unmasking her spell. 'In fact, it doesn't

152

precisely sail within our world at all, nor is this the gift we offer the Mahdek.'

'What is, then?' I asked, though I still couldn't take my eyes off that galleon half-buried in the soil.

Without warning, Ala'tris hurled herself at me. Her arms wrapped around my whole body and, before I knew it, she was hugging me again. 'I'm so glad it's you,' she whispered, her cheek pressed against mine. 'All the uncertainty, all the perils, waging battles against my own kind . . . But with you here, I *know* this is right. It's fate.' Louder now, so everyone heard, she declared, 'The Mahdek no longer need wander the length and breadth of this continent as refugees. They need no longer beg for shelter or charity, or fear those who would hunt them to extinction.' Tears of hope and pride shone in her eyes. 'Ferius, we have found the Mahdek people a homeland!'

Part 3

The Ship of Dust

Every disharmony charts a course different from the one we expected to follow, and yet an Argosi must be wary of abandoning their own path. Where the teysan sees contradiction and paradox, the maetri recognises a simple truth: it is not the road to which we must adhere, but the way in which we travel it.

Thus is made clear the danger of your disharmonies: that in seeking to rectify them, you may unwittingly allow them to alter your own spirit, until at last you wander the world as nothing more than the physical manifestation of a wrong that can never be made right.

20

The Spellship

'Hoist the halyard and trim the mainsail!'

'Steady to starboard and pull us hard to port, ye scurvy dogs!'

'Three sheets to the wind and drop the anchor, say I!'

The Argosi aren't exactly known for their maritime expertise. Neither Durral nor Enna ever explained why, only that the long roads and winding rivers are our homes, not the oceans. No surprise, then, that I wasn't familiar with the wide range of nautical terms sailors call to each other across the deck of a galleon. In my defence, the crew of the *Shadow's Gamble* didn't seem to know either; they just enjoyed the shouting.

Two days after our departure from the tower, I was leaning against the railing near the bow, lost in the impossible sights and sounds of my first voyage aboard a vessel that shouldn't exist, so filled with awe I barely remembered to breathe. Fields of tall grasses parted before the spellship's bronze figurehead of a rampant seahorse. The oak keel beneath the ship shuddered and shook as we sailed – *sailed!* – up wooded hills and over rocky plateaux, hurtling through dense forests and across sandy plains. Trees with trunks as wide as my outstretched arms and branches thicker than my legs that should've torn through the hull's wooden planking nudged us no more than a gentle an ocean swell. I kept expecting

159

to taste the salt of sea air on my tongue, but only got pelted by the occasional pine needle.

'Well, now,' I murmured to myself. 'Might be time to set aside my aversion to magic and get me a spellship of my own.'

'There are no others,' Ala'tris said.

I started, my right hand drawing a dozen throwing cards from my waistcoat pocket. It's not often someone sneaks up on me like that.

'My apologies,' she said, seeing the glint of steel in my hand. 'I didn't mean to disturb you. It's just that you've passed every waking hour at the bow, by yourself, and both nights sleeping alone on deck.'

That wasn't quite true; I'd spent plenty of time below decks tending to Quadlopo, which involved a lot of brushing and profuse apologising for having stuck him inside what he clearly considered to be the belly of a giant wooden demon.

'I worried your cabin might not be suitable?' Ala'tris asked tentatively.

So much grace in this girl. Hard to believe she was raised right alongside all those mages who'd tried to kill me more times than I could remember. Now she was concerned over my accommodation, which was funny because my arta precis had discerned from the sideways glances of her fellow mages that Ala'tris had given me her own cabin. I felt a little ungrateful, but how was I to explain that I couldn't imagine wasting one minute below decks if it cost me a single second of the marvels unfolding before me?

All I'd wanted since finding my Argosi path had been to travel this continent and witness its wonders – to feel the wind on my face and the wild beat of my own heart. Every moment since crossing paths with Chedran and the Mahdek runaways, my feet had been sinking so deep in the mud of my people's tragedies that

I worried I'd never go a-wandering again. Instead, Ala'tris had brought me aboard this incredible vessel, fuelled by incomprehensible spells, gliding across landscapes no other ship could sail.

'Ferius?' she asked. She reached out a finger and traced a line down my cheek. 'You're crying.' Stepping closer, her eyes catching mine, I saw the unspoken question on her lips. She leaned in, just a little – just enough to make me wonder if . . . but no.

Stand Ala'tris up on the forecastle next to Arissa, and you'd have the most lopsided beauty pageant in all of history. Both were beautiful in their own way, but one was luminous, graceful and idealistic. The other was a thief whose itchy fingers – even when they were stealing my own stuff – never failed to get me into trouble. One wanted to give me her heart, the other seemed content to steal mine and offer nothing in return.

No contest at all.

I took Ala'tris's hand and kissed the back of it with the chaste gallantry of a Daroman courtier. I almost made a joke about feeling seasick from the bumpy ride and who the heck was captaining this leaky barge anyway? I stopped myself. Memories can be precious candles full of stolen moonlight to brighten dark days, and this voyage, every minute of it, was something I wanted to cherish. 'You were saying something about there being no other spellships?' I asked instead.

Ala'tris didn't step away, but her withdrawal was unmistakable. She nodded with almost formal courtesy that only increased the distance between us. 'There are many spells that might harden a hull or propel a vessel along the water, but this . . .' The galleon was cruising through a narrow canyon barely wider than our sails. Ala'tris stretched her hand up high to where a rocky outcropping extended from the canyon wall right over the bow. The hard stone should've taken her arm off but instead passed right through flesh and bone, buffeting her with no more force than a strong breeze. She let that breeze turn her around so that she could point up to the forecastle. Sar'ephir stood with her back to us, the sun glinting on her shaved head, toned bronze arms outstretched to either side. The sigils of the tattooed band for sand magic were shedding golden sparks that winked out of existence almost as quickly as they appeared. 'Ba'dari holds the hull together with iron magic, Gab'rel uses his breath spells to channel Jir'dan's ember energies into our propulsion, and my own silk illusions keep the spellship from being seen, but only Sar'ephir can make the ship – and us – slip through solid matter.' Ala'tris smiled and shook her head in wonder, as if even she hadn't quite figured it all out. 'Ferius, we are literally travelling a fraction of a fraction of a second out of step with the world around us.'

'Incredible.'

'I know! It's as if—'

'No, I meant that literally. What you've just described isn't credible.'

The smile disappeared. 'Ferius, please don't ruin—'

I cut her off. I didn't want lies between us. 'Sand magic ain't so rare that only one woman among all the Jan'Tep could pull this off.' My gaze went back up to Sar'ephir on the forecastle, scouring for something my eyes weren't trained to see but I was absolutely sure was there. Hidden from me, maybe from all of us. 'Sand magic's not enough, Ala'tris. There's something else giving this ship its wondrous abilities. Something you're not telling me.'

She stiffened and a note of plaintiveness crept into her usually dignified tone. 'It's not my secret to tell, Ferius. Not yet.'

My arta precis and arta loquit played with her words a moment, the subtle shifts of tempo, the uneasy inflections. Arta loquit helps an Argosi understand what someone's really trying to say, in this case, '*I'll tell you when the time is right, but if I do so now, I would be breaking a promise.*'

Fair enough, I suppose. Ala'tris had taken plenty of risks for me already. She'd earned a measure of trust.

Arta precis, though, that's for detecting both what someone's trying to hide from you and what they're hiding from themselves. Sometimes it reveals the barest hint of a secret they're not even aware is being kept from them. There was something about Sar'ephir that Ala'tris was keeping from Chedran, Arissa and me. I was pretty sure she'd also been withholding it from the rest of her coven of 'restitutionists'. That worried her, because it could mean trouble once the truth came out. But buried in the uncertain, almost discordant notes in her voice was something confounding: a kind of . . . echo. Unspoken words that belonged to someone else, as if, when Ala'tris had been subtly conveying, '*I would be breaking a promise,*' she'd been recalling the secret Sar'ephir had told her, and something about that secret hadn't rung true.

I took my hat off and ran a hand through my unruly mess of red curls before settling it down again. My arta precis was giving me a headache, trying to untangle this spider's web of other people's secrets.

Ala'tris turned away. Maybe her silk mage's brain could tell when someone was poking through her private concerns, even when they didn't have any magic themselves.

You're just kicking the ball a few feet ahead at a time, aren't you, sister? I thought, watching the breeze play with the lustrous strands of her own red-gold hair. *You're betting that somehow, when we get far enough along, everyone'll have gone so far already that they'll agree to take that last step to where you're leading us.*

The deck shuddered as the starboard – I'd figured out that meant 'right' – side of the ship collided with the ridge of the canyon. An impact like that should've smashed it to bits, but the hull showed no sign of a breach.

'Pay attention, Gab'rel!' shouted Ba'dari, the iron band on her forearm gleaming. 'One of us needs to keep this wreck from coming apart, you know?'

Gab'rel didn't reply, just nodded sheepishly.

A massive whoop erupted from above. Chedran was leaning precariously over the edge of the crow's nest, laughing like a lunatic as the ship tilted this way and that. His arms waved in the air with the reckless enthusiasm of a kid balancing on shifting rocks while crossing a stream.

'I won't pry into whatever it is you're hiding,' I told Ala'tris, grinning as I added, 'especially since I'm pretty sure the spirits of all my ancestors would haunt me something furious if I ruined what is surely the only good mood Chedran's ever been in.'

Ala'tris smiled with a relief that pained me before throwing her arms around me, squeezing tight, then racing off to make sure Gab'rel and Jir'dan didn't ram us headlong into a mountain. I watched her go, and felt as if she was taking something precious with her.

'Now there's a heartbreak waiting to happen,' Arissa said, the shock nearly sending me tumbling over the rail.

Why does everybody keep sneaking up on me?

Arissa winked at me so I'd know that she was perfectly aware of how irritated I was at having failed to notice her leaning against the port-side rail not four feet away. 'Anyone ever warn that girl that if she keeps hugging people all the time they're apt to get confused about her intentions?'

No way was I taking the bait this time. *You want to finally have an honest conversation about what is or isn't between us, Arissa? You're going to have to start that conversation yourself – and be prepared for the consequences.*

164

The wind shifted, bringing a stench to my nostrils that made my eyes water. The stem of some sort of reed was dangling from Arissa's bottom lip, smouldering red at one end. I walked over to get a closer look, only to have her exhale and smother me in a cloud of smoke. 'What in the name of all that's unholy is that foul plant?' I asked between coughs. 'And what is it doing in your mouth?'

'Berabesq smoking reed,' she replied. 'Kharvir copper blend. Only grows from a single sand dune deep in the southern desert, if you can believe that. Found a stash of them in that horse trader's stable we raided.'

'You sure it didn't grow out of Quadlopo's poop?' The pungent aroma was clogging my nostrils. 'Pretty sure it's already been digested at least twice.'

Arissa reached a hand into the mottled canvas pack slung across her back and offered me a handful of the four-inch-long dark copper stems. 'It's an acquired taste.'

An Argosi's never supposed to turn down a gift that's sincerely offered. Reluctantly I took the reeds and slid them into the pocket of my leather waistcoat before Conch could jump up and snatch them in his teeth. 'Thanks,' I said, giving her a quick hug. 'I hope you'll accept my extensible steel rod in return.'

Arissa chuckled. 'More of your Way of Water? Cos I wasn't planning on giving you that rod back anyway.'

'Really?' I held up the six-inch cylinder for her to see. 'I just assumed you returned it out of politeness when I found it back in my pocket where it belongs.'

Arissa swore, spitting out the remains of her smoking reed over the side. 'An honest thief can't trust anybody these days.'

Golden autumn leaves on slender branches flitted beside us as we passed through a glade. A patch of dustier land lay ahead and, not far beyond that, a broken road leading to an even more broken-down building.

'The barracks!' Chedran called out from overhead. 'We've got back in less than half what it took on horseback!' He swung himself over the edge of the crow's nest and started climbing down the rigging.

The ship slowed as Jir'dan let his ember propulsion spell fade. He slumped down on the deck next to Gab'rel, who looked even more exhausted. I wondered how they'd fare on a much longer voyage to wherever this homeland was that Ala'tris was promising for the Mahdek people – and where, in fact, such an unlikely place could possibly exist.

Ba'dari passed me by as she walked up the steps to the forecastle, where she took up a position next to Sar'ephir. The smaller girl's shoulders tensed, her grey iron band pulsing as the sparks of Sar'ephir's gold band dimmed. The spellship seemed to stutter, skipping like a stone hurled across the hard ground and setting off an ear-splitting keening from the bottom of the hull as sand magic gave way to iron until, at last, the galleon came to a grinding halt.

Out from the barracks, twelve confused Mahdek teenagers raced over to behold in perplexed wonder the behemoth of wood and sailcloth.

'Anchor dropped,' Ba'dari mumbled, knees buckling. Sar'ephir had to hold her up, whispering in her ear words that I couldn't make out from where I stood.

'Will you make introductions?' Ala'tris asked. Offering me a precedence I didn't deserve, she gestured for me to climb over the side and down the ladder. The runaways waiting below were shouting a hundred questions over one another.

'Let him tell them,' I said, and pointed to Chedran, who was bounding across the deck. With a pirate's grin, he leaped up onto the railing, then somersaulted over the side to land with such grace as would put any acrobat to shame. I'd never imagined someone so relentlessly dour could look so happy.

Ala'tris caught my eye, reluctantly acquiescent. 'I don't fault your reasoning for deferring to these runaways the decision whether to allow us to proceed to the Mahdek enclave and present our proposal to their elders . . . but they seem so young, Ferius. Given Chedran's mistrust of us, how can we be sure he'll convey our intentions in the best light? Wouldn't it be better if it were you who—'

'I knelt down to pick up Conch and put him on my shoulder. Whatever his faults, Chedran loves those kids down to his bones. He'd cut off his own hands before he took from them what he believed to be the chance at a better life.'

'His beliefs are precisely what concern me.'

A fair point, but her sudden anxiousness raised a question in me that I hadn't considered until now: what would Ala'tris and her coven do if the kids turned down their 'gift'?

21

Attention

Trying to convince a bunch of kids to sit quietly and listen to a Jan'Tep delegation droning on about some theoretical homeland nobody's ever seen while a mystical galleon that can sail across any landscape sits half buried outside . . . well, such a task called for my best arta loquit.

'Everybody shut the hells up!'

Conch leaped two feet in the air, landing with his belly inflated and serving up an indignant glare so I'd know how perilously close I'd come to a well-deserved belching.

'Sorry, little buddy,' I whispered to him. 'Had to make an impression on these kids.'

A clearly unimpressed snort was followed by him turning tail and trotting outside the barracks to go swap Ferius-is-an-uncouth-brute stories with Quadlopo. Pretty sure he farted at me before he left. As for the runaways upon whose shoulders would rest a decision that would determine the future of the Mahdek, they just sort of froze.

Now, I get why, to an untrained observer, 'Shut the hells up!' might not seem the most eloquent of responses to their incessant questions, fidgeting and utter failure to stop trying to crane their necks past me, Chedran, Arissa, Ala'tris and her crew to peer out the door of the barracks to catch one more glance of the spellship.

168

But there's more to arta loquit than words, and not all shouts are made equal. Mine employed a variety of vocal techniques I'd learned from Enna (who'd mastered them in the perpetual pursuit of getting Durral to shut up once in a while). My pitch was carefully tuned to be neither so high as to sound screechy and desperate nor so low a rumble that it might frighten the young ones. I'd kept the grit out but also dropped the softness of the frontier drawl I'd picked up from Durral. My diction had been over-precise, turning each syllable into its own demand for their attention. And all that was just the audible portion of my efforts.

Arta siva, now that's a different talent. Ask any preacher or politician and they'll tell you the words are only a fraction of the art of persuasion. The rest is in the eyes, the lips, the movements of your hands, the way you stand and move, whether a little or a lot. Most of all, though, it's in the heart. To persuade is to open yourself up, find a truth inside you so convincing you believe it yourself. Only then can your arta siva move someone else to agree.

Telling someone to shut up is hardly any different than slapping them in the face. I needed them to really *listen*, to understand that what they were about to hear could change not just their futures, but those of every other Mahdek on this continent. I needed them, even the young ones, to recognise that part of their childhood was about to disappear, and their people needed them to grow up far faster than anyone should have to.

'We're listening,' Kievan said at last. She sat down cross-legged on the floor of the barracks. The other kids joined her, eyes flitting from me to the strange coven of Jan'Tep mages, barely older than themselves, I'd brought with me. Neither group viewed the other as the same species.

Only Remeny, barely twelve, resisted my arta siva. He approached Ala'tris as if she were a crocodile with jaws open, waiting for him

169

to get too close. 'You're the one I feel on my skin, aren't you?' he asked, fingers brushing aside the hair from his forehead to reveal the labyrinthine silver lines of the spell warrant. 'You took it over from the other sand mage?'

She nodded. 'It was the only way we could find you.' No apology, but something far more characteristic of her: compassion. 'You shouldn't have had to suffer such an ordeal even once, never mind twice. Is there a way by which I might make restitution?'

Remeny scratched at the markings. 'Can you take it away?'

You could see from the pinching at the corners of her eyes that she'd known this question was coming. 'What's your name?'

'Remeny.'

She leaned down so they were closer to the same height. 'There are two types of spell warrant, Remeny.' She scooped up a handful of dust from the floor, then held her palm out and whispered a few syllables. The particles of dust floated above her hand, each one like a tiny insect darting this way and that until at last they took on a circular shape whose twisting lines were similar to the ones on Remeny's forehead. Inside the circle, the specks of dust formed a grey-brown portrait of his face. 'One type is fashioned using breath and a touch of sand magic. It spreads out through the world like a kind of echo, repeating this shape you're seeing now for any mage with the right combination of talents.'

'Like those posters Daroman marshals sometimes nail up in town squares around the frontier when they're hunting fugitives?'

She nodded. 'And just like those posters that weather and crumble after a few weeks unless someone keeps putting more of them up . . .' She blew over her palm and the dust drifted back to the floor. 'A spell warrant fades over time on its own because—'

'Because a spell dies out without someone to keep it alive.' A trembling finger came up to the glinting silver lines on his forehead.

'But that silk mage, he burned these on me with some kind of liquid metal. That's why the spell didn't die with him . . . because the inks are still there.' The boy was struggling to keep the tears from his eyes. Guess he figured he'd done enough crying already and it hadn't done him any good.

Ala'tris wiped her dusty palm on her robe before placing it on Remeny's forehead as if she were checking him for a fever. 'The inks are made from veins of ore found only beneath an oasis. They're part of you now, drawing on your own magical potential. I can abdicate my influence over them, but then any Jan'Tep hextracker or bounty mage will be able to follow their call.'

Hearing her words, I couldn't keep my fingers from digging under the collar of my own shirt, over those near-invisible sigils around my neck. It had taken years for them to fade. Even now, they felt . . . asleep rather than gone.

I expected Remeny to start bawling then. There's only so much fear and misery a boy can hold inside himself after all. Instead he took away Ala'tris's hand and said, 'If they're part of me now, then I just need to learn how to change them on my own. The Mahdek used to work magic, long before the Jan'Tep came. I used to feel a pull, like there was a fish hook in my head tugging me towards the oases. I don't feel it so bad now.' He tapped a finger against the intricate silver symbols on his forehead. 'Maybe this is how I'll learn to work magic for my people.'

Ala'tris rose and took a step back, turning to glance at me like she was lost as to what to say next because she didn't want to break the boy's heart. I didn't know what to offer her. The Argosi don't believe in lying to make someone feel better.

'Look at them,' Chedran said, almost shoving Ala'tris out of the way when he came to kneel in front of Remeny. 'Can you see the doubt in their eyes, boy? Neither of them believes you'll ever

171

be able to shape spells the way our ancestors did. You know why?' He put each of his hands on either side of Remeny's head, squeezing him. 'Because these Jan'Tep have convinced themselves that the Mahdek are weak. They need to believe we're incapable of the feats they perform, even though we were working magic long before they fouled our lands with their presence. Our elders? They think we're weak too.' He turned Remeny around so that the boy was looking over his shoulder at me. 'This Argosi sees so little worth in us that she turned her back on her own people.'

'That's not—'

'You're going to prove them all wrong, Remeny.' He tapped the silver sigils on the boy's forehead. 'You're going to take this wound those mages inflicted on you and make it heal into something wondrous.' He thrust his other hand towards the open door and the spellship some fifty yards away. 'That galleon . . . it's a miracle. It's like nothing anyone's ever seen, even the Jan'Tep.'

'A compliment at last?' Sar'ephir asked, seeming amused at the parade of emotions inside the barracks. 'Perhaps the Mahdek are capable of surprises after all.'

Chedran turned that feral grin of his at her. 'That one, she's not like the others, Remeny. Before she came along, I'll wager every clan prince and lord magus of her people would've laughed at the thought of a ship that can sail through forest, mountain and desert as if they were merely different kinds of oceans.' He turned back to the boy. 'A thing is always impossible until someone comes along and decides to do it anyway.'

Now Remeny *was* crying, but it was from a fierce pride that had come over boyish features that didn't seem so boyish now. He gave Chedran a terse nod, and that was that.

'Now I'm unsettled,' Arissa said quietly to me.

172

'How come?'

'Because for a moment there I almost forgot how much I dislike Chedran.'

Remeny, though, he walked right up to Ala'tris and declared, 'You may deliver your proposal now, Jan'Tep. The twelve of us will grant your words such consideration as they deserve and inform you of our decision.'

Again Ala'tris looked to me, that same unspoken question in that otherwise placid expression. It struck me as funny that a coven of Jan'Tep teenagers who'd decided they knew better than their own elders should have so much trouble understanding why I was adamant that the Mahdek runaways had to be the ones to choose whether or not to bring this gift of a new homeland to their people.

Sometimes the best response to a question that keeps being repeated is no response at all. *Glare all you want, sister*, I thought, *I've won tougher staring contests against my horse, and he's a lot ornerier than you.*

Ala'tris gave in soon enough, and knelt down to gather up more dust from the floor before motioning for Sar'ephir to join her. The statuesque beauty removed a small black bag from one of the folds of her dusky gold robes and poured sand into her own palm. 'Some things are better revealed than described,' she said, her gaze sweeping over the twelve Mahdek runaways. 'There will be no need for panic.'

What I presume was meant to be a reassuring smile was so full of accidental condescension that I was sorely tempted to smack it off her face. But the Path of the Wild Daisy winds towards the Way of Wind long before it travels the Way of Thunder, so I found myself a spot near the wall and sat down on the floor. After all, any time it takes not one but *two* Jan'Tep mages to explain something, you know they're gonna put on a show.

22

The Gift

Ala'tris tossed the handful of dust into the air. As the tiny motes began to fall back towards the ground, three of the tattooed bands on her forearms sparked. Lights danced beneath the gossamer fabric of her sleeves, first the purple of silk magic to pull visions from her own mind. Next, pale blue breath swirled the still-falling dust, lending it form until it resembled a map of the continent, held in place by the greyish glow of her iron band.

Arissa sidled up next to me. 'You think they put on these little magical puppet shows any time they want to explain something because they figure we'll all be so gosh-darned bedazzled by the fancy lights and floating pictures that it won't occur to us to question if any of what they're saying is true?'

Not everyone was bedazzled though. One of the runaways, the youngest boy, buried his face in his hands and began to cry. Chedran sat down next to him, placing an arm around his shoulders and whispering something inaudible into his ear. Gab'rel, only a couple of years older, chuckled disdainfully, apparently finding the other boy's trepidation silly. Like so many Jan'Tep, he was oblivious to the terror Mahdek children experience when they catch sight of a mage's bands sparking. Ba'dari made an inconspicuous somatic

174

shape with her left hand that briefly lit up her own iron band. A second later Gab'rel was bent over, exhaling a loud 'oof' as if she'd elbowed him in the stomach.

Ala'tris had missed the entire exchange. She was passing her palm across her floating map in a snaking up and down motion. The dust particles rose and fell to form mountain ranges and river valleys, forests and deserts. 'This continent we share is vast enough to support many times the populations of the great nations that occupy these lands.' With the forefinger of her right hand she traced jagged lines that rose up to become iron walls delineating the borders of the countries she named. 'Darome, Zhuban, Gitabria, the Jan'Tep territo—'

'Mahdek territories,' Chedran interrupted.

The momentary loss of concentration caused the dust to begin drifting apart. Ala'tris furrowed her brow and the map once again took shape. She shot me a glance that asked, 'Must he remind us all of his patriotism quite so often?'

I gave her a shrug that replied, 'Best get used to it.'

Ala'tris resumed her demonstration, which I would've found tedious were it not for the fact that all her poise couldn't hide her unease from my arta precis. 'Not all peoples are sedentary,' she went on, tapping a rhythm with two of her fingers along first the northern part of the map, then the southern. 'The tribelands are filled with nomadic peoples.' The last trail of figures she conjured were smaller than the others, but moved across the entire continent. 'None travel as great distances or interact with as many nations as the Mahdek.'

I winced at her phrasing and tone. She'd made it sound like all that endless slogging in search of food and shelter was some inborn cultural trait to be celebrated. She was about to get another dose of Chedran's patriotism.

175

'It is remarkable how fast and how far a people will trudge to escape the ember mages ever at their backs!' he said with such a growl that the boy he was comforting began to cry again.

'Untrue!' Ala'tris declared, returning Chedran's outrage in spades. She swallowed like her mouth had gone dry, then took in a deep breath.

Here it comes, I thought, slipping my throwing cards out of my waistcoat pocket in case things got ugly. *This is the part where she tells a bunch of Mahdek teenagers the one thing they never want to hear.*

Despite her visible discomfort, she let loose with all the formality and precision of an advocate making her case before a jury. 'This convenient fiction, this vicious slander that stokes your rage, is the same one that blinds the Mahdek people to a far uglier truth they have refused to face for generations!'

The barracks went quiet, but it wasn't a peaceful quiet. Even the youngest of the runaways were practically choking with indignation. Fists clenched, eyes narrowed, twelve kids who ought to know better were starting to wonder if maybe they could rip a few Jan'Tep mages to pieces before any spells could be cast.

'Sister,' I said, infusing the word with all my arta loquit, reminding Ala'tris that she'd referred to me as kin before her coven – and letting everyone else know I viewed her the same, 'this game you're playing ain't—' The problem with arta loquit is that sometimes you can perfectly convey your meaning only to discover it's exactly the wrong one for that moment.

'It is not *my* game, Ferius, nor solely that of my people,' she shot back at me. Those pale blue and eerie grey bands of hers sparked brighter as she sliced down at the edges of her map, breaking them off to leave behind a hexagonal game board. The scattered dust floated back up to become stylised pieces representing armed figures

176

that drove the trail of Mahdek refugees away from their side of the board. 'The Faithful in Berabesq slaughter any *marquari* attempting to settle within their borders.' Ala'tris scowled, her voice thick with discomfort, yet she pushed through. 'The word means "plague rodents". It is the term by which the Berabesq viziers refer to the Mahdek.'

Her fingers darted across the board, adding sentries and chevaliers and myriad other pieces that each instantly began chasing the Mahdek pawns. 'Zhuban warrior-poets call your people *dabu bidaku* – the dead-who-do-not-know-they-are-dead. The killing of any dabu bidaku trespassing on one's land is prosecuted not as murder but with a fine for unlawfully culling a wild animal!'

'Enough,' I said, approaching her. The way things were headed, I was going to have to punch her lights out just to keep Chedran and the others from trying to tear her to shreds. 'You've made your point.'

This time her glare would've put Quadlopo right on his butt. 'No, Ferius, I haven't. I begged you to let me conduct these negotiations with the Mahdek elders, who have long known these facts yet repeat the same old myths to each new generation, blaming all their suffering on *my* people.' She glanced at the runaways, none of Sar'ephir's condescension in her expression, only pity. Her hands rose up high, the sudden tension in the muscles of her slender arms visible through the translucent gossamer of her sleeves. Her fists clenched as she brought them down on the map, smashing it into hundreds of shards that spun in the air before dissolving back into dust once again. 'Damn them, and damn you for leaving me no choice but to reveal such hideous truths to children!'

Silence held sway for a time, all of us watching the last motes of dust drift back down to the floor. Maybe she was right. Maybe I'd botched this whole thing right from the start.

177

'How's the taste of that guilt?' I imagined Enna asking. 'Must be real sweet the way you're drinking it down.'

'Don't start with me, Mamma. Pappy's the one who talks sideways all the time, not you.'

'Why should he have all the fun? Besides, you know his arta siva isn't near as good as mine.'

'Arta siva? Why would—'

My gaze went to Ala'tris, who stood there with her arms by her sides, looking almost as miserable as I was feeling. Arta siva is the Argosi talent for persuasion. Durral just called it 'charm', but Enna had never agreed with him.

'Making people like you is easy,' she reminded me now, as she had on those other occasions. 'Negotiations though, they're about alliances, not friendships. An enemy you trust is better than a friend you can't.'

I was still watching Ala'tris, but now my arta precis let me see past her guilt and shame, genuine as they were, to the cold calculation underneath. She hadn't been trying to impress the runaways with her display of magical floating grey dust; she'd wanted everyone on edge. That's why she hadn't let Sar'ephir start out by conjuring visions of this wondrous homeland that's supposed to protect the Mahdek from their enemies. These kids would never have believed it.

This time it was Durral's voice I heard: a memory from when he'd first named me his teysan. I'd asked why his teachings were always so damned confusing and irritating. The Argosi ways are full of wonder, a never-ending awakening deep inside yourself. Why make them seem so . . . infuriating?

'That's the problem with offering someone a gift that seems too good to be true, kid. Nobody ever believes you'd just give something so precious away.'

A clever gambit, maybe even a necessary one. But there aren't too many people on this earth who can pull it off like Durral Brown. Even before the scuffling of boots on boards had broken the silence, I knew Ala'tris had overplayed her hand.

Kievan was walking towards Ala'tris, strands of hair, red mixed with the blonde, across her face from staring down at her feet. 'You think to teach us about the world, Jan'Tep?'

I let one of my throwing cards fall into my hand. Quiet as she spoke, I heard the rumble of thunder in Kievan's voice. She reached down the top of the shabby, oversized shirt that had probably been worn by a corpse before someone had given it to her and pulled out a dingy little brass locket. 'When a Mahdek turns thirteen, she stands before her clan to reveal her chosen name and its meaning. It is a day of celebration, of singing and dancing long into the night until the stars themselves tire of us. Sometimes we even feast if the clan can afford it. Gifts, though? We Mahdek do not receive gifts on our name day.'

There was no threat in Kievan's tone, nor in the way she stood so close to Ala'tris. Even so, a blow was coming. I just couldn't see what it was.

Kievan let the locket dangle from its chain, so tarnished it barely caught the light. 'My mother waited until my father and brother were asleep. Would you like to see what's inside?'

Ala'tris never even looked down at the trinket. She kept her eyes on Kievan, which I suppose was wise. 'Does it matter what I want?'

The younger woman smiled, though there wasn't any joy in it, only acknowledgement. 'A question every Mahdek asks themselves sooner or later. That's what my mother wanted me to understand when she woke me and told me I was beautiful.' Kievan took hold of the locket and pressed the top with the nail of her thumb, popping it open to reveal a dollop of oily grey chalk with flecks of yellow. 'She offered to rub this on my face. It's easier to make sure none of it gets in your eyes that way, you see? There's no pain. The skin goes numb before withering and scarring permanently.'

Two simple facts hit me at the same time, far too late for me to stop what was coming. The one thing Ala'tris and Kievan had in common was that they were both pretty. Nothing else about them was evenly matched. One had been born to power and privilege, the other to crushing poverty and unrelenting peril. Ala'tris had spent her youth studying the ways of Jan'Tep magic, but Kievan had acquired something just as dangerous: a childhood expecting death at any moment.

I brought my arm back, let my wrist begin that first twist that would send my razor-sharp steel card past Ala'tris's right ear. The angles were lousy, so I'd probably leave a nasty cut on her cheek and slice off a chunk of her hair before the card buried itself in Kievan's left eye. No other shot would stop her in time. Like I said, lousy angles.

My hand failed to move.

At first I thought it must be some kind of iron spell cast by Ba'dari, thinking I was about to attack their leader. Instead, it was a hand wrapped around my wrist. 'You're reading this wrong,' Arissa whispered.

I'd been right though: Kievan absolutely intended to do Ala'tris harm. I'd just gotten the weapon wrong. 'I thought my mother would be angry when I recoiled from her,' the girl went on, staring at the ugly grey and yellow dollop inside her locket. 'She wasn't though. Merely kissed my cheek and said, "It's all right then, my love. When they come for you, swallow the chalk, and death will escort you to her bed before anyone else can force you into theirs."'

180

Chedran, quiet as a ghost, came up and placed his palm on Kievan's shoulder. 'Your mother was only—'

She shrugged his hand away. 'Kindly do not tell me what my mother was or was not doing, or how I should or should not regard her gift. She ruined my naming day, planting inside my chest a terrible blossom that I can never pluck from my heart, no matter how hard I try.' The locket snapped closed and disappeared back down the front of her shirt. 'But I keep her gift with me, always.' She leaned close to Ala'tris, almost as if she were about to bestow her mother's kiss on another. 'Long before a Mahdek child learns to hate the Jan'Tep, we learn that those who offer charity frequently expect something far more valuable in return.'

Ala'tris didn't retreat. She waited for Kievan to step back before speaking. Her eyes were red-rimmed and filled with as much outrage as shame. 'Is that what you believe of us? That we've risked exile and perhaps even death just so that we can exploit you in such a vicious, vile manner?'

Kievan walked around her, slowly, as if inspecting a statue in a museum. 'Your ancestors may have stolen the magic from mine, Jan'Tep, but they left us with a talent that rivals your spells or even Ferius's Argosi ways. Our gaze can discern a hundred different shades of hatred and contempt in the smiles of others. Our ears can detect a thousand cackles or snarls in their kindly words.'

'Speak then,' Ala'tris said, shoulders back, prepared for the worst. 'Put a name to the wickedness you see in my eyes and hear in my speech.'

When next the two were facing each other, Kievan stopped and lifted her chin to meet the other woman's eyes. 'Hope,' she said quietly. 'I see hope for your people, and compassion for mine. So much compassion for our plight . . .' She brought up a finger and traced the arch of one of Ala'tris's eyebrows. 'It makes you blissfully unaware of how much our weakness disgusts you.'

I couldn't see Ala'tris's expression from where I was standing, but I knew her eyes would be bloodshot, holding back indignant tears she knew she couldn't release. Too much was at stake, and besides, Kievan wouldn't care. I knew something else too, and this time I didn't need memories of Durral or Enna to make me see what had taken place here.

Smiles and kind words can hide evil intentions, but callousness can just as easily mask acquiescence, and a decision already made. Every negotiation begins with laying out the facts. Ala'tris had needed the Mahdek to accept the ugly truth of their situation on this continent. In turn, Kievan had forced Ala'tris to see that she didn't know a damned thing about what it meant to be Mahdek.

Turns out it was a lesson I'd needed to learn too.

Kievan strode over to Sar'ephir and looked down at the pile of sand still waiting in the taller woman's hand. 'You were going to give us another display of magic?'

Sar'ephir nodded.

'A beautiful envisioning of some strange, magical realm that can only be reached by your spellship? A bountiful land, uninhabited and inaccessible to the Jan'Tep or Berabesq or Zhuban?' She gestured absently towards Ala'tris. 'This was all a practice run for when you both stand before our council of elders. She destroys our people's three-hundred-year-old dream of resettling our own territory, and you offer us a bright and shiny new one.'

Sar'ephir looked more amused than concerned. 'Precisely.'

Kievan took the tall woman's hand and turned it over so that the sand fell to the barracks' floor. 'Then no more mystical demonstrations will be required.'

182

'Kievan, wait,' I said, my arta loquit searching frantically for the right words to stop this from falling apart. 'Just because th—'

'You misunderstand, Ferius.' Our eyes met briefly, and I knew in an instant that yet again my arta precis had failed to show me what one of my own people was planning. Turning on her heel, she faced the other eleven runaways. In their faces, beaming with excitement, I saw mirrored what must have been on her own. 'We ran away from our families because we couldn't endure the gloom and despair that left them unable to see even the brightest stars overhead. Wouldn't it be –' she glanced back briefly at Ala'tris and her coven, a wry smile on her lips – 'magical if we could return to them bringing the stars with us?'

There was an explosion then – an eruption of cheering and shouting, hugging and crying that shook the rafters and sent me scurrying out the door. It was all too much for me. Too much joy born of sorrow – the bright light that blinds eyes grown accustomed to the darkness. I ran from the barracks, down the dirt track to where Quadlopo was standing in a copse of sparse trees, munching on the same bush as Conch, who seemed determined to outpace him. I placed my hand on the horse's back, rested my forehead against his neck and waited for my breath to return or the fist to unclench from my chest. Either would've been nice.

Wasn't long before I heard footsteps, which was polite of her since she has to work against her own reflexes to be anything but dead silent.

'Well, that went real dark, real fast.' Arissa came and leaned her back against Quadlopo's haunch. Then she took out a smoking reed and lit it, taking a puff before staring at it quizzically. 'Then it just got weird.'

I nodded. Weird was definitely the right word. That's some pure arta loquit right there.

She took out a second smoking reed, lit it with the first and offered it to me. 'Sure you don't want to try it? The Gitabrian sailor who got me hooked on these things promised they were good for the lungs.'

'Pretty sure he lied,' I said, but took the reed from her anyway. It tasted horrible, thick and smoky and oily all at the same time. Then again, many of the finer things in life are an acquired taste, so I inhaled a second time, deeper. That set me coughing something awful and I decided that maybe some tastes aren't meant to be acquired.

'You okay?' Arissa asked.

'Funny thing to ask someone you just tried to poison.'

'Not that. The other thing.'

'What other thing?'

She nudged over, put her arms around me and held me tight like she didn't think I could stand on my own. 'It's a hard thing to realise you can see through a thousand mysteries with those Argosi eyes of yours, but can't recognise yourself in your own people.'

Yeah. That explained why I was crying so much.

23

The Refuge

Where do you hide nearly three hundred people from the rest of the world? Can you really house, feed, clothe and provide medical care to that many bodies without anyone figuring it out? Not their enemies, not your own government, not even the folks in neighbouring towns and villages? What's to stop the clerks, guards and labourers needed to keep the operation running from selling your secret to the highest bidder? Why wouldn't all those merchant caravans bringing supplies start making enquiries into how you go through them so fast?

A thousand different ways things could go wrong. So how was it possible that no one – not even the Argosi – had stumbled upon the secret Mahdek enclave?

As I gazed up at the tall grey stone arch practically inviting us into the luscious orchard beyond which lay a towering palace, my thoughts turned back to the seventeenth principle of arta precis, as elucidated by one Durral Brown: *'Keys are overrated.'*

I know, I know – what the hells does that mean? I'd asked my incomprehensible maetri the same question, and in return, got a riddle. *'A door with a thousand locks opens without a key. A door without any locks at all is easier to keep closed.'*

The solution to this particular riddle is pretty simple: if your door has a thousand locks, you're telling the whole world you've got something valuable inside. Sooner or later someone's going to break it down, no key required. If your door has *no* locks, most folks will assume there's nothing worth stealing inside and leave it alone.

Most folks. Not all.

What you need then, if you want to conceal the last remnants of a dying civilisation on your property without anyone noticing, is to build a door without locks that nobody dares open. Be the sort of person of whom no one asks any questions because the answer's never going to be worth the trouble.

Someone poor and unassuming? Nope. The poor get robbed a lot more often than the rich. Less reward but hardly any risk.

A king or queen perhaps? Show me a royal palace that isn't packed with foreign spies and corrupt courtiers and then we'll talk.

How about the abbot or abbess of some distant monastery? High walls, plenty of room, hardly any outsiders snooping around. Don't know what sorts of monks or nuns you've been hanging around with, but the ones I've met gossip more than drunken chaperones at a debutantes' ball.

A criminal overlord mending a guilty conscience by spending the spoils of their nefarious endeavours on a few hundred long-suffering exiles? Forgetting for a moment that crime lords aren't the most generous of souls, you can bet their lackeys aren't troubled by bouts of excessive charity.

A military general might be able to pull it off with enough loyal troops. Problem is, housing hundreds of illegal settlers without your sovereign's permission is an act of treason that would surely turn even your most devoted soldiers against you.

So here's what you need to house and feed all those refugees without anyone catching on: wealth, influence, a small army of loyal retainers and a reputation for being the sort of person nobody

186

wants to cross. All of that, yet without any of the encumbrances of political or criminal allegiances. Someone upon whom a vast estate might be bestowed by a grateful monarch who no longer expects anything from them.

Yeah, that's what I figured too: the legendary captain of the Royal Daroman Marshals Service. Retired.

Lucallo Colfax – or 'Luke' as his followers called him – stood with his legs wide, hands relaxed by his sides. He still wore the customary grey frontier hat and matching long leather marshal's coat over a pair of dusky riding trousers and black boots. Thick hair, white as the alabaster dunes north of the Seven Sands, hung down to his shoulders. His trademark moustache curved like a pair of bull horns down past his jaw. Placid as a butterfly on a marigold or a crocodile about to snap its jaws on an unwary rabbit, he gazed up at the galleon we'd left half-buried in a slope of grass outside the walls of his estate.

'You won't be leaving that out in the open,' he said in a deep baritone full of grit but without an ounce of concern over the five Jan'Tep mages whose bands glinted through the fabric of their sleeves. None of us failed to notice the absence of either a question or a request in his tone.

Jir'dan and a couple of the other mages were none too pleased by that tone, but Ala'tris settled them with a look before twitching her fingers and uttering a quiet spell. Beneath a cheerful early morning sun, the huge sails billowed in a wind that came out of nowhere to whirl around the ship, leaving first a shimmer in the air and then nothing at all as the spellship disappeared from view.

Without so much as an approving nod, Colfax then cast an appraising eye across each of the twelve runaways. Methodical, unhurried, no more concerned with any threat Ala'tris and her

187

coven might pose than he was with social niceties like welcoming visitors or even asking their names.

He's examining their injuries, I realised, watching his gaze sweep over every inch of the runaways in turn. *He's trying to determine whether any of their bruises or scars might've come from us.*

Ala'tris attempted to open diplomatic relations, but before she'd spoken the first syllable of her greeting, Colfax was already holding up a finger to quiet her. Hadn't even looked in her direction: just heard that first intake of breath before someone speaks and cut her off.

Conch was nestled close to me, his little goat stare never leaving Colfax. Periodically he made a little huffing sound that generally precedes him belching into oblivion anyone he suspected of being a predator.

'Stay easy,' I said quietly. 'Guy like that never risks trouble 'less he's got a plan to deal with any that comes his way.'

Personally I'd never spent much time around Daroman marshals, but even I'd heard of the famed Captain Colfax: finest fugitive hunter on the continent and the only man the previous King of Darome ever entrusted with the safety of his wife and son. Three years after that king had died and his son had ascended the throne, the marshal had finally tendered his resignation. Rumour had it the new monarch refused to let him retire, pleading that no one else could equal the old man's skill and devotion for protecting the crown. The matter was only settled when Luke Colfax finally convinced the only lawman tougher than himself to take over the marshals: his brother, Jed.

Standing there, outside those walls, with the marshal's grey eyes peering right through me, noting every scuff on my trousers and stain on my shirt as if they were mounting evidence in some case he was putting together against me without bothering to ask a single question . . . well, let's just say, I hope I never meet his brother.

'Okay,' he said at last.

From most people, 'okay' sounds like acquiescence. With Colfax, I would've sworn he'd just passed sentence on us.

'Revered Marshal,' Ala'tris began again, this time hitting him with that warm, graceful smile of hers that could turn a horde of cannibals into vegetarians, 'we come on a mission not only of mercy, but of hope for a brighter—'

This time he cut her off with a shake of his head, slow, never taking his eyes off her yet somehow seeming to keep watch on all of us. 'Got work waiting for me in the orchards,' he said with a gravelly rumble. 'More chores than hours in the day.' He started walking along the line of twelve runaways like he was inspecting fresh recruits. He never smiled or offered up a kind word, yet the Mahdek kids grinned up at him as he passed like he'd just ruffled their hair and grabbed them in a bear hug. 'When your aim is to keep a people alive, there's nothing more precious than their children. Lot of dangers outside these walls. Feared we might never get these unruly brats back to their kin.'

He paused a moment to stand in front of Kievan. Her shoulders slumped as if the weight of the world had fallen on them.

Colfax curled his forefinger and lifted her chin. 'You brought them back alive and unhurt,' he said quietly. 'Take pride in that.'

Kievan's back straightened and you could see the glow come to her cheeks. 'I . . . I had help, Luke.'

She hadn't so much as gestured towards me, but Colfax nodded as if he'd already worked out all the details himself. 'Argosi, I suppose,' he said.

'How'd you know?' I asked.

189

Still not bothering to meet my gaze, he brought up one finger in a lazy circle around his face. 'You all got that look.'

He didn't need to say anything more for me to know that the rest of that sentence went something like, ' . . . *and I've never much liked that look.*'

Conch pawed the grass with one of his hoofs. I saw his stomach expanding.

'Best that spire goat keep his intestinal gases to himself,' Colfax warned. 'He's too small to make a proper supper, but I do enjoy a snack in the afternoons.'

'Goat's hard to chew on when you ain't got no teeth,' I told him.

Don't care how big a legend you are, tough guy. Nobody threatens my goat.

Colfax ignored me though, and kept on walking past the line of runaways until he got to us. 'As for you, miss,' he said, tipping his hat to Arissa without stopping, 'you're welcome to steal anything you like, so long as you don't mind leaving your fingers behind as payment.'

Okay, the fact that he pegged her as a thief so quickly was a *little* impressive. Arissa nudged me with her elbow. 'Ooh, a challenge. You in, Rat Girl?'

When he reached Chedran, it was the first time he actually looked one of us in the eyes. 'You're the exile,' he said, again not bothering to make it a question. 'Murdered a coven of Jan'Tep mages in their sleep a few years back.'

'Sometimes I murder them when they're awake,' Chedran replied.

If he'd hoped that remark would cause the old marshal any unease, then he was sorely disappointed. 'You won't be killing anyone on my lands,' was all Colfax said. No threat, no warning, just a simple, incontrovertible fact.

Ala'tris was about to launch into her third failed attempt at diplomatic discussions. This time it was me who stopped her. 'Don't waste your breath, sister,' I muttered.

She turned to glance at me, confused and mildly irritated at my presumption.

I pointed to Colfax. 'He ain't gonna listen until he's finished his magic trick.'

'Magic trick?'

The marshal turned from the staring contest he was winning handily against Chedran, who'd been trying so hard to mesmerise the old man he'd given himself what looked to be a painful headache. 'Argosi,' Colfax said, imbuing the word with a bucketful of disdain. 'Rather be dead than let anyone forget how clever they are.'

'Marshals,' I shot right back. 'Rather start a war than let anyone forget how tough they are.'

Colfax chuckled at that. I thought maybe my arta loquit had cracked that stone-faced exterior of his. I was soon corrected when he gave a short, high-pitched whistle through his teeth that set the grey hairs of his moustache to twitching.

There wasn't so much as a rustle from the tall grasses of the field outside the walls, but I turned anyway, following a slow circle as I counted forty men and women emerging from their hiding places to surround us. Their brown, rough wool farmhand attire was utterly at odds with their soldierly posture. They were pointing long slender iron tubes at Ala'tris, Jir'dan, Gab'rel, Ba'dari and Sar'ephir.

Oh, and at me.

'Don't,' I warned Conch. The spire goat seems to understand only half of what I'm trying to tell him. I hoped this was one of those times.

'Gitabrian fire lances,' Colfax explained, referring to the long weapons. His troops held them at their right hip in a two-handed grip, waiting, I presumed, for the cue to twist the two joined halves that would then fire something entirely unpleasant in our direction. Colfax produced a lead ball from the pocket of his grey leather coat and held it up for us to see. 'Once the powder inside the tube ignites, it sends one of these at the target at around a thousand feet per second.' His gaze went to Ala'tris and her coven. 'I'm told the impact is like being hit with both an iron spell and an ember bolt at the same time.' He tossed the lead ball in the air, then caught it again. 'The only difference being that my friends over there can twist those cylinders in half the time it takes one of you to cast a spell.'

People who talk about how easily they can kill you rarely intend to do so, but still, this guy was starting to annoy me. 'Those mages helped save Remeny and the rest of the runaways, you foul-tempered old mule. They've risked their own lives to offer the Mahdek elders a chance at a decent future.'

Until that moment nothing had seemed to get through to Colfax. Now, though, he was so moved as to offer me an amused half-smile. 'A future?' He turned to Ala'tris, who did an admirable job of not looking terrified of the imposing marshal who could, without a doubt, have had her killed with a simple nod to one of his fire lancers. 'Thirty years I spent in the marshals service. Tracked down escaped criminals all across this continent. Crossed hundreds of miles, sometimes thousands, just to hunt down a single fugitive.' Without glancing at me, he asked, 'You know the difference between a fugitive and a refugee, Argosi?'

I never much liked answering other people's riddles. This one, though, mattered to him, which meant it was a chance to prove I understood his protectiveness over the Mahdek. 'A fugitive gets a trial before you kill them.'

192

He gave no acknowledgement that I'd given the right answer, but it was plain from the way he stared down Ala'tris and her coven. 'Thirty years of hunting the worst fugitives on the continent. Killers. Rapists. Traitors. None of their deeds held a candle to the foulness I saw left behind by bands of pretty young Jan'Tep mages like all of you.'

'That's not—'

It was his grey eyes that silenced Ala'tris this time. 'I was a marshal. Had a job to do, and that didn't involve protecting folks who weren't citizens of the glorious and just Daroman empire. Filed reports though. Dozens of them. Begged the king to convince his regional governors that the Mahdek should be allowed to settle in Darome. Waste of resources, I was told again and again. Too many complications. No Daroman king wants to be the one who started a war with the Jan'Tep.' He gestured back towards the tall stone walls surrounding his massive estate. 'When I retired, the king gave me these lands. Reminded me that it's not within the purview of a retired marshal to set domestic policy for the Daroman empire. On the other ha—'

'On the other hand,' I finished for him, 'kings have better things to do than visit the estates of retired marshals too distant from the capital for any Daroman nobles to venture, yet far enough north of the Berabesq border that the viziers don't pay any attention either.'

Colfax chewed his lip a moment. 'You ever wonder why decent folk dislike the Argosi so much?'

'I have better ways to spend my time.'

He nodded again, though this time it seemed to be a signal to his guards. They closed in on us, thirty of the fire lancers keeping their aim on us while the other ten strapped their weapons across their backs before splitting off into pairs. One would draw a long serrated knife that was the customary field blade of the marshals, the other unwinding a gleaming spool of copper wire.

'No,' Ala'tris said, her usually unassailable composure failing to hide the panic in her voice. 'I did not bring my comrades here so that some paranoid, vengeful old man could bind us in copper to prevent us from casting spells while he makes us his prisoners.'

Colfax held up the dull grey metal ball an inch from her forehead. 'Copper or lead. Your choice.'

Not much of a choice at all.

24

The Orchard

Colfax and his troops marched us through the welcoming stone arch and into a magnificent orchard that stretched out to the walls on all sides. Apples, pears and walnuts seemed to be most prevalent, but I also saw little copses of cherry trees with beautiful pale pink flowers.

'Hard work making them blossom so late in the year,' Colfax mentioned, noticing me staring as we passed them by. 'Worth it, though, just to add a little colour to the autumn.'

Unlike Ala'tris and the other Jan'Tep, neither Arissa, Chedran nor I was bound. We still had escorts though: two guards each to keep us in line. Well, two guards we could see.

'Those petals do draw the eye,' I observed. 'All that soft pink makes it hard to make out the iron barrels of your snipers.'

Colfax frowned, which I could only tell by the bobbing of the twin bull horns of his moustache. 'You spotted them?'

'Nope.'

The retired marshal chewed on that a moment as we walked along one of the many orchard paths towards what I presumed would be the estate's main keep. Conch, having apparently concluded nobody wanted to hold him hostage, ran around the various trees with increasing enthusiasm, leaping up in the air as he tried to nip various pieces of fruit with his teeth. He was doing a decent job of it.

Colfax gave a low grumble as he asked, 'How'd I give away the snipers? Your arta precis pick up something I hadn't meant to give away?'

I shook my head. 'Arta loquit. You saw me staring at the apple trees, then the pears, the walnut grove, but only when you caught me ogling the cherry trees did you bother to say something.'

Colfax considered my reply but only grew more irritated. 'Why would that be arta loquit instead of arta precis?'

'Arta precis is perceiving that which others seek to hide from you or from themselves, through their words, their deeds, or even the things they don't say or do at all. Arta loquit is just listening with your whole head and heart to what someone's telling you, seeking to learn *their* language, in all that entails.'

The gruff rumbling that preceded Colfax's utterances deepened. I was getting under the old goat's skin. He really did remind me of an ageing, curmudgeonly Conch – hopefully without the same digestive proclivities. 'You trying to tell me th—'

I turned to him and put on my most preposterously theatrical scowl, then dropped the pitch of my voice as low as it would go before repeating his earlier statement in an even grouchier tone than his. '*Adds a little colour.*'

The marshal kept looking straight ahead, walking with the unhurried stride of a man convinced the world only turns as fast as suits him. 'Wouldn't go making a career out of doing impressions.'

I repeated the words once more, this time adding a different emphasis to each one. '"*Adds*",' I began. 'Sharp, yet stretched out just a hair to deliver a subtle warning. Then you gave me "*a little*", with that diminutive delivered casually, almost jokingly, because you meant to convey its opposite. "*Colour.*" Ah, now we're in some

196

rich territory. You split the word into two parts: a "*cuh*" like the pulling of a trigger on a crossbow or whatever twisting mechanism sets off those fire lances of yours, followed by "*lehrr*" – the growl of a predator. You wanted me to know that the colour to which you were referring wasn't the pink of those cherry blossoms, but a much darker shade of red.'

The marshal halted, and just like that so did all of his guards. Maybe he was right to think the world only turned because it suited him. The men and women holding the lengths of copper wire that bound the wrists of Ala'tris and her coven behind their backs yanked the captives to a stop. The marshal's subordinates knew their business: the wire was wrapped not only around the mages' wrists, but then around each of their ten fingers to ensure they couldn't cast even the simplest of spells.

Colfax turned to me. 'You got all that out of four words?'

Ala'tris tried to catch my attention, then glanced towards Ba'dari. This was the tenth time she'd done this, signalling to me that I should free the raven-haired girl first when I made my move against the marshal and his guards. For the eleventh time – because I'd tried to warn her before our trek through the orchards had even begun – I gave a quick, sharp shake of my head. There wasn't going to be any escape from someone as experienced and prepared as Luke Colfax. Not yet anyway.

'You wanted me to know about those snipers,' I explained to the marshal, 'even if you didn't quite realise it at the time.'

Arissa sauntered over and rested her chin on my shoulder, looking up at Colfax. 'Okay, now you've even got me confused, Rat Girl. Isn't the whole point of hiding your snipers so the enemy won't know where they are until it's too late?'

Colfax swore something in archaic Daroman that I didn't recognise but which went on a while. 'Arta tuco,' he said at last.

'Which one's that?' Arissa asked. Unlike the rest of us, she didn't seem concerned one bit about the marshal or his guards. I was going to have to keep an eye on her; she's got a nasty habit of provoking people in authority.

'Arta tuco is how the Argosi refer to military tactics,' Colfax replied.

Durral Brown would *not* have liked the sound of that. 'We prefer to think of it as subtlety,' I said, a touch indignantly. My eyes caught those of Ala'tris. I needed her to make sure her people understood what was really happening here. 'Marshal, you have no intention of killing those mages or even imprisoning them. You just want them to know that their spells won't protect them here. But if something unexpected happens, say, if I make a move you haven't planned for, all hells could break loose. Those fire lancers of yours? I'll bet you've trained them to shoot the instant they see an ember or iron band flare. Which makes this one of those rare occasions when you really do want your enemy to know you've got snipers ready to fire.'

Arissa lifted her chin from my shoulder and pointed at Colfax, her finger dangerously close to his whiskers. 'Then why didn't Lord Marshal Grumpy Face here just show off his oh-so-scary snipers in the first place?'

Quit pushing him, girl, I thought, but didn't bother trying to convey that message to Arissa, since it would only encourage her to be even more belligerent. She badly wanted to give Colfax a metaphorical slap for bullying us into submission. Since I couldn't trust her to do that without setting off a firestorm, I had to do so on her behalf. 'Pride,' I replied. 'The marshal didn't want some eighteen-year-old Argosi knowing she made him nervous.'

The twelve runaways, who the guards were, with friendly politeness, keeping away from Arissa, the Jan'Tep and me, stared back and forth between me and the marshal, seemingly expecting one of us to lose our temper.

Colfax only chuckled though – not that there was any mirth in it. 'Guess we know a little more about each other than either of us would prefer.'

I shot him Durral Brown's most annoying, most *Argosi* smile – the one that's perfectly friendly yet rises just high enough on the left side of the mouth to express a little good-natured mockery. 'Speak for yourself, Lucallo. We Argosi love nothing better than wandering the wide world and learning from everyone we meet.'

That soured him good and proper. 'You ever wonder why some of those folks you're so fond of meeting dislike the Argosi so much?'

'Is it because they all cheat at cards?' Arissa asked excitedly. 'Please, Rat Girl, tell me you at least cheat at cards a little. This goody-goody act of yours is starting to depress me.'

Neither Colfax nor I laughed. Our eyes were locked like the antlers of two stags. I let my smile drop and offered the marshal a good, clear look at who I was underneath the frontier drawl and sunny disposition that so irritated him. Without breaking our gaze, I pointed to the trees ahead of us, lush with deep foliage. 'You didn't stop us here by accident. I reckon past this last stretch of orchard we're going to arrive at your fortress. Big place, right? High walls. Lots of guards armed with lots of weapons. By now, whoever you sent ahead has informed the Mahdek elders of our presence. They're in some finely appointed chamber waiting to hear why a coven of Jan'Tep mages rescued their runaways and risked their own lives to gain an audience.'

'Your maetri ever teach you it's better to be wise and silent than blurt out every thought you ever have just to sound clever?'

Now *that* made me laugh. 'My maetri taught me to love the sound of my own voice, especially when I was using it to remind

199

pompous bullies that their schemes aren't nearly so cunning as they like to believe. That's why I'd be powerful grateful if you could confirm for me that my estimation that where we're standing is about two hundred yards from your fortress is correct, and that, counting the time it'll take us to go inside, walk up a couple of sets of stairs and down a hallway or two, we're about fifteen minutes from where you're taking us?'

Had to give the ex-marshal credit: he was the very picture of unflappability. 'Fifteen minutes sounds about right.'

I took a step closer to him, noticed in my periphery the swivelling of a dozen fire lances in my direction. I couldn't hear Arissa snapping the extensible steel rod she'd stolen from me again to its full length, but I didn't doubt she'd done so. Colfax had to be near sixty, tall and rangy rather than imposing. Still, from that close I had to crane my neck to look him in the eye. 'That gives you sixteen minutes to untie those copper wires from my friends before you find out *exactly* why some folks dislike the Argosi so much.'

25

The Greeting Hall

Seventeen minutes.

I couldn't be absolutely certain that exactly seventeen minutes had passed before Colfax finally ordered his guards to release Ala'tris and her coven from those copper-wire bindings, because I wasn't carrying a pocket watch. Durral never was big on that particular Gitabrian invention. *'Time is the leash that yanks us all by the neck towards death,'* he always says.

When I'd pointed out that sometimes it's helpful to know what time it is, he'd gesture absently to the grandfather clock that Enna insisted on keeping in the entry hall of their cottage just to annoy him. *'Prove it,'* he'd demand petulantly.

So I'd tell him it was two o'clock or seven minutes after midnight or whatever it was. He'd stab a finger at me and shout, *'Hah! Wrong, kid!'* Then he'd find a bottle of something suitably unhealthy and say, *'It's whisky time, that's what time it is!'*

Enna, thankfully for my sanity, would later explain that Durral's point was that perpetually measuring time grants it sovereignty over our minds. *'Every hour, every minute, becomes something precious, to be hoarded all to ourselves or risk being stolen from us by others.'*

Funny thing was, both Enna and Durral could tell you exactly what time it was with near-perfect accuracy without ever consulting a clock or pocket watch. She was right though: those who obsessed over their time often became equally determined to control that of others. That's how I knew that Lucallo Colfax, who did indeed own a pocket watch and consulted it often, had kept track of how long it took us to arrive in the greeting hall of the massive country palace he'd turned into a fortress, and then made us wait exactly one minute longer before freeing the Jan'Tep.

'You know,' Arissa said, surreptitiously sliding another pocket watch – this one pilfered from one of Colfax's young handsome guards during some rather shameless flirtation – into the pocket of my waistcoat, 'I'm starting to think you and that marshal might be related, Rat Girl.'

By my count, the watch was the third item she'd pickpocketed during those seventeen minutes. I would've minded less were she not prone to hiding the evidence on me. 'Those smoking reeds of yours addlin' your wits, girl? He's Daroman and I'm Mahdek. Besides, we don't look a thing alike.'

She got serious a moment, which is rare for Arissa. 'Neither of you is Daroman *or* Mahdek. You're both lawmen. Only difference is the set of rules you're trying to enforce on everyone else. Besides, right here?' Her fingertip traced the line of my jaw, which I'll admit was clenched, then tapped my chin, which, sure, *might* have been jutting forward just a touch. 'Spitting image of the marshal, if you ask me.'

I never got the chance to respond – or even reclaim the miniature brass spyglass she'd filched from another of my pockets while distracting me with that nonsense – because at that moment a gong sounded. That's when I met the revered leaders of my people for the first time.

Whatever architect had designed the fortress greeting hall must've been inspired by a soldier's fever dream of heaven. The vaulted alabaster expanse must've been a good seventy feet long and twenty-five feet wide. The floor was like an ocean of polished oak, interrupted here and there by islands of circular mosaics depicting Daroman military triumphs. Stern-faced generals with perfect hair, their cloaks billowing in an unseen wind, led small battalions of wounded yet strangely placid troops to victory against snarling enemy hordes. Lone cavalry officers atop defiant steeds charged jeering villains mounted on tigers, wolves and even dragons. For a nation that derides religion as weak-minded superstition, the Daroman nobility sure do love to mythologise their own past.

A hall like this one would typically end with a throne set on a dais where a chamberlain would grant audience to visiting aristocrats or foreign dignitaries while his lord gazed down from the gilded-oak balcony above. The throne of Colfax's hall was long gone though; the gold fittings removed from the balcony railings. No doubt the dour ex-marshal had sold off such ostentatious furnishings shortly after being gifted the estate.

The dais remained though, as did a narrow gold-trimmed velvet carpet leading to it from the entrance. By custom, those seeking an audience were to remove their shoes by the arched double doors before approaching, their weapons stowed in the ornately carved mahogany racks overseen by stewards known as *custodir gladia*.

Another tradition Colfax had done away with, apparently.

Twenty of his fire lancers split off to take up staggered positions along the long walls on either side. That way, they could shoot anyone causing trouble without risking hitting their own comrade stationed on the other side. If negotiations got ugly, we'd have a devil of a time trying to run that gauntlet alive. A second contingent of guards escorted Ala'tris and her coven to the front of the dais, while Arissa, Chedran and I were penned in by our own little sextet of armed chaperones.

203

The runaways had been collected by their kin for what I could only assume would be a tremendous amount of hugging and crying followed by a whupping the likes of which none of those kids would ever forget. Only Kievan remained, defying both the tearful, heavyset but handsome man I assumed was her father and Colfax himself, who insisted on standing next to her by the entrance. I had the feeling she was just as much under guard as we were.

'What are we waiting for?' Arissa asked in a casual tone that warned me trouble might be imminent. She was bored and miffed in equal measure by the dull silence that offered no distractions for her to pick a few more pockets and see how far she could go before testing Colfax's promise to chop off her fingers.

'Kid, you are seriously gonna have to keep an eye on th—'

I cut off Durral's warning before he got to the conclusion I wasn't ready to hear – even if it was only in my own mind. Arissa had always tiptoed the line between audaciousness and outright stupidity. That wild, reckless streak was one of the things that made those dark eyes of hers shine so bright. The hell she'd endured in Soul's Grave should've spooked the stupid right out of her, but anyone could tell she was determined to prove she wasn't afraid of being caught again.

'Not long now,' I muttered, staring up at a twenty-foot-wide tapestry draped down the back of the balcony that overlooked the dais from a long brass rod attached to the vaulted ceiling. The weaving was unevenly tattered, the crowned black stallion rearing majestically clearly having seen better days.

'Why do you keep staring up at that ratty old thing?' Arissa asked.

'The edges of the canvas reveal the painting,' I said, reciting one of Enna's old axioms for arta precis.

Arissa rolled her eyes. 'I'm starting to sympathise with the marshal's dislike of the Argosi.'

'There's no art on the walls,' I explained. 'No finery in the entire hall. Why would Colfax leave up that tapestry unless it served a purpose?' I pointed to the horse's rear end. 'See that six-inch strip where the black is more faded than the rest?'

Arissa squinted. 'Hard to see, but yeah?'

'That's not just wear and tear. Those threads have been intentionally thinned out so that someone on the other side can look out over this hall without being seen themselves.'

'Why go to the trouble? I mean, those Mahdek elders are either going to meet with Ala'tris or not. Why lurk behind some dusty old tapestry making us wait for nothing?'

I didn't reply, even though I knew the answer. This was one of the few times I felt a connection to my people. The Mahdek spent their lives being looked down on by others, either with pity or contempt – no one more so than the Jan'Tep. For once the Mahdek were looking down on *them*.

Ala'tris knows it too, I thought, noticing how stoically she stood before the dais, waiting with that preternatural grace of hers. Not once had she looked back at Colfax or demanded to know what was going on. The other mages, especially Gab'rel, were doing a poorer job of not fidgeting. Strangely, none of them seemed nearly as flustered as Chedran.

Arissa poked my back as she whispered, 'He keeps shifting his weight from one foot to the other, and his shoulders are so tense you can barely see his neck. Any minute now, he's gonna lose it.'

Stupid, stupid, stupid, I thought, glancing back up at the tapestry. *You're all so determined to goad the Jan'Tep into losing their tempers by humiliating them that you can't see how close you're pushing one of your own people to breaking point.*

The six guards surrounding us would surely interpret any sudden outburst as an imminent attack. These guys were professionals, and they weren't oblivious to the way Chedran's whole body was practically vibrating with suppressed rage.

Moments like these, it's easy to get so caught up in trying to figure out how to keep the reins on one lunatic that you forget the one standing right next to you.

'Well, will you look at what I found?' Arissa shouted so loud I had to cover my ears. I turned and saw her right hand raised up high. A dozen steel throwing cards, taken from my pocket when she'd poked me in the back just now, shimmered in the light shining through the hall's sloped windows. 'Anyone want to see a card trick?'

'Arissa, don't!'

I tried to grab the cards from her. I was slow though, and she was unwilling to allow fear even the tiniest hold over her. What followed happened so fast I could only make sense of it by playing the events back slowly in my mind after it was already too late to stop them.

The instant she'd yelled her idiotic question, the six guards around us had shoved Chedran and me aside so they could level their short-bladed swords at Arissa. None of them had been carrying fire lances because weapons like that work best from a distance; the last thing you want is for your captive to snatch it out of your hands and turn it against you. Arissa now stood poised like the bud at the centre of a flower, the swords like six shining petals extending out around her. With the stolen steel cards fanned out, she spun like a dancer, using her momentum to knock the sword points out of line. Still twirling, she leaped straight up in the air.

The guards had clearly been about to thrust, so I'd shoved the one nearest me with my shoulder, hard enough that he stumbled into the two on his right. That left three who, seeing their comrades' blades coming at them, drew back a step before regaining their footing and thrusting again. By now Arissa had already landed on her feet and was bowing so low the swords went right over her. Their tips stopped just short of my sternum.

'Swords down!' Colfax bellowed so loud I swear I felt the floor rumble beneath my feet.

With such speed and precision you'd have to call it graceful, the guards had dropped their points and stood to attention. Arissa stood back up, hands held high as if waiting to catch some imaginary bouquet of flowers tossed by an appreciative audience.

Everybody in that hall froze. The guards surrounding us, the fire lancers on the wall, Ala'tris and her coven, their fingers still curled in somatic shapes for spells they hadn't had time to cast. Even Chedran was staring wide-eyed as if expecting me to explain what the hells had just happened.

I was shaking. Shaking so hard I couldn't move. Deafened by the blood rushing in my ears and my heart battering against the inside of my chest. My mouth felt strange. Tingly. There was moisture on my lips that hadn't been there a moment ago. Still trembling, I brought two fingers to my bottom lip, felt that hint of wetness before pulling them back, waiting for my eyes to focus. I knew what I'd find on them: the flecks of blood that had spattered from the wound about to end the life of this crazy girl who'd saved mine so many times.

There was no blood though.

The wetness I'd felt on my lips? That had come from something far less sinister, but nearly as unsettling.

'Did you . . . ?' I gawped at Arissa, unable to get the words out, refusing to believe it was possible even as my arta eres went back through every single step of what she'd done. Events of only seconds

207

before flashed through my memory like a deck of cards being riffled before the last deal of the game. 'You spun around, knocked all six sword points out of line, then jumped up in the air. You threw my cards, all while gambling that I'd manage to knock half the guards out of the way before you landed to give you enough space to duck down before the other three could complete their thrusts. And then . . . in that split second between narrowly surviving this insane manoeuvre and almost certainly getting skewered, you risked it all just to . . . kiss me?'

I have seen a great many grins in my eighteen years. I've worn plenty of them myself. But never have I seen a grin so fierce, so mischievous, so damnably smug as the one on Arissa's face when she said dropped a mock curtsy and said, 'Ta-da!'

As if on cue – and a part of me wondered whether somehow, on top of everything, she'd somehow timed it precisely that way – the cords holding the tapestry above the balcony gave way. The strands had been cut clean through by the razor-sharp edges of the cards Arissa had hurled while spinning in the air. With only twelve cards and a single flick of the wrist, she'd sliced through all six cords.

I was definitely going to need more practice.

We all watched as the tapestry fell, first across the railing to dangle precariously for a few seconds, before the weight of the top half caused the whole thing to slide over and land at the feet of the Jan'Tep delegation below. From the shadows of a narrow passage behind the balcony, seven figures emerged. They spread out along the railing to gaze down at Ala'tris and her coven. None of them spared the rest of us so much as a glance.

I thought something was wrong, that for some reason Colfax had brought us before not the Mahdek elders but a group of ageing Daroman nobles. Most were close to his age, a couple even older. They wore fine garments, men and women alike draped in long coats of varying colours and fabrics, ruffles of cream or pale grey down the front of the shirts beneath. Their sleeves glinted from the ornate inlay of silver or gold thread, and the bright ribbons at their cuffs matched those binding their elegantly coiffed hair into elaborate arrangements. I wasn't the only one who noticed this departure from Mahdek custom, which usually called for the hair to be worn down.

Laughter boomed throughout the hall, bitter as an early winter freeze, all of it coming from one man. 'Look at these parading dandies!' Chedran declared. 'Witness what has become of the venerable elders of the Mahdek, who cast me out for standing up to those who'd massacred our people! What has happened to you all? Some sad-eyed, slack-jawed Daroman marshal gave you permission to run rampant through closets filled with abandoned courtiers' clothes he considered too foppish to wear himself?' He started prancing about in a small circle like a show pony. 'Now you preen about his home, playing at being the aristocrats of a people too feeble and destitute to even feed themselves?'

The silence his performance left behind was a damning indictment. Six of the elders shuffled aside, making room for a woman shorter than the rest whose darkly tanned skin was crinkled like paper left out in the sun too long. When those wrinkled lips parted, I half expected a gasping wheeze to come out. Instead, hers was a voice as strong and clear as Chedran's, only more so because there was nothing brittle or frenzied in her response. 'A people on the brink of extinction do not have the luxury of hanging on to outdated traditions. Tattered and flea-ridden rags bestow no great dignity upon the wearer any more than childish outbursts confer moral authority to a murderer.'

Chedran's reply was quieter than before, less manic and yet with an edge sharp as a drawn blade and twice as threatening. 'You, above all others, should not speak to me of moral authority, old woman.'

The elder gripped the railing with both hands, fingers curled around the brass so tightly that I half expected her to leap over and hurl herself at him. 'And you, *beneath* all others, should know by now that I will speak however I must, *do* whatever is necessary for the survival of our people. That is no less true now than on the day I exiled you, my beloved son.'

26

Sovereign Diplomacy

There's too much pain in the world. Too much suffering.

That's not my bleeding heart talking, that's a fact, plain and simple. Some pain, some suffering, is inevitable: avalanches, earthquakes, disease, drought, old age, lost love. Every Argosi will readily acknowledge that these things are part of life, and must be, if not celebrated, at least recognised as the essential darkness without which light and joy would be meaningless.

There's another kind of pain though, another kind of suffering. It's the kind that shouldn't exist, that's unnatural. The kind that's just plain wrong. No wife or husband deserves to be beaten by their spouse. Nobody should be made to starve or have their body subjected to torture. Those aren't part of the natural order of things. They're not the consequences of fate or acts of the gods. The world could turn for a thousand ages just fine without any of those awful acts ever being committed.

There has to be pain, there has to be suffering, and, sure, maybe sometimes a boy has to be exiled into the wilderness, cast out by his own clan. But you tell me, is there any reason in this world or any other why the person who condemns him to almost certain death should be his own mother?

Therein lies the difference between some folks and the Argosi.

'You gonna lose it?' Arissa asked me.

She wasn't worried about Chedran any more. He was practically in his element: standing tall, chin raised, jaw clenched at the injustices heaped upon him. He almost seemed relieved when the Mahdek elders, far from being shocked at his return or, better yet, condemning their leader – Stoika, they called her – for having exiled him in the first place, pretended not to have heard the exchange between them. Instead they stood calmly behind the curved railing of the balcony, listening with studied indifference as Ala'tris presented the secret island she and the other restitutionists had found for the Mahdek people.

'They're acting like aristocrats,' I muttered, only dimly aware that Arissa had asked me something a moment ago. 'Like they've elected themselves sovereigns.'

The Mahdek never had much use for sovereigns these past three hundred years. The war with the Jan'Tep had ended in a series of escalating atrocities committed by both sides in response to the other. Eventually we'd run out of people and stopped being a nation. In most great conflicts, the conquered are assimilated by the victors or else disperse to become part of other countries. That didn't happen in the case of the Mahdek.

The Jan'Tep were obsessed with the idea that somehow the Mahdek might one day regain control of the oases and poison the magic against them. Tales of Mahdek spellshapers and shamans consorting with demons persisted until gradual genocide became a practice not only justified but considered necessary to preserve the peace. And, as everybody knows, peace is the one cause so just and noble that no amount of violence is too great a price to bring it about.

The funny thing was, without all those generations of young Jan'Tep mages going off to hunt us 'demon worshippers', without

212

their diplomatic envoys spreading accounts of our vile deeds and disease-ridden blood, there wouldn't *be* any Mahdek left in the world. Our ancestors would've settled in other places, mated with other peoples and slowly faded from history. But since nobody wants to make babies with a demon worshipper – especially when doing so might get you a late-night visit from some hextracker or bounty mage or even one of your own especially patriotic neighbours – the Mahdek bloodlines remained almost as pure as the hatred between our two peoples.

'What a coup it would be . . .' said one of the elders, a man with craggy skin and sallow cheeks at odds with the rich auburn locks tied in a gentlemanly ponytail with dark green ribbon. The hair of a Mahdek doesn't grey or whiten with age. In fact, some codgers like to claim it becomes ever more vibrant with the years. He banged the palm of his hand on the brass railing of the balcony from where he and the others looked down on the rest of us. 'What a triumph for a young coven of mages to return home with the scalps of the last two hundred and eighty-seven living Mahdek, eh?'

Neither the Jan'Tep nor anyone else, other than the occasional outlawed Berabesq religious sect, scalps their enemies any more. It makes a good story for when you're trying to terrify Mahdek children into never straying from the clan though.

'Then it would seem a poorly conceived plan, given we have turned ourselves over to you,' Ala'tris said evenly. Lines of weariness were beginning to show on her otherwise smooth forehead. She gestured behind her. 'Perhaps next time we attempt such a scheme we'll make the gift seem more enticing.'

A floating island constructed from shimmering, multi-coloured sand dominated the centre of the greeting hall. It rotated slowly for all to see, upon the calm waters of what appeared to be an ocean of pure onyx. Sar'ephir, who'd been holding the spell for

213

nearly two hours while Ala'tris attempted to explain the nature of the island and why it had remained undiscovered so long, was struggling to stay on her feet and pale despite the thick make-up she always wore.

'How better to rid your people of us once and for all,' coughed out a second man whose brocaded burgundy coat was a near match for the thick red curls ribboned in black, 'than by marooning us in the middle of what may well be a hell itself!'

Ala'tris sighed. Jir'dan threw up his hands and only kept quiet when Ala'tris gave a short, sharp shake of her head. Even some of Colfax's guards rolled their eyes as the endless cycle of argumentation returned yet again to its central proposition.

While the island appeared both beautiful and bountiful, from its lush forests with fruit trees to rival even those of Colfax's orchard to the magnificent mountain plateau at its centre, from which waterfalls depicted in silver sand flowed down to rivers no doubt filled with fish, it was that black ocean surrounding it that troubled everyone. Even me.

'The water is not truly black,' Ala'tris said for what must've been the seventh time since Sar'ephir had conjured the replica. 'We believe it is an optical phenomenon caused by the physical laws of the realm within which the island exists.'

'Not truly black, eh?' asked another of the elders, a woman of nearly seventy whose hair was a blonde more golden even than Arissa's. 'Why then do you call it by that name . . . what was it again?'

'The shadowblack,' Sar'ephir answered, though I'm pretty sure that this time at least three other people joined in.

You could see from the elder's self-satisfied smile that she hadn't forgotten the word, merely wanted to make them say it again. 'Strange that you, a Jan'Tep mage, would speak so casually about a form of magic so reviled that to reveal an attunement to it is cause for execution. In fact, is this shadowblack not the source of the notorious "Mahdek demon magic" your people have claimed is the justification for killing us all?'

'We—' Ala'tris hesitated, no doubt searching for an explanation that would sound more palatable than the three she'd tried already. This time, though, she was cut off before she could even make the attempt.

'Not "we",' Stoika said. Chedran's mother, the diminutive, sharp-eyed leader of the Mahdek council, had been mostly silent during the presentation. Now, though, I could tell she was about to take charge. 'You know nothing about this shadowblack, do you, girl?'

Ala'tris bristled. 'Do not call me, "girl", madam.'

'Then do not play me for a fool.' Stoika glanced at the elders to her left, then to her right, shooting them a look that let them know they'd said enough and she would be handling matters from now on. When they nodded their acquiescence she turned her steely gaze back on Ala'tris. 'The Jan'Tep know precious little of the shadowblack because so few possess the talent for shaping it. Yet here you stand, claiming that you've found this magical island within the shadowblack realm itself, even though you've never set foot on it yourself.' She pointed an accusing finger. 'Because you *cannot!*'

'Oh, by whatever gods grant mercy on poor thieves,' Arissa swore, 'are you really that thick, old woman?' She shoved aside the guards keeping her, Chedran and myself separated from the Jan'Tep and strode to the construct of the island.

Oh, spirits of my ancestors, I swore. *She's going to get us all killed.*

She began wiggling two fingers along a section of the illusory beach as if they were a pair of legs going for a walk. 'This is a

215

Jan'Tep, see?' She made her fingers buckle as if the person were collapsing. 'Pretty island make bad Jan'Tep sick.'

Ala'tris looked to me, silently pleading for me to intervene. I just shrugged. Irritated as I was with Arissa's incessant need to escalate every situation to the brink of bloodshed, diplomacy wasn't getting us anywhere. Maybe outrageous insult would shake things up.

'Oh, but what's that?' Arissa asked theatrically. She waggled two fingers from her other hand along the same beach. 'Is it . . . ? Yes, I think it is! It's a lovely little Mahdek.' The fingers walked cautiously along the sand while Arissa moaned loud enough for everyone to hear, 'Woe is me, woe is me, for the world is so cruel to we pure-hearted Mahdek.'

'Laying it on a bit thick,' I observed.

Arissa was too entertained by her own performance. She made her fingers wiggle faster, then jump in the air, the tips now a pair of feet clacking together in joy. 'Look at that! I think our little Mahdek likes the place. Maybe because –' she walked her fingers over to the dead body represented by her other hand, which she then kicked – 'the nasty Jan'Tep is all dead now!'

Arissa took a step back, stretched out her arms and bowed. 'I'm here all night. Don't forget to tip your servers.'

Okay, I know she's reckless, irreverent and utterly unconcerned with consequences, but are you seriously going to tell me you wouldn't fall for her too? Chedran, who usually seemed to despise Arissa, was the only one who clapped – much to the annoyance of his mother.

Still can't believe he's her son, or that she exiled him . . . or that Chedran emerged from an actual human womb.

He turned and took two steps towards the entrance before the guards stopped him at the same time as Stoika shouted,

'Where do you think you're going, boy? This council has not dismissed you.'

Chedran looked past the shoulders of the guards to where Colfax stood at the doors with Kievan, to whom he spoke, ignoring his mother. 'I rescued twelve runaways from being tortured and killed by Jan'Tep mages. As I understand my people's laws these days, that's grounds for exile – a sentence I am only too eager to resume. So either command your guards to kill me – I'd advise you start with the ones you'd be least concerned about losing – or get out of my way.'

The furore his words set off inside the greeting hall finally allowed me to see what was really going on here.

Enna once told me that the problem with diplomatic negotiations, like legal disputes or first dates, is that the participants are always putting on a show. Nothing nefarious about it – that's just how most folks behave. Unfortunately, those behaviours mask what they're thinking and feeling so deeply that often they aren't aware of their own thoughts and emotions. A moment like this though, when Chedran had shifted the axis of conflict from one between the Mahdek and the Jan'Tep to one between elders and their young? That brought all the masks down just long enough for me to get a good look. I reckoned I had about seven seconds before it all blew up.

I started with Ala'tris, taking in every detail I could in that split second: the narrowing of her eyes as she tried to discern what Chedran was doing, the faint beginnings of a frown that – combined with the slumping of her shoulders – told me she was ready to give up this mad quest for some sort of redemption for her people. There were tears waiting to be shed, but she wouldn't do it here, not in front of strangers. I felt a stab of shame for having begun with her, but didn't have time for self-flagellation, and so moved on to Sar'ephir.

You're way too beautiful and not nearly vain enough for all that make-up, sister, so what are you hiding under there?

The commotion in the room as Chedran took another step towards the guards – who hadn't yet been told whether to let him go or skewer him – was enough to make all the mages nervous. I caught the slight glints of colour from the tattooed bands on their forearms, but my attention was on Sar'ephir's shaved head.

There! The faintest darkening, like something swirling beneath the smooth bronze make-up coating her scalp. The Jan'Tep don't tattoo sigils anywhere but the bands around their forearms, which meant this was a different kind of magic.

That's how you found this island in a place where the Jan'Tep can't travel, and figured out how to spell a ship so that it can voyage through mountains, deserts and even into the shadowblack itself! I glanced just briefly back at Ala'tris, now convinced that must also be part of this mission she'd set for herself: she wanted to prove that those rare Jan'Tep like Sar'ephir afflicted with the shadowblack didn't deserve execution or exile.

I heard Colfax start to shout a command for his guards to step aside, and took that last instant before the masks came back up to set my arta precis on the biggest puzzle of all: Stoika.

The Mahdek weren't supposed to have monarchs. When your population has been decimated, the best chance for survival is when you split apart into smaller tribes and clans that can try different means of thwarting extinction and even thriving as they wander the continent. But Stoika? Everything about her told me she was sovereign over this 'council of elders', just as they were sovereign over the remnants of the clans that now lived in this enclave.

She's not planning on letting Chedran leave, I realised, seeing the urgency playing out in the wrinkles of her forehead and around her eyes, the tightness of her lips, pressed together as if it were the only way to keep herself from calling out to him. A mother's love? Perhaps, but something else as well: an unspoken admiration and a conviction that she needed him now for precisely the same reasons she'd exiled him years ago. He was a warrior. Dangerous. Unconstrained by either fear of the enemy or moral qualms over killing when it was necessary. But why would she need him now, when they've got Colfax and his troops and his fortress to protect them here?

Stoika must've sensed me staring because her eyes met mine just long enough for me to shoot her a grin.

You're not nearly so arrogant as you pretend, are you, Stoika? I thought, observing the clenching of her jaw as she saw that I'd figured her out. *The other elders buy into the old prejudices and grievances, but you're too smart for that.* Her eyes flicked down to Ala'tris, and I had my confirmation. *You believe her. You have all along. You know this isn't a trick. You just haven't figured out how to sell it to people you've told since the day they were born that all Jan'Tep are tyrants who can't be trusted.*

'Chedran, stop!' I called out. 'Colfax, don't let him go!'

'Stay out of this, Argosi,' Chedran warned. 'I may be an exile, but you *chose* to abandon the Mahdek. You have no business here.'

Oh, how I wished that were true. My heart sank in my chest, and my hand went to the pocket of my waistcoat where I kept my deck of debt cards. They felt heavier somehow. All I'd wanted was to pay off my debts so that I could truly begin my journey along the Path of the Wild Daisy. To wander free. To witness places and events strange, magnificent, even terrifying, but always, always as far from my past as my feet would take me. When I'd found Arissa in that cell in Soul's Grave, I'd almost let myself believe maybe she'd walk that path with me awhile. When Chedran had pushed

219

me to help him reunite with Kievan and the other runaways, I'd hoped maybe we could get them home and that would be that. The kids would be safe and I'd move on to repay my next debt.

Stoika's eyes held mine as if somehow she'd shackled our gazes. Now it was her turn to smile, because we both knew what it would take to convince the Mahdek to risk everything on the promise of a new homeland, to abandon the safety of this enclave to sail into the shadowblack aboard a ship piloted by their ancient enemy.

'We can't leave,' I said to Chedran, though I suppose I was really talking to myself. 'Our people need us.'

27

Love and Duty

They stuck me in a room on the second floor of the fortress. Any cell above ground rather than below it is a step up in the world, Durral liked to say, but this one was especially nice. Dark polished wood planks practically flowed along a hexagonal chamber. Well-situated brass wall sconces with conical oil lamps provided a lovely even lighting throughout the room. A huge, three-foot oval cameo made of alabaster or ivory adorned each of the six walls, depicting scenes of diplomacy and trade.

You'll find *diplomatiums* like this one in most Daroman palaces and fortresses. Never hurts to make a foreign dignitary feel special. They don't all have six walls of course, but this one, being in the deep south of the country near the Berabesq border, was designed to appeal to visiting viziers. Too bad nobody informed the architect that while the Berabesq do indeed worship a six-faced god, every vizier has their favourite, so making all the walls perfectly equal would always be deemed sacrilegious no matter who stayed here.

The bed was nice though: brass-framed with a proper mattress and coverings of rich burgundy wool that looked entirely too comfortable to waste on mere sleeping. Not that I would ever know for sure: Conch had decided the proper function of such a mattress was for rolling around on and occasionally bouncing up and down on while making what sounded oddly like chirping noises. Every now and then he took a break to chew on the pillows.

A more conscientious guest than myself would've reminded the spire goat that it's not polite to eat your host's furniture. On the other hand, a more polite *host* would not have stationed two guards armed with fire lances outside the door promising to shoot me if I took one step outside. Still, not a bad room to wait out the various negotiating, planning and other banalities of a people packing up and leaving the only safe place they've found in generations to set sail on a spellship into what might well be a hell itself.

'You stare at the walls as if there were some insight to be gleaned from them,' Chedran said with his customary derision as he paced back and forth in front of a window along the eastern wall. Well, given there were six sides, I suppose it was the mostly-eastern-but-one-third-northern wall.

'There are insights to be gleaned everywhere,' I said, tilting the brim of my hat down a little as I sat back in the pleasingly plush chair on the opposite side of the room. 'Just gotta open yourself up to them.'

His pacing came to an abrupt halt. 'You seem remarkably at ease.' I didn't bother to look up; I could imagine the sneer on his face just fine. Besides, you could hear it all in his tone.

'A congenital condition. Had it since childhood.'

Chedran was a guy who could move real quiet when he wanted to; it was just that he seldom did. The three stomping strides that brought him entirely too close to me were like a carefully written letter detailing the many, many ways in which I was a lousy, worthless human being. That didn't stop him from reciting them though. 'Six of the marshal's guards dragged Arissa – your supposed *friend* – from the greeting hall. Twenty others, armed with fire lances and spools of copper wire, escorted the Jan'Tep below

222

ground.' He paused in his litany, which I presumed was so that he could gesticulate at our opulent surroundings. 'I doubt their accommodation is nearly so pleasant as yours.'

An Argosi isn't supposed to sigh; that's what Durral used to say anyway. A sigh is a public pronouncement masquerading as private suffering. It's petty and impolite – a way of expressing exasperation over someone or something without taking responsibility for it. *'Most of all, kid, it ain't cool. And an Argosi should always be cool.'*

I sighed. Chedran snorted. Conch, not wanting to be left out and having been given a strict no-belching warning before being allowed to join me in my temporary incarceration, farted.

'Disgusting,' Chedran said.

'Less so than usual.' I reached over a hand to scratch underneath the spire goat's chin. 'Been eating a lot of them pears from the orchard, have you, buddy?'

Conch gave a little rumble from his belly, which I took as a yes.

'You truly care nothing for the torments your friends are suffering beneath this fortress?' Chedran asked, shaking his head in disgust. 'Fitting, I suppose, since you abandoned your people with equal ease.'

It's not up to you to explain yourself to him, Ferius, I told myself. He's a blowhard who can't handle being cooped up and deals with it by being an ass. Not your problem.

'They're fine,' I told him, unable to follow my own sage advice. 'The elders know the only way to transport the Mahdek to that fancy island is on the spellship. Without Sar'ephir, that galleon is nothing but a big old wooden tub halfway buried under the soil and rock. She won't go anywhere without Ala'tris, who would die before she helped anyone who'd hurt a member of her coven. All of which means your *mamma*—'

Okay, yeah, I know that was petty. Guess I couldn't help myself. I'm still new at being an Argosi.

223

'Your *mamma* is just messing with the mages a little, testing how skittish they get when she makes it seem like Colfax and his troops might beat them into confessing this whole restitution business is just another dirty Jan'Tep trick.'

'And Arissa?' Chedran demanded. 'She hurled sharpened steel cards at the elders and followed it up with intolerable mockery. Stoika will not have forgotten that insult, and the council has no need of a thief aboard the spellship.'

I'd already considered that unpleasant fact myself. Fortunately, Stoika was too cold and calculating to waste time on revenge. 'Nobody's going to lay a finger on Arissa. She's Stoika's bargaining chip to keep me in line.' I raised one leg and pointed the toe of my boot towards the door. 'Any minute now, she's gonna walk through there and detail everything she expects of me – even though I've already agreed to tag along on this little expedition to make sure the island's legit before I return with Ala'tris and her mages. Stoika intends to extract a whole bunch of promises and oaths from me in exchange for freeing Arissa and convincing Colfax to let her leave with all her fingers.'

'And you'll agree to whatever she asks?'

I leaned back in the chair and propped my feet up the edge of the bed, ignoring Conch's warning grumble. 'The Argosi don't swear oaths or sign contracts under duress. Your mamma gets nothing out of me that I don't believe the situation warrants.' I should've left it there, but truth was, part of me was curious. 'What about you, Chedran? You know she's going to demand absolute subservience from you as much as me. No murdering anyone unless she tells you – that's going to be the deal.'

He got quiet then. Not his usual sort of quiet that's half moodiness, half homicidal contemplations. Proper quiet. Almost Argosi quiet. I pushed up the brim of my hat. He was leaning against the window, looking out onto those pleasant orchards and the rolling hills beyond. You'd swear he was watching a massacre unfolding right before his eyes.

'Did you know that our ancestors really did possess the secrets of demon magic?' he asked.

'Always assumed that was Jan'Tep propaganda. Disinformation to keep other nations from interfering in the genocide.'

He kept staring out the window, bearing witness to some horror I couldn't imagine. 'Not entirely. The elders don't share this with their clans, but back three hundred years ago, some of our shamans really could commune with entities of such pure evil they referred to them only as the Gleeful Ones. When the war turned against us, the Gleeful Ones whispered to our shamans through the ethereal planes. They offered a pact. Agree to their terms and –' he snapped his fingers – 'victory. Just like that.'

'These "Gleeful Ones" don't sound like the sort of folks who do favours for free.'

'The bargain was equitable enough. Our spellshapers fashion a portal between the two realms, and the Gleeful Ones bring their armies across. They even vowed to leave – every single one of them – the moment the war was over.'

'Whose definition of "over" are we talking about?'

He shrugged. 'Nothing too unsavoury. Once the last Jan'Tep had been either eaten alive or shackled with copper so that they might be dragged through the portal to serve as slaves in that other realm, the Gleeful Ones would depart.'

'So, trade one genocide for another?'

The rage in his voice was a smouldering acid that seemed to burn his throat when he tried to hold it in. 'The Jan'Tep would've made that bargain in a heartbeat.' His fists clenched at his sides. 'Yet still our ancestors demurred, fearing such an atrocity would prove us no better than our oppressors.' His shoulders slumped as the anger drained out of him. He leaned his forehead against the glass, too weary to hold himself up any longer. 'Now our people are on the brink of extinction and the Jan'Tep have convinced the entire world that we practised demon magic anyway. Tell me, Ferius Parfax, why should those Mahdek elders of the past be remembered as anything less than war criminals? Should not the archer who refused to fire his deadliest arrow be held as guilty for the hundreds of thousands of deaths suffered by those he'd sworn to protect as the enemy who slaughtered them?'

Times like these, you pray for a knock at the door to save you from the question for which there's no decent answer. Knocking being a sign of respect for whoever's on the other side of the door, Stoika didn't bother. Instead, she strode right into the room. I knew instantly that she'd been out there a while, listening in on our conversation.

'Spoken like a child,' she said dismissively, 'with a child's inability to comprehend consequences other than not getting their own way.' She didn't give Chedran a chance to return fire, raising an imperious finger to silence him. 'You've never appreciated the complexities of what it takes to lead a fading people into the twilight of their existence. I doubt your years away have remedied that defect.'

I found myself in the unenviable and entirely unwanted position of defending Chedran. 'Doubt's a fine thing,' I told her, rising up from the chair to face her, 'until you let those doubts harden so much they aren't really doubts at all any more, just . . . What's the word for an untested belief about someone else that you never question?'

The old woman stiffened, her back suddenly straight as an iron rod inside that elegant burgundy and silver coat of hers. 'I won't

226

be accused of bigotry against my own flesh and blood by an Argosi who displays not one shred of allegiance to her own kind.' She turned to Chedran. 'Well, boy? What have you to say on this subject? Am I wrong to fear that your love of violence exceeds that for our people? Are you any more Mahdek than this Argosi wastrel who seeks at every turn to renounce the duty to which we were all born?'

Chedran turned at last from the window, and his eyes drifted to mine before they met those of Stoika. 'I cannot answer, Mother. Unlike Ferius, I have never been blessed with the burden of love, and so find myself ill-equipped to measure its weight.'

Stoika's jaw tightened at first as if Chedran had slapped her, but then she reached out a slender, wrinkled hand. 'Come then, my son. There remains a little time before we abandon this home that was never a home for yet another foreign land. Perhaps the hour has come at last for you and I to speak of love, and see whether, in the face of the fearsome duties awaiting us, there might remain enough of that love in us to spare a little for each other.'

Chedran gazed down at her trembling palm as if it were full of embers waiting to burn his flesh to the bone. Stoika smiled, a little sadly, as she withdrew her hand. Yet, when she turned to leave, Chedran followed her out the door.

Conch gave a snoozy grumble, dozing on one side, half-buried under the burgundy covers. I scratched his fuzzy head awhile, wondering about the terrible, precious chains of love and duty, and how anyone shackled with either could ever truly be free. Unlike Chedran, I'd known plenty of love in my relatively short life, along with the pain of leaving it behind. Maybe it was the Scarlet Verses swirling around in my skull, or perhaps just my arta loquit, but lately it seemed as if the very word 'freedom' had become a synonym for 'farewell'.

'They're gone now,' I said aloud. 'You can come out.'

A creak came from the wall adjacent to the bed. The big alabaster cameo swung open like the door of a cabinet. Arissa wrestled herself through, sliding head first onto the floor before rolling back to her feet with less than acrobatic elegance. 'Ta-da!' she declared.

I offered muted applause. Conch snored approvingly.

Arissa dusted herself off. 'How did you know I was hiding in the passage behind the wall?'

'Until three seconds ago, I didn't know there *was* a passage behind the wall.'

'Then how did you know I'd escaped?'

'Simple. I know you.'

She brought her hands up under her chin and pretended to swoon. 'Oh, you do say the sweetest things, Rat Girl. I do declare it's almost enough to make me fancy you.'

Get to it, I thought, holding back the bitterness. The playful banter she was trying to instigate between us was excruciating because I knew exactly where it was leading.

'Hey, you okay?' she asked.

I smiled as I walked over to hug her. 'Just relieved that I didn't have to rescue you again.'

She pulled away. 'Rescue *me*?' Her grin widened as she held up the disharmony card I'd painted of her. 'I only came back to return this stupid debt card of yours. See, my next heist is going to be my greatest ever.'

'Yeah?'

She planted her fists on her hips, turned her head to the side and struck a heroic pose. 'Like the intrepid princes of those sappy old Daroman shield romances, I've come to rescue me a damsel in distress!'

Please don't do this, Arissa. Please don't make it worse than it has to be.

228

I gestured to our opulent surroundings. 'I don't see no giant trolls or evil dukes guarding this here dungeon. Who is it you reckon I need rescuing from?'

'Well, there are those ex-marshals outside your door. But mostly . . .' Arissa leaned forward and kissed me on the cheek. 'I'm here to save you from yourself, stupid.'

She wasn't here to save either of us, though. Arissa just hadn't figured out yet that freedom and farewell are the same word.

28

Freedom and Farewell

Everybody's got their own way of saying goodbye. Maybe it ends with a tearful expression of bittersweet sorrow followed by a proclamation equal parts romantic and tragic: 'You were the best friend I ever had,' or 'So long as the sun rises in the east and sets in the west, I'll never feel about another the way I feel about you.'

Rebellious denials work for some. 'I refuse to say goodbye. Mark my words, we'll be together again sooner than you think!'

Disappearing in the middle of the night is always a classic. *It's too hard to say goodbye*, they're telling you, as if their silence were a mark of how much you meant to them.

Enna once told me that all goodbyes are performances, scripted as surely as any stage play, measured against how many tears the audience sheds once the curtain comes down. Pretty cynical for someone as loving as her, I'd thought, but she explained that the hardest things in life demand to be performed before they unfold. Rituals prepare our minds and bodies so they don't collapse in on themselves when the heart breaks.

'Weeping, hugging, raging against the universe. It's all part of arta forteize, Ferius. We make ourselves resilient to loss by enacting it before it happens.'

Sage advice. Unless, of course, your particular choice of ritual farewell leans towards violence.

'Time to go, Rat Girl,' Arissa said, grabbing hold of my pack and slinging it over her shoulder. She'd never carried my stuff before; this was the first step in showing me I didn't have a choice. 'You, too, Conch,' she told the spire goat as if this whole operation were being handled by the two of them. 'I've found us a way out of this monstrosity of a fortress. We'll need to knock out a few of Colfax's guards, but I was planning on stealing me a couple of them Gitabrian fire lances as souvenirs anyway.'

'Sure,' I said, not yet ready to play my part. I lifted Conch off the bed and set the sleepy-eyed goat on his hoofs. 'Where we headed after that?'

'I'm thinking north to the Zhuban territories. I'm not fond of the weather up there, but the Zhuban are reputed to be the most skilled astronomers on the continent. They import the finest glass from Berabesq and brass from Gitabria to make these telescopes that can make you feel like you're walking on the moon any time you look through them.'

She walked over to the large cameo spyhole and opened it back up, shoving her own pack through the gap first before sliding mine off her shoulder. I guessed my time was up.

'You figure the moon's far enough away?' I asked.

Arissa hadn't looked at me since she'd started this little farce. She didn't do so now either. 'Don't make me do this, Ferius.'

Don't make me do this. That wasn't the right line. I needed her to say, *'Don't do this.'* Three words, not five. Those other two? They were going to be trouble.

'I have to see this through, Arissa. The Mahdek don't trust the Jan'Tep worth a damn. The Jan'Tep can't trust them either, and Chedran, hells, he'd have the entire Mahdek–Jan'Tep wars start

231

all over again if he had his way. I'm the only one who can stop that from happening.'

She was still staring off into the darkness beyond the cameo opening. 'Think pretty highly of yourself these days, I've noticed.'

'Ala'tris trusts me, and the rest of her coven will follow her lead. Kievan and the other Mahdek teenagers will listen to me because I never let the doom and gloom of our elders hold me back. Chedran adores those kids, so he won't act up on the voyage if I'm around to keep him in check. Stoika and the council need him because he's their best bet for killing the Jan'Tep mages if they try anything funny. That whole spellship will blow up like a powder keg before it even sets sail unless I'm there to keep the peace.'

Arissa's next words were so quiet, spoken into the black depths of her intended escape route, that I barely made them out. 'They're going to ruin you, Ferius.'

'I can handle them. Stoika. Chedran. I'm tougher than they think. Tougher than you seem to believe.'

Conch gave one of his little snorts.

'You stay out of this,' I told him.

The spire goat took one of those heaving, gut-expanding breaths that precede him knocking me unconscious, then thought better of it and plopped down on a rug to go back to sleep.

'The goat's got it right, Rat Girl. You're not nearly tough enough, not in the way I am or Chedran is. We can be stabbed, beaten, locked up, but that's all anyone can do to us. We don't have . . .' She started to turn, then stopped herself as if she needed to keep staring into the shadows, drawing strength from them for what was to come. 'It's your spirit they'll destroy first.'

Funny choice of words, because my spirit was precisely what I was trying to protect. 'I can't walk my path if I'm carrying around unpaid debts. That's not the Argosi wa—'

232

'You've paid your debt to the Mahdek three times over. You freed Chedran from Soul's Grave, rescued those runaways and returned them to the safety of this enclave. You even brought the council of elders a chance of finding a bright and sunny new homeland.' She turned to face me at last. There was no mirth hiding in the corners of her mouth, no mischief in her eyes, only a hurt both raw and dangerous. 'You're done, Rat Girl. Time to hit the road.'

I crossed the hexagonal room, desperately searching my arta loquit for the right words. I chose poorly. 'I can't abandon them. They're my people.'

Yeah, it didn't sound right to my ears either. Arissa grabbed on to that fact with both hands, just as she grabbed hold of my wrists. 'No, Rat Girl, the Mahdek *aren't* your people.' She yanked up my left arm, placed her palm against mine. 'This. *This* is what's real. You find someone you trust, someone you . . .' She shook her head, refusing to say the rest out loud because it would've blunted the blow she'd had planned for me all this time.

When it came, I stumbled back from her, punch-drunk. I'd expected some kind of physical attack. Both of us knew a whole bunch of ways to knock a person unconscious. I'd been ready for those. Instead Arissa had taken me out with nothing but her words.

'I wish someone else had found me in that Berabesq prison.'

She always could surprise me with how quickly she took to weapons of all different kinds. Turned out she was just getting started.

Holding up the disharmony card I'd made of her, she asked, 'Why'd you paint this?'

'Because . . .' I couldn't speak. I was having trouble breathing, still reeling from that hammer blow. *'I wish someone else had found me.'* 'I painted that card because I owed you a debt,' I stammered. 'You'd saved me a dozen times over and I—'

233

The flash of her hand whipping past my face was all I saw before I felt the first cut on the edge of my jaw. Disharmony cards aren't sharp, but she'd struck so fast she'd broken the skin. 'Bullshit.' I'd never heard her swear that way before, devoid of any humour or joy, spitting out the word like it was a bad taste in her mouth. 'You have plenty more of these cards. Why come for me? Why not somebody else?'

I kept trying to regain my balance, awaken my arta forteize, but I couldn't. 'Luck of the draw. Your card happened to be the one I pulled from the deck.'

'*This* deck?' She was holding the rest of my disharmonies now, which meant she'd lifted them from my pocket when she'd snapped the other card across my jaw. She fanned out the deck with a flick of her wrist. 'You just happened to draw my card out of all these other folks who we both know are more deserving of your Argosi pity?'

'It wasn't pity. I told you, it was just chance.'

'Liar.'

With the deck fanned out, she sliced at me again. Even a regular card can cut deep if you strike at just the right angle with enough speed and force. I was ready this time though, and a split second later the cards were drifting down all around us like falling leaves. All except for the card depicting Arissa, which I was holding in my hand.

'Don't ever try to hurt me again. You're not the only one who's quick on the draw, Arissa, and I know a whole lot more card tricks than you do.'

She smiled, cold and joyless. 'You figure maybe one of those tricks is where you fool yourself into believing you picked a card at random when in fact you drew the exact one you wanted all along?'

I could've lied. I'm not great at it, but my arta valar is enough to fool most people. Would've been better for the both of us if I had lied. My mistake was that when I'd snatched the card depicting Arissa out of the air after knocking the deck from her hand, I'd caught it with the painted side facing me. Now I was staring both at the girl I remembered from years ago, captured in brushstrokes and dabs of paint and more longing than I'd ever admitted to myself, and the woman she'd become, who was seeing right through me.

'I was alone,' I confessed at last. 'My head . . . it's full of these damned Scarlet Verses. They whisper things to me, Arissa. Awful, awful things. I kept dancing around them, but I wasn't sure I could hold them back much longer. I needed . . .'

You know what I wonder sometimes? Why does anyone ever say goodbye anyway? What comes of giving voice to grief?

'Say it,' Arissa demanded.

My arta tuco failed me next. Hard as I tried, I couldn't see any way to avoid the calamity coming on faster and faster, a boulder picking up speed as it tumbles down the mountain. I could see it plain as day, but my feet couldn't seem to get me out of its way.

I stared at the card, at the smirk that seemed to rise up all the way from her lips to her eyes. 'I needed *you*, Arissa. I needed your stupid grin and your wild, reckless spirit that always makes me feel like there's no trap the world's ever devised that you can't escape.'

The card went flying from my hand. 'So you busted me out of Soul's Grave only to lock me with you in a prison of your own making?' I'd been staring at her painting so hard that I hadn't noticed her cheeks were now dripping with tears held back far too long. Only someone whose notion of being free is so absolute, so uncompromising that even bonds of affection are just another kind of shackle, would've hurled so much fury into what she said next. 'You had no business making me fall for you, Ferius Parfax!'

And there it was at last. The blow I couldn't take. Too sharp. Too bitter. It cut far, far too deep. 'Don't you dare pretend you love me,' I said, the words coming out like gravel soaked in venom. 'Not that way. Not the way I—'

She shoved me away, only to catch right back up with me, shouting in my face, her outrage burning bright as mine. 'How the hells am I supposed to know *how* I feel? You think because I haven't bedded a girl before it means I couldn't . . . that I'd never want to . . .' She shook her head, like someone who's downed too much liquor too fast, and now is trying to keep from passing out. 'I don't know how I feel about you, Ferius.' She stilled, and her eyes rose to meet mine. 'You should've given us both the chance to find out.'

A candle flame of possibility flickered inside me, so faint that only a fool would've followed it into unexplored territory. But maybe chasing hope into the darkness is an inevitable part of these performances, these rituals.

I kissed her.

Arissa, after only the briefest hesitation and with the same rash, headstrong, death-or-glory resolve with which she does everything, kissed me back.

Was it real, that kiss? Her lips pressed against mine, so fierce and firm, our mouths moving together, searching breathlessly for a rhythm that might signify more than just the impending loss we were both trying to forestall. Our hands met, fingers intertwining only briefly before coming apart so they could travel along the other's back and neck and thread into the tangles of each other's hair. The intensity was there, and the thrill, but was it real? Were the two of us giving in to wild abandon, or just clinging together in the dark, a pair of lost girls terrified of being abandoned?

Don't know. Couldn't say. My arta precis's pretty darned good, but it ain't *that* good. I broke it off first, knowing Arissa wouldn't because doing so might mean the kiss wasn't real.

'Come with me,' I said, breathless but determined to get the words out before she could stop me. 'Sar'ephir says the journey through the shadowblack will only take five, maybe six days. Add three weeks to make sure the island's safe and help the Mahdek get settled, then we come back. After that, we go anywhere you want to go. Find every unscrupulous merchant and corrupt king and we rob 'em blind. We'll be the most famous thieves the continent's ever seen. Courtly minstrels will write songs about us, and if they don't, screw 'em, we'll write the songs ourselves.' I kissed her again, then pressed my forehead against hers and closed my eyes so I wouldn't have to see what was waiting in hers. 'Come with me, Arissa.'

It was just the sound of us breathing for a while. Then she laughed.

It wasn't a cruel thing, but she didn't hold any of it back. Laughing's what Arissa does when facing the inevitable calamities brought on by her own choices. 'You, a thief?' Her forehead still rested against mine, the fingers of her left hand trailing down my shoulder while her right picked my pockets. She was too skilled for me to feel it happening; it's just that any time I can't see both her hands, I know she's stealing *something*. 'You've never been a proper thief, Rat Girl.'

'I was good enough to be your partner in our days with the Black Galleon gang.'

Her forehead rolled left then right against mine. 'Afraid not. Even back then, before you became an Argosi, you weren't a proper thief. You're a gambler, Ferius. You play your cards or roll your dice because that's your way of defying fate. When your hand comes up short or you roll snake eyes, you honour the wager because a proper gambler always pays her debts. Me, I'm a thief by nature, not circumstance. You know what makes a proper thief?'

'Loose morals and a complete lack of respect for other people's property?'

I could feel the skin on her forehead tightening when she smiled. 'The deep spiritual conviction that I don't owe the world a damned thing.'

Arissa stepped back, then knelt down and gathered up my scattered disharmony cards while I watched. After she was done, she stood up again and riffled the deck as if seeing the cards properly for the first time. 'For a professional gambler, you sure do lose a lot of bets, you know that?'

There was a line I was meant to say then, one as inevitable to this moment as the curtain coming down at the end of a play. '*It's not gambling if there's no risk,*' a better actor than myself would've recited, '*and some debts, well, paying them makes your life richer.*'

A decent line. I just couldn't get the words out.

Arissa handed me the cards, then squeezed herself into the passageway beyond the cameo. 'Listen, when this nonsense with spellships and magic islands and three-hundred-year-old wars is over, assuming you make it back to the continent alive, look me up, all right?'

A knock at the door and Ala'tris's soft voice told me that preparations were almost done, and my time with Arissa – or Arelisa Talédra, Contessa of who-the-hells-knew-where – was almost gone.

'It's a big continent,' I said, coming to peer through the opening in the wall. It was so dark on the other side, she was barely more than an outline among the shadows.

'How'd you find me last time?'

A smile came unexpectedly to my lips with the memories of those six frustrating months bribing lawmen and lawyers in three countries, following all those rumours of unsolved burglaries and outrageous heists. 'Easy,' I replied. 'I followed a trail of trouble. Led me right to you.'

Arissa appeared to give that considerable thought. 'Well, I hate being predictable, but –' she shot me a grin so big I could make it out even in the darkness – 'I've got a feeling that might just work a second time too.'

I never heard her leave, only saw that the shadows had somehow darkened and a candle flame inside my chest, small but bright, had been extinguished. I closed the cameo just before the door opened and Ala'tris entered. The two guards outside were gone, so I guess Stoika had gotten what she'd wanted out of the Jan'Tep and no longer needed to keep me from interfering.

'I'm sorry to disturb your contemplations,' Ala'tris said with her customary diplomacy, 'but the preparations are almost done and Sar'ephir says now is the best time for our departure.'

Not even three days, I thought, a finger tracing the elaborate design engraved into the cameo. *Nobody but the Mahdek could uproot their lives so quickly.*

My arta loquit picked up a trace of strain in Ala'tris's tone. There was a heaviness in her breathing. I knew even before I saw the paleness in her features and redness around her eyes what had happened. 'They roughed you up, didn't they? Colfax and his former marshals?'

She shook her head, and smiled in that way graceful people do when they're hiding a deep hurt. 'The interrogations were . . . as gentle as the situation allowed. Stoika needed to assuage the concerns of the other Mahdek elders. Your people have a remarkable talent for asking the same questions over and over again, and Lucallo Colfax finds great virtue in denying sleep to a suspect.'

239

'I'm sorry,' I said. 'It shouldn't be this way.'

Ala'tris stared at me a moment, and I had that uncomfortable sensation when someone who's just gone through hell is feeling sorry for you.

She walked over to the large window where Chedran had stood before, curling a finger to beckon me to join her. The sun was setting, but there was still enough light for me to look down the slope of the orchards and past the walls of the estate to where the spellship now floated upon an ocean that hadn't existed when we'd arrived. Waves of pure shimmering onyx rose and fell, the ship bobbing up and down among them, anchored by whatever magic Sar'ephir had used to summon that shadowblack sea.

Ala'tris placed her hand on my shoulder as she pointed. 'You and I, Ferius, are about to board that galleon and sail through realms never before visited by any of our ancestors. I don't pretend to fully understand the Argosi ways, but tell me, sister, are we not on the precipice of a magnificent adventure, you and I?'

I've known since I was a little girl that the world can be a desert so parched it'll drink up your spirit soon as you set foot upon the sand. When I became an Argosi I learned to stop fearing that desert, because no matter how dry and empty it gets, if you look hard enough, you'll always find something unexpected blooming atop the next dune.

'Come on, sister,' I said, retrieving my pack in one hand and Conch – who'd managed to sleep through all my emotional turmoil – in the other. I headed for the door, winking at the guards waiting there with scowls on their faces. 'I've a hankering to see what kinds of fish swim in a shadowblack sea.'

29

Thresholds

The most treacherous crossing in any voyage is the one that sees you stepping out your front door. It seems a small thing, and most folks barely mark its passing, but think about it: that single step carries you not only towards your destination and the dangers it surely entails, but away from all that has kept you safe until now. More importantly, once over the threshold, you're no longer the person you were before. The familiar rhythms of your life, big and small, fade as you leave that version of yourself behind to become one with the path awaiting you.

'What are they doing?' Ala'tris asked, bemused by the sight unfolding before us. The deck of the spellship rocked beneath our feet, despite the fact that we were still on dry land right outside the walls of Colfax's estate. Sar'ephir stood behind us on the foredeck, conjuring that eerie black water that touched nothing around it save for the hull of the ship. Two hundred and eighty-seven Mahdek were filing up the gangway, lugging their meagre belongings with them. They needed no packs or bags, but instead used an art unique to their culture in which a single long length of rope could be ingeniously wound around every item, big and small, holding everything in place and culminating in two equal lengths that served as straps so they could carry all their possessions on their backs. 'I find something odd about the way your people are boarding the ship,' Ala'tris remarked. 'I can't quite place what it is.'

'They're not looking back.'

She came a little closer and watched their slow, patient progress down the orchard path and through the stone archway, with Colfax's troops and retainers waving goodbye or handing them little gifts for the voyage, finally walking up the gangplank, to find their sea legs on the deck. 'You're right. None of them are so much as glancing back at the estate. Do you suppose they weren't so well treated as we believed?'

'Colfax treated them fine.'

That fortress had been, for a scant handful of years, the safest and most comfortable home most of the Mahdek had ever known. It wasn't in their nature to look backwards though. No complaining, no weeping. Not even the kids shed a tear, just kept putting one foot in front of the other, trudging to wherever fate led them to next. That too was a talent of the Mahdek culture.

Supplies were being brought aboard, overseen by Colfax himself. Meats, cheeses, dried fruit, vegetables, sacks of rice and grain both for the voyage and those first dangerous weeks in a new land, where you don't know what you're going to find or whether you'll have to turn tail and scurry back; canvas and wooden poles for tents, tools of all kinds, crates of wool for making clothes and blankets for warmth. Colfax even allowed me bales of hay for Quadlopo. Amidst that cornucopia, it wasn't hard to slip in a few other, sealed crates that no one except for Stoika seemed to notice.

I left Ala'tris to join the old woman by the railing where she was supervising both the passengers and the loading of supplies, a task she'd made clear would be performed by her council, not the mages offering them passage.

242

'You planning on telling our hosts what you and Colfax are sneaking on board?' I asked.

Stoika's steely-grey eyes flicked to me, but only for a moment before returning to continue overseeing the loading. 'You were occupied with your thieving companion when those crates were being packed. Don't waste your breath trying to goad me into revealing their contents, child.'

Child. Funny how people reveal so much of themselves when they attach labels to others. Didn't need my arta loquit to hear Stoika's conviction that my generation was vain, irresponsible and utterly incapable of being entrusted with the future of the Mahdek, any more than I needed my arta precis to tell me what was in those crates.

'Only one type of cargo you'd bother keeping secret,' I said, and pointed to another of the sealed wooden boxes being stowed beneath a basket of cucumbers and rhubarb. 'Six foot long, three feet wide, two foot tall? I'm just making a rough calculation here, but that would be enough room for a dozen fire lances. Third of those same crates you've snuck below decks.' I waved to Colfax, who was on the ground supervising the work from there. 'Gitabrian fire lances aren't cheap. Thirty-six of them is a princely gift.'

'Gift?' Stoika spat over the side. 'A gift is given out of love or respect. No Daroman has ever felt either for a Mahdek.'

'Pity, then?'

Lips wrinkled as prunes twisted upwards in a self-satisfied smile. Apparently I'd finally revealed my ignorance. 'If you still believe in such a thing as pity, child, then you truly are pitiable.' Stoika turned to lean back against the railing, casual as if she'd lived at sea her whole life. 'Why do you suppose I consented to this voyage?'

I. Not *we* or *the council.* That hadn't been a slip of the tongue. Stoika wanted me to know that she was in charge. I turned and

243

rested against the railing as she had done, adopting that position so I could see what she did. The deck was rumbling with activity. People, animals and cargo were being shunted this way and that. The process was quick, efficient, yet somehow with a plodding, joyless rhythm. Interwoven between those thumps and bumps and rattles, however, were brief sparks of bustling excitement. Kievan was holding up one of the children to look out over the mystical black river upon which the ship floated as it awaited departure. Most of the adults not busy loading cargo had gone below already, yet I saw Remeny and several other teenagers exploring the deck or pestering Sar'ephir and the other Jan'Tep with questions.

Conch trotted over to me, excitedly wagging his little goat tail. Usually that made me laugh, but now I shooed him away. 'You don't believe this island will provide a future for the Mahdek at all, do you, Stoika? You only sanctioned this voyage because you knew Kievan and the others would run away again if you refused. Only this time, more would follow.'

Stoika's next words were cold and precise, the voice of a woman convinced of the world's cruelty and unwilling to pretend otherwise. 'Don't talk to me of the future, child. The Mahdek have none. We are less than three hundred souls, barely enough to continue as a race even if the Jan'Tep weren't intent on hunting us to extinction. Yet it is not our enemies who will destroy us in the end. It will be our own children.'

For an instant I wished I could see through Stoika's eyes, understand what she saw when she looked at Kievan and Remeny. 'You're really ready to blame the downfall of the Mahdek on your own kids?'

Stoika's upper lip curled, like the stupidity of my sentiment had filled her mouth with the foulest taste imaginable. 'I blame our ancestors who failed to recognise the avarice of the Jan'Tep

244

before it was too late. I blame the generations that followed for turning us into migrant farmworkers and tin-cup beggars. I blame the young for being so reckless, so disloyal and gullible, that they would seek to emulate one who rejected her own people, and in so doing force us to abandon the only safety left to us.' She pushed herself away from the railing and strode away, but not before saying one last thing to me. 'Most of all, Ferius Parfax, I blame you.'

The ear-splitting screech of the iron tracks underneath the gangplank being slid aboard preceded Ala'tris shouting for everyone to hang on. She, Gab'rel, Jir'dan and Ba'dari joined Sar'ephir on the foredeck, their tattooed bands gleaming so brightly they practically outshone the sun. That ceased to be an exaggeration when Sar'ephir raised her arms up high and spoke words I barely heard on a breeze that appeared out of nowhere.

The sky disappeared. The shadowblack river widened all around us, becoming an ocean that stretched to the horizon in every direction. There were moans and mutterings from a few of the passengers, and a few cheers from Kievan and the other runaways as the ship lurched forward, pulled along the onyx waves as if a perfect wind were carrying us along.

'Quite a sight, isn't it, Conch?' I asked, looking out over the rail at a world filled with shadow yet whose strange physics allowed us to clearly make out glinting black stars against a black sky arranged in constellations I'd never seen before.

The spire goat propped himself up on his back legs, front hoofs on my thigh as he waited impatiently for me to pick him up. 'Okay, fella,' I said, and lifted him onto my shoulder, where he balanced himself confidently and made quiet, inquisitive noises as he stared out at the mysterious vista before us. Me, I was watching Stoika prowl the deck like some spectre looking for someone to haunt.

Arissa's absence was beginning to take on a far more tangible urgency.

I reached up a hand to scratch Conch under his chin. 'I'm gonna need you to watch my back awhile, okay, fella? Because suddenly I don't feel so safe on this ship.'

Part 4

Sea of Graves

There is one disharmony card that an Argosi must never paint. A debt that cannot be repaid, for it must never be accrued. Have you guessed what forbidden image would adorn this outlawed card? Gaze into a pool of water, or the polished surface of a tin plate or steel blade. In that reflection lies the person whose mind you must never deceive, whose body you must never wound and whose spirit you must never desecrate.

Misfortune is a word without meaning to an Argosi. With our seven talents we can outwit any opponent, escape any trap, endure any hardship, so long as our mind, body and spirit act as one. When we dishonour that bond, even in the service of others, we abandon our path and cast ourselves . . . adrift.

30

The Onyx Ocean

The Argosi don't look back. We don't ponder what's been lost, because once you step in that particular quicksand you never come out. That's how I knew I was in trouble; I couldn't stop thinking about Arissa. Worse, I couldn't stop talking to her.

'What's the problem, Rat Girl? You made your choice, I made mine. Find some other gorgeous, brilliant, devil-may-care darling to fall in love with. You know it never would've worked out between us anyway, right?'

I'll say this for my imaginary Arissa: she was a lot more supportive of my decisions than the real one had ever been. Now, there's nothing wrong with seeking advice from your memories. I do it all the time (even if Durral's is mostly annoying rather than helpful). But that's not the same as looking backwards. That's bringing your past with you into the present. Completely different thing.

What I was doing those first few nights aboard the spellship, though? That was definitely looking backwards, obsessing over the what-ifs and why-nots that had gotten me to this lonely spot near the bow of the galleon, staring out into the darkness ahead, blind to the shadows gathering all around me.

I must've known something was wrong . . . Somewhere inside that part of my brain where my arta precis and loquit, tuco and siva, eres and forteize, even my crazy arta valar, all meld together into a singular lens through which an Argosi sees the world . . . I knew. I must've known. Why else did I keep staring at the little golden-haired girl with her whole life ahead of her, and the ageing stoop-backed man who already had one foot in the grave, along with all the other Mahdek aboard that galleon. I kept seeing the same thing in all their faces . . . a shadow to which I couldn't put a name. I should've searched harder.

Six nights we sailed that shadowblack sea. You can't really think in terms of 'days' when journeying through a realm without colour. And yet, the nether-light shining down from pitch-black stars made the world glitter a thousand shades of onyx. The ocean swells were like dunes of black volcanic glass, rising and falling in a mesmerising rhythm. The galleon had taken on the inversions of this place, the hull now ebony, the once-white sails the black of a raven's wing.

When first we'd departed, our skin, eyes, hair and garments still appeared to match the colours of the world we'd left behind. Ala'tris had explained that this was an illusion: a trick of our minds transposing what we expected to see overtop what our eyes actually perceived. She was right too, because by the third night we began to see each other as shadows, our faces, our clothes, even the strands of our hair were as detailed and distinctive as ever, only now painted from a palette of vivid blacks.

The weirdest part, though? My horse.

You don't think much about a person's eye colour or skin tone once you know them, but a brown horse is always supposed to be brown, damn it. Something about Quadlopo's hide being black as a crow's butt disturbed the hells out of me.

'Not your fault, buddy,' I said to him when he caught me staring and neighed his irritation. Despite the eeriness of our environment, he preferred remaining up on the poop deck at the stern of the ship. Ala'tris asked me if this was because it was the highest part of the deck and he felt safer there. My own theory was that he just liked the name 'poop deck' because it reminded him of his favourite activity, which he engaged in frequently as revenge for my having dragged him to yet another place where no sensible horse would venture. 'I think you look dashing all in black like that. Maybe when we return to the continent, I'll dye your entire hide black as coal permanently. How's that sound?'

As I turned away, I heard him give an annoyed and threatening snort, followed immediately by an unpleasant and all too familiar plopping sound. Whatever the shadowblack did with light, it failed to do with odours; Quadlopo's poop stank just as bad here as it did anywhere else. He whinnied in a way that suggested he was mighty pleased with himself.

Durral, who always had just as troubled a relationship with Quadlopo as I seemed condemned to suffer, insisted that an Argosi treated a horse with kindness and respect. When said horse refused to return the favour, however . . .

'What's that, old pal?' I asked, grabbing the shovel for what seemed like the twentieth time that night. 'My arta loquit must be failing me. Tell you what, let's make it easy. If you *want* me to dye your coat black when we get back, just poop one more time on this deck right after I clean this latest mess up. If you'd like me to shave your hair clean off, on the other hand, poop twice.'

Quadlopo's tail twitched. He showed me his teeth. I showed him mine.

'Go on, you cantankerous beast. Test me. I dare you.'

That big ornery head of his swivelled out over the railing to stare at the onyx ocean again. Apparently I was being dismissed.

'Ferius, Ferius!' a young voice called out. Remeny was summoning me from the main deck.

'What's got you barking like a puppy?' I asked, though I couldn't keep the smile from my face at the sight of him practically jumping out of his shoes as he waited for me to climb down from the poop deck. The spell warrant was still there on his forehead, but it no longer troubled him. In fact he seemed to delight in following Ala'tris around, peppering her with questions about Jan'Tep magic.

'Sorry,' he said, 'it's just that the Lady Mage asked to see you on the forecastle.'

'The Lady Mage' was the title he'd given Ala'tris for reasons she could no more fathom than his insistence on opening doors for her or clearing ropes out of the way wherever she went. The rest of us weren't quite so blind to a twelve-year-old boy's obvious crush.

'Well, if the "Lady Mage" wants to see me,' I said, ruffling his hair, 'then far be it from a lowly Argosi card player to keep such a grand dame waiting.'

My breath froze in my lungs when I noticed Remeny wasn't alone. We could see each other clear as ever here, but sometimes you just didn't notice people unless they spoke or moved. It took me a second to recognise the chubby-faced little girl who'd been bouncing on Chedran's lap back at the mining barracks tagging along after Remeny. Her curls, golden then, were now, well, black. Even so, something else about her struck me as darker than before.

'You okay, darlin'?' I asked, kneeling down in front of her. 'You keep making that goofy-looking face and it might get stuck that way.'

Remeny laughed nervously. The girl didn't laugh at all. She stared back into my face but showed no interest in meeting my eyes. 'Are you dead?' she asked.

I took her hand and placed it over my heart. 'Do I feel dead?'

'No.'

254

'Then I guess I'm alive.'

She nodded, then slid her hand away. 'That's what I thought.'

'Well, good th—'

'I think I might be dead.'

I reached out to stroke her cheek, but she drew back into the shadows by the railing. 'Don't be silly, sweetheart. You're not dea—'

'Ferius!' Ala'tris called out, crossing the deck towards us. 'I need to speak with you.'

'I delivered your message,' Remeny said to his Lady Mage, sounding a touch hurt at not being trusted with his vitally important mission.

'Do me a favour, will you?' I asked him. Stepping over to the railing, I took the girl's hand before she could shy away and placed it in Remeny's. 'Take her below decks. Do you know her parents?'

'They reside in Gitabria.'

The Mahdek don't tend to speak of people as being dead, especially not around children. Instead they'll refer to them as residing in this place or that place, which happens to be wherever they died.

'She has a great-uncle though,' Remeny said. 'Do you want me to bring her to him?'

'Take her straight there, okay? Tell him . . . tell him I'll come down in a while to have a chat.'

Most of the Mahdek never came up on deck. They stayed below, cooking meals or mending clothes, sharing knowledge and skills that might be needed on the island or just singing songs to each other. All the things that made the hours pass as if this were merely an especially long night rather than a realm so foreign it might well be the land of the dead.

Ala'tris touched my shoulder, a gesture of urgency rather than familiarity. 'Ferius, I'm sorry, but Sar'ephir awaits us on the forecastle. There's a . . . matter of some importance that we need to discuss.'

'I'm coming,' I said, then turned briefly to Remeny and the girl. 'Go on below and find yourselves something sweet. A reward for being the best darned messengers on this whole ship.'

Remeny shot me a big, mischievous grin. The cherubic little girl saw it and then smiled up at me too, matching him tooth for tooth, as if her cryptic words of a moment ago had been a silly prank and suddenly everything was okay again.

That was the clue I missed.

31

Troubled Waters

Sar'ephir's graceful yet daunting figure dominated the forecastle. Her previously beige robes, now a rich sable that glinted as if woven from tiny grains of onyx sand, fluttered in a wind that touched no one but her. With her sleeveless, tightly muscled arms outstretched and facing away from us, she could've been mistaken for a living ship's figurehead. The thick make-up that had covered her scalp was gone, the winding lines that swirled like snakes upon her skull revealed for all to see as she guided our ship through the shadowblack.

'It isn't her fault,' Ala'tris said quickly, as if forestalling some anticipated revulsion on my part. 'The markings appear on those attuned to the shadowblack when they're young, and grow with the years.'

'I'm not Jan'Tep,' I reminded her. 'To me, she looks . . . majestic.'

'Does it matter what she looks like to you, Ferius?' Enna would've asked, reminding me that an Argosi has to see the world not only through our own eyes but through those of others. It didn't do Sar'ephir one lick of good whether I thought her markings were beautiful. What mattered was how her own people saw them.

'*Vile. Disgusting. Despicable,*' I thought, imagining myself a Jan'Tep lord magus or maybe even one of Sar'ephir's parents. '*All the good in our people, all the sacrifices we make to keep ourselves pure, and look at this vile thing you've become. Why would you allow yourself to live when your very existence threatens all those you profess to love?'*

'Ferius?' Ala'tris asked.

I'd meant to snap myself out of it, but when I turned to Ala'tris, she who was the epitome of the perfect young Jan'Tep mage, I caught the tightness around her upper lip that wanted badly to curl into a sneer. I saw too the lines on her usually smooth brow that spoke of concern for her friend's well-being and shame in her own prejudices. Durral always said that it was within the cracks of a person's innate goodness that we can find their decency – something none of us are born with but which is the more worthy pursuit of our shared humanity.

'You said there was a problem?' I asked.

Ala'tris nodded and walked up the stairs to the forecastle ahead of me. But before she reached the top, she stumbled, landing hard on her knees. I took the first two steps then vaulted the rest to help her up.

'Clumsy of me,' she said, attempting to deflect my concern with a frail laugh. As soon as she was back on her feet, she tried to take her hand back. I didn't let her. 'Ferius, please, it was just the rolling of the ship. You can let me go.'

'Ain't holding you that tight, sister. One good yank should do the trick.'

'You're being childish!'

I squeezed her hand, not hard, just enough to feel how feeble her attempts at pulling away were, and the tremors she was trying to conceal. 'You didn't trip because of bad sea legs. You tripped because you're not accustomed to the muscles in your legs being so weak. You're sick.' I glanced around at the lower decks. Hardly

258

anyone had come up here in the past two days. That wasn't unusual for the passengers, but the crew? I released Ala'tris's hand. 'Haven't seen much of Jir'dan or Gab'rel or Ba'dari lately. They all catch the same cold?'

'I told you, it's nothing.' She rubbed at her fingers as if I'd bruised them, but I saw that for the ruse it was – meant to distract me from pursuing this further.

'How about you, Sar'ephir?' I asked our navigator. 'You feelin' just dandy too?'

Her skin had been much darker than mine on the continent and even here, where everything was black, that was somehow still true. But when she turned I saw beads of sweat glistening like oil down her forehead. She was smiling, like always, but the upturned line of her lips was tighter now. Determined. Defiant. 'Tell her,' she said to Ala'tris. 'You know the Argosi will keep prying until she finds out.'

Six nights we'd been at sea. Ala'tris had promised the journey would take less than a week, and had repeated that promise several times. I'd assumed she'd been trying to reassure the Mahdek, who were naturally anxious about the duration of the voyage. Looking back, it now seemed to me her gaze had flickered to the members of her own coven just as often.

Gently I took her forearm and raised it parallel with the deck, the fabric of her sleeve soft to my touch. Beneath that gossamer silk, the sigils of three of her tattooed bands had lost their lustre, looking more like patterns of necrotised flesh than metallic inks that could summon the awesome magics of her people. 'The shadowblack is making all of you sick, isn't it?'

Ala'tris nodded, and a brittle, wry smile came to her lips. 'One of the reasons why the island will be an ideal home for the Mahdek.' She squeezed her fist and closed her eyes. A flash of pain crossed

259

her features before the sigils illuminated feebly. Gold, crimson and purple. The only true colours I'd seen since we'd set sail from the continent: a light sparked not by the physical laws of this realm, but drawn from a Jan'Tep oasis far, far away. 'The stronger a mage's connection to the veins of raw mystical ore beneath the oases – what we call the *Jan* – the greater the strain we endure inside the shadowblack.'

'What about you?' I asked Sar'ephir.

The galleon slowed, as if whatever invisible wind propelled us through the onyx ocean had dropped. The big woman reached a hand up to the back of her head and tapped a finger against one of the swirling bands on her shorn scalp. 'My shadowblack markings are more potent than ever. My other sigils however . . .' She sparked the gold band for sand magic on her forearm and winced. 'It's a bit like making passionate love while suffering a blinding headache.' Turning back to the bow, she raised both arms wide and the ship lurched forward. 'Now –' she turned to Ala'tris – 'tell the Argosi the bad news.'

'We . . . we are not where we should be,' Ala'tris admitted. She wouldn't meet my eyes.

'We're lost?' I glanced out over the port-side railing. The seemingly endless onyx ocean offered no landmarks of any kind. Then I looked up at the pitch-black stars of constellations which had changed any number of times since our departure, but never in a way that would allow someone to plot a course. 'I assumed you guys had some sort of hocus-pocus navigational spell or someth—'

'We're not lost,' Ala'tris retorted angrily. 'It's more that . . .' She swore under her breath. I only know a little Jan'Tep, so the finer points of their vulgarity are beyond me. 'You wouldn't understand, Ferius.'

She was wrong though; I understood perfectly.

Durral Brown was reputed to have the finest arta loquit of any Argosi living, and even he confessed mine might be better. Part of it was my childhood as a refugee, going from place to place with my clan, having to learn all the different ways a person's words might reveal genuine pity or disguise terrible cruelty. Those skills had been honed by subsequent years contending with the cursed sigils branded around my neck that could turn anyone's affection to me into murderous hate. Not a pleasant way to grow up, but damned good preparation for learning the Argosi talent of arta loquit.

Every word Ala'tris had spoken, every inflection in her tone, every hesitation, were all part of what she didn't want to say.

'We're not where we should be.'

No mention of travelling too slow or too fast, or even heading in the wrong direction. Just that we weren't where we should be – like it wasn't our course that was wrong, but the map itself.

'We're not lost. It's more that . . .'

The obvious correlate of declaring that we weren't lost, coming from someone like Ala'tris who's prone to educating everyone around her, would be to follow up with a specific reference to our location. She hadn't though; she'd equivocated instead with 'It's more that . . .' She'd trailed off because she couldn't find the words, which suggested the concept of 'location' somehow didn't apply to our current situation.

And the coup de grace: 'You wouldn't understand.'

The statement was inherently denigrating, which wasn't her style – especially towards me. Despite our radically different vocations, Ala'tris saw me an equal, almost a sister, so when she claimed I wouldn't understand what was happening, what she really meant was that she didn't understand it.

261

Which left me with the only logical conclusion: when you're not where you should be, but you're not lost, and no amount of magical knowledge can tell you where you *are*, then the problem isn't that you're in the wrong place. The problem is that you're not anywhere.

Ta-da. Where are you, Arissa, when I'm being so darned impressive?

I crossed the deck of the forecastle to stand next to Sar'ephir. The onyx waves rose and fell ahead of us like magnificent sculptures being moulded then flattened by unseen hands. 'That's not really an ocean, is it?'

The strain in her smile eased up a little. 'No, it's not.'

I shifted my weight to my right heel, made a full three-hundred-and-sixty-degree turn. 'The ship's not really moving then, either.' I returned to where I began and then pointed up at the constellations in the sky. 'You're . . . moving space around us, right?'

The tall, broad-shouldered woman pursed her lips in a way I found oddly charming. 'It is more that . . . we're all refashioning the space the galleon occupies until that space becomes more and more like the destination we require.'

'The destination that contains the island.'

She nodded.

'So we're not sailing to the island at all. We're . . . sailing the island to us. Only it's not getting any closer and you can't bring it to us.' Ala'tris had come up behind me. I turned to her. 'You never would've risked so many lives if you hadn't been absolutely sure you could pull this off. You've tested this journey before, you and your coven. The only thing that's changed—' I held up a finger to keep her from interrupting.

Sar'ephir wasn't what you'd call a talker, and hardly ever used unnecessary words. She could've simply said, '*We're shifting the space we occupy*,' but instead she'd said, '*We're all shifting the space we occupy.* That innocent little 'all' was the missing piece Ala'tris hadn't factored into her equations when she'd set us off on this journey into the shadowblack.

'The Mahdek . . .' I began, my mind racing, struggling to catch up with this bizarre phenomenon of navigating by shaping the space around oneself through spells guided by thoughts. *Thoughts.* That was the answer. 'Two hundred and eighty-seven Mahdek on this ship compared with five Jan'Tép. It's *their* thoughts, their *feelings*, that are affecting where we are. That's why we're not lost, yet not where we're supposed to be.'

Ala'tris nodded. She looked almost relieved at the look of confusion on my face. 'The spell draws on the caster's ability to envision a specific pattern of complex esoteric geometries. Sar'ephir and myself are capable of doing so, but Jir'dan', Gab'rel and Ba'dari cannot. In and of itself, this does not hamper our efforts because—'

'Having three people who don't know how to row the boat isn't a problem, so long as the two who *can* row the boat are strong enough.'

She chuckled, shaking her head at me. 'You do have a way of simplifying incredibly sophisticated metaphysical phenomena, Ferius Parfax.'

'Yeah, my talent for dumbing things down is legendary. So what's the problem? All those bodies making it too heavy?'

'That's not it. Weight is an almost irrelevant concept within the shadowblack. It's your people's spirits. Somehow they're . . .' Frustration sharpened her tone, though it was directed more at herself than anyone else. 'I don't understand how this can be!'

I found my hand drifting to the pocket of my waistcoat that contained my deck of ruses. Cards depicting different ways an individual without magic can trick their way out of a mage's spells. None of those cards described this particular situation, but many of those schemes relied on the fact that every Jan'Tep spell requires

263

an anchor, and more often than not, that anchor is the mind of the victim. That's why the Argosi are so good at slipping magical bindings: we spend our lives training our minds to work in twisty, turny ways, which makes it difficult for mages to anchor their spells to our thoughts. The Mahdek . . . well, they may not study the Argosi ways, but that doesn't mean their minds work like everyone else's.

'My people can't envision destinations any more,' I said softly. There was a heartbreaking simplicity to why the spellship had become dead in the water. 'You can't arrive at a place if the concept of arrival, of homecoming, has no meaning.'

'What are you talking about?' Ala'tris asked. The ship settled once more as Sar'ephir's arms dropped by her sides, her futile spell fading into the nothingness all around us. The two of them stared at me, waiting for an explanation.

'You wouldn't underst—' I stopped myself, the irony not quite lost on me of my instinctive prejudice that these two privileged Jan'Tep mages couldn't possibly appreciate how deeply ran the differences between them and their passengers. 'You both saw how fast the Mahdek picked up and left from that Daroman marshal's fortress. Two hundred and eighty-seven refugees, born into that life, all walking away from a place of comfort and safety into the unknown. No other people could do that.'

Ala'tris still looked confused, but Sar'ephir got it at once. 'The Mahdek haven't experienced permanence for hundreds of years. They perceive all places as temporary pauses in an endless journey. They can speak nostalgically of their former territory, even fight for a new one, but they cannot envision . . .' The last word came out as nothing but a sigh: 'Home.'

Ala'tris turned towards the railing, looking out over the black water that wasn't water in this place that wasn't a place. When she spoke, it was in a whisper that was quickly lost in the shadows, but I saw her lips move, and heard the shame in her words. 'There's no such thing as a destination in the mind of someone who's never allowed to remain anywhere.'

Sar'ephir took a more practical view, straightening her shoulders as if readying herself for battle. 'This emotional paralysis afflicting the passengers explains why the ship cannot shift the space around its hull, and why the constellations in the sky keep changing without ever holding their position.' She wiped beads of black sweat from her brow. 'No wonder it feels as if I'm trying to push a galleon through quicksand that only hardens with every inch.'

I followed her gaze over the bow. Quicksand was the wrong word for the way the onyx waves no longer moved at all. Clay, maybe, or concrete. Something more pernicious started to worm its way into my thoughts: if Sar'ephir's attempts to sail us through the shadowblack were being impeded by the hopelessness of the passengers, and the space the galleon occupied was beginning to reflect their anguish, then what would all that hardening despair be doing to the Mahdek?

And there it was. The peril I'd missed in the darkness gathering all around us. I leaped from the forecastle, racing across the deck towards a tragedy I couldn't yet see but knew deep in my bones was already taking place.

'Someone stop her! Someone stop—'

But I didn't know her name. Only her face. The face of a little girl smiling up at me because she knew that's what was expected of her. But it hadn't been her smile; it was Remeny's. She couldn't remember her own smile because she'd lost all sense of who she was – because she was convinced she was already dead.

I can run fast when I need to. Matter of fact, on a good day, I can . . . But there are no days in the shadowblack, only a single endless night, and this one that wasn't good at all.

The child whose joyous innocence had once been so potent as to melt Chedran's cold heart was perched atop the railing when I found her. Remeny lay unconscious on the deck below, black blood staining black hair, a black rock discarded next to him. The girl heard me screaming for her, calling out to her, but never saying her name because I hadn't bothered to learn it. Maybe that's why she said, 'It's okay. I'm already dead.'

Despite its name, the onyx ocean wasn't made of water. I guess that's why I never heard a splash.

32

Overboard

Spray glistened off the railing, a shimmering of black droplets beautiful as the night sky, deadly as raw, liquified despair poured down your throat. The beads that landed on my face and arms seeped into my skin, filling me with the morbid certainty that my time was done, draining me of hope for a future worth living.

'It's good, isn't it?' asked an old man a few feet to my left. He was pushing himself awkwardly up onto the railing, looking out into the dread sea where the little girl had disappeared beneath the onyx swell. Her great-uncle, I knew, just by the look of him, and the placid, fatalistic way he'd made the word *good* mean *proper*. Resigned acceptance of the inevitable slithered its way into my own thoughts as I mouthed that same word with that same awful meaning. 'She'll be with her parents now, my niece and her husband,' he went on, one knee on the railing as he awkwardly yanked the trouser leg of the other to get it over. 'We'll all be together.'

'No,' I said, but it wasn't a bold, unyielding 'no' that could deny his macabre 'good', but instead a whining, pitiful moan that asked, *'Why me? Why must I endure this?'*

Like a drunk, I stumbled towards the railing, hand reaching out to grab hold of the back of the man's tattered coat. Even in this,

I was too feeble, too slow. My fingers barely stroked the frayed wool before the old man plunged into the shadowblack depths. The last thing I saw of him was the smile on his face, devoid of any joy, longing only for oblivion. He found it too, disappearing beneath the onyx depths to leave behind not so much as froth in his wake.

'*Kid, don't let th*—' Durral's voice was so quiet it wasn't even a memory any more. More like the last gasp of a dying animal.

A strange envy came over me. What right did this old codger have to meet his end before me? What was so special about his misery compared to mine? I'd lost my parents as a child, my entire clan before I'd even chosen a name. I'd been tortured and tormented by Jan'Tep mages, faced every kind of death imaginable. Even now, the madness of the Red Scream whispered its destructive verses in my ears in an endless urging to utter them aloud, spread them to every living soul. If anyone had a right to tumble headlong into oblivion, it was me.

I slumped over the railing, drawing on the last remains of my arta forteize to give me the strength to push myself over.

No! cried a voice inside my head. This was no self-pitying whimper, but a rebellious clarion call to resistance. Too bad it hadn't come from me.

'*You belong to us!*' the Scarlet Verses screeched at me, clawing at my despair, chewing on those dark thoughts as if they could grind them into nothingness. '*You cannot die, that-which-once-called-itself-Ferius! Not until you have freed us! Not until*—'

The shadows settling over me like a burial shroud quieted the verses at last. The silence was . . . lovely. How long had it been since my thoughts were free of those nagging voices? Durral dragging me back to my path with his convoluted, indecipherable sayings; Enna setting me straight whenever my own doubts twisted me in knots; even Arissa lately, telling me to trust my gut when all that ever did was make me want to race back to the continent and find her again. My head's always been a mess of wayward recollections, especially after the Jan'Tep spell that had shattered my memories into a thousand shards of glass. The Scarlet Verses had made it even worse. All those memories, those insistent echoes, telling me what to do, what not to do. Now, though? Silence. Sweet, soothing silence. No more duty, no more debts.

'Oblivion is just another word for absolution,' I murmured, feeling the old man's smile come to my lips. That's what he'd been trying to say as he'd sunk beneath the black waves.

The ebony boards of the deck rumbled beneath my feet. A slow, plodding stampede of Mahdek were coming up from below. On each of their faces I saw that same resigned weariness that had first dulled the eyes of the golden-haired little girl: the sublime certainty that the world had no place for her. Only here, in this empty landscape sculpted from our own docility, had we finally found a place we belonged.

Two hundred and eighty-seven brittle spirits flickered faintly within two hundred and eighty-seven exhausted bodies. Two hundred and eighty-eight counting me.

The last remnants of my people trudged to the railing, each ready to inscribe the end of their own tragic tale onto the onyx ocean. The waves had stilled, yet the sea level had risen higher up the hull. The shadowblack sea bloated as if to make room for all of us to drown beneath its surface.

I shoved a few of the others back, reasoning that it wasn't their turn yet. It was mine. I'd *earned* the silence, *paid* for my shot at oblivion, at absolution. Nobody was taking that away from me. I accomplished nothing though; the others just grumbled as they shuffled around me to get to the railing. I turned, horrified to watch

269

as they tumbled over the side, stealing all that precious emptiness for themselves.

I stopped fighting and instead set my foot on the bottom rail to push myself up and over. In death, as in life, sometimes you gotta make do with what you get.

'Ferius, get away from the railing!' Ala'tris shouted. That girl sure could sound imperious when she was in a snit. Her footsteps thundered across the deck, only to falter as she tripped and fell. More of her Jan'Tep swearing with its lilting, almost sing-song melody. Funny how swearing always seems to have the quality of being both guttural and musical at the same time.

'Hmm?' I asked. Someone had whispered to me.

'Can't hear you,' I muttered, after it happened again. Some nonsense about . . . swearing? Maybe I was just remembering something from long ago. Durral had a peculiar obsession with swearing.

'Swear for me, kid,' he urged me.

'You know Enna hates it when I use vulgar language, Pappy.'

'That's just cos you're no good at it. Come on, kid, give me a good one. Something real nasty like what that Jan'Tep girl's spitting out.'

Ala'tris was indeed swearing her head off, lost in the crush of Mahdek passengers making their slow, steady progress towards oblivion. Jir'dan and the rest of the coven had come up on deck too. They were fighting to free Ala'tris from the swell of bodies, but she was packed in too tight. I saw glimmers of Jan'Tep sigils as they tried to cast their spells, but those sparks died almost instantly. Their magic was too weak here, in this ruined place to which Sar'ephir's shadow magic and my people's fatalism had unwittingly brought us.

Again I tried to push through the others, to get over the railing. The spellship had become landlocked. What had been an onyx

270

ocean had solidified into a flat, unmoving black landscape. The Mahdek who fell over the side landed on their backs, arms crossed over their chests in repose. An arch of pure obsidian rose up behind each body: an ancient Mahdek funerary custom. The grieving were meant to kneel on one side of the arch, from where they would speak to their dead relatives, listening for whispers from the other side that never came.

The bodies were sinking ever so slowly beneath the surface. Soon the only thing left of the last Mahdek families would be a field of black arches. Once, long ago, my people had built grand cities that flowed within and around forests and mountainsides. This empty necropolis would be the final piece of Mahdek architecture ever created . . .

. . . and still I couldn't bring myself to care. Though I hadn't yet made it over the side, I was being pulled under just the same.

'You did this. You brought us to our fate,' Stoika said from behind me.

The cold finality of her verdict shook me enough to make me turn to face her, but it was Chedran I saw, walking slowly towards the railing. His brow was furrowed as if he was confounded by his own smile – the same one I wore, that we all wore. Beads of black sweat were dripping down his forehead, his body's last rebellion against the oblivion to which his feet were inexorably dragging him. Stoika was behind him, shuffling closer, though she seemed both more resistant to the call of the void and yet somehow more accepting of it.

'Come, child,' she said, that same corpse's smile coming to her lips as she held out a hand to me. 'It was always going to end this way. Our doom was coming soon enough. What difference would a few more years of shaking our fists and swearing at the sky have done?'

Swearing at the sky. Why did that sound familiar?

271

Swearing. *Swearing*. Why did I keep thinking about swearing?

I turned back to the port-side railing, eager to get myself overboard and colonise my own private patch of emptiness in the necropolis that was rising steadily atop the onyx surface hardening around the ship's hull. Stoika was right: this was our new homeland.

'Ferius, for the sake of your ancestors and mine, stop this madness!' Ala'tris screamed. She was so busy berating me that she'd let herself get swept to the railing. Fitting, I supposed, since she was the only Jan'Tep I'd ever met who seemed like it wouldn't trouble her none to be buried among a bunch of Mahdek refugees.

She was going to need to change her attitude though. She elbowed a placid-faced elderly lady right in the nose, swearing all the while. First in Jan'Tep, then in Daroman – the one language that everyone on the continent knew. 'Snap out of it, you stupid bi—' That last nasty slur was cut off as Ala'tris was crushed in the press of suicidal bodies.

My old Daroman comportment instructor, Master Phinus, would've tut-tutted Ala'tris something fierce for uttering that particular word. Not a proper word for young ladies to use, no, sir.

'Go on, kid.' Durral's frontier drawl seemed to be drifting towards me from far, far away. '*Live a little, or, if you can't be bothered to live, die like a damned Argosi! Swear up a storm! Swear until you're so blue in the face, my darling, daring girl, that you'll blaze like a sapphire against all this darkness!*'

Guess that was supposed to sound inspiring. Didn't do the trick though – not when I'd finally got me a decent spot at the railing. I swung my left leg over. '*Enna says any Argosi who has to go around swearing hasn't learned their arta loquit, Pappy.*'

Looking out at the necropolis, I saw a lovely spot just the right size. Not so small that I'd feel cramped, but not so big that I'd ever feel lonely again.

'Ain't talkin' about no arta loquit, kid,' Durral blustered, though he was too far away now to matter.

Still, though, I'd hate to die with such an obvious question rattling around in my head. 'Of course it's arta loquit,' I insisted, bringing my other leg over the railing. Looked pretty far down from here. The shadowblack sea had frozen to a field of onyx ice that would surely break both my legs when I landed. No problem though; I'd just need to do some fast crawling to get to my spot before anyone else took it. I could already see my own obsidian arch rising up from the black ice, beckoning for me to lie down in front of it, cross my arms and seep into the onyx where I'd never have to deal with Durral Brown's crap again.

Except . . .

'Damn it, Pappy, if swearing ain't arta loquit, then what the hells is it? Swearing is a form of language, and the understanding of languages is part of eloquence.'

'Not when you're staring into the void!' Durral countered.

Smug bastard. I could feel his smirk all the way from here, and it wasn't the peaceful, accepting smile on the face of the people around me. No, this was his own trademark grin, full of bluster, mirth and . . . what was the other thing? I couldn't recall, and he wasn't making it easy, badgering me like that.

'When everything is lost, kid, and every ounce of your mind and body have given up on you, when fate itself looms over, hands outstretched to keep you from taking another step, that's when you tell fate to – Well, I sure as hells ain't gonna say the word myself. Enna might be listening. Now, where was I again?'

My buttocks were resting on the railing, my feet dangling over the side. All I needed to do was let go and this would finally be over. In fact, if I just sat here a few more seconds, somebody would surely give me a helpful shove soon enough.

273

I'd never have to hear Durral Brown's annoying voice in my head ever again.

'You were saying something about fate, Pappy?'

'Right, right. Fate. Worst invention anybody every came up with. Probably one of them Gitabrian contraptioneers with more brains than sense. Anyhow, kid, when it's all over and there's no escape, when the four ways have failed you and your will is gone, that's when you swear right in fate's pretty little face. And when you do that, Ferius Parfax, when you swear in that moment? That ain't arta loquit any more. That's arta—'

The word slipped out between my lips like the last bubbles from a drowning man's mouth. 'Valar,' I muttered.

'What's that, kid?'

I repeated the word, a little more distinctly – not that any of the bodies tumbling over the side of the galleon to take up their graves in the necropolis were listening. 'Swearing in the face of certain doom isn't arta loquit. It's arta valar.'

Daring.

Boldness.

Reckless, devils-may-care, gods-damned swagger.

My personal favourite.

Five things happened then, each one stranger than the others, and pretty much all at once. The timing matters though, so let's get it right.

First, my twisted memory of Durral's teachings shook me loose from the smothering acquiescence that had brought me to the precipice of my own death.

Second, a bunch of my fellow Mahdek, understandingly impatient for their own peaceful descent into oblivion, rammed into me from behind and accidentally shoved me over the side.

Third . . . well, that one shouldn't have mattered much at a time like this, but the third thing was, I swore. I mean, I really *swore*.

Think of the worst swear word you know. I'm talking the foulest, most vulgar, entirely unacceptable-to-your-comportment-instructor's-teachings epithet you can imagine. Go on – is that *really* the most obscene thing you can come up with? Pretty sure that, as I felt myself fall into the abyss, having snapped out of that fatalist fog two seconds too late to do me any good, I became the world's undisputed swearing champion.

Not a bad way to end, if you're an Argosi.

Oh, and the fourth and fifth things that happened almost, but not quite, at that same moment? Those were miracles. And as we all know, miracles almost always come on four legs.

33

Miracles

Let me be precise: the sound-for-which-there's-no-name probably came right *before* someone knocked me over the railing and I started swearing my head off. It's just that I only noticed it after I had begun to fall towards the black abyss waiting to swallow me whole.

But let's get to that sound – that raucous, cacophonous, discordant, unmelodious, gorgeous, gods-damned noise. Because, friend, *that* sound, no matter how big the world gets or how many centuries go by, only ever occurred once in history, and it was . . . I can't find the word. I'll get there though, I promise.

Neighing is the wrong word. A neigh couldn't describe that sound any more than the patter of a raindrop could be confused for a thunderstorm. Neighs are lilting and musical, sometimes even playful. There was nothing playful about *this* infernal, skull-shattering racket. But okay, since no language has yet been invented to describe this particular sound, let's start with what we've got: take some of that neighing, make it loud as hells, then deepen it. Lower the pitch. No, lower than that. I'm talking belly-deep fury that sparks a fuse dangling off that neigh until the whole thing explodes like the wrath of every god forgotten by their followers. The unyielding, soul-rending battle cry of a one-horse army. Now, underneath that roar, add the pounding of four hoofs as they thunder across the deck, hammering sturdy wood planks into pulp.

Think you can hear the sound yet? Because, friend, you ain't heard nothing yet.

If 'neighing' is too timid to encompass the first part, then 'braying' is positively timid compared to the incandescent honk riding on top of it – both figuratively *and* literally. This was the trumpet's blare of a war being declared on anyone and anything that got in the way of the chimeric beast that, as I turned during my fall in a flailing bid to grab the railing, was currently leaping over the side to my rescue.

Quadlopo, the most placid, apathetic horse ever born, had bounded over the crowd of passengers rushing to their respective oblivions with such unbridled determination that, in the paradoxical nether-space of the shadowblack, he somehow caught up to me. On his rump, facing back towards the ship and with his little spire goat belly bloated to bursting, was Conch.

Now came the punctuation to all those other pieces of the sound-for-which-there-is-no-name: the loudest belch in all recorded history. What Conch's spontaneous gastric emission lacked in dignity, it more than made up for in potency as he spewed enough spire goat gas to smother the entire mob in a billowing black cloud tinged with just a touch of defiant green.

Like I said, a miracle.

I wasn't entirely passive during all this, you understand. In the split second between Quadlopo's leap and our landing, my arms instinctively grabbed hold of his neck. I'd like to believe that I then swung my legs across his back, but I suspect it was more the way he contorted himself under me than any acrobatics on my part. Either way, by the time his hoofs struck the black ice of the necropolis, I was mounted on my horse, shaking like a leaf, my eyes so wide they couldn't focus on anything. So confounded was I by the strangeness of existence that all I could do was play that bizarre sound over and over in my head until, finally, I found its name. I even managed to say it out loud.

'Glorious.'

Next thing I knew, the smaller hoofs of my other four-footed hero settled on my shoulder, balancing with far more confidence than one would expect. Then again, he *is* a spire goat. I turned my head to glance up at the galleon trapped in the onyx ice. Beyond the railing, the crowd of Mahdek who'd been lurching towards their doom were now tumbling to the deck, one by one. Thump. Thump. Thump. Thump.

Conch gave a smug grunt of satisfaction with his handiwork.

'Proud of yourself, little fella?'

Quadlopo neighed at me. This time it was his regular, 'Ferius, why are you the dumbest human who ever saddled up a horse and how many more times are you expecting me to rescue you from your own stupidity?' sort of neigh.

I tried to compose a witty reply, but I was having trouble keeping myself from sliding off his back and falling to the onyx from which, I was pretty sure, I would never rise again. Sure, I'd shaken off some of the black fog of despair that had sent me lumbering towards oblivion moments ago, but I was still staring out at a shadowy necropolis where dozens of Mahdek lay beneath their death arches, slowly sinking into the black ice. Soon the effects of Conch's fumes would dissipate and the passengers on deck would reawaken. After that things would likely get real ugly, real fast.

That's the second problem, I thought, squeezing my legs around Quadlopo's sides for balance. *First problem is getting yourself together, Ferius.*

'*Thing about arta forteize, kid, is th*—'

'I don't need a lecture on arta forteize, Pappy. Just gimme a second here.'

Resilience comes not from ignoring pain or pretending you're not exhausted. It comes from building trust between your mind, your body and your emotions so you can align them to a single purpose. Right now, mine were running off in all different directions.

When your head is full of clamouring thoughts, breathe in emptiness so you can breathe out the stupid.

That was one of mine, not Durral's. Sometimes I forget that no matter how wise the maetri, every teysan must walk their own path, and in doing so chart their own Argosi ways.

I breathed in deep, and though I wasn't even sure that whatever existed in this strange place of shadows could be called air, I let it fill me up until there wasn't any room for idle ruminations about death, doom and the cruel misfortune of the Mahdek people. Took a couple of tries. Didn't help that Ala'tris was shouting something at me from the spellship.

Leave it for now, I told myself. *You won't be any good to her or anyone else until you straighten yourself out.*

Once my head was clear, I turned my attention to my body, listening to everything it had to say to me. Boy, did it have a lot to say.

'*Hey, Ferius, this is your heart speaking. Don't know if you've noticed, but I'm beating so fast you're going to lose consciousness any second now.*'

'*You think you've got it tough? I'm her muscles, and we're all clenched to hells. She's losing the feeling in her hands from squeezing so hard.*'

'*Uh, hello? Head here. Aching pretty bad. Blinding, actually.*'

I assume most people's bodies don't actually talk to them, but then most people don't imagine their old mentor nattering at them all day long either.

279

'Ferius? Don't mean to disturb you here, but I'm your bladder and I'm about to pi—'

Do what you gotta do, I told my body. Don't hide from the pain or the shame or whatever else is coming over you. Just let it be what it's going to be. One more step and then we can figure out what the heck Ala'tris is on about up there.

With my thoughts clear and my body doing all the shaking and stirring it needed to do, I went to work on the last part of myself that was in sore need of coming back into alignment with the rest of me.

'Go on,' I whispered to the maelstrom of emotions that my mind and body had been working so hard to keep me from feeling. '*I'm here, and I ain't afraid of you.*'

Much as I admire the Argosi talent of arta forteize and all the ways it can strengthen you, there's a reason why sane folks repress their traumas. Nothing more natural than burying the bad things deep until you feel safe enough to let them out, even if secretly you never intend to let them out at all. Our minds and bodies may fail us, but it's our emotions that can tear us apart the fastest.

Shame. Guilt. Grief. Inadequacy. Failure. Coward. You were ready to die. Had to be saved by a horse and a damned goat. Never been as strong as Durral or Enna or Sir Gervaise or Sir Rosarite or Rosie or Arissa or Arissa or Arissa or Arissa . . .

Arissa.

Yeah, Arissa. You left her behind. She left you behind. All a big joke. Nothing real between you. Just putting up with you, like everyone else. You let Durral down a thousand times. You nearly killed Enna. Remember that? Stuck your sword right through her lung, you ungrateful little sow. Ugly. Cruel. Mean down into the marrow of your bones.

Tears dripped down my cheeks, drops of black oil that clung to my upper lip, trying to get inside my mouth so they could repeat the journey all over again.

Crybaby. Eighteen years old. Supposed to be an Argosi. Dozens of your people out on this cold, black graveyard, dead because you couldn't keep them from killing themselves. And here you are crying because you're what? Lonely? You're lonely? You think you're lonely now, you stupid little bit—

Okay, now. That'll do.

I blew air out between my lips, almost like Quadlopo when he's telling me he needs a brushing. *Not a bad idea*, I thought. *We all need a good brushing now and then to get the dust off of us.*

Single best lesson of arta forteize Durral ever taught me was years ago when the two of us were trapped inside the mind cage in which Ala'tris had been ordered by her mother to keep us locked up. He'd started with jokes. Ear-splitting, belly-busting, pants-peeing jokes. That was arta valar: a declaration to the universe that he wasn't going to take his fate sitting down – or even seriously. I guess that's where I'd gotten that nonsense about swearing in order to break out of the summons towards oblivion that had been created by, and was now consuming, my fellow Mahdek.

What had come after the jokes, however, was something entirely different. Durral started telling stories about Enna. Big majestic tales of love. Little insignificant anecdotes, light as a lover's finger tracing the knuckles on the back of your hand. At the time I hadn't fully understood what he was up to. Part of it had been drawing our captor's emotions so deep that she couldn't hold her concentration on the mind cage, sure, but the rest? That was Durral strengthening himself for the real fight to come. That was him donning his armour, only his armour wasn't made out of metal but from the love he shared with Enna. Stronger than steel, impenetrable to despair.

That's what I had to do now, because I could hear what Ala'tris was saying and Sar'ephir was shouting. I knew that this abyss to

281

which my people's sorrow and her people's spells had brought us was swallowing all of us whole. The ship was sinking into the onyx ice of this shadowy land where death itself must come to die. Even as they lay unconscious, the Mahdek were still anchoring the spellship to the necropolis. Up on deck, Jir'dan and Ba'dari were near killing themselves trying to spark their bands so they could cast the spells necessary to rid them of that anchor. To save the ship, they were going to have to kill its passengers.

My own dark feelings assailed me, showing me the worst moment of my life, when I'd almost killed Enna in a sword fight. *She forgave me*, I reminded those cruel memories. *Enna came for me months later in the desert, helped me find myself and my path, never doubting – even in that terrible instant as the tip of my sword had pierced her lung – the woman I could one day become.* With my right hand I brushed the dust that wasn't there off my left arm. A simple, ritualistic gesture, but one that brought my mind, body and emotions a little closer together. I could almost see the vambrace and gauntlet of a knight's armour where I'd brushed away the shame.

'Jir'dan, no!' Ala'tris cried out from the deck.

'We must! We've followed you this far, given up our families, but I won't let you or any of this coven die for these people so consumed with their own doom that when we offered them paradise, they brought us to a hell!'

Durral's love now, his might be strongest of all, I reminded my self-pity, brushing off my right shoulder this time. The black dust that hadn't been there disappeared, in its place an armoured pouldron like those Sir Gervaise and Sir Rosarite might've worn over their shoulders.

'We must find a way to untether ourselves from this place!' Sar'ephir shouted. 'The ship is melding into the shadowblack, becoming one with this graveyard!'

Never thought I'd hear Sar'ephir lose her cool. She always seemed so—

No. Focus. Assemble your armour. You're going to need all your arta forteize for what comes next.

I brushed the loneliness off the front of my ratty travelling shirt, leaving behind a hundred hugs from Sir Gervaise and Sir Rosarite, and a breastplate that solitude's arrow simply could not pierce. Next I swept the doubt from the tops of my legs, felt them strong and sure around Quadlopo's sides. Cuisses and greaves, that's what they call the curved armoured plates that protect a knight's thighs and knees. I patted the horse's neck. 'You complain all the time, but you just keep coming back for me, don't you, old fella?'

He nickered. A reminder that I should pay attention to the task at hand, because Jir'dan, Gab'rel and Ba'dari were becoming overwhelmed by their own dread, and any second now they were going to overpower Ala'tris for what they believed was her own good.

A helm, I thought. *Can't have proper armour without a helm.*

I brought my hands up to my cheeks, wiping away the tears so that my fingertips could trace the kisses left behind by the Path of Thorns and Roses during those brief, impetuous hours in the mountains when we'd been stalking a mystical plague together. Sure, it hadn't worked out between us, but that hardly mattered at times like these. Besides, there were other kisses with which to complete my helm.

Arissa.

Foolish kisses, sure. Reckless and wild, just like her. They made an excellent visor.

The last vestiges of my self-doubt clawed at me, dragging my gaze downward to see that I wasn't really wearing armour. I was nothing but a rumpled, shivering girl so frightened of what lay ahead that she'd already wet herself. Didn't matter though. An Argosi always keeps a little self-doubt in her pocket, just in case she needs a good laugh now and then.

I made sure Conch was properly settled on my shoulder, then gave Quadlopo a gentle kick to get us moving. 'Come on, fella. Time we ride out a ways.'

I'd expected to get a gentle trot out of him, but I guess he was riled up some. That horse exploded like thunder across the expanse of that necropolis, tearing up the onyx ice with his hoofs, leaping over the still-sinking bodies of my people.

'Ferius, where are you going?' Ala'tris cried out to me.

'She's lost her mind,' I heard Jir'dan tell her, his frustration clear as a bell despite the growing distance between us. 'This mad venture has met its end. We must act to save ourselves now.'

'Sister, please!' Ala'tris kept on shouting to me, even as her words faded to dying echoes the further I travelled into the necropolis. 'Why are you abandoning us?'

O, ye of little faith.

I rode a few seconds more, just until we'd reached the last of the obsidian arches. There I pulled on Quadlopo's reins and turned him back around. He snorted a sort of *'What now?'* at me. My arta loquit doesn't extend to horses, but he sounded doubtful to my ears. Conch, perched on my shoulder, added his own nervous bray to the conversation. Heck, even Durral got in on the action.

'You sure you can pull this off, kid?'

'Now, Pappy? Now's when you start doubting me?'

In that shadowy haze, I could almost see Durral standing there, a few feet away, tilting the brim of his frontier hat up a little as he surveyed the landscape between us and the galleon that was beginning to capsize beneath the onyx ice.

'Ain't doubtin' you, kid,' Durral said. 'But what you're aimin' to do, they ain't gonna give it to you for free.'

He was right of course. There would be a price for this.

I was eighteen years old. I'd spent most of those years hunted, hungry and haunted by so many different kinds of misery I didn't know enough words to describe them all. Finally, *finally* I'd found my Argosi path, and before I could even take my first step along that road to joy and wonder, this was where it ended?

Well, as Enna might say, 'Whining ain't the Argosi way. You either do a thing or you don't.'

Wise woman.

'You fellas listening?' I asked silently to those darkest and most foul of voices that lingered in my skull like a fever that never goes away.

They didn't answer. Maybe they wanted to fool me into thinking they were asleep. But they couldn't hide their glee at finally having a taste – just a taste – of what they'd been craving since the day they'd wormed their way into my mind, implanted inside me by nothing more than a handful of stanzas.

'You want another shot at enslaving me? Now's your chance . . . but first, you've got to do something for me.'

Again the silent treatment. Most of the time I can't get the little chatterboxes to shut up. I wasn't troubled though; once I let the verses out and stopped dancing from their grasp, they'd be ready to play.

I cupped one palm and placed it to the side of my mouth, lifting my chin as I shouted across the necropolis: 'Whatever spells you need to sail the ship through the shadowblack, best get 'em ready!'

I couldn't see Ala'tris or the others any more. The black fog of the necropolis was too thick now. Maybe I was too late, and the mages had already killed one another over whose ghastly plan was the most noble. Didn't matter to me now though. I knew what I had to do.

The problem was simple enough: Sar'ephir couldn't propel the spellship through the shadowblack while the fatalism of its passengers anchored it to this graveyard of their own making. No one, not even a coven of Jan'Tep mages, with all their mental discipline and training in esoteric geometry, could overwhelm the despair of so many. The raw, unshakeable will required to break through such desolation would be . . . well, it would be pretty much indistinguishable from madness.

Which I happened to possess in plentiful supply.

I nudged Quadlopo to a gallop back among the black arches separating us from the galleon. Soon we were nearing the first of those grave markers. I tightened the straps of my imagined armour, the arta valar forged from all the wild, wonderful moments I'd accumulated during my short life.

I'm not the toughest Argosi out there. Rosie now, she's tough. The Path of Thorns and Roses, she calls herself. More thorns than roses, if you ask me. Durral and Enna surpass even Rosie for toughness. Those rambling thistles are almost unbreakable.

Let me ask you this though: what's tougher than a wild daisy, sprouting from dead soil in a place where even weeds ain't supposed to grow?

Let's find out, shall we?

Okay, you little rat bastards, I told the Scarlet Verses, reaching a hand up to my brow so I could pull my non-existent helm's visor down over my face. *Let's find out who wins in a war between madness and despair.*

34

Bad Bargains

The deal was dead simple, and neither party required a contract. The Scarlet Verses were, in essence, a language plague. Once heard, the words and syllables from which the verses were composed began restructuring the brain, tearing down the feeble, crumbling edifices of our moral foundations and sense of self. In their place, towering new architectures of malevolence arose that were as impervious to pain and physical weakness as they were to the victim's pleas for mercy. They also had a lousy sense of humour.

'*Come on, fellas,*' I urged the Scarlet Verses as I began my hell ride through the necropolis on Quadlopo's back. '*Not even a little joke?*'

Silence. Which wasn't to say they weren't busy: with me no longer dancing around the twisted, loathsome meanings with which they'd tried so many times to imprison me, the verses were now erecting pillars inside my mind with carefully chosen words.

'*Resolve. Spine. Testament. Doggedness. Tenacity. Single-mindedne—*'

'*Nuh-uh, sorry, fellas,*' I told them, pirouetting around that last one. Tricky though, because it had so few inherent meanings. *Single-mindedness . . . Single-mindedness . . . Ah, there we go!*

'*Single-mindedness: the state of an intellect directed only by itself, freed from influences outside or within the brain.*'

The verses weren't pleased with my interference. '*You demanded a will so powerful it could overwhelm the petty, scattered desires of those conjuring this necropolis. Why do you oppos—*'

'Because your notion of single-mindedness is precisely the knot I'm trying to untangle. The world's been telling the Mahdek for generations that they've got no future. Now they all believe it with, shall we say, your sort of single-mindedness. So I can't have you pushing that word onto me.'

A moment's resistance, then finally, '*Agreed. You may have your own interpretation of single-mindedness. We will encompass the rest of your mind soon enough, now that you've allowed us to—*'

'Can we get on with the job at hand? The first black arch is right there in front of me.'

'*Resolute. Unyielding. Unfaltering. Bone. Diamond. Stone.*'

Stone. There we go. That last one works for me!

I pulled up on Quadlopo's reins, halting him before the first of the black arches that served as the gravestones in Mahdek tradition. Conch let out an angry bray as he scrabbled to keep his balance on my shoulder. I let go of the reins, nudging the horse to a slow walk with my knees and giving Conch a reassuring scratch under the chin before setting my will upon the shadowblack arch.

'I am Argosi,' I informed the black stone arch. '*I walk the Way of Stone. Resolute. Unyielding. Unfaltering upon my path. There is no place for markers of death before my will. From shadow were you cast, back to shadow I return you.*'

The arch resisted, drawing strength from the rest of the necropolis, on the unifying despair that gave form and structure to this graveyard. Beneath it lay a Mahdek woman, arms crossed over her chest, the placid smile of oblivion on her face.

Sorry, sister. No time for naps. Especially permanent ones.

288

Again I set my will on the arch. Again it resisted. But the shadowblack is a place of mind as much as matter, and my thoughts were propelled by the madness of the Red Scream that bound my every thought into a single purpose. Cracks appeared in the curved obsidian like tiny spider's webs. The arch tried to repair itself, but something began to sprout from one of those cracks: a tiny black daisy.

Conch leaned over, made that chewing noise he makes right before launching himself at food. I grabbed hold of him and set him on Quadlopo's neck between my legs. 'Those are *not* for eating, understand?'

The spire goat curled his lip, showed me his teeth and made it plain he did not appreciate being told what he could and could not eat by a skinny, gangly-limbed human who was long overdue a lesson in manners.

I was saved from that unpleasant education when the obsidian arch collapsed into rubble. The Mahdek woman lying beneath it blinked her eyes open. She crawled out of the indentation her body had made in the black ice all around us. She was thick-bodied for a Mahdek, curvaceous and with features that reminded me of those portraits Daroman noblewomen pay exorbitant amounts of money to have painted of themselves. She got to her hands and knees, stared down at the daisy and then up at me. 'I was content,' was all she said.

It was hard to form words with my mouth. The Scarlet Verses instinctively tried to take control of my voice, eager to disseminate their madness to others who would then spread it far and wide until the entire world spoke a single, perfect language in which words were no longer necessary because all thought was one. Such notions have no place in the Way of the Argosi, however, so I forced my lips to dance around the words they wanted me to say and spoke my own.

289

'You have kids?' I asked.

'Two daughters,' the woman replied. 'Both reside in . . . They're dead.'

I glanced around the necropolis until I saw the young yellow-haired girl who'd been the first to leap over the side. 'Like her?'

The woman shook her head. 'She's not dead yet. Soon though.'

I nudged Quadlopo closer, and snapped my fingers to get the woman's attention again. When she turned, I slapped her across the face. 'Then what the hells are you doing standing here?'

I shouldn't have struck her. Violence isn't the Argosi way. But I had the Scarlet Verses whispering madness in my ears and I was barely holding it together. Not much of an excuse, but it was all I had. For her part, the woman stared at me a moment longer, like she hadn't felt a thing, then shrugged and trudged off to where the little girl lay beneath her arch.

Okay, I thought, holding tightly to my intention, focusing it through the unshakeable will the Scarlet Verses were infusing me with. My entire mind hardened, becoming an engine of raw determination. I had to make sure that determination served the right purpose.

I was about to give Quadlopo a kick, but the horse didn't need any cue from me. He bounded ahead, racing to the next row of obsidian arches. I let go of the reins, reached my arms out wide and set about tearing this wasteland apart and leaving a garden of my own design in its place.

One by one the arches cracked, black daisies bursting from the obsidian, leaving mounds of those blooms behind. Some of the sinking Mahdek awoke on their own, others needed help from the woman I'd slapped or one of the people she'd awoken after the little girl. Quadlopo's hoofs began to shatter the black icy ground, leaving cracks behind that collapsed in on themselves.

Over and over, the death arches of those seeking oblivion resisted me, struggling to keep the necropolis together. The Scarlet Verses were a lance in my hand that smashed through the wills of others. I'd never seen a joust, other than in some of the old shield romances Sir Gervaise and Sir Rosarite had shown me of their homeland across the water, but I revelled in every collision as my tenacity shattered that of those who resisted me. Never before had I understood how good it felt to be powerful.

'Yes,' the verses whispered in my ears, adding more and more columns to prop up the walls they were constructing in my mind. *You begin to comprehend our gift. You begin to see. Abandon your silly dancing, that-which-once-called-itself-Ferius, and let us build you a palace so fine you will never again wish to leave it.*

'Friends, you make a convincing argument,' I agreed.

Half the arches were gone and the black ice behind us was crumbling, first into shards of obsidian, then melting into waves of glittering onyx. Those Mahdek now awoken were running for the ship. I felt no desire to join them.

The Way of the Argosi is supposed to be wondrous, but all it had ever done for me was force me into one hard choice after another. I thought I'd be free when I found my path, but that only led me to debts I never knew I owed and duties I never wanted. Every moment of happiness had been nothing but an interlude between deeper hurts and longer solitudes.

'Yes, yes, yes,' hissed the Scarlet Verses, diligently reconstructing the foundations of my consciousness. *At last you accept what must be! No other before you rebelled against us for so long.* I felt a surge of gratitude, like the purest liquor pumped straight into my veins. *Your resistance has refined us. We will make you our herald, and your voice the harbinger of a new worl—*

I swore. A bad word, that no gentle person should say aloud, but I filled it with mischief and joy borrowed from Arissa.

'*What are you doing?*' the verses demanded as one of the beautiful, perfect columns of fixed meaning they'd erected inside my thoughts cracked and crumbled. '*You begged us!*'

'Beg is a mean little word,' I told them. '*Never liked it much, myself. Sets one soul beneath another. Let's play with it a bit, shall we?*' I struck down another of the arches, my daisies now cropping up everywhere, first splintering the stones, then, when the rocky ground liquified, floating on the waves. Inside my mind I painted butterfly wings on a word and made it fly. '*The best kind of begging, if you ask my opinion, is begging the question.*'

'*No!*' the verses shouted, their hammers pounding the inside of my skull as they tried to smash my little butterfly. '*We struck a bargain! We forged your will, made it irresistible. In exchange you must serve us!*'

Quadlopo whinnied anxiously, pouring on more speed. Conch hunched low between my thighs. The last of the arches were coming down of their own accord now, the necropolis losing its hold on the Mahdek, and they, in turn, letting go of their obsession with oblivion. Up ahead, the galleon was loose from the ice – or whatever the hells that shadowy stuff really was. Ala'tris was leaning over the railing with Chedran, helping the last of the Mahdek back on board. She looked across the ice at me, screaming for me to hurry.

'*Never,*' the verses told me, abandoning their hammers for spikes as they tried to shred my sanity with the sharpened fingernails of their outrage. '*If you will not serve us, then we will—*'

'*Serve ain't a word I'm too fond of either,*' I reminded them, squeezing it into a ball and tossing it to them. '*There, see? I just served you. Happy now?*'

Quadlopo's back hoof slipped. I nearly fell off as his hind legs went into the water. He managed to scramble back onto solid ice again, but his coat was soaked with black sweat. Conch, usually the fiercest little monster I'd ever met, was huddled low, making quiet moaning sounds.

'Almost there,' I told Quadlopo, patting the side of his neck as he renewed his mad gallop towards the ship.

Seven strides. Couldn't have been more than that left. We just needed seven more of Quadlopo's good, long strides. The galleon was low in the water, like it couldn't decide whether to float or sink. The hull listed back and forth, port to starboard and back again as if caught in the mother of all storms.

Six strides. The onyx was cracking all around us. There was barely a big enough patch before the ship for us to leap from, and even with the ship low in the water like that, Quadlopo wouldn't be able to jump high enough to clear the railing.

'*You lied to us,*' the Scarlet Verses said. '*You promised us—*'

'Damn it, I don't have time for your crap right now,' I said aloud, shifting the meaning of 'promise' in my mind from an oath that must be fulfilled to potential, aptitude, flair. '*The deal was for you to build up my will so I could break through the despair holding the necropolis together. Never said I'd let you turn me into a mindless, brainless mouthpiece for your foul intentions.*'

Five strides. The Mahdek were all on board. Be a shame if everyone got out of here except Quadlopo, Conch and me.

Four strides. Something blacker than black was sparking near the bow of the ship. Standing atop the forecastle, Sar'ephir was waving her arms up and down, the ship lilting along with her movements. People on board were screaming, confused by what was happening. I understood though.

'She's trying to make the side of the ship low enough for us to jump over the railing,' I told Quadlopo. 'You're going to have to time that leap perfectly.'

Don't know why I felt the need to say that. He's a horse. Doesn't speak a word of Daroman. Still, he nickered in that way that convinced me that, despite my sounding like an annoying gnat in his ear, he figured I was probably saying something irritatingly obvious.

Three strides is when I heard the laughter. It wasn't coming from me.

'Your betrayal is meaningless,' the verses tittered. They weren't even hammering at me any more, just . . . swirling there inside my head, admiring their own handiwork. 'There is enough here now.'

Two strides. The ship was taking water over the sides with each sway of Sar'ephir's arms.

'Something funny, fellas?' I asked the verses.

They giggled and snickered like cruel children. 'Your mind is more rigid now, Argosi. All your wit and will barely kept you from our grasp before. The path you are on will lead you to more peril, more pain, more confusion. When next you falter, the flawless noose of our words will wrap around you for the final time, and you will be ours.'

Quadlopo's haunches bunched, and I felt us lowering nearly a foot as the last patch of black ice began to sink under the surface. The port side of the ship swung back downward, all those frantic Mahdek hanging on to whatever their hands could find as they protected those too young or old to do so themselves. The explosion of Quadlopo's muscles compressed my entire spine. I hugged Conch close to my chest, his horns pressing under my chin. My stomach nearly came out my throat as we sprang into the air, the ship already starting to tilt back to starboard.

We aren't going to make it, I thought, convinced Quadlopo's hoofs would strike the railings and we'd go down the side and into the icy black depths. At the zenith of our arc, I hurled Conch at

Ala'tris, figuring at least one of us ought to survive. *Sorry, little fella. Should've left you munching on blue moss on that spire of yours.*

I was right about it being too high for Quadlopo to jump over. I flinched as the very tips of his hoofs collided with the wooden railing, felt the bravest, most dauntless animal I'd ever known sag beneath me as failure and death became inevitable. Then, in that same split second as that nasty old hag fate had me and Quadlopo in her clutches, something else grabbed hold of us.

Grey ain't a colour, everyone knows that. That's why it always struck me as strange that the Jan'Tep band for iron magic could somehow violate that simple fact by sparking with grey light. But in that blackened world, the grey sparks erupting off Ba'dari's arms blinded me so bad I had to shut my eyes tight as I waited for me and Quadlopo to either hit the deck so hard one of us would end up with a broken leg for sure, or sink down into the frigid shadowblack waters below.

'Ferius?' a voice asked. It was Ala'tris. 'You can open your eyes now.'

'Nope,' I said, keeping them shut tight and my arms wrapped around Quadlopo's neck.

'It's all right, you're—'

'Shut up.'

'What's wrong with her?' Chedran demanded. That guy was always demanding something.

Nobody understands, I thought, holding back the tears. *They're going to want to cheer and clap me on the back. Tell me how heroic I was. Those stupid runaways are going to start peppering me with questions about being an Argosi and would I teach them because they want to be just like me.*

'Sounds awful,' Durral said. 'Positively, stultifyingly horrendous. I don't know how you've endured the agony of being admired this long, kid.'

He's never been good at sarcasm.

For once I didn't give my imaginary mentor the satisfaction of a response. Instead, as I lay there slumped against Quadlopo's back on the deck of the spellship, my eyes still squeezed shut, I went through the slow, painstaking work of removing the armour of my arta forteize, releasing each and every one of the memories that had protected me out in that land of onyx ice and obsidian gravestones. The Way of Stone can be tempting to hold on to. It makes you strong. Certain. Unbreakable. Pursued too long, though, it becomes a trap as pernicious and inescapable as despair. You become hard and unforgiving.

That ain't the Argosi way, I said silently, mimicking Durral's favourite denunciation so I wouldn't have to hear him say it.

I love his voice, that frontier drawl of his that so often infects my own tongue, and when it does, I know I'm at my best. But I wasn't ready to hear it yet, nor Enna's, nor Arissa's, nor anyone's.

At last I opened my eyes, slid off Quadlopo's back and handed the reins to Ala'tris. Conch leaped out of her arms so he could start butting my knees. I shooed him away and slipped through the throngs of well-wishers to the stairs that led below decks. I needed to be alone a while.

A hissing laughter inside my head followed me all the way down.

35

The Cabin

Those next three nights were hard. I'd stumbled into what I'd thought was a small cabin with a narrow cot that took up almost the entire floor and blocked the door from the inside. Turned out I'd crawled into a storage room and collapsed on a bunch of grain sacks. On those rare occasions when someone knocked to inform me there was a proper cabin available or offering to bring food, I'd tell them to go to hells. Impolite, to be sure, but I blamed it on the fever that left my entire body slick with oily black sweat.

When awake, I shook and shivered, wrestling with my darkest thoughts. No longer a dancer, I'd become little more than a punch-drunk boxer on her last legs, tripping over words and meanings that sought to ensnare me with their insidious shackles. When asleep, I tossed and turned, reached for dreams of brave smiles and stolen kisses. Sometimes I'd shudder awake, the soft tickle of lips pressed to my cheek. My hand would reach out in search of some presence next to me on the pile of sacks. I never found anyone, but always it seemed as if the rough fabric was warmer than it should be. Fever makes for a strange bedmate.

None of this was unexpected. On that hellish ride through the necropolis, I'd pushed myself to the brink of madness. You don't

297

return from something like that all at once. You almost never come back all the way.

Eighteen is too young to feel so old, I thought.

A chuckle roused me. '*Seventy-two is too old to be burdened with the work of the young.*'

There was that same foggy, muffled distance to the words that I associated with memories or imaginings, but since neither Durral nor Enna are more than forty I realised the voice wasn't coming from inside my head.

Drawing once more on my arta forteize, I employed a technique for bringing myself out of sleep quickly: three sharp, shallow breaths followed by a sneeze you don't let out, but instead send through your entire body like a whip-crack. Try it sometime. Wakes you right up, all at once.

The door to the storage room creaked open and my first visitor entered. Almost certainly the last person I wanted to see. Guess I hadn't blocked the door like I'd thought. Stoika stepped inside, bearing a tray with two wooden cups and a steaming clay pot. A travelling people learns to brew a great many kinds of tea over the generations. I disliked pretty much all of them.

Stoika ignored the look of distaste that was surely plastered on my face and sat down on my most favourite grain sack, balancing the tray shakily across her lap. 'Don't pout at me, girl,' she said, making herself unduly comfortable. 'Petulance is unattractive at the best of times, and entirely unconvincing in one's saviour.'

'Saviour?' I barked that one out. Not quite a laugh, not quite a cough. Something in between. Something a little poisonous.

Stoika folded her hands on the tray. 'Tell me, child, is it considered virtuous among the Argosi to deny the heroism of saving nearly three hundred lives? Or is it that, to you, those lives are worthless because they are Mahdek?'

298

'Don't start that we-are-the-forgotten-people crap with me, lady.'

I sat up, which for reasons beyond understanding unleashed all the stenches I'd been carrying with me in an all-out assault on my nostrils. I needed a bath almost as badly as I needed to punch this mean-spirited woman in the face, just once. Alas, necessity and circumstance had been twisting my path too far from that of the Wild Daisy already. I needed to get my head straight before I stumbled off the road entirely.

I put up a hand, pivoted my palm to the right in the traditional Mahdek gesture of repentance. 'My apologies, elder. My words were ill-considered, my insinuation unfounded and churlish.'

Stoika's eyes widened for an instant before she broke out laughing so hard she almost tipped the tray over. 'Oh, how honoured am I, that the legendary Ferius Parfax chooses to express repentance to me with such graciousness.' She wagged a finger in my face. 'Don't use me as some sort of . . . totem to settle your nerves, girl.' She leaned back, resting against the side of the narrow storage cabin with a weary sigh. 'How perfect I must seem for such a purpose, eh? Bitter. Domineering. Unfeeling. If you can force yourself to show me courtesy, find a way to tolerate my presence and even forge some sort of fledgling rapport with me, then you haven't abandoned your Argosi ways at all. Isn't that so?'

'That is so, revered elder.'

'Oh, do shut up with your fumbling attempts at proper manners. I never liked you before you saved all our lives, and, somehow, you manage to make me like you even less now that I owe you everything.' She began pouring hot water into the wooden cups, dropping in leaves that looked black and bitter in this realm and I was pretty sure were black and bitter in any other too.

My arta precis wasn't coming back very quickly. Something about exerting too much arta forteize makes one less perceptive.

But I didn't need any arta precis right now, because Stoika wasn't trying to hide her intentions from me. I just needed to allow my arta loquit to hear what she was really saying.

'*Oh, do shut up.*'

Tone's too sharp, too much like some dockside fish trader shooing away unruly kids. Not controlled or haughty like she usually is.

What she'd really wanted me to hear was: *I need you to move past your impressions of me. I need you to trust me, just for a moment.*

'*I never liked you before you saved all our lives.*'

Again, too much heat, the words spoken too quickly. *When you came to the enclave, you scared me. Scared all of the elders.*

'*And, somehow, you manage to make me like you even less now . . .*'

Guilt. Confusion. Trepidation. She uses the word 'like' to mean 'understand'. *I never understood you until you led us out of the necropolis, and yet I understand you even less now.*

'*. . . now that I owe . . .*'

Owe. So much emphasis on that one syllable, stretching the vowel until it no longer carries a sense of debt but instead one of . . . gratitude? *Now that I am so grateful to you for . . .*

'*Everything.*' The last word, the destination to which she was trying to lead me, even though she couldn't bring herself to say it aloud. *Everything.* Everything in what? Possessions? No. Lives? More even than that. This was an everything that encompassed not only that which *was*, but that which *has yet to be*. The future.

So what she'd really wanted to tell me was: '*I need you to move past your impressions of me, Ferius. I need you to trust me, just for a moment. When you came to the enclave, you scared me. Scared all of the elders. I never understood you until you led us out of the necropolis, and yet I understand you even less now – now that I am so grateful to you for the future.*'

My unwinding of her utterances had taken only a couple of seconds, and I hadn't spoken any of them aloud, but Stoika was staring at me, wrinkled lips parted a little, her exhale sending the foggy fumes of the tea across the tiny cabin. 'You already know what I came here to say, don't you?'

'I believe so, elder.'

'How? Have the Argosi uncovered the secrets of Jan'Tep silk magic that you can pluck from my mind words not yet spoken?'

'No, elder. It is that you . . .' I searched for a way to explain the third tenet of arta loquit. 'Conversations such as the one you came to have are not linear in nature. They're more like . . . like a single painting cut into hundreds of tiny scraps and kept in a bag. With each sentence, you reach into the bag and toss a few more scraps onto the table between us, reassembling the picture ever so slowly. Yet, in one sense, each of those scraps is—'

'Part of that greater whole,' she finished for me. 'And from it, one might infer the rest?'

'Yes.'

Stoika reached inside her coat and took out a tiny leather pouch. Mahdek teas are often combined with mixtures of spices and sugars. This particular melange smelled overly sweet. Maybe she was tired of smelling me already. She tapped out a thimbleful of the sweet-scented crystals into one of the cups, then asked, 'Would you like some as well?'

I stared at the little pouch, listened to the flat tone in her voice. 'Yes, please,' I replied. 'A little more than you've put in yours.'

Stoika nodded but didn't actually pour even a fraction of her own portion into my cup before she began stirring it in. 'Do you suppose you might allow me to speak awhile without telling me what I intend to say before I've even found the words?' she asked.

I grinned. 'I make no promises, elder.'

'The young,' she complained as if that were a complete sentence, then sat there chewing and watching me in relative silence as the creaks and groans of the galleon went on around us. The hull listed a little, so I reached over and steadied the tray on her lap. She batted my hand away before finally beginning what anyone, regardless of whether they'd ever studied arta loquit, would have instantly recognised as a confession. 'The council thought we were helping our young,' she began quietly, 'shielding them from the heartache that our generation and all the ones that came before us experienced when realising there was no future for our people. Our ancestors had failed us, and we, in turn, had failed ourselves. We thought . . .' The words trailed off. She lifted her wooden cup to her lips.

'Go on,' I urged her.

She put down the cup. 'We believed that Kievan and the others would be the last generation of Mahdek, that, whether through disease, violence or simply neglect, our people's lineage would end within these next few decades. When Marshal Colfax offered us a place of safety on his estate, the council decided that this would provide a gentler life, an easier passage into oblivion for our children.'

Shouts from the deck above seeped through the wooden planking. Something about 'the causeway' being in sight. I ignored the cacophony though. When someone's struggling as hard to get their words out as Stoika was, you don't rush them. She seemed to sense this and smiled a silent acknowledgement before reaching for one of the wooden cups.

'That one's mine,' I said.

She looked down at the tray. 'Really? I could've sworn—'

I picked up both cups, and made a show of sniffing at each one. 'See?' I asked, holding up the first. 'This one stinks of too much sweetspice and ginger.' I handed it back to her and then turned to the second. 'This one just reeks of good old-fashioned Mahdek tea.' I set mine aside. 'Either way, there's a commotion above decks, so if you've got something to confess, now's the time.'

She stared into the steam coming off her cup and sighed. 'Do you remember what I said to you when the ship ran aground in the black ice, or rather the black ice had surrounded the ship?'

'You said, "It was always going to end this way. Our doom was coming soon enough. What difference would a few more years of shaking our fists and swearing at the sky have done?"'

Stoika nodded, and paused to wipe away a tear that was barely more than a hazy wetness in the corner of her eye. 'We brought the black ice with our despair. The necropolis came into being through the melancholia we elders had sown deep inside the soil of our people's hearts. I knew it. In that moment, I knew that we . . . that I had delivered the Mahdek to oblivion.' A trembling hand came to brush at her cheeks clumsily. 'For three centuries the Jan'Tep sought to wipe us from the world like an unsightly stain upon nature's beauty. They failed.' Her fingers closed into a fist. 'All their magic, all their power, and yet they failed.' She slammed her fist down on her own thigh, rattling the tea tray. 'Not we elders though. Not the council whose duty it was to protect and guide the young. When we realised we could not give them a better life than the one we'd lived, we instead destroyed their hopes and dreams so thoroughly that they . . .' She stopped again, shaking her head.

A dozen phrases came to mind. Kindly, reassuring sentiments meant to ease her anguish. Some came from Durral, some Enna. Sir Rosarite always had a few good sayings for times like these. None belonged to me though, and none would have done a lick of good. Sometimes pain is pain and you have to go through it, not around it.

303

Stoika pounded her fist against her thigh a few more times, lighter though, a kind of punctuation to give herself time to breathe. The galleon's movements slowed a little. I had to remind myself that it wasn't the ship moving through the shadowblack waters but the waters moving around us. Either way, we were arriving somewhere. Stoika sensed it too, and pushed herself through the rest of what she'd come to say.

'When I saw you out there, on that mad horse of yours with that nasty little goat on your shoulder, I thought, *What a fool that girl is, riding off to an arrogant, vain ending as if fate were an opponent you could challenge to a fist fight.* And yet, ride you did, and fight you did. One by one you shattered the death arches. One by one you dragged our people out of the pit into which the folly of their elders had consigned their spirits.'

A knocking at the door. 'Ferius, we're here!' Ala'tris called out excitedly. 'We've reached the causeway.'

'I'll be out in a minute,' I called back.

Stoika smiled wearily. 'Our time grows short, and our tea is getting cold.'

I sniffed again at the fumes from my own cup. 'That could only improve the flavour.'

'Heretic.' She drained her cup all the way to the bottom, then set it back down before carefully placing the entire tray on the floor between us. 'All right, old woman,' she muttered to herself, 'no more hiding from the truth.' Her eyes met mine, and there was so much ease there, so much gratitude, that I almost wondered if I was staring at the same stern woman as moments ago. 'You saved our people, Ferius Parfax. More than that, you've proven something I never would have believed possible. The Mahdek *do* have a future.' She glanced around at the tiny cabin. 'This preposterous galleon, these damnably polite Jan'Tep mages.' She cast an arm back towards

304

the door. 'That island waiting for us. It's as if you slammed down the blade of an axe in the centre of a dead-end road and somehow forked a path into the future. Our destiny was to end in misery and despair, I was sure of that, but now . . .'

More cries came from the deck above us, full of excitement, trepidation and wonder.

'Now we have an island to explore,' I said, and poured my cup out onto the floor, never taking my eyes from Stoika.

She chuckled, softly. 'You think I came here to poison you? Perhaps we have both overestimated your Argosi talents. Which would be a terrible pity now.' She leaned back against the wall as if she never meant to leave this little cabin. 'Our people need someone to lead them. I'd hoped that one day it might be my son, but Chedran is . . .'

'An arsehole?' I suggested.

She didn't appreciate the joke. 'A warrior. As pure a warrior as was ever born to a peaceful people. But he only knows one way to fight – with fists and blades and a heart full of rage.' She pointed an accusing finger at me. Her arm was shaking. 'You, Ferius. You make a foe of suffering and despair, but never of people. *That* is the war the Mahdek must learn to fight. *You* are the leader they need.'

I rose to my feet. A little unsteady. Three days lying on grain sacks doesn't make for a refreshing rest. 'Get up,' I told Stoika.

She smiled the way a gambler does when slapping the winning cards down on the table. 'I haven't long left. You presumed I poisoned your cup, but it was mine, and your rather unsophisticated attempt at sleight of hand didn't fool me for an instant. The moment you started that nonsense about me reaching for your cup, I switched them.' She waved dismissively towards the door. 'Go. Guide our people to a better fate than the one I foresaw for them. Leave a woman too long past her prime to die alone and miserable as is our most sacred right.'

I bent down and hugged her. 'You're a crazy old bat, you know that?'

She was so stiff it was like hugging a board. She patted my back awkwardly. 'I still dislike you, Ferius Parfax.'

I laughed. The bitter coot had excellent delivery. Durral would've approved. 'On your feet, elder,' I said, extending my right hand to offer support.

She tried to swat it away, but I slid my hand under her arm and offered it to her again. 'I told you, child, it's too late for me. Go save someone who wants it.'

'Okay, first, stop calling me "child". I'm eighteen.'

She sighed and her eyes drifted closed. 'Still a child.'

'Second, never try pulling a con on an Argosi. It's embarrassing for both of us.' I noisily rattled the tiny leather satchel that I'd picked from her coat pocket.

'Suit yourself,' she said in the slightly distracted way of someone waiting for sleep to come. 'I've no use for it any more.'

I stuffed the satchel into my waistcoat, then reached down with both hands and hauled Stoika to her feet. 'Third, in case you're ever playing poker with a card sharp . . .' Her eyes opened, full of fury and outrage, both of which I ignored. 'When you *think* you've caught them palming a card? That's the one they *want* you to spot.'

She pushed herself away from me and seemed surprised that she didn't fall back down. She rubbed her thumbs and forefingers together. 'No numbness,' she mumbled. 'They should be numb.'

'The first switch of the cups was when I steadied the tray on your lap, you ill-tempered buzzard. I only pulled the second one because I knew you'd expect me to try to swap them.' I headed for the door, stopped just outside it. 'You keep thinking our people need leaders to guide them. Maybe that's true, but you know what

306

I think? I think it's high time our leaders learned a thing or two from their people. You reckon you can endure *that*, Stoika?'

She came to the doorway and stepped outside with me. Now that she'd figured out she wasn't dying, the steel had returned to her spine and she stood straight as an arrow. Her hand, though, was unexpectedly soft as she cupped my cheek. 'When I first knocked, you were mumbling something about eighteen being far too young to feel so old.'

The cheering from up on the deck was becoming a raucous chorus. I could even hear Conch bleating excitedly. 'I was tired, that's all.'

Stoika's hand remained on my cheek. 'Did the elders of your clan never teach you the old Mahdek saying about wisdom?'

'I was only eleven when my clan was killed,' I reminded her, 'and the elders had a great many sayings. They always seemed to be about wisdom.'

She smiled, but there wasn't any joy in it. '"Wisdom is never free, and the price is paid in either years or in pain."' Her hand fell away from my cheek, leaving behind a little warmth. She rose up on tiptoes to kiss that same spot. 'No one so young should have had to purchase as much wisdom as you have, Ferius Parfax.'

The Letter

To Her Esteemed Ladyship,
   Arelisa Valejine Talédra,
   Contessa of Corveon,
   You didn't think I was gonna let Ala'tris keep your full name a secret from me, did you? What was so awful about being called 'Arelisa Valejine Talédra' anyway, that you had to give up all three and just went by 'Arissa'? On the other hand, I seem to recall that the entire county of Corveon got swallowed up by its northern Daroman neighbours some fifteen years ago, so I can understand why you dropped the 'Contessa' part. One of these days you're gonna have to tell me the whole story of how the only living daughter of the famously honourable Talédra family became a notorious cat burglar and sneak-thief.

   I wish I knew for sure that this letter was going to reach you. Who knows how many thousands of leagues of shadowblack sea lie between us? Even if the spellship makes it back to those shores where you and I parted less than two weeks ago, you could be anywhere, rambling around any city in any nation across the entire continent. Ala'tris reckons her silk magic can follow your trail wherever you've wound up, but I've told her to start with the prisons just in case.

   Anyway, if you're expecting some tear-stained, poetry-inspired lament to lost love, you can remove the smouldering end of that hideous smoking reed of yours from the edge of the paper. This letter isn't about loneliness or heartache. It's about finding beauty in unexpected places. It's about the Path of the Wild Daisy.

Durral once told me that a true Argosi, skilled in the seven talents, walking the four ways, is prepared for anything the world can throw at them except beauty.

Yeah, yeah – typical sort of Durral nonsense I'm always complaining about.

Thing is, beneath all his sentimentality you can always find some cold, hard logic, and this one's no exception. An Argosi armed with arta eres knows how to defend themselves, with arta forteize, to endure all kinds of hardship; arta tuco sharpens the mind in evasion and arta siva in persuasion. On and on the seven talents go, each one stacked up like a deck full of trump cards waiting to be played. Yet, to what purpose? Why does someone become an Argosi at all? First and foremost, we're wandering gamblers. But gambling on what? And wandering where?

Spend enough time on those questions – and I've spent plenty – and you realise that every Argosi's path is a search for wonder, meaning and beauty. And when we find all three . . .

'How can you be staring at scraps of paper with *that* out there?' Gab'rel asked.

I balanced the quill on the railing next to the little jar of ink and kept one hand on the letter while absently reaching out the other to tousle the fifteen-year-old's hair. Gab'rel was sorely in need of a reminder that, while he might see himself as a promisingly powerful Jan'Tep breath mage, to me he was just an annoying kid.

The Mahdek passengers filling the deck of the ship had generously made a path for me to come to the bow and witness the prize that had brought us all here. Ala'tris was shedding tears of relief and pride, hugging Sar'ephir. The winding black markings on the tall woman's skull were still swirling, but not so intensely as when she was navigating the spellship through the shadowblack. Her forehead and shoulders were glistening with sweat. Jir'dan and Ba'dari were grinning from ear to ear. The Mahdek were holding each other close, whispering promises of better days to one another. Even Chedran seemed dumbstruck by what awaited us.

Everyone – Ala'tris and her coven, the Mahdek, young and old, and yeah, even that arsehole Chedran – had waited for me to say or do something. I'd given some thought to what I wanted to say, then asked for some paper, ink and a quill.

Anyway, Arissa, where was I? Oh, right. Beauty.

So, the thing about the Argosi is that all of our talents are built on opening ourselves up to the world, not closing ourselves off. Arta precis requires us to see that which others do not wish seen or fail to even recognise in themselves. Arta loquit embraces the voices and eloquence of others. Even arta eres, defence, teaches us how to let the opponent in rather than keep them out, turning the fight into a kind of dance.

When we come face to face with something wondrous, something beautiful? All those talents can cause us to become . . . well, mesmerised.

As I write this, the spellship has docked next to a long, narrow strip of shimmering black onyx, smooth and flat. The causeway can't be more than ten feet wide, but it stretches out a full half-mile before reaching a landscape so lush it practically bursts with colour, defying the eternal night of the shadowblack. Even from here, I can see the sandy beach glittering all golden, reflecting the rays of a sun whose light shines no further than the shore. Beyond the beach, grass and brush thickens as it leads to lush forests. There's an astounding tapestry of trees and bushes crowned in lustrous leaves of shapes and colours both familiar and strange waiting for us. The streams and rivers . . . I shouldn't be able to hear them from so far away and yet my ears delight at their babbling. Towards the centre of the island, I can just make out the wild, emerald landscape sloping upwards, gently at first, then more steeply to a mountain range that rises all the way up to kiss silver-white clouds. All this, Sar'ephir and Ala'tris had tried to show the Mahdek elders back at the enclave with their lightshaping magic. The real thing makes their spells look like parlour tricks.

'We must send a scouting party,' Stoika just announced. You remember her? The pompous, sour-faced elder who nearly had you locked up in Colfax's dungeon for having hurled a dozen of my throwing cards at the entire Mahdek council? Anyway, she's already gazing at the assembled passengers as if preparing to announce her choices.

Sorry, had to pause a moment in writing this so that me and Stoika could have us a staring contest. In my eyes, she saw curiosity that she'd so readily take the reins when minutes before she'd intended to die and leave leadership of the Mahdek to me. In the glower she returned, I read a more portentous message: I had refused to take power, and she would neither offer to give it up again nor shy away from wielding it in the best interests of our people.

When I first came back up on deck, Ala'tris had sidled over to me and spoke quietly so no one else would hear. 'This is as far as we can go.' She'd held up her forearm to show me the angry red rash forming around the sigils of her tattooed bands. 'The mystical ores within the island are interfering with the ones that bind Sar'ephir, Gab'rel, Ba'dari, Jir'dan and myself to our own continent. We will grow sicker the closer we get.'

I took her arm, traced a finger around the reddened lines on her skin. They felt hot. 'How long can you wait for us?'

311

'Seven days, perhaps a bit longer. After that we'll be too sick to make the return journey.' She smiled wryly. 'At least Stoika and the elders can be reassured no Jan'Tep invaders will ever come knocking.'

I thought about that a moment, about the sacrifices Ala'tris and her 'restitutionists' had made to bring her people's ancient enemies to a place of safety. There would be no parades for her back in her home city of Oatas Jan'Dal, if ever she was allowed to return at all. Yet, she had undertaken this hard and harrowing quest because she knew, deep down, against the teachings and traditions of her own family, that it was right.

'Ferius?' she asked.

'Yeah?'

'Why are you staring at me that way?'

Conch had been battering my knee, no doubt to let me know he wanted off this ship so he could get started on eating every bit of foliage on that island. I winked at Ala'tris. 'I'm staring because I'm an Argosi, sister. We can't help but be mesmerised by beauty.'

Ain't trying to make you jealous here, Arissa. It's not like I fancy to Ala'tris, not in that way anyhow. Just speaking the plain truth. Doesn't much matter now, anyway, because here's what's going to happen next. I'm about to hand this letter to her and remind her to be kind to my horse while I'm gone. Then I'm going to snatch up Conch and run to the side where the gangplank is being lowered. I'll leap over the railing to slide down that plank just as reckless and wild as you would if you were here. Stoika can send whoever she wants to scout the island, but me and the spire goat? We're getting there first.

Hold that image in your mind for me, will you, Arissa? Picture me bounding across that onyx causeway, rushing into

312

who-knows-what new dangers with a spire goat in my arms and a gambler's grin on my face. I ain't fooling myself, you understand? I know there are perils aplenty waiting for me. Undiscovered lands and treacherous magical forces; wondrous adventure and heartbreaking betrayals.

You're probably wondering why I'm writing this letter to you now instead of later after I've gotten a good look at that island and can make you jealous for not exploring it with me. You remember how you told me I shouldn't let myself be weighed down by debts I never really owed in the first place? That's good advice, but the thing is, I've finally come to understand that the debts that brought me to this island weren't debts at all. They were . . . gifts.

An Argosi's path is more than a road we walk. It's a theory about how a person can transform this cruel and often treacherous world into someplace wondrous with every step we take. The Path of the Wild Daisy winds away from the self-doubt and melancholy that shackles my people as surely as any mage's binding spell. Truth be told, I've spent too long held back by those same chains. So now I'm going to do this thing, this hard, terrible thing, because I'm gonna prove once and for all that even in the coldest, darkest moments of our lives, something wondrous can bloom if you just look hard enough.

Oh, before I forget: enclosed you'll find a card. I'm not the one who made it – that's Durral's surprisingly gentle hand painting all those beautiful brush strokes. He gave it to me years ago. Technically it's not a debt card at all, but I reckon it'll serve the purpose. I'm hoping that every once in a while you'll take it out and spare the red-haired girl with the frontier hat and the righteous gleam in her eye a passing glance. Maybe wonder what kind of trouble she's gotten herself into and ask yourself whether maybe it's time to look her up. I've a feeling she might be in need of rescuing.

　　With equal parts admiration, irritation and love,
　　Ferius Parfax,
　　The Path of the Wild Daisy,
　　Your Rat Girl.

Acknowledgements

The Deck of Harmonies

Faithful readers of my books will recall that I make a habit of blending my acknowledgements with details about the various decks found within the Spellslinger and Argosi series. With this third book of Ferius Parfax's adventures, however, I decided to break with tradition.

The Disharmonies, or deck of debts, represent unpaid obligations for which an Argosi must some day make restitution. While I have, indeed, accumulated a great many debts to those who have assisted me over the past several years in putting these tales of unruly card players, troubled spellslingers and somewhat murderous squirrel cats into your hands, referring to them as 'debts' feels wrong. The Disharmonies represent situations in which the Argosi has left someone else poorer for their passing: the suit of thorns represents pain caused to another, the suit of chains leaving them bound in some way, the suit of graves denotes an untimely death and the suit of dust – perhaps most sorrowful of all – a state of unknowing.

Blessedly, no one who's ever worked on the Spellslinger and Argosi books has ever expressed anything but joy and comradeship throughout the process. Therefore, let me propose a new deck of cards, one not yet found within the pages of these books but perhaps to appear in a future story: the Deck of Harmonies. Let the suits of this most grateful of decks and those individuals who represent them be hereby enshrined.

The Suit of Beacons

Darkness comes in many forms, the absence of light being only one. An Argosi may find themselves lost in forests so thick they cannot see past the branches and leaves blocking their way, or in deserts so wide and open all sense of direction is quickly lost. The Suit of Beacons represents sources not of simple illumination but of guidance and wisdom. An Argosi should always be grateful indeed when such cards appear along their path.

Maurice Lyon: an editor who never cracks a whip but instead nudges his authors towards the best version of their stories.

Jon Wood: an agent who tolerates rather a great many business meetings with authors who don't earn him nearly enough money to justify all their complaints. I'm referring to those *other* authors of course. Not me. I'm a joy to work with, right, Jon? Jon? Umm . . . Jon? Are you still there?

Christina de Castell: when she smiles, I am happy; when she enjoys one of my books, I've found my story. It's as simple as that.

The Suit of Melodies

Songs can be lonely things when sung alone. A single voice rarely produces the sweetest tune, just as a single mind rarely conceives the perfect path forward. An Argosi is well served when listening to the ideas of others, for in such insights are found unexpected harmonies that make one's song all the sweeter.

Kristin Atherton: when Ferius speaks a line in my books, it's your voice I now hear.

Sally Taylor: ingenious deviser of interior illustrations for the many, many Argosi decks of cards.

Gavin Reece: visionary cover artist. Your illustration for Durral in the first Argosi book captures his essence so perfectly that I'm still amazed every time I see it.

The Suit of Wings

Distances can be too vast for even the most tenacious of travellers. A shoulder to lean on can be as a pair of wings to the Argosi, and even the tallest peaks can be ascended when one is borne aloft by the kindness of others.

Emma Matthewson: many thanks for once again publishing Ferius Parfax and having faith that one day she'll come back from her journeys bearing bags of gold (or at least some very fine stories of her travels).

Talya Baker: as always, brings sparkle to the prose and only rarely asks me to remove a dirty word.

Melissa Hyder: proofreader without peer, caught every single spelling mistake ecxpet this one and, more importantly, vigilantly guards the integrity of the characters as they journey through the story.

Nick Stearn: the wonderfully inventive design lead who defined an iconic style for the Spellslinger and Argosi series.

Jake Cook: thanks for putting together the cover for this book, which might be the trickiest of the series.

Giulia Caparrelli: the production of a beautiful book is a truly complex feat of alchemy and engineering. Thanks for keeping all the trains running in the right direction!.

DataConnection: typesetters extraordinaire!

Clays: if you're holding a physical book in your hands, they printed it with loving care.

Marina Stavropoulou: with great attention to detail, brought the audiobook into being once more.

Lauren Campbell: excellent author's assistant who had to read every chapter as I wrote them and warn me if I'd gone off the deep end.

Kim Tough and Kristi Charish: the next two people to read the first draft of this book, provided contrasting yet equally insightful perspectives that made the final manuscript much better.

Suit of Garlands

The Argosi are many things: wanderers, gamblers, frontier philosophers and frequent troublemakers. Always, always the Argosi are storytellers. Gladly – and often without prompting – they will recount tales of quests great and small, seemingly innocuous anecdotes or snatches of conversations that stuck with them, demanding to be revealed as if the insights hidden within can only be gleaned when shared with others. How strange, then, that the Argosi are so reticent to tell their own stories. Grateful they must be for those who so enthusiastically and eloquently spread word of their deeds . . .

Mickey Mickelson: an honourable publicist who always takes my call and somehow hasn't yet figured out I'm not nearly as famous as he assumes.

Emma Quick, Isobel Taylor, Pippa Poole: the stalwart marketing and publicity teams at Hot Key Books.

Rob Power, Jessica Webb, Kate Dewey, Stephanie Bramwell-Lawes, Stacey Hamilton, Alan Scollan, Jeff Jamieson, Jennie Harwood, Robyn Haque: who manage to convince what I suspect are often reluctant booksellers to take a chance on my books.

Sharon Miller Gold, Holly Powell: who convince other publishers around the world to translate my books into an ever-increasing number of languages.

Jade of Jadeyraereads: my favourite YouTuber!

Librarians and booksellers everywhere: who so kindly recommend my books to their many patrons and customers who wisely trust their judgement in sorting through the seemingly infinite number of choices out there!

And, as always, the thousands of readers who are my fellow travellers along the winding ways of the Argosi. My thanks for sharing my books with family and friends, for being generous with your time in reviewing and recommending the series, and for your wonderful letters and emails that are the highlight of my day!

Sebastien de Castell
London, England
May 2023

Curious to read about Ferius Parfax's first appearance in the Spellslinger series? Read on . . .

SPELLSLINGER

4

The Thunder

What happened next came mostly in flashes – little sparks between the shadows that would envelop me on the journey from the city's oasis back to my family home. It began with my father lifting me up from the ground and whispering in my ear.

'Do not cry in front of them. If you must cry, hold it in a little while longer.'

A Jan'Tep must be strong, I told myself. I'm usually not much of a cryer anyway, never having seen any evidence that it does any good. But I was exhausted and frustrated and more than a little scared, so it took a surprising amount of self-control for me to say, 'I'm not going to cry.'

My father gave me a small nod followed by the barest hint of a smile. I felt a warmth inside me that made me wonder if he'd just cast a fire spell, though of course there was no way he could have made the somatic forms while holding me in his arms.

Everyone in the oasis stood stiff and silent, except for Osia'phest, who still lay on the ground, though from the mumbling noises he made I presumed he was gradually regaining consciousness. Panahsi, Nephenia, Tennat and the rest of my fellow initiates just stared at us.

My father was a big man, over six feet tall with deep black hair – a sharp contrast to the blond colouring that both Shalla and I had inherited from our mother. He kept his moustache and short beard meticulously trimmed and exuded an air of imposing dignity wherever he went. He was strong in all the ways a Jan'Tep was supposed to be: physically, mentally and, above all, magically. Even Panahsi's eyes reflected a kind of disbelief that I was really the son of someone as powerful as Ke'heops.

'I can stand,' I said to my father, embarrassed to appear so weak in front of the other initiates. He didn't let go of me.

Shalla walked gingerly towards us. 'Father, don't be cross with—'

'Be silent,' he said, and my sister closed her mouth. I watched as my father scrutinised the scene in front of us, his eyes moving to each of the participants in turn. I knew he was reading them as easily as if he could unlock their minds, watching their reactions to his presence, sifting through furtive glances and shifting eyes. I could see him work through recent events by considering and cataloguing each person's fear or guilt under his gaze. Then his face took on a slightly puzzled expression. I turned my head and saw him looking at the woman who'd saved my life.

'You. What is your name?' he asked.

She took a step closer as if to prove she wasn't afraid of him. 'Ferius Parfax,' she said, and reached out a gloved hand to wipe something from my face. I saw grains of green and grey dust against the brown leather of her glove. 'You'll want to bathe him. That powder can start acting up again something fierce when it settles into the skin.'

My father barely let her finish the sentence before he said, 'You will come with us now.'

Ferius Parfax, who, despite the single lock of white sticking out from the red tangle kept in check by her frontiersman hat, looked to be several years younger than my father, nonetheless put her hands on her hips and laughed out loud. 'Now, see, I thought you Jan'Tep were supposed to know *all* the magic words.'

There was grumbling and sharp intakes of breath from my fellow initiates, the loudest coming from Shalla. No one spoke to Ke'heops that way, especially not some magic-less Daroman wanderer. I looked up at my father and saw his jaw tighten just a little, but then he said, 'Forgive me. Would you please accompany us to my home? I have questions that may be important to my son's recovery.'

Ferius looked at me and winked as if she'd just conjured a thunderstorm on a dry day. 'Surely I will.'

I felt oddly compelled to contribute to the conversation, so I said, 'My name is Kellen.'

'Nice to meet you, Kellen,' she said, taking off her hat only to put it right back on her head a second later. The Daromans have weird little rituals like that.

A commotion nearby drew our attention. Osia'phest, with precious little help from the students standing next to him, was struggling to rise. 'My Lord Ke'heops–'

'Someone assist him,' my father said.

Immediately two of the nearest initiates took Osia'phest by the arms and lifted him to his feet. The old spellmaster took a few awkward steps towards us. 'If I could perhaps explain more fully the circumstances . . .'

'Rest,' my father said. 'Some of these others will help you home. We will speak tomorrow.'

Osia'phest looked as though someone had just read out his prison sentence. Ferius gave a snort of disgust. 'Mages,' she said, as if the word meant something different in her language than it did in ours.

Watching the old man having to be practically carried by his students, seeing the way they rolled their eyes at him and the way they glanced back at me, filled me with shame. 'I can stand by myself,' I said to my father.

His eyes narrowed for an instant but he set me on my feet. The sudden weakness in my legs and blurring of my vision were the first clues that I'd made a terrible mistake.

'Never seen a man recover so fast from a stopped heart,' Ferius said, patting me on the back. Only she wasn't patting me on the back, not really. Her hand was gripping the back of my shirt as she kept me from falling forwards onto my face.

My father did an admirable job of pretending not to notice. He took a step forward, blocking the view of the others as Ferius now used both hands to keep me up. 'The rest of you have homes and families to return to,' he said. 'Do so now.'

It took only seconds for the oasis to clear out. No one stopped to say anything to me. Not Panahsi or Nephenia. Tennat didn't even bother to insult me.

When everyone but Shalla and Ferius had gone, my father turned to the Daroman woman and nodded. She removed her hands and I immediately felt myself falling backwards. My father caught me effortlessly in his arms. 'You should sleep now,' he said.

It wasn't a command or a spell. I could have stayed awake if I'd tried hard enough. But, see, there was this tiny, almost infinitesimally small possibility that if I fell asleep I would wake up later to find that this had all been a terrible, humiliating dream. So I closed my eyes and hoped.

Thank you for choosing a Hot Key book!

For all the latest bookish news, freebies and exclusive content, sign up to the Hot Key newsletter – scan the QR code or visit lnk.to/HotKeyBooks

Follow us on social media:

bonnierbooks.co.uk/HotKeyBooks